THE RISK AGENT NOVELS

"The perfect way . . . to acquire a new reading addiction."
—BookReporter.com

CHOKE POINT

"[Knox and Chu] make a good team, with his brawn and her brains . . . Plenty of action and some steamy sex help make the pages fly by." —*Publishers Weekly*

"Pearson has written another compelling thriller. Knox and Chu are protagonists who engage the reader . . . A winner."
—*Library Journal*

"The action is . . . nonstop." —*Kirkus Reviews*

THE RISK AGENT

"Brace yourself for a thrilling afternoon: Pearson's introducing a new action series that stars a Shanghai-based security agent named John Knox." —*Chicago Tribune*

"A cunning thriller worthy of the promised series . . . Exotic locale. Credible heroics. Vicarious thrills. Fans will want more, and soon." —*Kirkus Reviews*

"Entertaining . . . Thriller fans will look forward to seeing more of Knox." —*Publishers Weekly*

"Rich with the atmosphere . . . filled with breathtaking suspense . . . Readers who love international thrillers won't be disappointed." —*Library Journal* (starred review)

"The perfect summer read." —*Christian Science Monitor*

continued . . .

"Solid, reliable Pearson in a whole new suit and country. This is the first in a projected series, and if it's any indication of what's to follow, I would happily wait patiently for each one with my cold, wet nose pressed up against the bookstore door glass . . . Full of action, twists and turns, double crosses, and good old-fashioned thrills." —BookReporter.com

PRAISE FOR RIDLEY PEARSON

"A multilayered thriller." —*Houston Chronicle*

"[A] page-turner." —*The Seattle Times*

"[An] edge-of-your-seat crime novel." —*Tucson Citizen*

"Pearson can plot a heist with ingenuity and delicious complexity." —*St. Louis Post-Dispatch*

"A gripping page-turner of a novel." —*Rocky Mountain News*

"A master of that all-too-rare book: the read that is both exciting and intelligent." —The Associated Press

"Ridley Pearson has outdone himself." —James Patterson

"Ridley Pearson writes thrillers . . . that try to yank you to the edge of your seat and keep you there." —*Boston Sunday Globe*

"Ridley Pearson . . . [is] fully worthy of comparison to Michael Connelly." —Scott Turow

"Consummate entertainment." —*The Baltimore Sun*

"Ridley Pearson packs a wallop." —*The Cincinnati Enquirer*

"If we had a Thriller Hall of Fame, Ridley Pearson would be a first-ballot certainty, both for his technical virtuosity and his intensely human stories." —Lee Child

TITLES BY RIDLEY PEARSON

Choke Point

The Risk Agent

In Harm's Way

Killer Summer

Killer View

Killer Weekend

Cut and Run

The Art of Deception

The Diary of Ellen Rimbauer
(writing as Joyce Reardon)

The Pied Piper

Beyond Recognition

Undercurrents

BOOKS FOR YOUNG READERS

The Kingdom Keepers series

Disney After Dark

Disney at Dawn

Disney in Shadow

Power Play

Shell Game

Dark Passage

The Insider

Peter and the Starcatchers series
(with Dave Barry)

Never Land series
(with Dave Barry)

Steel Trapp series

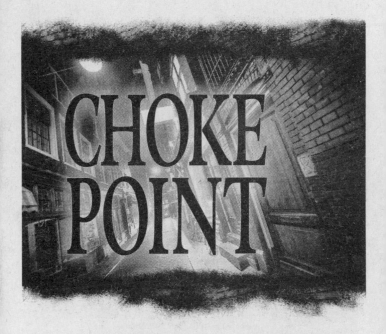

CHOKE POINT

RIDLEY PEARSON

JOVE BOOKS | NEW YORK

THE BERKLEY PUBLISHING GROUP
Published by the Penguin Group
Penguin Group (USA) LLC
375 Hudson Street, New York, New York 10014

USA • Canada • UK • Ireland • Australia • New Zealand • India • South Africa • China

penguin.com

A Penguin Random House Company

CHOKE POINT

A Jove Book / published by arrangement with Page One, Inc.

Jove Books are published by The Berkley Publishing Group.
JOVE® is a registered trademark of Penguin Group (USA) LLC.
The "J" design is a trademark of Penguin Group (USA) LLC.

For information, address: The Berkley Publishing Group,
a division of Penguin Group (USA) LLC,
375 Hudson Street, New York, New York 10014.

ISBN: 978-0-515-15464-1

PUBLISHING HISTORY
G. P. Putnam's Sons hardcover edition / June 2013
Jove premium edition / May 2014

PRINTED IN THE UNITED STATES OF AMERICA

10 9 8 7 6 5 4 3 2 1

Cover design by Andrea Ho.

For Kathi

ACKNOWLEDGMENTS

Thanks to the U.S. Department of State for sponsoring a speaking trip to Germany that allowed for research in Amsterdam. To Jen Wood and Nancy Zastrow for their help in the office. To David and Laurel Walters for the repeated copyedits. To Dr. Genevieve Gagne-Hawes for her brilliance. My editor, Christine Pepe. Agents Amy Berkower, Dan Conaway, and film agent Matthew Snyder.

And to Marcelle, Storey, Paige, Louise, Betsy, and Brad for keeping the family close.

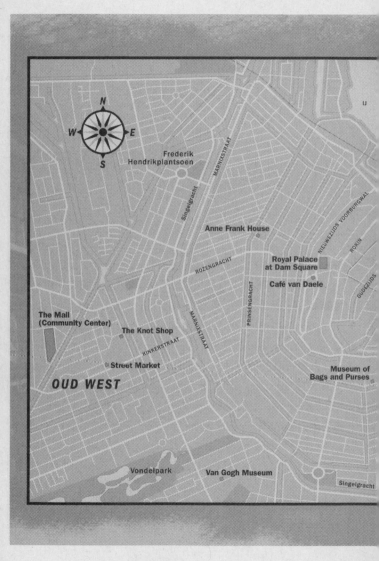

NOORD

AMSTERDAM

IJ

Ferry Terminal

Centraal Station

IJ Harbor

VOORBURGWAL

PRINS HENDRIKKADE

Oosterdok

Natuurhonig

Red Light District

Nieuwe Waart

Singelgracht

First Houseboat

Second Houseboat

Binnen Amstel

0 Miles   .25   .5

0 Kilometers   .8

© 2013 Jeffrey L. Ward

1

The air is visible. It smells of camel dung and human sweat. It tastes worse. It comes in hot waves, stealing any appetite he might have had and stinging his eyes. Flies buzz past his ears and light on his face. He waves them away, his right hand a horsetail of constant motion.

The sun-soaked skin of the man who sits cross-legged before him looks shrink-wrapped over long, thin bone. Unflinching rheumy eyes stare back at him beneath wild white eyebrows. John Knox studies the man's long flat-nailed fingers as they punch out numbers on a battery-operated calculator that serves as their translator—money, the only language spoken here.

The chess sets before him are things of beauty. Knox is offered such sets everywhere he trades; he's tired of them. But these are hand-carved inlaid stone boards and intricately carved jade pieces—fine jade, not the cheap stuff. What they're doing in Kairouan, Tunisia, is anybody's guess. Knox used to try to think through such anomalies. No longer. He doesn't care where they came from or who made them, just craftsmanship and price. Weight, sometimes, because shipping has gotten so expensive. Profit is not in quantity but quality. He needs to reach a price that will allow him to sell them for ten times cost. His mind grinds through figures—taxes, shipping, breakage, shrinkage. The merchant taps the calculator, signaling a new asking price. Knox blows away a fly and reads the number upside down.

It could have been a gust of wind, the touch is so light. A moth-eaten cat that appears by his leg offers another possibility. The poor thing looks like it was put in with the laundry and hung out to dry. But accompanying that touch came a sour odor. Not cat urine; something distinctly human. Trailing faintly behind, a pleasant, almost intoxicating, sweet warmth of milk chocolate.

It's the chocolate that causes Knox to react reflexively. Turning as he does. He misses the boy's left ankle but feels hairs brush the tips of his fingers.

Up and off the rug and into the melee of the market, the grit of sand against stone under his Tevas as he dodges the colorful robes and linen wraps that move about randomly, unintentionally blocking him.

The kid got his wallet belt. Sliced the nylon webbing with what had to be a razor—Knox takes note of that— and was gone. Just like that. Ten, maybe eleven years old, and with the uncanny touch of someone who'd done this

for many years. And fast? The kid is Usain Bolt in miniature. Knox's one advantage is height—able to leap tall
buildings. He keeps his eye on this kid despite the kid
pulling away from him.

They turn left down a narrow lane passing wooden
birdcages stacked high, noisy colors darting around
inside. A stall of stringed peppers like an astringent in the
air. Silver bangles chiming in clumps on pegs while sea-
shell necklaces clatter in the same breeze. The kid with
blurred legs like the Road Runner.

The cash would be a loss. This is a buying day, the last
of four days in the market, the first three devoted to
research. A fat wad of bills he can't afford to lose just now
at a time when every shekel counts. But the passport is
the most important. He'd rather avoid the U.S. Consulate
if given a choice. Has no desire to spend another several
days here awaiting the reissue. He's heard a rumor of
Queensland Boulder Opals arriving into Marrakesh by
the weekend. Never mind that he must travel to Morocco
to buy Australian gems—it's a global economy.

The kid turns right: a mistake. Knox has him, unless
he proves to be a good climber. That lane is a rare dead
end, terminating at a tobacco café serving the best coffee
in the city—which is saying something here. Knox
increases his stride, coughs up some phlegm and spits—
enjoying the aerobic hit.

He reaches for his waist pack that isn't there. *Shit*. The
kid has his knife. He slows infinitesimally; it doesn't affect
his speed, but it places his feet under him more substantially. If the kid is a pickpocket, fine. But there's a larger

possibility he is only to serve as bait to lead Knox into a real mugging and full robbery—jewelry, shoes, even teeth if they have gold fillings.

Two guys he can handle. If it's more than that, he's in trouble.

Doesn't see the kid anywhere. Gone, like a special effect. Laundry hangs out to dry. Some fish suspended by the tail alongside the underwear. And his waist belt on a café table in front of an empty chair.

Knox skids to a stop, dust catching up with him from behind.

David Dulwich's shoulders pull at the seams of the gray XXL T-shirt reading OHIO STATE ATHLETIC DEPARTMENT in cracked, silk-screened letters. His scarred hand engulfs the demitasse to where it looks like he's drinking steaming coffee out of a white thimble. A torn-open Hershey's bar rests by the ashtray.

"Really?" Knox says, working hard not to appear out of breath.

"Sit down," David Dulwich replies, kicking back the empty chair.

2

The rush of the hotel room's forced air is all she hears. Or maybe it's blood rushing past her ears, chased by adrenaline. Hours earlier, it was a cox-swain's rhythmic chants rising from the Charles, but the boats are long in their racks.

Her nakedness is a liability; she isn't herself. But it's the only price she has paid thus far to reach the endgame. The kissing and touching she found distasteful, but it never went further than that. Her decision, she reminds herself. She owns this op.

She crosses to the bathroom on tiptoes, having always found the idea of hotel carpets disgusting. She imagines colonies of bacteria engaged in an orgy, a single-celled frat party feeding on ground-in beer, vodka and cocaine.

The needle goes first with a simple snap. It splashes into the toilet and the sound startles her. She wraps a facecloth around the rest of the syringe, places it carefully onto the tile and stomps her heel, crushing the plastic to pieces that quickly follow into the open bowl. She flushes everything down, waits to make sure it's all gone. Gooseflesh ripples up her arms and neck as she catches herself in the mirror. Grace Chu, former forensic accountant.

She flushes the toilet a second time for good measure.

She stands there seeing all the imperfections in her naked form. Always the same. At first a flash of "isn't she pretty?" followed by disappointment: she sees her lean, attractive figure as marred by sallow skin and etched by an abundance of black body hair—the curse of every Chinese woman. She invents sad eyes and small teeth. A short neck. Never mind that men call her "alluring," "intoxicating," "beautifully proportioned." Men see breasts and legs, a waist and bottom. And little else. Losing the staring contest, she terminates it.

Grace locates her underwear on the carpet and shakes it vigorously before stepping in. Her bra is next. Strapping it on. Bending forward, adjusting. She feels surprisingly safer. She searches her purse for a tube of Vaseline while she studies the man in bed. The clock reads 1:33 A.M.

She uncaps the Vaseline without looking. Approaches him cautiously, not quite trusting the combined effect of Rohypnol and ketamine. Asleep yet awake. Paralyzed yet conscious. As the drugs began to take effect she was able to milk him for the VPN password, which he gave up freely. He will have no memory of that—of any of the past hour—in the morning. No memory of her. Possibly, even, the hotel bar. Getting Rohyped turns the Etch A Sketch upside down and shakes it, hard.

She swallows away her fear as she confronts his open, blank eyes. For a moment she wonders if she's killed him, but then the throbbing of a neck vein convinces her otherwise. Smearing the Vaseline across his open eyes does not bother her the way she imagined it might. Without the ointment he would suffer permanent eye damage. She reminds herself she's helping him. There's something sadistically pleasing about that, causing her to smile ruefully. With the Vaseline smeared across both open eyes the man looks frightful. He was no Romeo to begin with, but this clouded-eye look is hideous.

Sitting at a reproduction leather–topped desk, she attacks his laptop like the digital predator she is. Her fieldwork has increased steadily since a Shanghai op that took her out of her desk chair—though technically, this job is unrelated to a paycheck. It's off the books.

Cloning a large data hard drive can take forty to ninety minutes. But she can't pass up the opportunity. Strictly speaking, all she needed was the password—access to the mutual fund's corporate server. But the contents of the CFO's laptop offer the possibility of a rich prize. Possible leverage over the man down the road: the kind of sordid thing Rutherford Risk thrives on.

She raids the minibar for a bottle of vodka. Wipes it down and places the empty in her purse for good measure. Can barely take her eyes off Mr. Smear-n-Off where he lies in bed. Expects him to sit up and march toward her like a zombie.

She downs another vodka quickly and preserves its bottle as well, leaving nothing to chance. After consideration, she keeps the drinking glass as well.

At some point, she redresses in the formfitting mini that won his attention in the bar. Her head feels as if it's stuffed with gun cotton, and her mouth is dry. She cautions herself to leave the minibar alone; she must remain lucid. At 102 pounds, only a very little booze can push her into la-la land.

She fusses in front of the bedroom mirror, peeks out occasionally at the tiny, flashing blue LED on the external drive. Still copying. Checks Mr. Smear-n-Off. He hasn't moved a centimeter. Her throat tightens. She feels sorry for him. Guilty. Swallows it away. This op represents job security; Dulwich will owe her for this. John Knox will thank her.

This is progress.

3

A steaming demitasse is delivered the exact moment Knox sits down. The waiter says nothing. All prearranged. All trademark David Dulwich. Although never technically a spook, the man could give the CIA a run for its money. Knox notices the burn scar beneath the man's collarbone. It immediately calls up the smell of diesel fuel mixed with cordite. At the height of the extended Iraq war, a VBIED explosive took out Dulwich's truck. Knox dragged the man from a flame-ripped truck cab across packed sand while shrapnel whistled past his ears. No medals were awarded; they were working for a private contractor, a resupply and transportation firm based out of Kuwait. Dulwich rarely mentions the debt that hangs between them. But he lives it. In his current job, Dulwich manages field operations for a private security firm, Rutherford Risk. When opportunity arises, he offers Knox the choicest work. Short term. High pay. What are friends for?

"A phone call or an e-mail would have done just fine," Knox says. He resists the fieldwork. He has a brother who relies on his good health.

"I'm goofing with you. So what?"

"Don't."

"It was harmless."

"Not for the kid if I caught him."

"You wouldn't have."

Knox lifts his travel belt, studies the razor cut first, then unzips the pouch and carefully searches the contents.

"You're getting careless, if there's anything in there of value," Dulwich says.

"I'll let you know when I want your advice."

"Testy."

"There's a certain look to a buyer like me. A role to play. I'm trying to run a business here."

"As am I," Dulwich says. "Besides, you're done with that. Castanets? Incense burners? You? Please." Eschewing the showiness of an aluminum briefcase, Dulwich draws a camouflage backpack into his lap and withdraws a folded *International Herald Tribune*. He pushes it across the table at Knox as if it were toxic.

"That's a week old," Knox says, having not touched it. "Already read it. Thanks anyway." He suspects a photo is folded into it, or a contract, or both. He wants the money—desperately—and Dulwich knows this, but Knox has to play like he doesn't want or need it, and Dulwich plays along. A long-standing friendship, this.

"Our client is Graham Winston."

Knox works the miniature spoon against the rock sugar at the bottom of the demitasse, impatient for it to dissolve. *Good things take time to develop,* he reminds himself. Women, for one. There's a stunner under the shade of the café's torn awning who has now looked his way three times. His imagination is sometimes a liability. He forces himself to focus on Dulwich, which is not easy.

Knox doesn't need to ask which Graham Winston. Instead, he has to try to be a step ahead of Dulwich and figure out the angle. Without consulting the newspaper, he's at a loss, so he concedes a round to Dulwich by pulling the newspaper low into his lap in order to shield any possible contents beyond news. He wonders how he might have looked right at something yet not have seen it. How transparent is the obvious? This is more than a game; it's part and parcel of his survival. He knows it. Dulwich knows it. Retention is ten-tenths of the game. He knows when he sat down there were six people at tables behind him. Four coffees, two teas. He knows that's the fourth furtive look the attractive woman has given him, and it's starting to bother him. He knows he read this paper and yet can't recall the last time Graham Winston's name appeared in a story. Knox took a chance.

"An interest of his, not a direct mention." He unfolds the paper. No added contents.

"Correct."

"A cause."

"More like it," Dulwich says.

Graham Winston is famous for supporting causes:

Greenpeace; Human Rights Watch; Doctors Without Borders.

Knox supports Starbucks and Anheuser-Busch, Victoria's Secret and Apple.

Knox doesn't read every article in every edition. He skims. He headline-hops. He absorbs. Read the lead. Follow the jump. He likes newspapers. Mourns their passing.

"'Little Fingers, Big Problems,'" he quotes.

"Who says you're stupid?"

"Careful."

Winston turns causes into headlines and, though he comes across as self-aggrandizing, is nonetheless someone Knox can tolerate. In this instance, their stars align; Knox's predisposition against the servitude of women in general, and young girls in particular, fuels his interest in Winston's cause. He doesn't allow Dulwich too close a look at his face, doesn't want him to pick up on the fact that this is work he would do pro bono if asked.

"A girl, nine or ten, was treated in a local health clinic. Malnourished. A circular lesion—massive infection—on her right ankle, suggesting she'd been chained. Gets treated and either flees or is kidnapped from the center. It was the shape of the ankle wound that set off all the alarms. That, and the discovery by the docs of wool and animal hair in the wound. Her fingers were observed to be heavily calloused: thumb, index, middle."

"I may have skimmed the article."

"Graham Winston did not skim it."

"He wants some rug factory shut down?"

". . . they're called knot shops."

"I think of Winston as one of those names you hear on Terry Gross. He writes checks he can deduct. What's he want with financing a battle with a bunch of Afghan thugs? If it backfires, he'll bring them to his door. I hope you warned him."

"He'll bring them to our door. And it's believed they're Turks, not Afghans."

"That article was a couple weeks ago," Knox said, suddenly interested in the contents of the more current newspaper.

"Bottom of page six."

Knox locates the article. Three inches alongside a two-column ad for couples performance videos. He knows that Dulwich is monitoring the telltale vein in his forehead. He attempts a Zen technique to control his heart rate. But it's like trying to hold back a barn-sour nag.

"A car bomb," Knox says. "A choke point."

"Indeed."

"Killed the driver and passenger."

"A low-level EU bureaucrat who was sadly so insignificant they had to work the obit to make him appear otherwise."

The paper's placement of the article—buried deeply—speaks to Knox: the man's death was insignificant as well.

"It's better than sex, isn't it?"

Knox says, "You're treading on the sacrosanct."

"This EU guy is so far down the ladder, he's holding it for others. So why kill him?"

"Why are you screwing around with me? If you want

me for this—and we wouldn't be here if you didn't—offer me the job and be done with it. I can tell you why: you think you're on such thin ice that you have to let me sell myself. You condense this down to a couple of lines and you know I won't be interested."

"But you are interested. They killed the bureaucrat because he was a source for the article. They're trying to kill the truth."

"Spare me!" But there are style points to be awarded here. Dulwich is beating a drum and making it louder with every hit. He has it all choreographed. He assumed it would be a tough sell. Knox wants to make sure to see it from both sides before feeling the trapdoor give way. Graham Winston. A knot shop. Some low-level bureaucrat reduced to toast.

Knox still can't see it perfectly. He's pissed at himself.

"Why would Brian Primer," he says, mentioning Dulwich's boss, president of the Rutherford Risk security firm, "accept a job to shut down a sweatshop ring? It sounds more like something for a police task force."

"Because he has a paying client."

"Brian has plenty of paying clients."

"Because these guys are scum holes. They kidnap ten-year-olds and chain them to posts and make them work eighteen-hour days. You know the drill. It's repugnant."

Knox needs no reminder why the op appeals to him—Dulwich had him at ten-year-olds in chains; he's less sure about Rutherford Risk's motivations. No matter how Dulwich pumps him up, he has always assumed he is expendable to these people. Rutherford's clients pay well for a reason: the work is typically unwanted by, or too dangerous for, others.

"I'm appealing to your savior complex," Dulwich says, being honest for a change.

"The girl."

"The girls. And you need the money."

Knox is in financial quicksand. A $300,000 nest egg to provide for his brother's exceptional medical needs was embezzled by a woman who took advantage of his brother's diminished abilities. Without that nest egg, should anything happen to Knox, his brother, Tommy, will be institutionalized. The irony Dulwich forces upon Knox each time he makes an offer is that Knox must risk his own safety to win the money to provide for his brother in case he's not around.

Dulwich reaches down and comes out with another newspaper that contains the original article about the young, injured girl fleeing the health clinic.

"I did read this," Knox says, remembering. The byline is Sonia Pangarkar. It's as much a story about the poorer neighborhoods of Amsterdam and the European struggle with immigrants as it is a cry for this runaway girl's life. The reporter is smart, thorough, and the piece engaging. There are names and places to back it up.

One of the names jumps out at him. "The car-bombing victim was one of her sources," Knox says. "We discussed it already. So, it's hardball."

"Bingo."

"In addition to wanting to protect those who cannot protect themselves, the benevolent Mr. Winston draws a line at murdering those willing to whistle-blow," Knox says. "I'm touched."

"Winston stands for liberty and justice for all. Terry Gross. Rachel Maddow. Anyone who will listen."

"Graham Winston is intending to run for prime minister."

"You said that. I did not."

Knox sets down the paper. "I'm not a political consultant." Hard-to-get is the only play with Dulwich. It's time to negotiate.

Knox downs the rest of the coffee. It's like swallowing a six-volt battery. "I've got Tommy to think of. The Turkish mob is not going to like being exposed. Just ask your low-level bureaucrat."

"Winston will pay four times the last job."

The number 200,000 swims in Knox's head. It's a lot of thimble cymbals.

Knox signals the waiter and orders another shot of espresso, wanting to ramp it up to twelve volts. Dulwich does the same. The curious woman stands up to leave. Knox senses a missed opportunity. "I'll need Grace."

"Done."

"Resources."

"It's Graham Winston, Knox."

"A reliable contact in the police department would help." He wants the young girl recovered safely. All the girls recovered safely. He resents that Dulwich knows this about him.

"Know just the guy. Name of Joshua Brower. We go way back."

"I've got to believe that someone in power is looking the other way on this thing. Right? So the police piece is a tricky one."

"Brower's trustworthy. I'm with you."

"You wouldn't be leaving something out?"

"That's not in anybody's best interest."

"Listen, we both know, given the choice of losing me or Grace, Brian Primer's going to protect Grace."

Dulwich is silent.

Knox decides not to push. He suspects Grace Chu's star has risen within Rutherford Risk. First and foremost a forensic accountant, she has recently proven herself a quick study of computer hacking and, because of her former training with the Chinese Army, is no slouch in field ops. Knox knows he's not in the same category—he offers Primer and Dulwich his cover of a legitimate international exporter and a growing passion for stomping the ugliest bugs that crawl out of the dark.

There's sand in Knox's teeth. Or maybe it's coffee grounds. He can't afford to get himself hurt or killed with Tommy's ongoing medical care unfunded. The money being offered would help him to eventually cover his brother's long-term home care. He bridles at the thought of an institution.

He's pissed as he accepts the job.

4

I n another life, Grace would've been a witch doctor. A digital witch doctor. She balances between several worlds: her father's traditionalist Chinese versus the reality that is Shanghai, Beijing, Chengdu and the other major cities joining the Western world; a love life that has lost its way; a woman in an overwhelmingly male-dominated world of private security; numbers on a page versus numbers in the cloud.

As her fingers hit the keypad, all that changes: she's transported into a digital realm that both absorbs her and fascinates her. She is in control, despite the vodka. Her eyes stray over to Mr. Smear-n-Off—the digital gates open before her like she's marching on Troy. She's through three barriers and onto the corporate network, marching with her army of education, training and experience and pushing her horse through with its belly full of surprises.

The investment firm has thousands of clients—tens of thousands—and she's trying to find just one. No name. No account number. She's exhilarated. Electric. Part of it is the voyeurism. Part of it, the excitement of exploration. Part of it, superiority. All she has is a number and a date, and the chances are the number has been broken into smaller numbers. But that's part of the fun. So it's down to the date in sorting through hundreds of deposits, knowing the mistake that's always made is the cents. She's hunting for fifty-four cents. Over three hundred thousand dollars stolen, and she's going to find it with just fifty-four cents.

With any luck, that will just be the start of this. She suspects the three hundred thousand may be only the tip of the iceberg.

Mr. Smear-n-Off moans and rolls over but isn't even close to REM—he's not coming around anytime soon. Her eyes are to the right of the decimal point, the numbers scrolling in what to others would appear a blur, and there it is like a flag waving: FIFTY-FOUR CENTS. Her index finger skids the scroll to a stop. She has to back up a page to find the actual entry, but it's there. A date that makes sense. The alcohol helps her to make a joke just for herself. *It makes cents.* She chuckles. She captures a screenshot almost automatically, saves it to the external drive and deletes it from the laptop. As a hunter she has raised her bow, but is far from firing. This smells of the game she pursues, but only time will tell. And the amount is small: forty-seven thousand, two hundred, eighty-three and *fifty-four cents*, leaving much more to find. Possibly much, much more.

The LED on the external drive stops flashing, the cloning complete. She's all efficiency of motion as she packs up, wipes down the desk and laptop and makes for the door. She can almost move herself to feel sorry for Mr. Smear-n-Off.

Almost.

5

The air in the room hangs heavy, snowflakes of wool lint mixed with tobacco smoke swirling beneath the rows of arched skylights. An occasional deep-chested cough interrupts the quiet. Four girls to a rug, sometimes six. Ten to twelve rugs. Feet tucked under the girls' bottoms to ward off the cool concrete floor. Maja, a "local," ties at station three with two "residents."

It is a joyless space. A place of deep concentration—mistakes are not tolerated. Furtive looks are exchanged between the girls; they share a language of minute gestures, undetected by the watchers. These messages and warnings travel from station to station as the girls attempt to protect one another. A team of nameless strangers, yet some have known each other for years. Some go back only a few months. Five of the girls arrived less than two weeks ago.

A warning flashes across the room, carried by a dozen hands.

"Inspection!" a watcher cries out sharply.

The shop is a place of routine and schedule. Most of all, it is a secret place. No one leaves—not even the watchers—once the door is closed and locked. The sound of the door coming open means only one thing: Him.

The girls continue their work, shoulders hunched with dread and anticipation.

More frightening than the dog is the man who leashes him. The leader. His face looks like it's been through a shredder. But it is his deliberateness that terrifies Maja. His calm covers a churning machine inside. He may not exactly enjoy punishing the girls, but he has no problem doing so. He makes the watchers look like nannies.

The clicking of the dog's nails on the concrete and the animal's rapid panting send chills up her spine. The inspections are like Russian roulette. Sometimes the girls pass muster, sometimes not.

The leader's running shoes squeak as they flex. The timing of the inspections, every two to three weeks, is unpredictable. What the leader is searching for remains unclear. Electronics? Forbidden. A camera? Forbidden. Candy? Gum? Forbidden.

The minutes stretch out interminably. Maja is restless. She works furiously at her rug. Even from a distance, she can hear a watcher take a drag on his cigarette and exhale. She hears a gob of dog drool splash on the floor next to her. She does not pause.

The beast is upon her, its nose active. The dog snorts and

huffs as it circles her head, her back and pauses at her bottom. Despite her being fully clothed, she's embarrassed. The animal works around to her crossed legs and stuffs its nose into her crotch. Still, she cranes forward, continuing to tie.

The dull rattle of its choke collar signals that this time she has passed. The dog is led to the girl to Maja's left. The process begins again.

The dog growls roughly.

Why? Maja wonders.

"No, no! Please!" the girl cries. The leader coils the girl's hair around his hand and lifts her straight off the floor. Maja doesn't even know the girl's name.

"Too slow!" the leader calls out.

But she is one of the most efficient of them all. Surely one of the watchers will defend her! But nothing is said.

Maja's partner hangs by her hair, tears streaming down her cheeks. The girl bites down on her knuckles, not daring to scream. It would only get worse for her. They would beat the soles of her feet with the sock—a knot of rocks tied into the toe of a white Reebok athletic sock.

"You dare look at me like that?" the leader spits at the crying girl. "This one!" he tells the nearby watcher. The leader passes the girl by the hair. The watcher lets her settle to the floor and drags her off.

"Faster!" the leader shouts.

All heads are trained down. All hands are busy.

Ten minutes later there's a ruckus at station nine. "Sloppy!" the leader says in Dutch.

This girl cries out and is slapped repeatedly. She settles into a blubbering sob.

Maja knows better than to look. A moment later, the leader leaves. Two girls are gone, never to return. Taken to where, Maja doesn't know.

Her fingers twist the length of red yarn. Grab, tuck and pull tight. If they see her tears, she's in trouble.

6

Sonia Pangarkar's newspaper article haunts him as he makes the call to his brother. The reporter was interviewing doctors at a local clinic about the cost of immigrant health care when an emaciated, unkempt girl arrived at the desk, feverish from a festering ankle wound. The writing is excellent—too good for Knox; too many well-crafted images left swimming in his head. Now he wishes he hadn't read it. They had to include a photo because what would the article be without some nausea to go along with it? A girl of nine or ten, her face all bone and eyes. Pleading. Helpless. These children are used for their small fingers. Their knots can be tied tighter and more quickly. It's efficiency, at any price. But now it's their turn to pay the price, whoever's behind this. Dulwich has his mission; Knox has his own.

Before calling Tommy, Knox tries to settle himself.

His brother knows him way too well, and in an uncanny, telekinetic way, his condition—whatever name they're putting on it this week—allows him insight nearly to where he can penetrate Knox even over a phone line, discerning his mood or state of mind. Knox will use the new job offer as an excuse to delay his scheduled visit; it's not the first delay, nor likely the last, and he doesn't want Tommy seeing through to the truth—whatever that truth may be; it continues to elude him. Knox has been focused on Tommy's financial health for so long that he's beginning to see himself as avoiding the realities of his brother's physical and emotional health.

"Hey."

"There you are!" Tommy comes in two flavors: apathetic and charged. It's the latter today, which is easier for Knox. When apathetic, Tommy is unreachable.

"How are things?"

"You know." Tommy feels responsible for the embezzlement of over three hundred thousand dollars by their company's former bookkeeper, Evelyn, a woman Tommy became infatuated with. No matter how many times Knox explains Evelyn fooled them both, Tommy can't forgive himself. Part of the guilt revolves around Tommy's crush, allowing her to manipulate him. Knox has plans for Evelyn when he finds her, and he will find her.

"I'm taking a job with Sarge. I don't know for how long, but it will pay well."

"How'd the buying go?"

Knox isn't sure he's heard him. Tommy can be funny that way. "Good. You got my e-mails?"

"Yeah."

"Then you know it went well." There are those who treat Tommy like a ten-year-old. Not his brother.

"You shipped to the warehouse."

"Correct." They're getting somewhere; Tommy is staying on top.

"We can put the new stuff online as soon as they're inventoried." There's pride in his voice now, making Knox happy.

"Yes. That's right. You can take care of the inventory?"

"No problem."

That a boy. "You heard what I said about Sarge?"

"Yeah."

"It doesn't mean you can't call me."

"I know."

"I want you to call me."

"Yeah, okay."

"Seriously."

"But not too serious."

Knox can't wipe the smile off his face as he answers. "You got that right."

"What kind of job? With Sarge?"

"Just a thing."

Much as he knows he needs to keep the lines of communication open, Tommy is a liability. Someone might try to track down Tommy to get to Knox. Ignorance is bliss. People who run sweatshops are not to be messed with. The kind of person who chains a ten-year-old to a worktable thinks nothing of taking out a thirty-something Curious George. He and Dulwich rarely discuss the risks.

The pay grade reflects them up front. None of that does Tommy much good if Knox doesn't come home. Knox is wearing a bull's-eye on his back before he ever leaves for Amsterdam.

"Yeah, okay." Tommy knows the rules.

"So we're good?" A loaded question.

"You're saying you're not coming to see me."

The question hangs over Knox like an executioner's blade. He can't speak. Who's the child now? Knox resents the responsibility for Tommy even as he moves to meet it.

"Take care, Johnny." It comes out as a memorized line.

7

Grace enters the Netherlands on her own passport. One of the fallouts from 9/11 for companies like Rutherford Risk is the difficulty in forging identities. It can still be done, she knows, but it's expensive and time consuming. It has been two weeks since Dulwich offered her the work. Two extremely busy weeks of conference calls with Dulwich and Knox, and Knox alone; CV creation and corresponding background support so that by the time she hands the hotel desk clerk her European Union business card everything will check out. Not exactly a new identity, but a solid academic and employment record that will hold up under all but the most intense and high-level scrutiny.

She is dressed in a conservative gray suit with low black heels. It was bought off a used-clothing rack in Hong Kong specifically for the slight fraying of both sleeve cuffs.

She wears the worn, tired expression of an overtraveled low-level bureaucrat. At hotel registration her speech is clipped, but polite, and she displays a road warrior's knowledge of everything expected of her: passport, credit card, business card, signature. She waves off the bellman and hauls her roll-aboard to the elevator, barely lifting her eyes as she punches her floor number.

Once into her room, she unpacks, maintaining the routine of an experienced traveler. Her mobile alerts her to an e-mail with an attachment she'd rather open on her laptop, so she takes a minute to set up her traveling office. Chargers, wires, the laptop with a Bluetooth mouse. She carries a data/Wi-Fi device that goes on the desk as well. The encryption between the laptop, the data device and the cell network requires a piece of USB hardware, the software equivalent of a tempered stainless-steel lock. Three passwords later, she's into her corporate mail and is downloading a PDF sent by Dulwich—which turns out to be a scanned copy of an Amsterdam police report. The existence of the report should have been good news, for it signals Dulwich's having established a local police contact for her and Knox. But it's anything but.

She responds to her situation physically—an elevated heart rate, sweaty palms. This assignment is important, if not critical. Her moment has arrived; she intends to capitalize on it. Brian Primer will not be sorry he approved her participation.

Grace's Dutch is better spoken than written and read. It's true of her Italian, Russian and Arabic as well. But she's fluent in German and finds it useful as she attempts to decipher the police report.

An Egyptian-born male, one Kahil Fahiz, thirty-two, was the victim of a mugging/robbery just west of the central district. He sustained multiple minor injuries and lacerations, was treated at a hospital as an outpatient and was discharged. On the surface it looks common enough. But for Grace, it is a minor shot of adrenaline. She reviews the initial newspaper article, skimming it for a name that's echoing around her head. Finds it:

Kabril Fahiz.

Sonia Pangarkar's article quotes a Kabril Fahiz, a local merchant who took a dim view of child labor sweatshops in his neighborhood.

Kahil . . . Kabril.

She places a call using the laptop.

"Have you opened it yet?" she asks Knox over the VPN's voice-to-Internet protocol software. As he speaks on his mobile, it is conceivable Knox's end of the conversation might be eavesdropped on. Not so for her. In a perfect world they would both be on the VPN.

"The police report? I have. My written Dutch is a little lacking."

"It's the victim's statement, short as it is, that interests me—us. That, and his family name of course."

"Okay," Knox says.

"It states that they beat him and robbed him. But at the end of the beating, one of them said something in Farsi along the lines of: 'That'll teach you to open your mouth.' The victim said he spent hours trying to figure out what he might've said and when he might've said it, but came up blank."

"We all say things we later regret."

"No . . . it is not that. Not in this case. The sergeant filing the report made an interesting observation. Entirely speculative, but important to us."

"Okay?"

"Ka*br*il Fahiz," she says, emphasizing the second syllable, "the man Pangarkar interviewed for her story, is from the same neighborhood—Oud-West—and is the same approximate age as the victim, Ka*h*il Fahiz, the one they assaulted."

"These apes go asking around intending to pound this guy who's speaking to reporters into a different postal code—"

"But they mispronounce his name. Kabril and Kahil— an easy mistake to make."

"They beat up the wrong guy," Knox said, speculating. "I like the way you think. Have I told you that?"

"It wasn't me, it was the police. It is speculation. You're jet-lagged. Stay on point."

"They got the wrong guy. Mixed up the names. Listen, I get it!"

"Avoided using a car bomb this time because they didn't want the assault connected back to the earlier murder. To the newspaper article. But the police made that connection. The police report suggests a follow-up on all of Pangarkar's sources mentioned in the article. They will have sent them to ground, John. Protect them from the possibility of more reprisals."

"That won't help us. Is there contact info in the report?"

"There is."

"You should interview Fahiz."

"Who do you think you are dealing with?" She hears herself slip into her Chinese dialect—she sounds like her mother!—and resents Knox for triggering her anger.

She resents a great deal about John Knox—his singular focus, his single-mindedness. The arrogance. Theirs is an evolving relationship. She imagines this is what an older brother would feel like—a combination of love, hate, respect, embarrassment. Together, they wander a no-man's-land booby-trapped with buried mines of sexual innuendo but lacking the chemistry to go along with it. He is at once fascinating and intriguing, boorish and disagreeable.

"If you go talking to . . . well . . . you know how I feel about it."

He had objected vehemently to Dulwich's plan for Grace to take the cover of a low-level EU bureaucrat arriving to replace the victim of the car bombing. Dulwich believed it not only gave her an excuse to follow in Pangarkar's footsteps but also might "attract the bee to the pollen." Dulwich showed little concern over using her as bait—a gamble given her increased importance to Primer. For Dulwich, it's all about efficiency—getting the most out of his assets to reach the endpoint the quickest. He would argue that that included suffering the least collateral damage. But the way he stages an operation often runs contrary to that objective.

"I don't need hand-holding," she claims.

"Just make sure to keep the 'Find My iPhone' feature turned on. I want you on a leash."

She pulls the phone quickly from her ear not wanting him to hear her laugh. She knows he'd rather be shopping in Marrakesh than pursuing a bomber in Amsterdam, knows that for him this is about his brother—always will be. Senses there is residual guilt there, but has never heard Tommy's full story. It bothers her that he has coaxed more out of her than she has from him.

"And you?"

"Don't worry about me," he says.

"Who said I was worried?"

8

Knox has never been in a newsroom before. His only impressions are from the movies—the noise, the confusion of dozens of reporters in small cubicles, phones ringing, pages running up and down aisles. About the only thing that matches with the image now in front of him is the glass wall at the end of the room beyond which are the offices of various editors, including the editor in chief. It's quiet, subdued, many of the cubicles empty. It has to do with the world economy, the state of the newspaper business. If once this newsroom thrived, it does no longer.

"Emily Prager?"

The woman who looks up at him is tired and needs to wash her hair. A package of nicotine gum rests by her keyboard, along with a blue spongy ball and a black hair tie.

He introduces himself as John Steele, the freelance photographer who called looking for Sonia Pangarkar. The receptionist told him where to find her. "You said you might be able to help me find her."

"I did not expect a visit."

"I can be impulsive."

"I told you: she's not coming in to work right now. She's taken a leave. I'm sorry."

"A leave, or on holiday?"

"She and Mark had a falling out. Our city editor."

"Over?"

"Not for me to say." Her eyes tell him she's uncomfortable speaking to him here. "You'll need to take that up with her."

"Can I buy you a cup of coffee?"

"No, thank you."

"Please."

She lowers her voice as her eyes appraise him. "Sonia is sometimes a little too independent—a little too creative for Mark."

"The sweatshop article. The girl. That's exactly why I'm here."

"She was assigned a piece on medical care. It's not exactly what she filed."

"But a strong piece just the same."

"But Mark . . . he writes the paychecks. He knows what he wants. He and Sonia . . . believe me, they have both benefited from the other, but it is push and pull with them. Right now, Mark is pushing. So is Sonia. So, her leave of absence."

"The car bombing didn't carry her byline." Knox had a crash course in journalism over the phone with a friend at the *Detroit Free Press*. He hopes to hell he has his lexicon straight. He feels he's inching closer to something, doesn't want to give himself away.

"No."

"And that upset her."

Emily Prager's consternation gives way. "There's a Starbucks on the corner. Ten minutes."

After twelve minutes he's beginning to worry, but she arrives soon thereafter, a sweater around her shoulders. She orders a coffee and waits for it, and joins him at a small table. The place is jumping. The streets are busy.

"Look," she says, "it's not like I have a lot to say to you."

"Yet here we are."

"I searched online for your work. It's good. You're good."

Dulwich and the Hong Kong office have made John Steele credible. "Her phone number?"

She appraises him. "I don't think so."

"You could text her for me. Let her know I'd like to meet with her."

"I could, but I won't. Sonia doesn't need a photographer; she needs time away. This story got to her. It happens."

"Good photographs carry a story," he says. "From the moment I read her piece . . ." He shakes his head. "You could just let her know I'm available."

"I can't get involved." Again, she studies his face. This time her expression softens. "There is a café on the corner of Paleisstraat and Nieuwezijds Voorburgwal. Southwest corner, close by to the tram stop. I forget the name of it. We have met there several times. Couches. Lamps. More like a home than these Starbucks," she says. "She favors it."

"I'll give you my number." He pulls out a business card for John Steele, circles the mobile number in pen, and passes her the card. He compliments himself for having the cards made. Best thirty euros he's spent.

"I won't," she says.

"You might."

"It's personal for her. For Sonia. There was a niece, I believe it was. It's a mistake to allow that into your stories. Mark knows that. Sonia should. But that's the thing about the personal—it creeps in, and you don't see it for what it is."

Knox thinks about Tommy, and his heart is heavy. "A niece."

"In India. Similar circumstances."

Knox senses her reluctance. Isn't going to push. *Similar circumstances.* The words swim around.

He says, "She's going to freelance the story."

"It happens."

"And the paper?"

"Mark won't like it. He'll throw a fit. But in the end, Sonia will win. Sonia always wins. She's very, very good. A reporter like her comes around only a few times a generation. The language skills. The people skills. Aggressive to the point of dangerous. To herself. To others. She is pretty enough for television, but has not given in to it fully yet. She dabbles, for her own amusement. She is still a writer first." She drinks the coffee, her eyes searching him over the rim expectantly.

She looks like she's beginning to enjoy this.

"It's a compelling story," he says. "Child labor. Poor working conditions. Impoverished neighborhoods. Unwanted immigrants. Why would an editor turn away from that?"

"The neighborhoods are not impoverished, Mr. Steele. Amsterdam is a city of immigrants—but only for the past three centuries. Do your research! Mark got a story he didn't ask for. It's as simple as that. He's a control freak. If he assigns the story, it has value. If it's brought to him in a meeting and discussed, it has value. If it shows up in his in-box unassigned . . ."

"What editor can work that way?"

"Now you're sounding like Sonia."

"You have my card."

She fingers it, flicking the corner. "Yes."

9

Grace doesn't know if it's her being Chinese, or the EU credentials, but no one at the health clinic attempts to stonewall her. She asks for and is given a printout of the emergency admission records for Kahil Fahiz. It goes too easily, a rarity. She commits the home address to memory, along with a mobile number. A few minutes later, she has entered them both into her phone. Without Sonia Pangarkar's tendency toward graphic journalism she would not have known the hospital. But now all that's left is navigating her way through a busy city, finding bridges across canals, and wending her way toward the address.

When mapped, Amsterdam sits like the left half of a bike wheel with crepe paper woven through the spokes; the crepe paper is the canals, with Centraal Station as the wheel's hub. Over the centuries, the city has expanded ever outward from the thirty blocks of its central historic district—devoted entirely to tourism, the canals lined with picturesque three-story Dutch timber and Tudor houses—to a postwar district of nearly identical brick and white-trim apartment complexes. These outer neighborhoods, all identical, stretch for miles in every direction.

Grace double-checks not only the building number but the street name. The architecture and street layout are so homogeneous as to be dizzying.

No one answers her repeated tries on the Fahizes' door. The first hiccup. She tries the phone number but gets voice mail in Farsi. She understands this. She imagines no matter how many times she called, it would go to voice mail. The victim of a beating, Fahiz will strive to remain as anonymous and invisible as possible. Because of this, she has her work cut out for her. But a person has to work.

The third neighbor she tries cringes at the mention of Fahiz's name; a reaction to his face following the beating, or his personality? She tells Grace of a shisha café, La Tertulia, that Fahiz frequents. How this woman knows this, or whether it's accurate, is anybody's guess. She asks directions, thanks the woman and heads off. She pauses at the bottom of the stairs; the neighbor is still watching her. There seems to be a question hanging between them—as if Grace forgot to ask this woman something. It's a strange and haunting feeling, and she can't shake it for the entire walk to the café.

La Tertulia is located on the ground floor of a brownstone. The smell of cannabis overwhelms as Grace enters, despite what are supposed to be vaporless pipes. New Age murals cover the walls—whales in blue oceans—with cannabis plants spreading above the couches and opium beds that proliferate. It's a pot shop primarily aimed at tourists, but there appear to be locals in residence as well, some of whom are of Middle Eastern descent and are smoking tobacco, not cannabis, from hookahs. The piped-in music reminds Grace of massage spas. A waitress with three studs in her lower lip and blue dye streaking her dark hair waves Grace toward a beanbag.

She thanks the girl, speaking Dutch, but heads directly to two men in the corner, one of whom has a face like a punching bag.

"Mr. Fahiz?" She speaks English first.

Fahiz looks up at her with mild interest. He has sleepy, dark eyes, a heavy shadow of beard, expressive thick eyebrows and a full head of hair. He's easily seventy years old.

Not the man described in Sonia Pangarkar's article.

Not by a long shot.

10

Knox walks along the avenue, Nieuwezijds Voor-burgwal, beneath an oppressive quicksilver marine layer that makes everyone look small, the tram and cabs toylike. The only relief to the impervious gray comes in the form of an occasional umbrella—of little use against the steady mist. He wears nondescript brown shoes, blue jeans and a tan Scottevest windbreaker with sixteen zippered internal pockets all containing various necessities. A roll of coins to palm in a fistfight. A penlight. A pack of waterproof matches. A pick gun for the occasional locked door. A sewing kit in case he's wounded. That he blends in is never in question. The Detroit Tigers cap helps to hide his face with its two-day beard and Tunisian tan. He passes a dozen of himself. Keeps his right shoulder to the store-fronts to reduce his exposure. Uses reflections off the glass to his advantage.

The coffee shop is abuzz with conversation as he enters. This is his fifth visit here in as many days and it's always the same. The crowd is a sprinkling of tourists on top of a foundation of firmly rooted locals. English is spoken as much as Dutch. There is an intensity to the conversation that one doesn't hear as much in the U.S. The women look masculine in their short haircuts. Only the piercings give them away. Knox is a fan of femininity, and mourns its passing.

He finds a chair at a table occupied by a young couple, and installs himself. A waitress with a lip stud and midnight purple eye shadow takes his order for an espresso. Knox pulls out his mobile—an iPhone on a prepaid SIM—and sends a text across the room. Of the twenty or so in the café, twenty or so have their phones out. Including Sonia.

Wait for signal. Leave cafe. Take tram to Centraal. Take 13 to Westermarkt. Proceed south on Keizersgracht to the Dylan Hotel. Wait in the lobby.

He hits SEND, his eyes straying over the balcony. Knox uses the camera to surreptitiously get a closer look, just as he used it a day earlier to capture her number as her phone rebooted. Her elegant fingers with their close-clipped black polished nails nudge her phone almost absentmindedly as the text comes through. She eventually drags the phone to a reading distance, and—if he had to guess—she reads the message twice.

His camera is on his lap by the time her head snaps up

and she scans the room. He can only wonder what she's experiencing. He's banking on a journalist's curiosity; an investigative reporter's paranoia; a woman's intuition. Given the controversy of the topic she's been covering, and the unfortunate outcome for at least two of her sources, she must give weight to the possibility that she herself is being watched. He won't know until he tries.

It's everything he can do to keep himself in the chair. Time crawls. The overhead fans spin more slowly. He sees every twitch of character on every face, hears the scrape of chair legs on marble, the sputter of lips sipping steaming coffee. She's on heightened alert, observing everything taking place in the café. She not only awaits the signal mentioned in the message, but wants to identify who's responsible.

Knox waits. He's in the business of opportunity. He stands. Lets a girl screen him. Crosses to the man with the heavy eyebrows and expressionless face.

"I hope you don't mind," Knox says, reaching his target. He speaks English.

He fires off a photograph. A volley of four flashes burst, blinding the man.

"Thank you!" he says. He moves and takes another picture, placing himself between the man tailing Sonia and the door.

He sees his plan has worked perfectly. Sonia is outside and moving across the street.

Her tail realizes she's gone.

Too late.

Knox uses the iPhone's camera to take a photo of the Nikon's small display. He texts the photo to Grace.

Sonia boards a tram. Her tail is too late.

GRACE'S PHONE BUZZES in her right hand. Even though she expects the text, the sensation nonetheless startles her. Standing outside Centraal Station, she feigns studying the tram schedule display. Her jaw lifted, her eyes are nonetheless trained on the faces of all the passengers disembarking a Line 5 tram. She raises the phone to where she can see Knox's photo of the man in the café, while studying the faces of those departing the tram.

She slips her iPhone into her black leather bag.

The area outside the station is jammed. Busier than she'd expected. She works to filter out the noise and confusion, to focus. She's noticed three pairs of police on patrol. One is behind and heading away from her. Another is to her left dealing with a vagrant. The third pair enters the station.

And yet, despite the chaos, there is something reassuring that everyone has a place to be, a place to go, a schedule to keep. *If only the world were more like a train station,* she thinks. When had the comforting sense of order been replaced by randomness?

Sonia appears from the door of the number 5 tram, as expected. She has a beautiful face: wide-set dark eyes, gorgeous Indian skin. She's shorter than Grace expected, perhaps her same height, wearing a soft purple scarf over her head, designer blue jeans and a flowing top beneath a tailored brown leather coat. She doesn't hurry, doesn't look back. Grace has the sense she's paying attention to her surroundings. Her body language is magnificent, that of a bored commuter, but a close look at her eyes tells the observer she is alert and busy-minded. Grace is immediately impressed.

A half dozen outdoor platforms serve the station. Platform 4 is currently serving Line 13.

Sonia is following Knox's directions to the letter.

Grace waits, sipping a coffee and swallowing her impatience. It is a deficiency her trainers have worked hard to remove. Not easily done. But she has learned to overcome it with small tricks, aware of its destructiveness.

Sonia's tail appears only minutes later on the next number 5. He's a clever one, this bastard. He inspects the schedule display, turns around. Grace does as Knox asked. She moves toward him and they collide. Her coffee spills across him.

"Shit," he curses in Dutch-accented English.

As Grace catches sight of Sonia climbing onto the number 13 tram, she rattles off an apology in Mandarin. She's brushing his side now, feeling a lump under his coat that is the weapon, down his leg as she kneels. He swipes at her hands, not wanting the contact. The delay is effective. At least twenty seconds and counting. She is telling him in Mandarin that she wishes to pay for the stains she has created. She proffers euros he has no use for, making sure that he knocks them from her hands in the process of his refusal. Making a scene. Forty seconds. Fifty. Head held low in an act of contrition, when the real point is to keep him from getting a good look at her. There may be cause for them to meet later. Grace cannot afford to be recognized.

It's over quickly. He steps out of the puddle and makes physical contact with her as he pushes her aside in his disgust. A simple shove to the shoulder, but she goes over like a feather duster, impressed. He's on the scent like a hound, pulled by the same string that aimed him at Platform 4. She could follow, but Knox has instructed her not to, and though it was difficult at first, she has learned to trust his areas of expertise. She has come to respect, even admire, his abilities—his street savvy, his people instinct, his understanding of crowds. He is capable of things most people don't ever think of. But she does think of these things because she has been trained to, because it interests her. She enjoys the role of the predator, the voyeur, the phantom. She thrives in shadow. This man understands these worlds in ways others do not; there is much to learn from him, though she is loath to admit it. It comes to him naturally, a second nature; he's like a natural-born musician who doesn't understand his own talent. But she understands for him. She knows what he does not: that there are few like him, that he teaches without meaning to, that he can frighten with a look, calm with a word or two. For now, she is content to follow his lead in some areas while making sure he never thinks she is. So she lets the tail go. The minute delay was all that was asked of her and she has accomplished it. The rest is now on Knox's meeting with Sonia. Grace can get back to what she does best—though what exactly that is, she's still working out.

11

Having received a text from Grace that her delay tactics went according to plan, that Sonia Pangarkar departed on the number 13 without her tail, Knox slows as he approaches the Dylan Hotel's front doors.

Three people occupy the far sidewalk—an older couple with a dog on a leash, and a woman crouched and petting the dog. Four other people on his sidewalk, a good distance away and moving.

He carries the camera bag. The Dylan Amsterdam is four interconnected Keizersgracht canal houses. A courtyard at the entrance. It's a European mix of contemporary and classical. Once into the hotel, the guest is enfolded in cream walls with white enamel trim; large windows flood the rooms with light. An eclectic collection of contemporary furniture coddles the weary. Knox enters the hotel lounge, a floor of reclaimed barn wood. He looks around.

She isn't here.

According to Grace, Sonia had followed his instructions to the letter. So why not to their conclusion? Has he helped her lose her tail only to get nothing in return?

Only now does he realize Sonia Pangarkar was the woman petting the dog. She'd checked him out—might've even snapped a photograph. The cautious and curious journalist.

He's an ass for making such a sophomoric mistake. He orders a beer and sits on the love seat with his back to a stone wall.

He sends a text:

cute dog. if you trust no one, you have no one. you have 15 minutes.

The cold beer goes down smoothly. There's a long hallway with windows that look out onto gardens and the canal beyond, and she comes down it like a runway model—all alone, arms swaying by her side, a boldness to her walk. Not a woman easily intimidated. She trusts the safety of the surroundings. If he'd chosen a city park, she never would've showed.

His moment has arrived. He doesn't consider himself much of an actor, but presenting himself to women is easy enough. Second nature. As smooth as the beer. He's never been afraid of women. Appreciates the companionship.

He'd rather see a movie with someone than alone, would rather share the Sunday paper, a meal, a drink.

The coffee she describes to the waitress has so many adjectives and descriptive clauses that the two might as well be speaking a foreign language. The waitress apparently has no trouble with interpretation and is off.

She stares at him. Not exactly sizing him up, but not letting him off the hook. If he were an artist he might consider painting her. He'd like to see her naked; it's one of the first thoughts that pops into his head, and it surprises him. It's her skin that is the elixir. He wants to see what that coloring does to all the various parts. His imagination is a little wild with it, and he blames it on the beer. He doesn't consider himself the type to first undress a woman, and yet that's exactly what he's done. He can imagine she smells different—exotic, sweetly perfumed, but heavy with the musky scent from between her legs. It's not a reaction he's comfortable with. He's aware it can give her an unfair advantage, a leverage that he has no intention of giving. He has only seen her at a distance. Sitting so close is disarming.

She possesses a professional edge that allows several minutes to hang in the air between them, the pendulum swinging back and forth between their nearly unflinching eyes. Each is waiting for the other to say something. Both understand that in a hand of bridge the lead carries a great burden: it establishes hierarchy, it sets the suit to be played. Better to let the other lead, and then elect to match suit or trump.

"John Steele," he says. He has always gotten a kick out of the surname. Strong. Heavy. He pulls a business card out of his pocket knowing she isn't the type to care about a business card, but he went to the bother—for her sake—and he has planned this out, and the business card is part of the plan. So he slides it across the table to her, and she flicks it by the corner in order to pick it up. Reads it. Flips it over. Looks back across to him. Maybe it has had more of an effect on her than he thought it might. Europe and Asia put much more stock in business cards than America. She's a reporter. Maybe it's enough evidence.

"So?" she says.

"The article on the sweatshop. Good writing. Bad photo."

"It was carried on the wire, that photo. Published all around the world." Her English is very good, though her accent thick.

"McDonald's operates all around the world. I still don't eat there." He'd hoped for a smile, but she isn't volunteering.

"Canada? The U.S.?"

"Once upon a time. And that time was a long time ago. Have you not seen my work?"

She studies the business card for a second time. "What is it you want?"

"I've been trying to get up my nerve to make you a business proposition. But you don't make it easy. And I'm not exactly sure what's going on with you. There are two of them. They take turns in the café." He waits for that to sink in. "Watching you."

"You were able to text me."

"I sat above you in the café. Your Nokia shows its number when it boots up. You might want to change that."

She wants to scoff at this; appears about to do so. He assumes it's the look he gives her that convinces her otherwise. Knox never shies from allowing his confidence to show.

"Are you so resourceful? I don't like this."

"If you're going after the story of the people running the sweatshop," Knox says, "and I believe you are, it needs photographs. A hidden camera? Video? You know it. I know it."

"The paper has photographers." Dismissive. She scoots back her chair. "Besides, I filed that story. I'm on to other things."

"No, you're not." He waits just long enough for her anger to stir. "You're on leave. You're working freelance."

"And who are you working for, Mr. Steele?"

"One of your sources is dead. Another, assaulted."

"And you're my guardian angel."

He doesn't answer. For a moment he is at a loss for words. She's not what he'd expected.

"What kind of photographer spots people watching other people? Or maybe you made it all up to impress me. Maybe you hired that man. It's a lot of trouble to go to for some photo credits."

"It's a tough economy."

Her laughter carries across the lounge. She covers her mouth, reminding him of Grace. Her eyes shine. A closer look tells him she's exhausted.

"I don't trust you, Mr. Steele."

"Google my work. A picture's worth a thousand words. You have my number." Dulwich and Rutherford Risk have established both as part of his cover. He's credited from Melbourne to Monterey.

"If you follow me again, if I see you again, I will call the police."

"These people weren't afraid to kill an EU bureaucrat. What chance do you think a reporter has?"

She stands, a pillar of righteousness. "A photographer has a better chance?"

"Do you trust them?" he says.

"They're killers," she returns.

"The police, I mean," he says, surprising her. "Do you trust them?" She sits back down, weary now, fearful even.

Her silence reaches across the small table like the smell of fear.

"Can a sweatshop be run without police on the take?" he asks. "I'm asking. I don't know Amsterdam well."

Her eyes burn with hatred and resignation. He knows which one is meant for him.

"You intend to find the sweatshop."

"Knot shop," she corrects. "The young girls are recruited because their fingers are so small. Faster knots. Women, too. But the girls are far cheaper—a few euros a day if they're lucky."

"And then? Do you stop if you get the story?"

"Would you stop there?"

"I would not," he says.

"Neither shall I."

"And they will kill you. What is the point of that?"

"Were you sent to warn me?"

He laughs. "The man in the café should have been enough for that."

"Indeed." She nods thoughtfully.

"You're out of your element."

"And you are not?"

He doesn't want to oversell. Doesn't want the shrug mistaken as a promise. Doesn't want to scare her off. There's a connection between them, but it's fragile at best.

"Two is better than one. We proved that at the café."

"How do I know you didn't set that up for my benefit?"

"You don't. Though to be honest, I'm not that smart."

She can't fight the curl at the edge of her lips. "I doubt that," she says. "All for a photo credit or two? I doubt that as well."

"And you? Strictly humanitarian? No whiff of prizes, of peer recognition?"

"So crass."

"I know who you are," he says. "Professionally speaking, of course. I know what this story would mean for me. I don't deny it. Do you?"

"I do. Absolutely."

"All right then, I'll accept you at your word."

"We are at cross-purposes," she says.

"Not at all. You need a wingman. Clearly."

She considers this. She doesn't like him, but there's the promise of tolerance as she purses her lips and looks down at her hands.

He senses she's not the type to shave her legs or under-arms regularly. European. Her perfectly plucked eyebrows contradict the stringiness of her hair. He wonders if her present circumstances are responsible or if this reflects her personal grooming.

"Don't follow me. Don't text me."

"You will come to find out that you don't have to tell me things twice." She stands and heads to the door without looking back.

He considers letting her go. Can't stop himself. She's gotten under his skin. He reaches her just before she opens the door to the street. Takes her by the arm, brings lips to her ear.

"Let me tell you something," he whispers. "You had better adopt a new attitude. Check your surroundings. Switch sides of the street. Reverse directions. Learn to follow no patterns—none. Assume—do you hear me?— you assume you are being watched or followed at all times and you do everything in your power to lose them, to make them work at it, to expose themselves to you. Remember faces. If not me, you let someone close to you know when you suspect something. Stay at hotels and switch often. Pay cash. Do not use your apartment. Avoid your regular crowd. Maybe you stay alive. You march out of the hotel without precautions, as you are about to do now, you won't last a week." He releases her. She has been pulling against his grip, and he's held her too tightly. Her perfume or deodorant—something—envelops her in a warm, earthy glow.

Her arm is free. They meet eyes.

"Thank you." She leaves his head spinning as she now takes in the lobby's clientele and slips out the hotel doors and onto the busy sidewalk. She pauses, studying the passing pedestrians and the vehicles along Keizersgracht.

A quick learner.

12

Following the address contained in the police report, Grace arrives at a nondescript brick apartment building, one of a line of identical structures on Kinkerstraat in Amsterdam's Oud-West. The suburban neighborhood has all the elegance of a community college campus.

Grace double-checks the house number against the photocopied report.

The door is unlocked. She passes an umbrella stand and a boot brush. Finds a two-person elevator and a door marked as fire stairs. The staircase holds the unpleasant aftereffects of curry and cigarettes. The space is well lighted, with no graffiti. Posters warn of AIDS.

The man she confronted in the shisha café knew nothing of a newspaper reporter; had no bruises or signs of having been attacked. The man who'd checked into the hospital had provided a bogus address, but one that was registered to a man with his same name. Clever, yes. But also premeditated. He'd known how he would fill out the forms well before arriving at the emergency room. The beating had scared him. Finding such a cautious man will not be easy.

She walks the second-floor hallway, past doors muting the sounds of music and television, conversation and radio. She stops, recalling the police report. She grins, amused. The address is apartment 9. There are only eight apartments.

She retreats and knocks on the door. A Slavic woman answers, too pretty for such a place. She's wearing a clean yet well-worn frock.

Grace displays her EU credentials. She speaks Dutch slowly. The woman has no trouble understanding. There is no man named Fahiz, Grace is told. Not that she knows of. People come and go. It is hard to keep track. We don't know each other well, the woman confesses.

A second dead end from the elusive Kahil Fahiz, a man mistaken for another.

Grace is about to inquire if the police have been around, but thinks better of it. She thanks the woman and compliments her on her child, asleep in a springed rocker. Grace's attention lingers a little too long on the infant.

"You have children of your own?" the woman asks.

Grace offers a half smile, reminded of the wedding ring she wears as part of her cover. Thanks the woman.

Descends the stairs in something of a trance. She feels weary. Old. She has left her high school sweetheart behind in China for a second time. Twice she has felt the skin peeled from her body; twice she has been forced to heal. She calls Knox, wondering why this is the first thing she thinks to do.

"Can you talk?"

"And listen," he says. "With pleasure."

She throws an internal switch: back to Grace the spy. "He provided a fake address. Twice, actually, but the second time to the cops."

"That's ballsy."

"Afraid the police report would leak," she says.

"And it did. He was right about that. You and I should not forget."

"I'm going to try the mobile number he provided to the police. I thought you should know."

"First, can you get into billing records for the mobile carriers?"

On their first job together, a kidnapping case in Shanghai, they had used a third-party hacker. It had bothered Grace to involve an outsider. Since their return to Hong Kong she had devoted herself to studying with the Data Sciences division at Rutherford Risk, a group that included a cadre of prepubescent freaks who kept their own hours and could drill into any server unobserved. Knox can tell by her silence that she takes offense at his asking.

"To see if the number's valid, et cetera, before dialing it yourself," he says. "There could be more accurate billing information with the mobile carrier."

"Point taken," Grace said. "And for the record, I had not planned to call from my own mobile."

"No. I didn't mean to imply—"

"Of course you did."

"I want to back you up."

"We'll see," she says.

"Just as you helped me at Centraal."

"It is possible."

"It's nonnegotiable."

"Did you connect with Pangarkar?"

"In a manner of speaking. We were in the same room for a few minutes."

"We need her."

He returns the silent treatment.

"I will check the carrier. Then I will call." She hangs up. She finds a wireless connection in the lobby of the Hotel Pulitzer on Prinsengracht. The mobile number Fahiz supplied to the police is a pay-as-you-go, rechargeable SIM card from SingTel, a Singapore cellular provider. The pay-as-you-go cards are not registered because there's no billing; their owner remains anonymous. She and Knox carry several such cards, providing them different, untraceable numbers. But use of a SIM card from a faraway country is an interesting choice for an Amsterdam local. A foreign provider means far-higher costs: ten times what one would pay using a local pay-as-you-go card. Fahiz's use of a foreign SIM tells her that the increased cost doesn't matter to him, and that distance—real anonymity—does. She wonders if he bought it after the assault to ensure he can't be easily found. But a second check reveals he's been recharging the card for nearly three years. This takes her into interesting territory.

"Fahiz is something of a curiosity."

"Aren't we all."

She fills him in on the man's use of a SingTel SIM card, pointing out the added expense, the implication of long-distance travel. She juxtaposes this with the false address he supplied to the police, and his listing his employment as "consultant."

"You and I, it's much the same," Knox says. "Three different cards, three different numbers, three different uses."

"But an average person?"

"None of us is average," Knox says. "He could owe child support. He could be a closet billionaire who just wants his privacy. Doesn't make him a person of interest in and of itself. Maybe he has five wives and five different families."

"Whose fantasy are we talking about here?"

"It would explain," he says, "why he gives the police a false address, but a working phone number. He wants to be contacted; he doesn't want to be able to be found."

She doesn't like it when Knox outthinks her. She loses her train of thought.

"All we care about," Knox says, "is that someone beat the snot out of him in a case of mistaken identity."

"For safety's sake, I will call him from a landline. A hotel over on Prinsengracht," she tells Knox.

"Good idea," Knox says.

"You wanted to know when I was going to call him."

"If you make arrangements to meet with him, I want in on that."

The call is placed from the hotel lounge, brown faux-leather chairs and couches grouped around black marble coffee tables on stainless-steel legs. Grace leaves a credit card with the desk to pay for the call. An automated voice tells her to leave a message. She does so.

Twenty minutes later, she receives a call.

"Ms. Chu?"

"Speaking."

"Fahiz, here."

She reintroduces herself as an EU official investigating hate crimes. The police report implied he'd been beaten for something he may have said. She would like to speak with him, if possible.

"The police were not to share my information," the man protests.

"I am afraid in instances such as yours they have no choice. Brussels is always notified in the case of hate crimes."

"I was . . . It was a mistake. It was an attack aimed at someone else."

"Yes. The man quoted in the newspaper article. Similar names. It is horrible." He says nothing. She continues. "This man, this other Fahiz, has left the city, along with the other sources quoted in the article. It might be wise for you to do the same."

"Impossible at the moment. I told the police, I want

nothing more to do with it beyond being notified *prior* to whatever arrests may be made. Should they miss someone, I do not want to bear the brunt of their reprisals."

"Then please, help us."

"Please, do not call me again."

Hearing his soothing and melodic voice, she's reminded of fantasies she had believed long buried.

"I found you," she says. "Others could as well. We should talk."

A protracted silence results. "Are you there?" she finally asks. "A few minutes is all. A few questions and you are done with me." *You called me back,* she wants to shout.

There's a steadily approaching sound in the background of the call. At first, she can't place it, but then she knows what it is: a tram. Fahiz is in the inner city.

"Hate crimes?" he asks. "To them, we all look the same."

To *them*, she notes. Plural.

"Your attackers were Dutch? European?"

She expects he may have hung up. When she hears his breathing, she says, "A few minutes is all." She gives him time to think. "You pick the time and place."

A long silence hangs over the line. Finally, he says, "Number fifty-four ferry to Noord. Alone. If I don't contact you on board, then walk straight up the promenade. Stay on that road. The first departure after the top of the hour. You have forty minutes." Fahiz ends the call.

Grace stares down at the screen of the phone, her thumbs poised to send Knox a text message. *Alone.* She follows through with the text, ending in all caps:

Agreed to meet: #54 ferry to Noord. 40 mins. Alone!
YOU CANNOT BE ON FERRY

She wishes she could trust Knox.

THE NOORD DISTRICT, with its postcard villages of
Ransdorp and Durgerdam, is separated from the touristy
central district by the brown turbid waters of the IJ harbor.
Pedestrians, bicycle and scooter riders, as well as any commuters using Centraal Station forgo the various traffic
tunnels, riding the three free ferries that round-trip in ten
minutes. The Venice of the Netherlands, Amsterdam is
home to ferries, water taxis and myriad private canal boats,
lending the city a romantic, historical seductiveness.

The easiest way to reach the Noord ferries is to cut
through Centraal Station. It's late afternoon—nine minutes remain until his deadline at the top of the hour—and
the always busy station is bedlam. The coffee and news
shops bulge with customers, choking foot traffic on the
concourse. A woman's voice over a loudspeaker grumbles
train numbers and track numbers and times and destinations to where it sounds like a quiz show. There is every
form of life here, from the stoned vagabond youth attracted
by the city's open pot cafés, to well-heeled businessmen
and -women, mothers pushing strollers, gray-bearded
seniors struggling to place their canes into the sea of shoe
leather. Grace holds herself back to move with the pace of
the crowd, not wanting to stand out. She wonders not if,
but from where, Knox is watching. She hates to admit that

along with the anxiety of having included him, there is an underlying sense of comfort that he's likely nearby.

Outside the station, she crosses with pedestrians and turns left to the ferries. Electronic signs announce the Noord destinations and the countdown to departures. Grace slows, but does not stop completely on her approach. Uninterested in the destinations, it's the numbers painted on the ferry pilot cabins that register with her: 55, 59, 71 . . . There's an enormous two-level barge tied up to the wharf that contains thousands of chained and locked bicycles. It's a bicycle parking lot for commuters who use Centraal Station. Sight of it stops Grace and she chastises herself for appearing the tourist.

54

The dock's electric timer counts down from 3:46. Bicyclists and scooter drivers push into a tangle on the right of the vessel. Pedestrians enter through doors to the left and move forward in a knot as the clock is down to under two minutes and there's a final rush to board. It's jammed, only inches separating people. There's the smell of humanity—perfumes, soaps, sweat, tobacco and wine breath. The stern gangway raises automatically and the ferry's under way. She is stalwart in her refusal to scan the faces of the passengers, to search for a man studying her. She doesn't want to spot Knox breaking promises. She can't allow anger to poison her. She must remain calm and objective. A low-level EU bureaucrat following up on something she'd rather not.

The crossing is fast. Five minutes, tops. The air fills

with blue motor oil vapor as the scooters start. The cyclists and pedestrians mix. It's an orderly off-loading. People fan out. Bikes are mounted, backpacks slung on. Grace joins a flow of pedestrians walking straight ahead on a wide, tree-lined artery with pavement for cars, a substantial bike lane and a sidewalk for pedestrians. The transition to pastoral from the concrete of downtown is immediate. Lawns. Freestanding homes with wrought-iron fences. Birdsong. The air tastes cleaner. A different city, five minutes from Centraal Station.

Still no contact.

"We will turn around now," speaks a male voice from behind. "I will take your phone."

Grace hesitates. It's like handing over her weapon.

"I'll put it in airplane mode but there is no—"

"Shut if off." His voice is sharp and icy, causing the opposite reaction in her: a spike of heat. He reaches for her. She pulls away.

"Easy!" she barks. The phone powers down. She shows it to him.

He holds out his hand, expecting its delivery. "No phone, no discussion," he says.

"Such cloak and dagger," Grace says.

He pockets her phone, turns her toward the ferry dock. "Walk." He stays at her side, a quarter-stride behind. In the distance, two electronic ferry signs.

She has yet to get a decent look at him. In profile, he's strong-featured, tall and unshaven. His left eye is swollen and he's sporting three stitches above the cheekbone. He has lost a layer of skin. Confident this is finally the Fahiz she's sought, she doesn't allow herself a sense of satisfaction. His preparedness is a warning. If he wants to come across as an ordinary man in extraordinary circumstances, he has failed.

Since a young age she's been drawn to the irrepressible overconfidence and swarthy looks of Turks. She finds their penetrating eyes hypnotic and their words carefully chosen. Appreciates that, as with Italian men, there's no ambiguity about what it is they are after. Conquest is all that matters to them, and she controls them because she controls access. She's never slept with a Turk. Can't say the same about Italians.

Is Knox watching? she wonders.

The walk back to the ferry takes only a minute. The approaching vessel is mid-river and closing fast.

Several cyclists arrive and queue up, standing alongside their bikes. It takes her a moment to recognize the man wearing the beret. His bike has to be twenty years old. He's stolen it. He will call it borrowing.

"After what has happened . . . someone with your particular credentials . . . the car bombing. My being assaulted. You must be half mad to investigate this." ·

"Only half?"

"You joke? A man was killed."

"Assistant deputy directors are allocated five minutes of humor a month."

"Again," he says.

The return ferry arrives. She repeats the boarding process, and there's Knox chatting up a blonde while eating a candy bar and laughing into the gray mist that's thick as teapot steam. He's so deeply in character she wonders if he remembers why he's here.

"Your . . . the people who assaulted you . . ." she says, "did they condemn you, make any kind of racial slur or—"

"My mother was a Turk. My father, Chechen. I no longer hear such things when they're said. My ears filter them out." He lights a cigarette, savors the first inhale. Barely any smoke escapes as he exhales, or maybe the wind caused by the movement of the ferry carries it away.

She does not quote the police file directly. She wants him to volunteer the same information a second time. People say strange things—incorrect things—when in shock and under duress. People will blurt things out to the police, invented on the spot, having no idea why.

Give me what you gave the police. Convince me.

"What can anyone do about such hate crimes?" he asks.

"I'm a civil servant. Trained as an accountant. I'm not much of an investigator. I ask questions I am told to ask. I write reports. We build statistics."

"I'm a statistic."

"Soon. Yes. Of course."

"Earlier you said you were investigating."

"Following orders."

"The police report. I would not have filed in the first place, except for my attackers' comment about me keeping my mouth shut."

Thank you.

"How many?" she asks.

"It is this Kabril Fahiz they were after. I know that now. You should be speaking to him, not me."

"He is on my list, of course. But he was not attacked. He is not the victim."

"Victim," he repeats. "So you *are* investigating."

"I am doing what I am told. Seriously. No more, no less."

"I'm not sleeping. If I am to see even my close friends," he said, meeting eyes with her for the first time, "it's like this." He motions out to the river. The ferry is pulling up to the dock. "Precautions. Paranoia."

"What exactly did they say?"

"You have read the report."

"Can you give me some descriptions? We often remember more a day or two later. Hmm?"

"Not I. I want to forget, not remember."

"We don't control our memories. They control us."

"A philosopher?" he says, mocking her. Again, eye contact. "What I ask is simple enough. This is not my fight. But they brought it to me. They know my face. My habits. How would I know until it's too late? You . . . and the police . . . you owe it to me to let me know what's going on *ahead of time* so I am not made a victim a second time." He touches the fresh scar on his cheek. It's an angry red. "You owe me."

"I need more," she says. "If I am to—"

She's cut off as the gangway begins its groaning descent. The passengers surge forward as a unit.

"Listen, from what I experienced, you should not pursue these people. They will hurt you. Worse. Go back to your superiors and tell them it was a dead end. Give this up."

"Height? Weight? You must remember something."

She sees Fahiz trying to time his next comment, his eyes shifting toward the lowering gangway.

"Three of them. One who spoke Dutch, but like a German speaks Dutch."

She says, "You did not tell this to the police."

He doesn't look at her, seems not to have heard her. "I have your number. If I should remember more . . ."

"The longer your assailants remain at large, the longer you are at risk. Help us find them, and your trouble is over."

"Once started, trouble is never over. That is a myth." He returns her phone. Then he's off into the departing passengers, putting a wall of flesh between them.

You owe me, echoes in her ears.

Behind him follows a man walking a twenty-year-old bicycle.

13

The bicycle's rear wheel squeaks on each revolution, its rhythm steady as Knox keeps his distance behind Fahiz. He, and a few hundred others in and around Centraal Station, wears stereo earbuds on white wires. His are connected to an iPhone zippered into his Scottevest windbreaker. But Knox is not listening to Coldplay; he's waiting for the call from Grace. He slings the camera bag over his shoulder.

Fahiz circumnavigates the station, rather than taking the shortcut through it. An interesting choice that puzzles Knox. Fahiz arrives at the outdoor tram platforms. Riders crowd the stops. Jiggering the camera bag, Knox mounts the bike and rides ahead of Fahiz and stops at a crosswalk, looking back to see Fahiz board the number 5. Knox knows the line. He can get a jump on the trolley and beat it to its first stop if the lights are favorable.

His ring tone purrs in the earbuds and he reaches into the windbreaker to connect the call, though he doesn't answer at first.

"Clear," comes Grace's voice.

"Got it."

Grace has executed a series of procedures to determine she's not being followed, and Knox trusts her. She's as good as—or better than—him in the field, having spent a year in Chinese Army Intelligence.

Knox hangs up and dismounts the bike. The number 5 passes. He likes the bike too much to ditch it. He walks it across the pedestrian crossing, over another grouping of multiple tram tracks, and follows up a sidewalk, the bike off the curb. The island to his right is a vast construction site and parking lot behind wire fencing. Its top boundary is Prins Hendrikkade. The neighborhood is coffee shops, T-shirt stores and restaurants, all aimed at tourists. At the next light he hits speed dial and mounts the bike and rides straight.

"Go ahead," answers the deep voice of David Dulwich.

"I'm shorthanded."

"I arrive this evening. I'm at the Sofitel Grand on Oude-zijds Voor . . . burgwal." The Dutch words come out sounding like a soap brand.

"I was thinking of someone half your age and twice your speed."

"Tell me how you really feel."

"A lot of balls in the air."

"So hire a juggler. You have a sizable expense account."

"Two men. Maybe three."

"Not going to happen, unless you agree to waive half your fee."

"Our client is rich."

"Every client has limits. My job is to see there's something left for Brian Primer to put on the P side of the P-and-L."

"One more man, then."

"You're talking to him."

Knox dodges a taxi and runs a red light. The street narrows a hundred meters ahead. Knox pinches the iPhone through the fabric of the windbreaker and kills the call.

THE TUDOR ALE HOUSE Knox has named as the meeting place has a view across the Leidsegracht canal. The magnificent canal houses are out of the nineteenth century. A slim waitress serves him. She has a platinum bob and black ceramic ear gauges the size of buffalo nickels. Without her to interrupt his fantasy, he might have been time traveling. He might have been spying on Vermeer or Jan van Goyen across the dimly lit room, with its heavy, exposed wooden beams, plank tables, wrought-iron candelabra. He can imagine a big-breasted woman wearing too much rouge delivering warm dark beer. Instead, he gets a scene-kid waitress smacking chewing gum in a room filled with people in T-shirts.

"I have caught you in meditation perhaps?" The older man with the scrubby white beard speaks his English with a Dutch accent so thick he's hard to understand. His nose is cratered with acne scars and spiderwebbed with broken blood vessels. His ice blue eyes study Knox from behind wire-rimmed glasses. His meaty hand is inhumanly cold as they greet each other. He sits down slowly, perhaps painfully, and looks as if he could use help pulling closer to the table, but Knox fears humiliating him by offering.

"I was wishing for a different waitress," Knox says.

"I can procure for you any girl you want. Certified clean."

Knox's jaw muscles knot. "I'll pass."

"Pussies soft as lambs. I can arrange it. Not the window girls. Much classier. Any age, any skin color."

Knox struggles to relax his fist, which has tightened beneath the table. He blames himself for starting the conversation. For an instant he visualizes the other man's bulbous nose pushed through his face and into his brain, his blue eyes lifeless.

Gerhardt Kreiger can procure *anything*. Knox knows this; he has purchased a variety of goods from him for nearly three years, one of his longest business relationships. But this is the first time Kreiger's offered to pimp. Knox wonders if the wholesale business is that bad.

He'd wanted to start with pleasantries but is reminded how unpleasant Kreiger can be. Instead, he jumps in, hoping to network his way into the rug business.

"We need another gross of the Delftware dinner plates and salad plates, a gross of the beer steins and a half gross of the glass yards."

"So send me an e-mail." Kreiger cleans the wire rims with a checkered cloth napkin, blowing on each lens. He orders a Grolsch as Knox's Heineken is delivered. "Not that I do not enjoy you buying me a beer. And the company, of course."

Knox keeps his voice low despite there being no one within earshot. "Rugs," Knox says.

Kreiger studies him pensively. "Turkey. North Africa. I realize the quality Afghans have dried up temporarily, but that's your country's fault, not mine."

"Too many middlemen," Knox says. "Prices are too high. Government's too unstable. I need quantity and quality and not six Turks between me and the manufacturer."

Kreiger fights off a devilish grin and shakes his head. He waits for the beer to be delivered. They clink steins. He makes sure the waitress is another five strides gone. "I didn't know you read Dutch."

"I have no idea what you're talking about."

"No, I am sure of it," Kreiger says. He savors the beer and licks his mustache. He eyeballs Knox again, a mixture of cunning and respect. "You impress me, Knox. Such ambition."

Knox says nothing.

"I do not picture you as the type to condone the manufacturing *methods*."

"Gerhardt, these are trying times. The euro zone is in recession, so it's a buyer's market. At home, we're stuck with customers wanting everything for less, if they want anything at all. If I buy from the Mideast, the margins will kill me, and between the shrinkage and the bribes to longshoremen, there go the profits. By the time I see my container—hopefully sometime this millennium—I'm looking at pennies on the dollar. To hell with that. I need that ratio reversed. Your city's got one of the biggest shipping ports in north Europe. If there are rugs being manufactured here—hand-tied, natural dyes, high-quality wool—and I buy from a single agent, as in you, I can trust the container to arrive with its original count and contents on time. Clean and simple, just as I like it."

"You do make a girl blush," Kreiger said. "But who says the article was accurate? You know journalism these days."

"Hypothetically speaking," Knox says, "there must be others like me . . . a market for high-end knockoffs."

Kreiger wipes foam off his mustache and grins wryly. "There's always the UK. And you'd be surprised: the Russians will pay these prices. So much goddamned money there now. All of them wanting to be as Western as money can buy. St. Petersburg is a gold mine for these rugs. Anything north of Prague is a viable market at these prices."

Knox hears price mentioned and thinks only of the girls. Kreiger reads him.

"Who says I would know anything about such a despicable place? I happen to like children. I have seven grandchildren. Did you know that? Four boys, one named for me."

"Congratulations." Knox works on the beer, but can't keep up with Kreiger, who signals for another. "Maybe you could ask around."

"For you? Anything." He leans closer. "Hypothetically speaking, what count and cuts are you interested in?"

Knox gives him an overall number and the breakdown in sizes. Kreiger rolls his eyes, exaggerated by the spectacles. He scratches out some numbers onto a napkin. "This number would occupy three-quarters of a full-sized container. You can't be serious."

"I take delivery once. If I have to wait a few months before you ship, I can live with that. My experience says that manufacturers like this don't stay in business all that long. I won't get the chance for a repeat buy, much less establish regular shipments."

"No. I would agree."

"So I'm front-loading inventory. Stocking up."

"You are looking at"—he refers back to the napkin—"a hundred thousand euros minimum. Cash, you understand?"

"Fifty. And you handle the port costs on this end."

"You have become a comedian. The act needs work, I'm afraid. Ninety-five."

"Sixty."

"Eighty, and it is final. Also, I must check with the supplier first."

"Seventy-five is my limit."

"I will look into it."

Knox writes a phone number on a napkin. He'll have to remember to swap the SIMs a couple times a day and check for messages. He pushes the napkin back to Kreiger.

"I need to see the work. All three sizes, various dye lots," Knox says. "You decide the where and when. I am at such an advantage knowing someone like you, only one middleman, not three."

"Someone like me." Kreiger hoists his beer stein, and the dull clank that sounds off Knox's half-empty stein sounds to Knox like a judge's gavel lowering.

14

A damp settles over the city, an impenetrable gray mist thick enough to taste. It hovers and swirls but does not dissipate. Grace has waited until evening to catch those heading home from work. By early evening, the market on Ten Katestraat is thick with bodies moving from one tented stall to another. Fruit and vegetable vendors compete by turning their displays into colorful art worthy of still-life photography. Merchants offer athletic clothing, bedding linen, office supplies and kitchenware.

She joins the crush and sets her sights downstream. She is carried in a clot. Manages to reach the edge of the flow and grabs a tent's corner pole to check her progress. She takes hold, appreciating the diversity of faces. Indian, North African, French, Italian. Yet she's the only Chinese. She hears Russian, Yiddish, Dutch, English.

"Yes?" The vendor addresses Grace as he punches a

calculator. A young woman stands before a variety of vegetables collected onto the portable table.

Grace pulls out the newspaper article and photograph—the young girl's sullen face appealing to the camera. She shows it to the vendor, whose eyes stick to it before rolling up to find Grace's.

"She lives around here," Grace says with authority. "I am looking for her."

His eyes are angry and deeply suspicious. "Who is next?" he says, calling out to his patrons.

Grace moves back into the thick of the crowd and bullies her way forward, wondering what to make of the look the man gave her. She's almost certain he knew the newspaper article or recognized the girl from the photograph. This tells her the neighborhood knows about the girl's story. They expect people like Grace to nose around. They assume her to be police. She must overcome their initial distrust.

She spins fully around once, as if looking back at a missed buying opportunity. Of the hundreds of heads and faces shining in the glare of bare bulbs, one stands out. Grace does not linger on it, but sweeps her gaze past it and alights on a tent across the crowded street. A tall woman of Mediterranean or Middle Eastern heritage, a light-colored scarf worn over her head. Her attention was fixed on Grace—that she turned away convinces Grace—thrills her, if truth be told. She's been followed. Identifying a tail has nothing to do with luck; it is a skill set taught, an instinct developed and developed until second nature. Grace moves on without so much as a crease to her brow or break to her step, leaving no trace of her detection.

She's on alert now. Ready. For what, she's unsure. Twice more she inquires with vendors or their helpers, this time displaying her EU credentials. Her third effort is to a middle-aged woman selling kitchen supplies. The woman suddenly won't make eye contact. She straightens stacks of dishes that don't need straightening. Grace loves it. Feeds off it. When she turns to move on, the tall woman in the scarf is gone. Grace carefully checks around her as she crosses through the melee for a fruit stand. Not only is the woman with the scarf nowhere to be seen, but she hasn't been passed off to another surveillant. Grace bounces between several more stands, her guess confirmed. No one.

Two stalls later she asks a younger woman with a lip stud and a plump mouth. She takes one look at the photo and motions Grace to the side of a table bearing bedsheets, towels, lace tablecloths. Her action is deliberate and carries authority; she wants Grace out of the way, but she doesn't want her to leave. It's a full five minutes before she comes to Grace's side of the stall. She doesn't look at Grace, but neatens a stack of folded items. Grace takes the hint and rummages through a pile for the right color.

The vendor's lips don't move, like a ventriloquist. She throws her voice softly. "Van Speijkstraat. North. You will see a blue sign for the Mall De Baarsjes. Be careful."

"Talk to me," Grace says.

"Not possible."

"Later. Name the place."

"Not possible." The vendor moves back to a waiting customer.

Grace feels a rush of heat flood through her. She's

addicted to this work. Only breaking through a firewall comes close to the thrill of fieldwork. She wants to prolong the moment, but it's not to be and she knows it. The vendor acts as if she no longer exists. A reluctant Grace moves on, her pulse elevated, her breathing excited. She barely notices the crush of people surrounding her as she moves wraith-like among them. By the time she reaches the end of the market street and the horde thins, she realizes she has neglected to keep an eye out for the tall woman in the scarf. She makes a passing effort at it, but she's coming down from a high; almost impossible to focus.

She wants to return to the vendor's stall and live it all again.

Knox receives a text from Sonia's number.

I have reconsidered.

It names a tram line, direction and time.

The woman is out of her element; a tram is out of the question. He returns a text:

I'm pleased. No tram. meet @ "chow fun" in rl district.
1 hr.

It's a Chinese restaurant that offers pizza and video games, a place where people their age will stand out, which is just the way he wants it. There are three exits—the front door, another by the restrooms and another that connects to a head shop by day but is closed by night. Knox takes a table next to this door. He has sight lines to the street entrance thanks to a mirror behind a small drinks bar, and to the corridor housing the restrooms.

Sonia turns a few heads with her entrance but then takes a place at a table and orders a beer, never looking in Knox's direction but instead concentrating on the pedestrians passing by the front windows. *Smart,* he thinks, *a fast learner.* When she's satisfied, she joins him. Most women would sling the strap of a purse over the back of their chair, but Sonia steps her right leg through the strap as she sits down and places the satchel at her feet. He wonders at the contents of that bag.

"Think of a tram as a trap," he says. "You can't get off until and unless it makes a stop. It gives the enemy time to identify you, physically reach you and detain you."

"The enemy," she says, scoffing. She thinks of him as a little boy. "Photographers think like this?"

"This photographer does," he says. "I'm here at your request." He waits for her to say something. "You have a shoot for me?"

"It is possible." She works her phone and slides it across the table to him. He reads. It's an e-mail in English. The message is brief. A woman has been reported as missing. Knox recognizes the name from Sonia's article. Another of her sources.

"From the police?" he asks.

"A contact. Reliable."

"And then there were three," he says.

"I'm sorry?"

"You quoted six different people in your article. This leaves three remaining. There's an old black-and-white movie. You like movies? *Ten Little Indians.* 'And then there were three.'"

She nods mournfully. "I must find Berna. The girl in my article."

"The chances of that are slim," Knox says, gloating that he now has the girl's first name. She's not asking for a photographer, but a bodyguard. He feels relief. He will maintain the pretense.

"I don't expect a shared byline, but I do expect you to fight for my photographs to run along with the article wherever it's published."

"You know I have no say over that."

"You have influence. You're well known. I am not."

"My editor and I will do what we can."

That's out of the way, allowing them both to tackle the unmentioned: that Knox brings other skills and qualities to the table.

"You must warn the other people you interviewed."

"I tried to do this, following the car bomb. Of course I did! Several were unreachable, including this woman."

"I forget her role in the piece."

"A teacher. Not Berna's teacher," she says. "When a young girl failed to enroll in school this year, her teacher from the previous year thought the family must have left the district—moved residences. She then encountered the girl's mother at a local market and confronted her. The mother shunned her, refusing to speak with her. I believe the school records are filled with such missing children."

"A place to start," Knox says.

"Acquiring enrollment records is not so easy. I have a contact, willing to help, but I would not anticipate much progress. Protecting children—" She cuts herself off, attempts to rub fatigue from her eyes.

"What about your remaining sources?"

"I was told they'd all left the city. Shows you what I know. If they have not, I'm sure they will now."

Knox thinks what good bait the three would have made. Lost opportunities.

He doesn't dare push his delicate relationship with Sonia too far toward investigation. He reminds himself he is a photographer, first and only.

"Honestly . . . I feel awful saying this . . . but it's Berna I care about. I should never have let her escape."

"Do you know the girl personally?"

Sonia views him curiously.

"You refer to her by name. I feel something each time you mention her."

She eyes him skeptically, but secretly impressed. "It is personal, but not with this girl, not with Berna. A niece. Another time and place entirely."

"You can't fix the past in the present," he cautions, wishing he hadn't spoken. She questions him with heated eyes, requiring more of him. "Based on personal experience, I'd say it's a mistake to try."

"I'm a problem solver, Mr. Steele. It is what motivates me to write in the first place."

He stifles what would be a cynical comeback. "I'm only saying: if your motivation is to help a niece who cannot be helped, you're setting yourself up for failure."

"When I want a therapist I'll let you know."

He hesitates. They're into the thick bushes now. It's darker here.

"You couldn't have possibly known she would run."

"She's just a child, Mr. Steele. If you'd seen her."

"Then we'll find her," he says. "We'll find her, and the authorities will shut this thing down." He's feeling authoritative.

As she bends down, something slips from her satchel. He leans back trying to steal a look at its contents, but it's out of sight. Her hand pushes a tourist map across the table. There are seven smaller inked circles at the center of seven larger dashed circles, also in ink. It looks like a Venn diagram, the dashed circles overlapping.

"Health clinics," she says.

"Berna." Pangarkar's encounter with the girl.

"Yes." Her eyes chastise him for interrupting. "But here is the point. Seven areas of coverage."

"Got that."

Another dismissive look. "This is the clinic where I found Berna. When I was interviewing for my story." She points to a small circle in the northwest of the city.

Knox understands she's testing him. "You're thinking that with so many clinics available, she'd go to the nearest one. That or one she was familiar with. One in her neighborhood, if she's a local." He pulled the map closer. "She lives somewhere within the dotted circle."

Her eyes come alive, overcoming the fatigue and anxiety. "You're good at this," she says somewhat suspiciously. She's in over her head.

Knox wants to help her, but reminds himself of his role. He can't reveal the *S* on his undershirt just yet. He senses she's glad to have someone to share this with; oddly enough, he appreciates being that person. Dulwich believes in straight lines—he does not condone working Pangarkar. He has Grace working the streets. Believes Knox should be taking this route as well.

"Someone within that circle knows her," Sonia says.

"It shrinks the net. It's good work."

The compliment arouses more suspicion from her. Occupational hazard. Knox cautions himself.

"I suppose she could work outside the circle." He sounds uncertain. "Or not. The clinic might be a place she knows from her family, or it could simply· be a store-front window she saw."

"It must be walkable, either from her home or the sweatshop."

"Interesting." He was there already.

"So, perhaps we widen the circle." Sonia draws a slightly bigger ring around the outer boundary. The darker circle around the clinic becomes a bull's-eye.

"You find a picture worth making and I can be there in ten to fifteen minutes."

"Two of us—" She's not going to beg.

"I'm interested in Berna's story," he says. "More

generically than you, but interested. Finding the knot shop would make a nice image. A school, not so much, but it might lead to something more worthwhile."

"The streets. The kinds of places people like Berna live."

She's crafty. He likes that. He'd sensed this cunning in her article as well. While exposing the larger problems of health care, she'd personalized the problem by bringing in Berna's story. By the end of the piece, the reader was ready to shut down every sweatshop between Amsterdam and Beijing. Sonia Pangarkar brought passion to her work, but she allowed it to possess her—which could make for bad decisions.

"I could spend a day or two shooting the streets as background."

"You could ask after her while you do that work. I'm known on the streets. My face. The television."

"I suppose." He nods. He's not accustomed to making a game out of being sought after. He finds it interesting to be on the receiving end of such attention. Marvels at her ability to manipulate. Realizes the longer and deeper he allows his ruse to stray from the truth, the more damaging the eventual revelation will be. He's locking himself into an identity he's uncomfortable with.

"It would help us both," she says. "I don't want to end up next on the victim list." But of course he does. If he becomes the target, the entire operation is expedited. The risk is also a rush.

"It might move the story forward, get us paid sooner."

"I like being paid," he says. "Until something better comes along, why not?"

Sonia uses the pen to cross-hatch half the wider of the two circles around the clinic. The dividing line falls on a street. "We will start from the clinic and work our way out."

"We? You said you're too well known."

"Yes, well, how much time do you think Berna has? Her face is known as well. She's a threat to them. Her story's out there." She hesitates. "My fault."

"The school records," he says. "Expediting that search—"

"I'm on it."

THE SIGN IS where the vendor told her it would be. MALL. Grace expected a retail center, but the sign is above a darkened alleyway. She walks past on the opposite sidewalk and continues to the next street corner, where she pauses and leans against a wrought-iron railing. It's five thirty-five but feels more like midnight.

The entrance to the building to the left of the dark alley is up four steps from the sidewalk. It's an unattractive brick box, a single structure occupying the space of four canal houses. There are security bars across most of the lower-level windows, potted flowers on either side of the steps. She's guessing five to ten apartments. Was this the address the vendor meant to give her, or did she mean the alley itself? Grace has no idea what to expect: Berna? her family?

a school chum? a girl who looks like Berna? the thugs responsible? Had the vendor called ahead to make sure that a curious EU official is greeted appropriately? There can't possibly be a shopping mall down the dark alley beneath the sign.

She double-checks her iPhone confirming the "Find My iPhone" feature is activated. She texts Knox.

if no text in 10 mins use Find My iPhone

Her finger hesitates above the blue iMessage bubble. She knows if he's not back there watching her already, he'll take the text as a call to action. She regrets it, but she can't be responsible for Knox's decisions.

She hits SEND.

A CHINESE GUY speaking Dutch and wearing Tom Ford gets takeout.

Sonia's voice is tight when she speaks. "I shouldn't have published the piece."

"It's a sweatshop," Knox says. The restaurant has become claustrophobic. "They need workers. They don't get rid of what they need."

"Berna was not going home at night. You don't chain girls who go home."

"So they'll keep her alive."

"I believe we're talking about two different kinds of workers. Those who are recruited locally, and those who were not offered a choice. This second group of girls never leaves."

"Locals and residents," he says.

She grimaces. "There's another more lucrative market for girls this age."

Knox's collar is suddenly too tight. He reaches there only to realize he's wearing a T-shirt under the windbreaker. "We have a girl in a sweatshop. That's all." She forces images into his thoughts. Maybe he's a photographer after all.

"We," the writer says.

The buzzing of his phone rescues him. He reads the incoming text.

"I have to go," he announces. "I'll start tomorrow morning."

15

The enclosed alleyway reminds her of a subway tunnel. One with no lights. One that smells sour and sordid. Tobacco. Marijuana. Stale beer. Human piss. Dog excrement. The entire urban experience reduced to olfactory overload. She enters the dark with trepidation. The woman in the scarf haunts her. *Be careful*, haunts her. The path beneath her is covered in a viscous goo, a residual sediment not washed away by rain. Her soles smack with it. It seems to move beneath her. She's through the space in less than thirty seconds, but in that short time her heart accelerates to an aerobic level and her mouth goes dry. She'd give anything for a Coke.

God hears her: there's a lighted vending machine alongside the entrance to a two-story brick building that fills the front half of an inner courtyard. Its windows hide behind black chain link. Graffiti has been sandblasted and chemically removed, leaving the brick two-tone.

She time-checks her phone, remembering to call off Knox. But not yet. Not so soon. She senses six minutes could prove to be an eternity here.

Corner lights on the building have either burned out or been stoned and broken. The interior lights are ablaze. She checks behind herself. Her long thin shadow stretches behind her like a crooked finger. No one back there. No one coming for her.

But they could be waiting. This could be a trap.

She walks fully around the building, behind which she discovers a blacktop playground. She puts her face to a back window. It's a recreation room. A half dozen kids sitting at battered folding tables in battered folding chairs. There's a kiddie station at the far end: a blue plastic fort and slide, some yellow plastic cubes and an orange airplane that can be straddled like a horse. It's a neighborhood youth center. She sucks down some Coke. Nothing has ever tasted better. She pauses for another sip before letting herself inside.

It's study time and quiet. Against the wall are long-outdated computers, their screens glowing. She's approached by a woman in her sixties who has a slight limp to her right leg, a face creased by the sun and dull blue eyes.

She speaks Dutch, welcoming Grace, who returns a thank-you and continues in Dutch. After two or three exchanges they have settled into English without discussing the switch.

Grace identifies herself as being with the EU. She offers

her business card. The woman slips it into a sweater pocket without looking at it.

"How may I help you?"

Grace proffers the newspaper photo of Berna.

The woman sees it, studies it, but it's radioactive; she does not reach out to take hold of it.

"I am familiar with the story," she says.

"I am trying to find the girl."

"It exaggerates. You know this, yes? The story? These ankle wounds described are more likely from a game or an accident. We see every kind of thing on our playgrounds."

"You do not believe the article?" Grace says, trying her best to mask her own surprise.

"You cannot possibly believe everything you read in the papers."

Grace says, "I believe this."

The woman openly displays her cynicism.

Grace crosses her arms tightly in annoyance. "No matter what caused her health issues—malnutrition and dehydration among them—she is a minor who fled the clinic and has not been found."

"I understand." Genuine concern seeps through the woman's cold exterior. "How many others each week? Each month?" She motions to the kids studying. "No one has it easy. Just because a reporter happens to be there one afternoon . . . all this attention. How many since then? How many before?" She lowers her voice. "Listen to me: If this little one is working in a shop, as reported, she has it good. Do you understand? Prostitution is legal here. Do you know how many girls enter Amsterdam each year looking to be a window girl? And what happens to them? Where do they end up? Is anyone counting them? Looking for them? All this—the EU"—she motions to Grace—"for one little girl. It's touching," she mocks, "but pardon me if it strikes me as hypocrisy."

"These children have families," Grace says, indicating the kids studying at the desks.

The woman looks over her flock. "Most have a parent, or an aunt or uncle, it's true. A place to sleep. Someone to feed them a meal a day if they're lucky. They might sleep five or more to a room. They come here to do the book work. They are good children."

"And during the day?"

"The little ones. Day care. Physical recreation after school. That is when we are busiest. Seventy-five to a hundred each day. I have one other on my staff. We receive donations: balls, pencils and paper, clothing. A local bakery provides yesterday's unsold pastries. We get by."

Grace takes it all in.

"I would say . . . it is impossible to know . . . but I would say at least one a month goes missing. Running away? Sex slavery? Or this labor shop of yours? Of the choices, I would take the shop."

"You are saying she has it good?" Grace is on the edge of indignant.

"I hope you find this girl."

"Do you know her? Recognize her?"

"Does her face look familiar to me? If I say yes, I give you false hope. If I say no, maybe you give up. I would prefer to say nothing."

"She is familiar then."

"Listen to me: there are no jobs out there. None. No fathers, half the time. The children who find work provide for their families, no matter how meager the wage, no matter the working conditions. You take away that small amount of income and many would starve. If you think you will find support here in the neighborhoods, you are sadly mistaken. Communities like this solve problems others cannot or choose not to solve for them. Is the solution always legal? No. But the mothers would rather have their girls sewing or gluing trainers than selling themselves or dealing dope. It is the lesser of two evils."

"I won't get help?"

The woman shrugs. She says nothing.

THE CLICK OF THE DOOR behind Grace feels ominous. She leaves the community center, heads for the alley tunnel leading back to Van Speijkstraat. She walks the ten meters to its entrance and stops, aware of the charged particles in the air. The unexpected whiff of fresh cigarette smoke. She turns.

Two men come at her in a blur of shadow and muscle. The first thing she notices is their height; neither is tall. They are fast and they are strong, and while one twists and pulls on her purse, the other blocks her left arm as it comes forward and runs his hand up under her skirt and between her legs and cups her. She surprises him by clamping her legs together so fast that he has no time to remove his hand. She traps it there and then head-butts him in the nose. The other one has her so tangled in her purse that by the time she lifts her knee to finish off the one in front of her, she's turned and her knee misses. The hand comes free and punches her left breast with such force that sparks fly and her stomach lurches. She's dizzy and going down. No more than a few seconds have passed.

The purse strap slips down her arm but she grabs for it. With her right hand she claps the one in front of her on the ear and he cries out. She stabs him in the eye with a locked finger and a manicured nail. He cries again, this time louder. She kicks at his knee, but misses.

He winds up a clenched fist. She regrets everything she has just done. She can't take a second chest punch.

Her opponent collapses, all joints failing simultaneously.

Grace slumps into the disgusting, sticky goo of the tunnel floor amid the sound of the other mugger thief fleeing. She's kneeling. A shadow looms over her.

The headlights of a passing car flood the tunnel with light. Before her stands the woman in the scarf from the market. It's not a gun in her hand but a stun stick, explaining the doll-like collapse of her assailant.

"You ask too many questions."

"Thank you for your help."

"You will get yourself killed."

Grace extends her arm for the woman to help her up. The woman reaches for her, but stops.

"Grace?" It's Knox, a backlit figure at the end of the tunnel. He switches on a small penlight that casts a faint blue light at this distance like a train's dim headlight.

"Here!"

Before the word is out of her mouth, the woman in the scarf is gone.

KNOX DRAGS THE KID by the back of his coat collar—a kid, not a grown man. Eighteen? Nineteen? Pulls him through the door of the community center.

"What's this?" the director asks, her voice breaking.

Knox lifts the semiconscious kid with one arm and deposits him into a vinyl chair. The studying students are all made of marble and are turned toward them.

"You must take this outside," the director says, sensing Knox's intentions.

The kid's left eye is swollen nearly shut and oozing. His nose is a bloody mess.

Grace enters last, a ripe bruise already forming on her forehead, her right shoulder lowered to favor her painful chest. Her skirt has slipped down a few inches, revealing the elastic of her bikini underwear.

"The toilet?" Grace speaks Dutch.

The director helps Grace by the arm, guiding her across the room. "What happened? What has happened?" She looks back over her shoulder at Knox. "Not in here."

Knox takes in the studying kids frozen in their seats. "He slipped and fell," Knox tells them, "but he's going to be all right." He hauls the kid to his feet and leads him back out the doors, pounding him against the brick wall and allowing him to sag to the concrete. He keeps him close to the doors for the sake of the ambient light. Knox squats. The kid is still dazed from the stun stick, though no longer paralyzed. Knox unlaces the kid's military-style boot and uses the lace to tie the boy's hands behind his back.

Taking the boy by the chin, he lifts and turns his face into the light. The eye is worse by the minute; the nose is clotting.

Knox speaks Dutch. "If you play tough, it will get rough. Understand?"

The one good eye fills with contempt. Knox grabs the boy's crotch. Takes a handful and twists. The eye rolls back into its socket. "She tells me you touched her like this." He twists harder. The kid groans. "One good tug and you're singing soprano for life. Your call." He tightens his hold. "Who put you up to this?"

The eye rolls back, filled with an innocent terror. The kid tries to shake his head but Knox holds his chin firmly in hand. But not with his right hand; that one turns a few more degrees clockwise. "Who? And where do I find him?"

"The purse. A little fun. That's all."

Another half turn and Knox will do permanent damage. He squeezes instead. "Fun yet?"

The color drains from the boy's face. He's not breathing.

The earlier look of fright goes a long way to convincing Knox the kid was not on orders, but he doesn't want to believe his own intuition. Fahiz was attacked and beaten. For Knox, this kid will do. An act of random violence won't satisfy his craving for conspiracy and connection.

He wants an easy route to follow back to the knot shop. He takes the kid's wallet, but removes the cash and a debit card and stuffs them into the front pocket of the boy's jeans. Confirms there's ID with an address.

"If I should ever see you again, I am coming after you with the full intention of ending your life. Do you understand?"

The boy is slow to respond. Knox loosens his grip on his testicles. The boy's chin tries to nod.

Behind him, Grace stands framed by the door, looking out. She has put herself back together; her dark hair covers her forehead.

Knox opens the door for her. Says to the director, "Do you know this boy?"

The director shakes her head without looking. "These are hard times. There are many such boys. Too many."

"Fix the lights in the tunnel," Knox says.

The woman nods. "Yes. Of course."

"Do not untie him. He can make it home without his arms. Lock the door until he's gone. If he doesn't leave, call the police."

Another nod from the director. "I already have."

The boy struggles to get up. Knox kicks him back down. "Ladies first."

Knox offers his hand to Grace, and to his surprise she accepts it.

KNOX HELPS GRACE feed the key card into the hotel room door, her hand shaking too violently.

"I can come in," he says. "Make you a drink. You could use one."

"If you wouldn't mind." She pushes open the door but doesn't move. Knox slips past her. He checks the bathroom, the closet and the rest of the room.

"Clear."

She enters. "Vodka, rocks." She is unbuttoning her blouse as she enters the bathroom. Shuts and locks the door.

He hears the bath water running, not a shower. She'll be a while. He's got her room key. He fetches ice and waits to make her drink. Takes a Scotch for himself. Drinks it from a plastic cup that he removes from a plastic wrapper.

The water stops running.

He hears the door lock pop as she cracks the door.

"Thank you," she calls out.

"No problem." He pours the vodka and approaches with his back to the bathroom door, then passes the drink inside. They touch hands. Hers is ice cold.

He heads back to his chair. Hears the shower curtain sing as she slides it aside and hears her ease down into the water.

"Why were you there?"

"A vendor in the market. I'm not so sure she recognized Berna in the photo so much as thought the community center director might help me."

"Some help."

"The director painted a different picture," Grace says. "The girls providing income for broken families. A way to battle the poverty."

"I'm not buying that," Knox says. He tilts the Scotch in the cup and swirls it.

"I'm not selling. But she was."

"It's a load of shit."

"More like realpolitik. No matter, it doesn't help us any."

Locals and residents, he thinks. He tells her about Sonia's theory of two classes of workers.

"If we can't get help from the mothers of these girls—" Grace says.

"Yeah."

"Graham Winston wants this shut down. We have our work cut out for us. If it's finding someone to hang this on, you have a wallet in your pocket. I will testify. Fahiz, I'm not so sure."

"Finding Berna and closing the shop are one and the same. Concurrent." The Scotch warms him. He uncaps another minibottle and dispenses it into the plastic cup. "Refill?"

"Please." He hears the shower curtain being adjusted. "You can come in." He enters the bathroom. Her clothes are neatly folded on the counter. Grace. Her arm is extended from behind the curtain. He takes her empty cup and pulls the door nearly shut behind him. Hears her chewing ice.

"There was a woman . . . in the market. It was she who rescued me."

It was she. Grace. "I'm listening."

"In the tunnel . . . She knew who I was. My EU persona. Warned me."

"Threatened?"

"Warned."

"Were the boys hers? Was it staged for your benefit?"

It's a long time before she says anything. "I don't like the way you think."

"It's the Scotch," he says.

"No, I am afraid not," she says. "She told me I ask too many questions and that I'd get myself killed."

"Hardly a warning. That's a threat."

"It wasn't. I'm telling you. She was hiding—waiting—in the tunnel. Waiting for me to leave the center."

"And we have no idea who she is."

"None."

"You're going back to Hong Kong. We're getting you out of here."

"Foolish. This is exactly what we'd hoped for. It just does not happen to be connected to the knot shop."

Knox's phone buzzes. A text.

in the lobby

"Dulwich is downstairs."

"Your doing?"

"Yes," he says. "Assaults, robberies and sexual assaults tend to win his attention."

"He can't come up," she says. "My room could be watched. One man in my room can be explained. Two is an orgy."

"No one is more careful than Sarge. Let me handle it."

Ten minutes later, after Knox has walked the hallway

and scouted the stairs, the three are in Grace's room. The hotel doesn't offer robes, so she's in pajamas with a towel wrapped around her head. She sits cross-legged on the bed. She looks about fourteen.

Dulwich drinks beer. Grace and Knox are on their third. They've run the minibar out of vodka and Scotch. Knox feels good for the first time all day.

Grace gives the recap.

Knox adds in enough of his meeting with Sonia to complete the picture. He looks over at Grace. "You've got to go," Knox says.

"Not the way the EU would see it," Dulwich explains. "They might assign a driver. That could be you."

"Can't be me," Knox says. He reminds them about Gerhardt Kreiger's efforts to connect him to a rug merchant, about his serving as Sonia's photographer, about already being stretched thin.

"Me, then."

"You limp. Some bodyguard."

"All the better," Dulwich says. "I look like a driver, as it should be." He asks Grace, "Good with you?"

She nods. She looks like she's in shock. *Or maybe drunk is more like it,* Knox thinks.

"Can we talk about Fahiz?" Grace asks.

"No," Knox says.

"Sonia Pangarkar interviews Kabril Fahiz, but Kahil's the enigma. Are we accepting that he intentionally lied on his health clinic admittance form *and* on the police report, all to protect himself? Is anyone that cognizant when admitted to a clinic in such bad shape?"

"He's collateral damage. Forget him." Knox sets down the rest of the Scotch, vowing not to touch it.

"Agreed," Dulwich says. "Wrong place, wrong time."

"You didn't speak to him. His attackers were Dutch or Europeans. He saw it as a hate crime. I don't think so."

"Your attackers were Dutch," Knox says.

"My attackers were kids." She wraps herself in her own limbs more tightly. She can't rid herself of the boy holding her down there, feels on the verge of screaming or vomiting.

"Has anyone spoken to the doctors?" Dulwich asks.

"Waste of time," Knox says. "We're off track."

"We're trying to stop whoever's intimidating Sonia Pangarkar's sources," Dulwich says. "Kahil Fahiz was a victim of those people. Mistaken identity or not, we're hardly off track."

Knox thought Sarge was on his side. The adrenaline is wearing off. The booze is swimming around his head. He upends the waiting cup. *Better.* "You want this short and sweet," he tells Dulwich. "That means we go for beheading, not cutting off fingers and hands. Who gives a shit that Kahil Fahiz was mistaken for someone else? Who gives a shit what condition he was in? They got the wrong guy. How can that possibly be worth our time?"

"What if we find out his attackers were two kids in their late teens?" Dulwich asks. "For instance."

"I had this kid by the short hairs. He was not hired to attack her. Trust me."

"Maybe he was led into it by his friend."

"The doctors are going to tell us that? I don't think

so. Why am I the one drinking, but you're the one talking like a drunk?"

"People explain their injuries. They're in shock," Dulwich says, casting a sideways glance at Grace, "their adrenaline's screaming. They're given sedatives. Their tongues wag. More secrets are spilled in the emergency room than the confessional. You two can carry on." He sounds disgusted. "I can do this. I will do this."

"My cover's better," Grace says, still in a tight ball. There's only ice left in her cup.

"Suit yourself," Knox says. "Waste of time."

"Ours to waste." Dulwich is angry with him.

"Between Sonia's work and Kreiger wanting to sell me a container of rugs, we're aimed at the top of the pyramid. Grace should chill out for a few days. Lose the fieldwork. We get a suspect and she goes to work on the person's finances. If and when we have our evidence, we make our move."

Dulwich cannot believe what he's hearing. "So *your* work is the only work that matters?"

"For now."

Grace rocks forward and back on the bed. She's biting down on the hand that holds the cup. She removes her lips long enough to say, "I found a piece of your money." Her dark eyes, wet now from the liquor, stare over her hand at Knox.

"Come again?"

"Grace and I have been involved in a little extracurricular activity."

Knox looks suspiciously between them. "What the hell's going on?"

"I found forty-seven thousand," Grace says. "It's a good lead. I'm going to find the rest. And then I'm going to find more."

"My money? The money Eve—?" Knox says, though he can't finish the sentence, can't hear himself say it.

"If we find the money—*when* we find the money—we will find Evelyn Ritter along with it," Grace says imperiously.

Dulwich hunches his shoulders. "It was a bum deal."

"It was my deal. Is my deal."

"What are friends for?"

Grace explains, "It was the change. The fifty-four cents. It's all in the details. We're having fun, John. Don't spoil our fun."

"And don't talk to me about returning favors," says the man whose life Knox saved—*twice.*

"Forty-seven thousand?"

"I do not have the money, but I know where to find it. I can determine how it got there—that is the key. Getting it back . . . That is not of primary importance at the moment. First, we find it. We find it all."

"Don't look so surprised," Dulwich says.

But Knox is surprised. Flattered. Impressed. Guilt-ridden that they've taken the time to pursue his loss when it has nothing to do with Rutherford Risk.

"Does Primer know?" Knox asks.

"Hardly," says Dulwich.

"But you're on his payroll. His clock." He looks over at Grace. "His gear."

"Field-testing the gear is critical," she says.

"There are more than eight hours in a day," says Dulwich.

The comment is laughable, though Knox doesn't laugh. Dulwich lives his job—fourteen- to eighteen-hour days. He doesn't have time to tie his own shoes—he wears Top-Siders.

"Thank you." Knox wishes he'd saved some of the Scotch. He thinks about suggesting a trip to the hotel bar, drinks on him, but knows that's absurd. The three of them can't be seen together.

"Thank us when you have her head on a stick," Dulwich says.

"And the funds back in your account," Grace says, still rocking.

She looks like a scared little girl. Knox considers reaching out to comfort her, but the timing is wrong; she'll think it has to do with the money.

16

The rug shop is on Kinkerstraat, sandwiched between a bra shop and an *optiek*, hardly a neighborhood for upscale rugs, but then again, looking around the narrow shop, Knox realizes the rugs are more Pottery Barn than Heriz.

Gerhardt Kreiger is smoking in the back with the floor manager. Kreiger looks like a history professor in a tweed sport coat and black turtleneck. The manager needs to gain more than a few pounds. Knox searches the stock for anything of quality.

"You're wasting my time, Gerhardt." Knox turns for the door.

"Easy!" Kreiger has all the panache of a Buick salesman. "Not these! Wait, my friend." Gerhardt hasn't had a friend since 1978. He sidles up to Knox. "This is our gallery, nothing more. Patience, please."

It isn't going the way Knox had hoped. He'd wanted a tour of the facility and says so. "As much as I appreciate you, Gerhardt, I'd hoped to talk directly with the seller."

"For obvious reasons, my friend, this is impossible."

Knox whispers, "For this much cash, nothing is impossible."

"You wanted samples. I have brought you samples. Third stack, rugs two through five." He points, his fingertip yellowed by years of cigarettes.

Gerhardt is being far too smart about this. Knox had hoped for incompetence.

Knox peels back the top rug from the waist-high stack of rugs. It's like looking at high-def television: an eye-popping clarity with wonderful dye-lot imperfections and gorgeous symmetry to the traditional design. Knox has run himself through a crash course and he's shocked by the quality. He'd expected something passable; he's looking at floor and wall art. He realizes Gerhardt had no idea of a price range when they'd spoken earlier. These have five to ten times the value Knox had expected.

"Remarkable work," he says, moving slowly back and forth among the four samples.

"It is," says the store manager, trying to worm his way into the conversation. "Oushak, for the region in Turkey. Vegetable dye. Hand-knotted. Two hundred fifty thousand per square meter. Persian tea rug design."

The number swims around in Knox's head. His jaw locks. He pictures Berna and her friends in leg irons circled around a rug tying all those knots. Each rug several meters. Enough rugs to fill a shipping container. It's like looking at the Great Wall. It's slavery at any wage.

As he speaks his voice cracks. "Gorgeous. But are you sure it's not Chinese?"

The man approaches the stack. He ignites a cigarette lighter and places it close to the wool. If synthetic or plastic, the fibers melt quickly in a tiny puff of black smoke. Nothing happens. Natural fibers. He pockets the lighter and inspects the jute backing. "Turkish," he declares.

Knox and Gerhardt know otherwise—this is a product of the sweatshop. That it convinces the merchant of its Turkish origin is impressive.

"I am sure you are right," Knox says. He eyes Gerhardt, who arches his eyebrows declaratively. Knox thanks the merchant and moves to the door, Gerhardt alongside him like a dog heeling.

"Nothing is impossible," Knox repeats. "Call me when it's arranged."

THE MOMENT THE TEACHER'S EYES fall upon her, Maja knows the man—her "father"—is waiting at the classroom door. As the teacher heads to the door, Maja slides out of her desk chair like every bone has gone to jelly. On hands and knees, she gathers her books and looks to the window. The steel-framed half windows hinge at the top and open out. She steals across the room to the jeers of her seldom seen classmates and opens a window. It comes open only fifty centimeters, forcing her to throw a leg over the frame and wiggle to get through. When no one else comes to Maja's aid, a girl finally jumps up and helps get her books out the window. This child then leaps back into her chair as the door opens and the teacher turns around.

The visitor wears a heavy one-day beard. His face is florid and his eyes are glassy with rage. Many of the children stiffen, knowing such expressions well from home. Their teacher's wide eyes and the sharp cry of Maja's name are followed by her hurried approach to the window, from where she sees only the empty asphalt playground.

Maja wisely holds to the exterior wall, ducking beneath windows, racing to the end of the long building. Her first concern is for her mother.

She knows the shortest route through the streets, which bridges to take.

Maja won't know until she gets home how bad it will be for her. She can stay into the evening if she chooses, making up for most of the lost money—two euros a day.

She has been betrayed. Either her shop boss contacted her father, or someone at school reported her. Neither of her parents owns a phone. The likelihood the shop would bother to contact them is slim, and then it would be her mother—not her father, who is rarely at home. So who and why? Whoever it was has earned Maja's mother a beating. Her own sentence is unknown.

Tension grips her tummy as she nears the shop, unsure

if they'll take her in. If they've reached their quota for the day, there will be no space for her. What then?

Home is not an option.

GRACE PLAYS THE EU CARD AGAIN, trying to speak with a health clinic nurse about Kahil Fahiz. But it's soon clear the daily volume of walk-in patients results in a bleary-eyed anonymity. No one remembers him, or if they do, they don't want to get involved. She abandons her effort after fifteen minutes of being annoying, having lighted on a better idea.

Dulwich drives her to the southern boundary of the Oud-West neighborhood, to the health clinic where Berna was treated. She requests a stop at a computer store on the way.

At the clinic, she asks for Dulwich to remain in the car. "It could be a while." She enters a crowded waiting area. She could stay in here an hour or two without sticking out. She may need to.

Vinyl flooring and overhead fluorescent tube lighting. Parents with kids. Adults with casts, or walkers, or their hands gripped tightly on the arms of the contemporary stainless-steel furniture. Flu and STD posters line the wall alongside Elmo and Tinker Bell. A TV running a cooking show hangs in the corner above the fire alarm and a water dispenser.

No EU card this time. The Great Wall of corporate IT is passwords. Sophisticated high-bit encryption schemes have made hacking more difficult and time consuming. Cracking a password can take weeks, not hours.

Grace comes prepared, having anticipated certain impossibilities: she won't be able to get a video camera in place to watch a keyboard; she can't install key tracking software without the password.

The Achilles' heel of such systems is complacency. Working a computer terminal has become second nature. Employees are accustomed to the look and feel of the terminal—to switch out a keyboard might sound an alarm or win an inquiry. Conversely, they pay no attention whatsoever to the snarl of wires and blinking lights at the back of the machine, and Grace knows this. This is where she has been trained to attack. She will need thirty seconds.

Phase one is simple enough: a prescription bottle with a small amount of lighter fluid and a cotton wick lit as it's placed into a trash can. This goes off smoothly. Grace steps up to the counter, her purse open. Inside her head the clock is running.

"Name, please?" the nurse asks.

Grace explains she's waiting for a friend who asked to meet her here.

Poof. The trash can ignites: her cue.

Grace, alarmed by the sight, knocks her purse across the counter, its contents spilling onto the desktop and the floor. The nurses rush the fire as a team. Grace comes around behind the counter and begins collecting her spilled items. On hands and knees, she scrambles under the desk's ledge and, locating the body of the PC terminal, pulls the keyboard's USB connector. In her hand is a thumb drive, a USB passthrough. One end of the device plugs into the terminal; the keyboard plugs into its opposite end. It's a Wi-Fi memory stick tweaked to record and transmit each keystroke. She hears the discharge of a fire extinguisher.

"May I help you?" comes a voice from above. "Excuse me, please!" Irritation.

"My purse," Grace says. "I apologize. The fire . . . I bumped my purse." She motions to the Tampax on the desk and the lipstick, wallet and change on the floor beside her.

"No problem. May I be of help?" A nurse, by nature, is more kind than suspicious. She's alongside Grace collecting her personal effects.

"The fire," Grace says, "it rattled me."

"Did me the first time as well."

"The first time?"

"Are you kidding? Some fool dumps a cigarette in there at least once a week."

Grace had not anticipated this. She fights off a smile.

Back in her seat in the waiting room, her tethered iPhone creates its own Wi-Fi network and is connected to the USB passthrough. She checks the device's log. The nurse hit the spacebar to clear the screen and then typed her ten-character alphanumeric password. Grace has what she needs. The USB can transmit up to sixty feet.

It's a waiting game now. Grace has an iPad sideways in her lap, her purse supporting and screening it from view. She can only take over the terminal when the nurse is away, which isn't often. She builds macros to automate the process. The first time she has access, it takes her over a minute to menu through to records. The nurse returns.

The second time, Grace has only to push a macro button to access the records, saving her the minute. She builds on her past accomplishments: records, sorted by first name, Berna. Now she's studying the admittance form: last name, Ranatunga.

Her country of residence jumps off the page: Belgium. Her language, French. A runaway, or a kidnap victim. There's a note: *indigent.* A "citizenship" box checked: *immigrant.* It's unclear if Berna walked in on her own or was dropped at the clinic. There's no money trail to follow. She is required to have private insurance, but has none. The state takes over. Grace follows this in a series of checked boxes.

The nurse arrives. Grace returns the screen to how the nurse had left it.

Grace Googles "Ranatunga." A common Sri Lankan family name. Berna is an Irish version of Brenda. Irish/ Sri Lankan—that accounts for the young girl's intriguing look. Irish/Sri Lankan living in Belgium. Chances are the parents can be found if they're alive, if they didn't sell their daughter into child slavery.

Grace is desperate to find connective tissue to follow back to the knot shop. Some hint, some clue to where Berna was being kept. She has to wait for the nurse to leave her station again, and the wait is interminable. Ten minutes, fifteen, twenty. Finally, Grace macros through to Berna's form. About to give up, she discovers two tiny paper-clip icons. She touches the screen.

Photographs. Her age or her situation required them to document her condition upon admittance. Grace gets a look at Berna prior to the hospital gown that she escaped in. She's wearing a pair of filthy blue jeans and an equally soiled blue-and-white-striped long-sleeved tee. Her hair is matted and filthy. Her eyes are sullen and her face malnourished. She appears exhausted. Grace saves the image and the next—Berna shot from behind—to the iPad.

It's the two dark stains below the girl's knees that capture and hold Grace's attention. The same height up the legs for both stains. *Water.* Berna had waded through water before arriving at the clinic.

A woman's voice. Grace looks up sharply to see the nurse has returned to her terminal. The woman sees an image of a young girl's backside on her screen instead of the screen where she left off. She calls over a colleague to have a look.

Grace's finger hovers over the icon that will return the screen to the nurse's last page view. She doesn't dare trigger it until the nurse looks away . . .

"Maghan!" the nurse calls out. Her eyes lift.

Grace touches the screen, hoists the iPad and drops it into her purse. She leans her head back with her eyes closed.

Maghan joins the nurse, who is clearly befuddled by the terminal's miraculous return to her original page.

Grace hears a discussion about how there was a picture of the girl—"*the girl!*"—just a moment prior. Berna is famous here since the publication of Sonia's article.

It's everything Grace can do to keep her eyes closed. Five minutes later she approaches the counter and, in an irritated tone, tells the nurse that if Julia Schmidt checks in, please tell her that her friend has left.

Muttering to herself, Grace leaves.

KNOX IS SUPPOSED to be going door to door showing Berna's photograph as he agreed to do for Sonia Pangarkar. But Knox is not great at following orders; he's better at following people, and so it's Sonia he follows.

She knows more than she is letting on. Reporters make their livings exploiting secrets. He has yet to determine where she lives, but she's a creature of habit. She has chosen Melly's Cookie Bar and Gourmet Coffee bakery several blocks west of Café van Daele on Nieuwezijds Voorburgwal. It's a small space that offers only a few bar stools looking out at the street. She arrives promptly— predictably—at 9:30. He needs to talk to her about that.

By ten A.M. she's on a tram, Knox bicycling close behind. Each time he's about to lose the tram it makes a stop, allowing him to ride at an even pace while still keeping up. She disembarks, walks four blocks west and rides another tram. Ten minutes later, she's moving store to store showing Berna's photograph as Knox is supposed to be doing. She's depressingly predictable. He stays with her another ninety minutes and is about to give up when she checks her watch. It's the first time she's done that. Right or not, he grants this weight. Encouraged, he stays with her, having little better to do.

At 11:30, she's on the move again. He can see it in the urgency of her strides and her passing up storefronts she might have gone inside only an hour earlier. A second check of her watch less than ten minutes after the first confirms it for him: she has an appointment.

It might be a hair appointment, or a lawyer, or a deadline filing, but her body language says differently. Excitement and anticipation show in her every step, in her eagerness to cross streets. She is charged, and he along with her.

At 11:45 she enters Plaats Riche, a restaurant undeserving of its name by the look of its pub exterior. Looks more bratwurst and Guinness than duck pâté and foie gras. The size of the place prevents him from following her inside. There's no question in his mind that she's meeting someone. If Sonia has arrived first, then Knox stands a chance of identifying her company. If she is late, then he'll have to hope for after the meal as she departs.

He wins a break five minutes later, when a fairly tall woman arrives at the door. She wears a head scarf and carries a shoulder bag. She pauses at the window, cupping the glass to see inside.

Grace didn't give him much of a description, but Knox is not shy about jumping to conclusions. He likes pieces to fit. Doesn't expect them to, but isn't one to fight it when they do. A tall woman wearing a scarf was seen in the market. A tall woman Tasered Grace's attacker.

Knox shoots a long-distance photo from waist high, as if reading e-mails, having no idea if the resolution will be good enough to see the woman's face. He considers some way of getting inside Plaats Riche for a salad. It's a small enough place to eavesdrop on any table.

He messages the photo to Grace.

look familiar?

She texts back:

where are you?

But it's Dulwich Knox texts next, asking how far he is from Knox's current location. The answer comes back:

15 mins

Knox considers all that he's missing inside the restaurant. He texts:

leave G and meet me. hurry. you just got hungry

"WASTE OF TIME," DULWICH SAYS, "except they make a damn good burger. Did it ever occur to you that both 'frankfurter' and 'burger' sound German? We're in the land of plenty over here."

"Nothing?"

They are walking on the canal side of a street, a block behind the woman in the scarf, who is alone. Dulwich's limp is causing them to lose ground; Knox will have to ditch him soon, and both men know it.

"They talked so quietly I'm not sure they could hear each other half the time."

"That's something," Knox says.

"That's bullshit. Coulda been pillow talk, coulda been nukes. Who knows?"

"But they knew each other?"

"Couldn't tell," Dulwich answers. "I would say no. Too many uncomfortable pauses between them. Leaning back, studying the other person. Nice rack on the tall one, by the way."

"Focus," Knox says. For once, they've reversed roles. "Ethnicity?"

"Indian? Pakistani?"

"Working for Sonia?"

"You two on a first-name basis, huh?"

"Maybe we are."

"They do not know each other. Not well, if at all."

"Was Sonia conducting an interview?"

"Maybe. Could be. She definitely took notes. But the way it looked, that wouldn't be my first guess."

"The tall one was spying on Grace. Rescues her at just the right moment. Meets with Sonia the next day for lunch."

"So maybe they do know each other," Dulwich concedes.

"Or maybe she's freelance. Someone Sonia hired, someone a friend recommended. Poses the question how she knew about Grace, how she knew where to find her."

"Grace has been making some noise," Dulwich says. He burps loudly. "Meal so nice you enjoy it twice." Dulwich laughs at his own joke. Knox does not.

Dulwich limps straight ahead at the next intersection, where the crossroad spans a canal to the left. Knox crosses the bridge, moving away from the woman, picking up his pace to catch up and stay even with her while across the canal. Natural barriers create mental barriers; she won't be looking for anyone over where he is. Knox quickly overtakes Dulwich, but has to run hard as the woman in the scarf turns right, away from the water, away from downtown. Knox has guessed wrong. He crosses back at the next bridge and staircases his way through the neighborhood's blocks trying to intercept her, but he has lost her.

He finds himself in a regimented, neatly planned residential zone of tree-lined narrow streets with endless four-story brick buildings, some with retail at street level. It's a massive housing project done with class. Block after block. Kilometer after kilometer. A dizzying place where it's easy to get lost because of the architectural similarity. An easy place to stand out. Small shops and banks are all he sees. No supermarkets or car dealers or theaters. No hotels or shopping malls.

No people.

The place appears inhabited by only cars and bicycles. The machines have taken over. It's a back lot for a science fiction film. It's the Blade Runner no one ever saw coming. It's suburbia.

He spots a tall woman at a distance; she's wearing the same color head scarf as the woman who'd dined with Sonia. She's walking away from him. He follows, careful to stay so far behind that he's still not sure he has the right woman. But anyone who can surprise Grace Chu in a crowd has his respect, is a formidable mark. He's not going to push it. Holds back several blocks trusting his good fortune; he found her once, he can find her again. He's a dog on a scent, a spy behind enemy lines—he lives for this shit. He can see, hear, smell and taste everything, everywhere: the couple coming out of the building a block behind him; the truck about to turn onto his street; the taste of winter in the air. Realizes why he loves this work, why import/export is a waste of his talents. It's like the ghost of Dulwich whispering over his shoulder. He thinks about Tommy. Feels the weight of the burden, regrets both their situations, is angry at his parents for dying on him. He's something of a mess when, a few dozen blocks later, he sees an oasis rise out of all the brick.

Frederik Hendrikplantsoen—Frederik Hendrik Park—rises as a forest to his right and across the wide boulevard before him. He has instinctively closed in on her, following now by a block, and on the opposite sidewalk as she slows nearly imperceptibly. They've arrived at her destination; she has telegraphed this unintentionally but clearly.

It gives him the chance to get the jump on her. He doesn't doubt his instinct. Advantage is a gift given in glimpses. With no time to consider pros or cons, Knox has only to choose a side of the boulevard that divides the park. He can be wrong and he's still okay; if he goes right and she goes left, a park is a place where a person takes her time; he'll have a second chance.

He crosses the street and enters the park's manicured lawns and gardens. He loses sight of the woman immediately. The smell of car exhaust is traded for loamy earth and sap. This is the part of his import travel he misses: the jungles, deserts and beaches. He walks a route that bisects the green ahead. Sensing more such space, he navigates to the right and reaches and crosses an asphalt path, moving deeper into the grounds. Parks himself on a bench with a view of the next path, realizing it leads back to the street. A man occupies a bench twenty yards up the same path. A woman runner approaches, then passes him.

Knox waits with his ankles crossed on outstretched legs, his shoulders back—a man at rest. In the periphery of his eyesight he sees the woman in the scarf coming up the path toward him. He sighs and closes his eyes. When he opens them again, she's nearly upon him. Then passing him. For all his apparent calm, his chest is tight behind a heart twice its normal size. The man to his left comes off the bench, a cell phone pressed to his ear.

Knox has to judge the coincidence of the timing. It feels like a baton pass, the runner in front gaining speed to match the runner approaching. He doesn't stare, doesn't study. Closes his eyes again. Another deep breath.

He's grabbed from behind. Two of them, both going for an arm. Knox rocks forward, slamming both men into the back of the bench. The grip holding his left arm lessens; he breaks free, swings a fist into the throat of the man on his right.

He sees the uniform too late to pull the punch. Slugs the patrolman off him and into a choking, coughing slurry. Throws his hands up, but again too late. Takes a club strike to the side of his head that sends him into a purple fog. Manages to keep his arms overhead as he spins to face them from the other side of the bench.

"Okay! Okay!" Knox says in English.

The one patrolman has recovered. The other is ready to punish him again, the club held high, but his red-faced partner waves him off.

"You will come with us," the patrolman croaks out. He spits into the grass and stares at his phlegm, looking for blood.

They're standing too close together. Another few feet apart and it would make things much more difficult. Knox can take them out. Debates doing just that. But what are they doing here in the first place, and why the rough treatment? Why the surprise? They aren't after an indigent, they're after Knox in particular.

Knox jerks his head to the right: no one there. But he's thinking: the guy on the bench; the cell phone; the arrival of two uniforms.

His mark has a meeting with the police. Knox is unwanted. They can't hold him; they have no real charges against him. Though that won't stop them if they want to. Advantage is a gift given in impulses. He lets this one pass.

He interweaves his fingers atop his head. "Okay, okay," he says again.

THE INTERVIEW ROOM OWNS a predictable blandness. Vanilla cream walls, a no-smoking poster burned by a match on the lower corner, a single table, two chairs, one bolted to the floor. A compact fluorescent bulb fails to provide enough reading light, like a hotel bedside lamp. The sergeant adjusts a pair of supermarket reading glasses to read Knox's exploding passport. It has gotten wet too many times, dried in the sun, stuffed into tight pockets. He has promised himself to renew it, not because of its condition but because there is barely space enough left on any page for a new stamp, a quality that catches the eye of customs officers. They study his passport like it's a piece of archaeology. The sergeant does the same, flipping pages, adjusting the orientation in order to read a date or location. He looks over the top of his glasses at Knox. Suspicious? Impressed? Jealous? It's hard to tell.

"You will please tell me what you were doing in Hendrikplantsoen," the sergeant says.

"I told the constables—the two who abducted me."

"Detained."

"I also told them I will speak with Chief Inspector Joshua Brower. No one else."

"You are hardly in a position to make such demands."

"Not a demand, a condition."

The sergeant puts down Knox's passport deliberately.

"Import, export," Knox says.

"Uh-huh."

"As you can see, I often trade here in Amsterdam. As I have for several years."

"You 'trade' in thirty or more cities and countries, Mr. Knox, many of which are not on the best terms with your government."

"Do not make the mistake of jumping to conclusions,

Sergeant. I am an importer. It's what I do. Period. Chief Inspector Brower, please." The sergeant thinks he's a spy.

Knox has a dozen questions he would like to reciprocate with, all having to do with the rendezvous in the park. But he can't go there. He and the sergeant bat the birdie over the net until Knox folds his arms and bites his tongue and challenges the sergeant to a staring contest that the sergeant cannot possibly win. Knox is the world champion.

The sergeant is too prideful to contact Brower. He returns Knox to a holding cell believing he can break him down this way, but the hours stretch out, and it's only then that Knox realizes Brower's absence can be attributed to his having the night shift.

They've taken Knox's possessions, including his watch, so he has no idea of the time when two officers lead him back to the same interrogation room and leave him.

Chief Inspector Brower is a freckled redhead with pale green eyes, a round face and thick bones, a man who might be ten years younger or older than the forty he looks. He wears chinos, a white shirt that was ironed at home and a Scottevest, a source of amusement for Knox, who wears the same coat.

He shuts the door.

"I'm sorry about this," Brower says. "Not terribly hospitable of us."

"I don't think we ever met in Kuwait," Knox says.

"David and I . . . we go back a little further than Kuwait."

Knox puts that down as military service but he's not

going to push. Dulwich's time before Kuwait remains foggy; despite the closeness and length of their friendship, Knox has heard little to nothing about it.

"Your sergeant didn't like me."

"We take a dim view of people following our superintendents."

Knox takes note of the superior rank of the cop in the park. The mystery woman is well connected. He tries to measure how much capital the Dulwich connection gives him. He believes he misjudged it initially. Brower's eyes suggest a stubbornness and a loyalty to his department that concern Knox. He waits him out.

"Do you want to tell me how you ended up on that bench?"

"I was following the woman."

"We take an even dimmer view of stalking."

"She's of interest to us." Knox strives to remind Brower of his connection to Dulwich.

"I can try to find out for you, but chances are it will only impede your efforts."

"Poke the nest."

"Just like that. Yes."

Knox shrugs. "Her name would help."

"I'm sure it would."

"She had a colleague of ours under surveillance." Knox can safely go this far, but not much further. Brower knows more than he's telling—how much more, Knox can't tell.

"You received the police report," Brower says. It might be a question.

"That was helpful," Knox says. "Extremely helpful."

"You and David must not make the mistake of inter-fering with an active investigation."

"Of course not."

"The young girl, Berna, is ours. The article caused a political firestorm. You get in the way—"

"Never our intention," Knox lies. "Our interest is"—Knox vamps—"protecting the free speech of the people interviewed in the article." He's been told this is how Dulwich pitched it to Brower. Private concerns don't shut down illegal sweatshops; that is reserved for authorities.

"Important, certainly. But should that work interfere—"

"It will not."

"This woman you were following has nothing to do with those interviewed."

"There you go," Knox says. "That's all I was trying to find out."

"So there's your answer."

"So it would appear." Knox hesitates, wondering how honest he dare be. "I can't tell if we're on the same side or not."

"David is a good friend."

Knox nods.

"You will be released. You must appear before a mag-istrate in the morning. I will vouch for you—it was mis-taken identity. There will be no charges."

"Thank you." Knox is surprised it must go this far. "Who is she?"

"It is not my case."

"Can you find out for us?"

"It is possible. I will let David know, if so."

"What do you know about the community center on Van Speijkstraat?"

"In regards to . . . ?"

"There was an assault. Two teenage boys. On a woman."

"Was this reported?" Brower's concern is genuine.

"No. We didn't want to make our efforts any more difficult. I'm sure you understand."

"Teens?"

"Yes."

"This is a good neighborhood. But these are difficult economic times for everyone."

"Unusual?" Knox asks. "We need to determine if my colleague was the real target."

"This woman . . . the one you were following. She sent your colleague there, to the *stichting*?"

Dulwich knew how to pick them.

"I can understand your interest in her," Brower says.

"Nice to know who your enemies are. If the police are—"

"She is not ours."

Knox ticks this off his list. Brower looks confused. Knox says, "A CI for your superintendent?" He adds, "Confidential informant," though it's unnecessary, perhaps insulting, given Brower's dismissive reaction.

"Doubtful," Brower says.

Knox has to make a judgment call. He decides this is not a time for holding back. "A vendor at a street market put my colleague in that alley. This other woman—who later met with your superintendent—intervened during the assault." He cuts off Brower before the man can interrupt. "There's no question it was her. The question is whether or not the vendor created the assault to allow a partner to intervene and appear the hero, or if that's overthinking it."

"And you stayed with this woman all night?" Brower sounds dubious. "This is how you came to connect her with our super?"

Knox doesn't answer, which to him is not technically lying to the police. "The next thing I know, she's meeting some guy in a park. And here I am."

Brower is warming up to Knox. He considers him carefully for the better part of a minute. It seems like much longer. "The city government is in the midst of a face-lift that is politically charged and possibly economically suicidal, at least in the short run. There is a transformation under way from the Amsterdam of marijuana bars and open prostitution to a city with core family values. We are doing what your Las Vegas did over a decade ago. We're a little late. This newspaper article, the idea of child slave labor and all that implies—child prostitution, sex slaves—this is exactly what the city can ill afford at the moment. It also hurts the Netherlands' standing in the EU. Which is a long-winded way of saying your presence here is ill-advised and unwanted. This is not to say child labor is in any way condoned, or that we would turn a blind eye. Quite the opposite, I assure you. It's more the outsider element, and of course the international publicity. The existence of a sweatshop is being investigated. It is an active investigation—any interference in an active investigation is itself a crime. You and David and this colleague of yours—I'm assuming it's a woman because of the assault—should take note of this. How and if this woman you were following connects to our work as opposed to yours . . . as I have said, I will look into it and report back to David. In the meantime . . ."

"I appreciate both the explanation and your efforts. It will be taken under advisement. But to remind you: our concern is freedom of the press."

"One other piece of unsolicited advice," Brower says, his concentration fixed, his brow tight. "These black market operations are well organized and well defended. I suspect the bottoms of the canals carry the bodies of many who tried to cross them." He pauses and lowers his voice. "I cannot vouch for *all* my colleagues. There is a great deal of money at play."

Knox refuses to react. His only response is a slight nod. Brower is trying to save his life.

"Until tomorrow morning, then," Brower says, leaning back.

Knox provides him the phone number of one of the SIM cards he carries. Brower will text the time and location of the hearing.

As Knox leaves the constabulary, he keeps an eye over his shoulder as he advised Sonia to do, Brower's warning echoing in his mind.

GRACE'S DRIVER, DULWICH, catches her eye from across a crowded Starbucks where a good deal of English is spoken. She packs up and joins him. He holds open the rear door of the rented Mercedes for her and then climbs behind the wheel himself.

"So?" she asks.

"Your scarf lady had lunch with Pangarkar."

Grace has been waiting impatiently for his return. It has been nearly an hour, and the wait has been killing her.

"And?"

"I had the burger."

"Please."

"Knox may have lost her. It's unclear. He played a hunch that didn't work out. It happens." He reviews for her what he and Knox discussed about the meeting between the two.

"They *know* each other, Pangarkar and this woman?"

"They do now," he says. "What about Berna?"

"Her full name is Berna *Ranatunga*. She's from Belgium."

"Well done."

She passes her laptop over the backseat. It shows the two photos of the girl. Dulwich drags it toward him at the next light.

"Wet legs."

"She arrived there that way. I am working on it."

"Working?"

"The canals are not knee deep. I'm looking for ponds and fountains . . . someplace a child might have waded through." She hauls the laptop back over the seat. "Turn left in two blocks."

"You have a nicer voice than the GPS," he says. The device speaks female robot in Dutch. It's hardly a compliment. Dulwich zooms out to try to see where she's directing him.

Four blocks later, as his eyes leave the mirror, he says, "Interesting."

She knows better than to turn around to look. There isn't enough tinting to hide her actions.

"A tail?" she says.

But Dulwich has his mobile out and is one-eyeing the street as he navigates the phone's screen.

He speaks Dutch. "Inspector Brower, please." He pauses intermittently. "Josh? It's me, David . . . He's not great with authority . . . I'll tell him. Question for you . . . How quickly can you run a vehicle registration plate? . . . Please." He consults the mirror and begins reciting the plate information when he's cut off. He ends the call, placing the phone in the cup holder. He explains, "Our contact at the police. His guys grabbed up Knox. Our guy, Brower, smoothed the waters."

She didn't hear the groan of a motorcycle. "The car behind us."

"Uh-huh."

"No one followed me," she says absolutely.

"No one's accusing you of anything."

"You're assuming it was me," she says. "You're wrong."

"We *want* you followed," Dulwich says, reminding her. "This is a good thing."

"But I wasn't followed."

"It's a taxi. A private taxi."

"I do not understand."

"We've underestimated the reach of our adversaries,

as well as your celebrity." He pauses. "The same thing happened to Knox in Shanghai. Money gets spread around the taxi drivers, the tram operators, hotel doormen. A private network of informers who have their eyes everywhere."

She experiences a chill. Doesn't want to acknowledge she was spotted. "Four blocks, and then a right," she says, directing him. "Let me out anywhere along the green. I will meet you on the opposite side, at the film museum, in ten minutes."

"Too risky."

"You are getting exactly what you want. We will see to what lengths they will go. I can handle him . . . them. You would not have chosen me otherwise." She's eager to make her points with Dulwich where she can. Her Army training and her performance in Shanghai are worth reminding him of.

Their eyes meet in the rearview mirror and she knows she has him exactly where she wants him. Men like Dulwich are so predictable. Knox, far less so. Dulwich is the drill sergeant type: he'll push to the edge of sanity, but ultimately believes in both a person's abilities—as he defines them—and the expendability of any one player to the greater cause. She's glad it worked out for Dulwich to drive her; she knows how to play him.

He pulls to the curb. She's out of the car and headed into the park. It is a beautiful setting of lawns and paths interlaced with a dozen ponds. The sudden change from brick and asphalt to grass and birdsong has a calming effect on her. The cabdriver has followed her, but he's lagging behind, and she can feel the tug of his parked vehicle drawing him. Whatever money he's been offered doesn't measure well against the hassle of a parking violation and abandoning his cab. She quickens her step, and by the second intersection she's lost him.

The pond she encounters has a three-flume fountain shooting water thirty feet into the air. There are couples on blankets despite the cold. The lawn tapers into the water, where a child could easily wade. There are bushes along the water's edge behind which a child could hide.

She passes a gazebo where the water is behind a retaining wall, and offers an unlikely place to hide. The park is enormous and would take an hour or more to circumnavigate, but she puts it on her list of possible locations.

She is well trained at increasing her pace without the appearance of doing so. Much of her sudden increase in speed over ground is the product of flexing her ankles with each step. It results in an incremental burst of speed which is unseen to the eye—a sprinter's trick—along with a slight increase in stride and standing up straighter, her posture implying a body more at rest than one leaning into her efforts. A person attempting to follow her will find himself losing ground, distance he can't make up without revealing himself. Her Army Intelligence instructor, a woman in anatomy only, used video and timing drills that, at the time, seemed overly harsh and exhausting. Only now does Grace appreciate them.

Fifteen minutes later, she and Dulwich are driving the streets surrounding the park. The real estate doesn't match her needs. It's hard—*impossible*—to picture a knot shop in such a classy neighborhood, where brand-name compa-nies occupy converted mansions along the park's perime-ter. This isn't an area to recruit hungry girls or to have them seen entering and exiting a building at all hours.

"We are going about this all wrong," she says, blurting it out before she realizes she's challenging Dulwich's orig-inal plan.

"Are we?"

"That is, I may have an alternative plan to bring these people to us."

"Are you going to share?"

"How committed is our client in terms of investment?"

"Less ambiguous, please."

"I will need . . . That is: it will require substantial investment in infrastructure. Five figures easily."

"If it means we can shut it down, I believe the client will bring the necessary resources to bear," Dulwich says.

"Not all of the funds will be recouped."

"I'm listening," he says.

17

A figure lurks in a dark corner of a dismal bar in the heart of the red-light district. Knox holds off, eyeing things in the reflection of the bar mirror. The bar is peopled with men of every age, stoned and drunk and smoking cigarettes. The women, far fewer in number, are overweight and overly made up, with piercings and too much pale, pimpled skin showing. The bartender looks like he could hold his own in a fight. He nods at Knox, Knox taps the bar and another beer is delivered. Knox pays cash. No tabs are run in a place like this.

He takes his beer over to the corner. Sonia Pangarkar is revealed out of the shadow. Knox sits down on a bench next to her.

"Hello."

"Mr. Steele," she says.

"I can think of nicer places to meet."

"No one knows me in a place like this. My television work . . . it comes at a price."

"You don't want to be seen in my company?"

"It is dangerous, this work, Mr. Steele. We've discussed this."

"You're afraid."

"I am careful."

"Can't be too careful," he says.

"She's a teacher. She knew the other one I told you about. She has a student who attends infrequently. She noticed the calluses I wrote about in my story. The girl's father, or a man claiming to be her father, because the teacher has never met the father, showed up at school yesterday. The girl escaped out the window. She's willing to talk—the teacher—if I keep her name out of it."

"Not much for me to work with. For you, yes, of course."

"There is, or I wouldn't have contacted you." Sonia is abrupt, verging on dismissive. He hears a new tension in her voice. She isn't sleeping well, judging by her gloomy eyes. The gin in front of her isn't her first.

"Are you sure?" he asks. "Maybe you wanted the company." He has a role to play; he has to fight to stay in character.

She hangs her head. "Leave," she says.

"Time and place." Knox upends the beer. He sets the half-empty bottle back on the table and stands. "Text or voice mail. Give me at least an hour advance notice." He only checks his various SIM chips once an hour.

She glances at her watch. "Forty minutes. You'll need your camera, unless I'm mistaken."

Knox is surprised by the timing.

"I'll come with you to get it," she says. "And I'll take your phone until we're finished."

"I thought we trusted each other."

"Why would you think that?"

"You've confided in me."

"Have I?"

He thinks of her meeting with the scarf woman. "As far as I know you have."

"Stick to the arrangement." She holds out her hand. "I will return it after our appointment."

"You'd better turn off your own first," he says, passing her the iPhone. "It's your phone these people would track, not mine. No one knows me."

She calls a number from memory and speaks Dutch, telling whoever's on the other end that she's on schedule. Knox smells a setup as he contemplates why Sonia Pangarkar would lead him into a trap. She turns off his phone and pockets it.

"How do you know I don't carry a second phone?" he asks.

"Do you?"

"No."

"Then we can go now."

She pulls a beige scarf up over her head and leads him out of the back of the pub, a door he should have known existed.

Knox is hit by something hot below the ribs. He's thrown back and his knees fail and he's down on the cobblestone. Tourists and pedestrians make room around him, barely breaking stride. A second man grabs Sonia, pulling for her bag. Knox cracks this man's knee with the sole of his shoe, causing him to cry out and let go of her.

The first guy leads with the cattle prod, lunging at the fallen Knox like a swordsman. He wears a shiny black leather jacket and designer jeans. Knox rolls into the cobblestone lane and chops at the hand holding the cattle prod. He manages to force a miss, but fails to dislodge it. He's hit in the right arm, and his arm goes instantly numb. His head spins. The device is designed to punish but not knock him unconscious. It's riot gear, either stolen or bought on the black market, or the guy's a cop.

Knox has use of only his left arm.

Sonia kicks the man who's down.

"Go!" Knox manages.

She's off at a run.

Knox pulls on a leg nearest him. A woman in her twenties falls across him and takes the brunt of the next burst of voltage. She tries to scream, but no sound comes out. Knox pulls his legs out from under her and drags himself across the cobbles.

Two guys attack the man with the cattle prod. Friends of the fallen woman. They go at him with haymakers. They're rugby types, and drunk enough to want the fight. Knox keeps back-pedaling, one-armed, awaiting any sensation in his legs. When the tingling arrives, he draws himself to his feet and limps off in the direction Sonia ran. By the wet, thumping sounds behind him, the ruggers are winning.

Knox rounds the corner and nearly coldcocks Sonia as she grabs him by the arm. She leads him down into a waiting boat, the engine running, and they speed off in a water taxi.

"What the hell?" Sonia shouts over the motor.

John Steele can't say what he's thinking: *police*. The look of the guy, the leather jacket and jeans. The fact that he'd checked all three SIMs when just outside the bar, prior to the meeting. He'd given one of his numbers to Brower. He wants to trust the chief inspector, but he doesn't trust the sergeant who first interviewed him, or the superintendent who busted him. John Steele can't know any of this.

"They must have been after you," he says, "but wanted to neutralize me first."

"It didn't seem that way."

"I don't think you're paying me enough." She isn't paying him anything.

"If you want to quit, I understand."

"Are you kidding? We just confirmed this is a hot story. I'm in."

"I can talk to my editor. Maybe he can offer our per diem. Not that that helps all that much. Our paper is very cheap."

"They wanted your bag," Knox says.

She clutches it firmly.

"You should back up to the cloud, and you should erase stuff once you do. You can't leave anything important on your laptop. They're clearly coming after your laptop." He hopes a photographer would say things like this. "I'm something of a tech nerd."

"I am not so good. You can show me how?"

He contrasts this with Grace, who is capable of hacking high-level systems, who rarely admits her limitations. He's concerned he should think of her, wonders why it's happening.

"Yes," he says. "No problem."

The yellow water taxi works through the labyrinth of canals that expand out from city center like concentric-ring roads. Knox requests a stop near his hotel. He leaves Sonia waiting in the water taxi. A historical plaque on the hotel doorway steals his thought. He'd rather not be reminded at a time like this of the city's history. But one can't pick such things. The city dates back eight hundred years to a bridge built by fishermen. They put doors on the bridge creating a dam, holding back the spring floods of the IJ. The protected town became important to the shipment of beer, and eventually grain from the north. But it was a religious miracle that made it a place of pilgrimage, elevating its population and importance. Now it is seen more as Europe's city of sin; the turnabout strikes him as ironic and even sad.

He retrieves his camera bag from the room. The windbreaker is disgusting from his rolling around the alley. He leaves it behind. Ten minutes later they're under way again. Sonia returns his iPhone to him, her eyes apologetic.

The water taxi driver makes turn after turn, and soon Knox has lost track of their location. The narrow canal houses—their high gables designed to hold winches for hauling up prosperous merchants' goods and furniture— give way to the ubiquitous brick buildings of the outer neighborhoods, providing Knox with some indication of the distance they've made. Travel by water is so much faster than by surface streets, further complicating his task. He would like a GPS fix. The current SIM card in the phone doesn't allow for GPS; the other chips are in his jacket, back in the hotel.

Sonia's holding her hair out of her face and looking across the boat at him. Not exactly the way a reporter would. More like a woman. A curious woman at that.

"Where'd you learn to fight like that? Back there?"

"U.S. Army," he lies.

She studies him. "Thank you."

"I could say 'My pleasure,' but I'd be lying. Tell the truth," says John Steele, the photographer, "I was scared shitless back there."

"Be careful, John. It will serve you well to not forget I have built my career on conducting interviews." She leaves it there, but they never lose eye contact in the flickering streetlight that struggles to reach the canal through trees and bridges.

"Did you recognize them?"

"No. But it was dark. They were dressed well for a pair of thugs."

"How do thugs dress?"

"Better than I thought, apparently."

Another turn and the taxi slows. It pulls up to a dock that rocks in the wake. The driver holds on to a cleat while they climb off amid the slap of water against the canal wall. Sonia pays him. The boat pulls away.

"Are you coming?" she asks.

But Knox is keeping his eye on the driver, whose cell phone is already out and to his ear. "We're here to interview the teacher?"

"Yes, of course."

"We have ten minutes to get out of this neighborhood. Maybe less. I hope the house is close by."

"That's ridiculous. How can you know that?" Nervous. Apprehensive.

He wishes she wouldn't do that. Appreciates Grace for her levelheadedness.

"The driver. The boat operator. I think he may have recognized you. He was on his mobile phone the moment he pulled away."

"So?" She leads the way across the street and to the right.

Knox looks for a landmark or street sign. These neighborhoods all appear the same.

"It's common enough practice for certain elements to seek outside assistance when trying to find someone like you," he says.

"The police? I have nothing to hide from the police."

But she walks faster, pulling away from him. He gives her the space, gives her time to think about it. She stops abruptly and turns to face him. "Do not patronize me. I confess I'm unfamiliar with being someone's target, but that does not give you the excuse to take advantage of me. If you are implying what I think you are implying, I do not accept this at all! The entire city is looking for me? Who is the naïve one?"

"Seven minutes," he says. "Maybe less."

"You're the big expert."

"I'm the big expert. In this, yes. I may not have many useful skills." He glances down at his camera bag to make the point. "But I've done some things I'm not so proud of, and I know the streets—evidently better than you. This would be the wrong time to doubt me."

"Only the police have that kind of reach."

"Six and a half minutes."

"It's going to go longer."

"Then we need an exit strategy. We can't be walking the streets. No taxis. No trams."

"You are overreacting."

"The Fiat across the street. I'll need a tennis ball."

"What?"

"Better if you ask her for it. And I'll need you to stall her long enough for me to get a knife out of the kitchen."

"This is part of that street savvy of yours, I suppose?"

"You suppose right. Six minutes."

At the next door, she lets them inside. Her finger roams the board and rings an apartment one flight up although there's no inner door to breach. Knox remains two steps below her as they climb, his attention divided to include the door to the street. He can move his arm, though it's numb. His side hurts where he was zapped. He would like to believe he's thinking clearly, but knows better. It leaves him paranoid and prone to overreact. A door coming open above them sparks a wave of adrenaline.

The woman who awaits them is in her early forties, with tired eyes and crooked eyebrows. The apartment is modest. Two tweens study at the kitchen table. There is no sign of the husband, but there's evidence of him—an extra-large sweatshirt draped over the arm of the couch, a hunting magazine next to the well-used television remote. She shows them inside. They decline the offer of something to drink. Knox checks his watch, making sure that Sonia sees him.

The conversation starts awkwardly with the teacher issuing concerns and denials. This is not something she would usually do. She would typically consult with a parent first. She doesn't hold the press in high regard, and yet is quick to make Sonia an exception. She is understandably nervous.

Sonia is an adept interviewer. Knox takes mental notes. His wrist is angled on his lap so he can see the watch face. Two minutes. While Sonia works the woman, Knox excuses himself to the washroom. He passes through the kitchen in order to say hello to the kids. He steals a knife.

By the time he returns, they are into the crux of the interview.

". . . only occasionally," says the teacher, in Dutch.

Sonia recaps for Knox, also in Dutch. "Elizabeth was just telling me that this student of hers, Maja, misses more days than she attends, but is an eager student when in attendance."

"Truancy is often just like this. Yes?"

"American?" Elizabeth asks.

"My father was an American serviceman," Knox lies, staying with the spoken Dutch.

"Elizabeth has a picture the girl, Maja, drew in class. Perhaps you could set up for that over there," Sonia suggests, pointing to the other side of the small room. She indicates the pen-and-ink watercolor on the coffee table. It shows several young girls around another piece of colorful art—a rug? One of the girls has what looks like a rope coming out from beneath her crossed legs. Sonia is right: it's a compelling visual.

"So this girl, Maja, attends only intermittently." It's a statement.

"Yes. Just yesterday a man who identified himself as the father showed up with the intention of bringing her home. However, Maja fled out the window before he could take her."

"You contacted me because . . . ?"

"Well, the artwork, of course. And the man as well. And her reaction, of course. She isn't the only girl, I can tell you that much. But the teachers don't talk about it amongst themselves, and there's very little done about it, and I'm not sure why that is. But I have a niece, you see? Your article, and of course the bombing . . . if I called the police I would have no choice but to be involved. With you it is different."

"It most certainly is," Sonia says, attempting to reassure her. "These other girls you refer to . . . do you have names?"

"No."

"Your colleagues, then."

"Carefully, please. I can ask. Yes, of course."

"But the more names, the more sources for my story, the more credible."

"You do not believe me?" Her eyebrows join above her nose as she expresses her offense. She's turned toward Knox in distrust.

John Steele is preparing his camera by testing the flash and adjusting exposure for the close distance, using a magazine cover as his subject matter. He retrieves the artwork from the coffee table.

"It is not that at all," says Sonia, "merely the ways of journalism, as I'm sure you can appreciate."

"Yes. I see." The woman's anxiety has given way to vulnerability. She's leaning forward now and on the attack. "You want me to spy for you, I suppose? You want me to put others at risk as I've done for myself. My principal will most certainly not tolerate my addressing the press this way. I am not about to involve others without their consent."

"As I've already promised, you will be an unnamed source."

"We all know how that works out," she says sarcastically and clearly afraid.

Knox is incapable of remaining quiet any longer. "There is a degree of sensitivity to this story, of security risk, that we are well aware of, believe me. Ms. Pangarkar and I have no intention of seeing anyone else hurt. Least of all, the children."

She tightens with the word.

"We all want the same thing," Sonia says.

The woman repositions her chair to include Knox, who's firing off shots of the watercolor. "I will ask my colleagues. It is all that I can do."

Sonia passes her a business card. "In the short term, I would appreciate a chat with Maja's mother."

"No. I do not have that information. Besides, it is impossible."

"I will be discreet. A good reporter is a good storyteller, Elizabeth. She will never know I started first at the school."

A television is playing through the wall. A teakettle sings farther away. "I will try," Elizabeth says.

Knox is about to warn her that should anyone come knocking on her door in the next thirty minutes, she should remain silent and avoid answering. But she's slipped into a fragility that dictates otherwise.

"This might seem like an odd request, but I was wondering if you might have a tennis ball I could take with me?" Uncomfortable about asking the question, Sonia does a poor job of it, making it sound too serious.

"It's for me, actually," Knox says. "A dog I must contend with. Better the ball than my leg." He winces a grin.

The woman is befuddled. "Around here somewhere, I suppose." She calls out to her son and puts him on the task. The boy returns in short order with a bald tennis ball. Knox thanks him and pockets the ball. With Sonia looking his way, he taps his wristwatch.

She thanks Elizabeth and manages some mindless chatter as they find their way out. As the apartment door shuts, Knox feels a profound sense of relief.

"Tricky," he says in English. "You were good in there."

"You don't have to sound so surprised." She adjusts her scarf to slightly below her hairline. They are nearing the stairs when she adds, "You could use a little work on your accent."

Knox stops to stab the tennis ball with the knife. The rubber is thick, the task not easy. He creates a small slit in the seam, squeezes the ball and it sighs. "We all serve a useful purpose," he says.

His pulse quickens as they reach street level. His us-against-them mentality warms him. He turns to Sonia in the faint yellow light of the foyer and sees her eyes shining. She's either terrified or excited, but it turns him on, whatever her present state. His urge is to take her here, now. Her eyes soften and she smiles.

"Follow my lead," he says.

"Of course," she replies, her voice raspy and hoarse.

It's her face that would be recognized, not his. He tugs her scarf farther forward, the contact intimate. "I will go first. Watch me before you follow. We're going directly to the Fiat, you to the passenger side. If there's trouble, you run in the opposite direction from where I turn. If we separate, avoid any place familiar to you." He picks up a piece of junk mail from the floor beneath the buzzer box and writes down Dulwich's phone number. "Call this number. He can help you." Seeing suspicion on her face, he says, "He's an old friend, the only person I know well here, a good man. And resourceful." He has gone too far, poisoned by the combination of hormones and adrenaline.

Knox is out the door before there's room for discussion. He pauses between two parked cars, using them as screens as he listens and looks for anything unusual. He'd prefer a busy street to this. But his hesitation is infinitesimal; he's out across the street, heading for the Fiat, the tennis ball gripped in his right hand. He hears the door pop shut behind her—does not look in that direction. Guiding the slit in the tennis ball to the keyhole in the car's door handle, he holds the ball firmly in his left hand while punching it with his right. The ball collapses and the driver's-side lock pops up. He's inside a beat before she arrives. He stretches to unlock her door while his left hand probes the wires beneath the dash. He's chosen the Fiat for its age. As she slides into the seat, he's already contorting to reach below the dash. He's pulling apart and biting the ends of the wires, spitting plastic onto the floor. He twists three of the wires together and touches them to a fourth. It sparks and the engine turns over and starts. One final twist of wires. As he turns on the headlights and the dash comes alive, Sonia's indicting expression weighs on him.

"An ill-spent youth," he explains. He catches a single, slow moving headlight in the rearview mirror. It approaches at a patrol-like speed.

Sonia notices the vehicle as well and pulls Knox into a kiss. Knox would've held the kiss if he thought it would've fooled anyone. But with his eye on the interior mirror, he grabs the door handle and throws open the door as the motorcycle comes alongside. The bike swerves to miss the door. Knox charges out into the street. He tackles the helmeted rider from behind, throwing him off. Kicks the man twice while hollering back to her, "Come on!"

He pats down the writhing rider, finds a mobile phone and throws it into the canal.

Sonia springs out of the car, dragging Knox's camera case. He rights the bike. She throws her leg across. They're off. She clings to him tightly as he leans the bike into the first turn.

"Who the hell *are* you?" she shouts too loudly for the closeness of his ear.

Knox doesn't answer. Accelerating the bike, he seeks out the cover of traffic.

18

I t's unnecessary," Knox complains to Dulwich as if
Grace weren't part of the conversation. "We're making
progress."

They sit at different tables in Café Papeneiland, a
brown café—the Amsterdam equivalent of a London
pub—at the intersection of Prinsengracht and Brouwers-
gracht. The mood is lively, the beer flowing. It's so dark,
due to the wood-paneled walls that stretch back to 1624
and the thick smoke in the air that might be as old, it's
difficult to make out Dulwich in the corner by the main
door. Grace is visible where she sits on a bench seat alongside a table of men, most of whom can't keep their eyes
off her. The three speak into their cell phones, a Skype
conference call initiated by Grace.

Grace places her hand across her mouth as she speaks
into the mobile. "The object is to bring them to us. Not

the soldiers, but the generals. The soldiers outnumber us. We have been lucky so far—all of us. If we are to expedite results, if we are to survive, we need a new strategy."

"I can't argue with that," Dulwich says.

But Knox wishes he would. The plan as proposed presents unnecessary risk to Grace. It amounts to a frontal attack instead of the guerrilla methods they've been using. While certain to win the attention of those behind the knot shop, there's no guarantee it will have the intended results, and Knox says so for the third time. He finishes with, "They'll have your head."

"They would rather know my business," she says. "They will be impressed by my investment capital. Before you kill the competition, you win all their assets. Who knows? Maybe they would welcome a silent partner with deep pockets. Expand the business."

"And maybe they're content to just kill you and move on."

"Not without having a look at me first."

Dulwich intervenes like a boxing referee. "Let's remember, she's not proposing that they will set up something face to face. It's stealth warfare. It's a good plan, Knox. Give it a chance."

"At what cost? We're doing fine. Kreiger is going to connect me to them as a buyer. We're so close to that. There's a teacher . . . If we can get to one of the parents . . . Let's give the current plan some time."

"No one is suggesting one plan over the other," Grace says. "We continue working every angle."

"If she's going to set up shop, she has to find a shop,"

Dulwich says, attempting to clarify things for Knox. "That means—"

"I get it, Sarge," Knox snaps. He's left Sonia. He doesn't trust her to stay put and is therefore anxious to be out of here. "My vote, for what it's worth, is no." He can't see her face clearly as Grace turns to look at him across the barroom, but he knows her expression must be disappointment. Wonders when that came to matter to him. Is he opposed to the idea because he didn't come up with it or because it's ill-conceived? "We have too many balls in the air. We don't need another." His last push.

"That's for me to decide," Dulwich says.

Knox leaves five euros on the table for the empty beer and heads to the door without looking at either of them. He wants badly to catch Grace's eye, but is afraid it might be the last time he sees her alive.

"Get a load of that," Dulwich says to Grace, Knox having left the conversation, "I think he cares about you."

"John Knox cares only about his last lay and his next meal."

"Not necessarily in that order." Alone at the table, Dulwich laughs to his stein of beer. People sitting nearby purposefully avoid looking at him.

GRACE HOLDS ON to a cool brick wall behind the line of street market tents on Ten Katestraat, where empty coolers and stacked crates, cardboard boxes and plastic milk cartons spill out of cars and microvans raked up onto the curb. Taking a drag on a cigarette, she sees through the tents to the quickly emptying center of the street, the pedestrian lane down the market's middle. It's a disgusting habit she picked up in the Army and dispensed with shortly after her discharge, but one that comes in handy at times like this. Truth be told, she misses it, though knows she's better for the decision to quit.

The stalls are joined one to the next, their aluminum tent poles secured with plastic ties. They stretch two blocks on either side of the street, sandwiching the milling crowds and squeezing money out of pockets. The regular shoppers bring their own bags, making the tourists easier to spot. Grace buys a green tote from a nearby vendor and carries it on her forearm. The linen vendor who steered her to the community center packs up by category: napkins, bath towels, kitchen towels. Each unsold stack goes into its own plastic bin, the bin into the back of a beat-up Volkswagen. The woman is methodical, robotic in her movements. Her lip stud catches the light from the string of bare bulbs that runs the length of the tents, sparking like an animated hero's teeth. She is forced to shut the hatchback door twice in order for it to latch.

Grace grinds out the cigarette's ember with the toe of her shoe and crosses to intercept. She grabs the vendor by her upper arm, twists her against the vehicle and blocks the woman's right hand as she raises it defensively.

"You listen carefully." Grace leans against the woman to pin her, but the contact is more than that—both threatening and intimate. "Remember me? Your idea of a little fun?"

The vendor's eyes remain at half mast. She's on the

wrong end of having been stoned for the past two hours. Grace represents a buzz kill.

"Marta?" calls a man's rough voice. "Everything okay?"

Grace releases the woman's right hand, and the vendor waves off her retail neighbor. "A lovers' quarrel is all." Until the woman smiles, Grace had forgotten what beautiful lips she has.

"Your son? Brother? Lover? Who was it that attacked me?"

"Screw you."

"You only sent two? Do I look like I am so easy?"

"Yes, you do."

Grace chokes the woman's upper arm tightly; isn't afraid to turn and crush her hip against the woman's pubic bone. She blocks the woman's free arm with her elbow and cups the woman's small breast painfully. "I am looking for a dozen girls to start. Twice that within a month. Five euros a day. Decent conditions. Working toilets. A true lunch break. No chains. No one held against their will. No questions asked from either side. But I can tell you this: my shop will be run by women, not men. The highest quality garments. You tell the mothers that. If trouble follows me or finds me, a colleague knows where to find you. And he—yes, *he*—will find you. You will be punished." She exerts enough pressure to know the woman is by now light-headed. "Clear?"

The woman's lips are bloodless, her eyes squinted shut. She manages a nod.

THE WAY BACK TO HER HOTEL challenges her patience. She doesn't trust any form of public transportation, and the walk is a long one. She stops to use storefront glass as mirrors; she takes four consecutive right turns, walking squarely around the block in an attempt to spot tails, not just once, but three separate times. She shakes off the dirty feeling of being watched, not knowing.

Wanting to avoid her room, needing an outlet for pent-up aggression, she makes eyes at a man in the hotel bar. Men are so easy, so predictable. A plunging neckline and they're putty. She lets him buy her a drink.

This encounter is just nuts-and-bolts. He twists and she receives and soon there's a fit of convenience. His small talk lacks originality; her flirting lacks interest. As it wears on into a second drink, it's clear to both that it's to be purely physical—a grinding struggle to find some sense of satisfaction amid unfamiliarity that borders on embarrassment. Finally upstairs to the man's room. She demands it remain dark. She's rough with him and he climaxes too early. She pulls off, raw and annoyed at herself, disappointed and unsatisfied. It isn't the first time she has screwed a stranger, which makes the experience all the more loathsome.

She begs a shower off him. He's snoring by the time she's toweled off.

Grace sleeps in the overstuffed chair. Wakes to rain on the windows. The self-loathing burns her stomach. This is not who she wants to be. It disappoints her. She wishes the sun would never come up.

19

Great care is taken by Knox in his return to where he left Sonia. He rides the stolen motorcycle, doubling back repeatedly; he watches vehicles and pedestrian traffic; he parks several blocks from his destination and spends an inordinate amount of time getting there on foot.

The B&B is one of hundreds of boats that line the canals. It offers two bow cabins for sixty euros a night. Knox has paid cash for both cabins and has tipped the night manager of a nearby small inn, the Bed on Board, to text him if anyone arrives asking questions about recent check-ins. His bases covered, he slips through the line of trees that all but hides the canal boat; a narrow flagstone path is the only indication of its whereabouts.

It's not the perfect cover—a small, contained space.

But the boats that take guests are cash only, off grid and operated by independents.

He knocks lightly on the door to the port cabin, pauses and knocks once more. He hears her move a chair blocking the door and she admits him. Forced to duck by the low ceiling, he takes a seat in the chair she has just moved. It's a small but warm space—teak and varnished hardwoods, nautical-themed fabrics, a clock fashioned after a captain's wheel. Her laptop is running, and plugged in, the pillow on the narrow berth crumpled where she leaned against it as she worked. An empty mug of tea sits in a gimbaled holder attached to the wall. He has never known her to look anything but tired, and she does not disappoint him.

"You never answered me," she says.

A thoughtful and exhausted Knox leaned back in the chair. "Refresh my memory."

"Who are you?"

"You've researched me online. You know who I am."

She wants to contradict this. As she considers how to, Knox speaks.

"Can you make me one of those, please?"

Sonia fills a small electric teapot with water from a ceramic pitcher. The thing starts boiling nearly immediately. She wipes off her cup, pours over a fresh tea bag and hands it to Knox, who cradles it in his big hands.

"You're writing."

"What else? It's how I relax."

"About the teacher? Maja's artwork?"

"Compelling stuff," she says. "A young girl's insight into the criminal world. A clue worth sharing with the general population. Maybe other girls have drawn similar images."

Knox sets the mug on the floorboards and unzips two of the many pockets inside the Scottevest, retrieved while he was making arrangements. Inserting the three different SIM cards and rebooting the iPhone takes several minutes. "You have more than one SIM?" she says, a challenge in her voice.

It has become so routine, Knox failed to realize how it would look to others. "Business and personal. Easier for tax records. U.S. taxes . . . don't get me started."

"A lot of bother for a struggling freelancer."

"Who said I was struggling?

"I just did." She returns to her typing, but her furrowed brow lingers longer than it should.

He checks texts, e-mails and voice messages for the chips that provide the various services. He scratches out notes onto the back of a receipt. Tommy has called several times on his private number; Knox feels badly about not having been in touch over the past few days. There are a half dozen business calls on his second card that need following up. The last of the three phone cards connects him to a voice mail from Chief Inspector Brower. Knox saves the message, reminding himself to return to it later. Grace will want to hear this one.

"You've made yourself a target, that much is obvious."

"Making enemies is making yourself significant," she says. "It comes with the job."

"Your enemies apparently have a long reach."

"If it's more than you can handle, no problem. I understand."

He takes a sip of tea. John Knox can think of several ways to turn that statement around and sting her; John Steele's reluctance to do so frustrates Knox.

"You don't need me until and unless there are some good photographs to make. Anyone can photocopy children's artwork."

"I feel safer with you around." The walls are thin—they can hear conversation from an adjacent boat—and so they have been speaking quietly. Her comment is barely audible.

"Maybe some kind of day rate is in order."

"If I want a bodyguard, I'll hire someone trained for the job."

"You are outnumbered. We are outnumbered. These people have clearly spread money around the town in an effort to find you. They got people to that neighborhood quickly. That suggests what, a half dozen guys on bikes? More? That's a big payroll."

"I appreciate what you've done for me, Mr. Steele. This place . . . I live here and it wouldn't have occurred to me. I probably would've gone to a friend's house, and I now see what a mistake that would have been. I'm not ashamed to tell you I'm afraid." She pulls her knees to her chest and places her chin on her knees, contemplative and vulnerable. "But I consider my own fear and magnify it ten times, and I still don't come close to the fear these children must be living with."

"Your niece."

She appraises him, openly pondering telling him. "Similar circumstances, I suppose."

He waits her out. The people on the nearby boat are making it a four-person party.

"Similar, but not identical. My niece disappeared the week after she turned thirteen. There is a worldwide market for virgins—did you know that? Upward of fifty thousand dollars U.S. All races. Boys and girls. Three girls—all friends—from the same school went missing on the same night. Never to be seen again. To this day, I search Craigslist each day for her initials: KP. She is called Kala. This is how the ransom demand is made.

"My brother," she continues, "asked me to get involved, to write about it, to raise awareness in hopes of getting her back. This series won me awards, led to many good job offers. I took the best of these. Yet my niece never came home. My brother says he's happy for me."

"Rough."

"Sometimes life offers a chance to correct one's previous mistake."

"I don't see the mistake," Knox says.

"The series did nothing to uncover the human trafficking. Did nothing to slow it down. It provided me job opportunities, that's all."

"And you're supposed to feel guilty about that?"

"Whether I'm supposed to or not, I do."

"If you'd wanted to solve crimes, you'd have been a cop, not a reporter. You can't have it both ways."

"Of course I can. What is it you think an investigative reporter does? If we don't follow an investigation, we cause one."

"Your niece again."

"It's what I do. I shine a light where there is none."

Knox has spoken before he thought it through, and regrets doing so. "So we're supposed to find Berna and bring her home. But we don't happen to know where home is. We don't know where she is. That's biting off a big chunk."

"I don't define the outcome. I pursue a story, or a series, to where it leads. That pursuit is not yet concluded. The more intimidation, the more inclined I am to believe I'm closer to the truth. It's really that simple."

It's about the money for Knox—Tommy's endowment, a way to keep him independent. He's going to need millions; he had barely started before the embezzlement. Now . . . he admires such altruism, but is too pragmatic to dwell on it. He has finished the tea. He reaches to return the mug to the holder. Sonia helps guide his hand, and makes eye contact as she touches him.

"Stay," she says. "I won't sleep with a man until he owns my heart, but in India we know a thing or two about pleasure."

"In Detroit, too," he says. He shouldn't have looked into her eyes, not if he'd wanted to keep this uncomplicated. Her eyes have been his downfall since they first met.

"THIS NEEDN'T COMPLICATE THINGS," he says, studying the grain in the cabin's dark-paneled ceiling.

"Of course it will," she says, rolling onto her side and staring at his profile. "It already has."

"There's something I want you to consider."

"The answer is no."

"They clearly have a long reach."

"They have killed one source, assaulted others, attempted to intimidate me—"

"Kill you."

"We don't know that."

"We're outnumbered."

"This is my cause, not yours. Let's call this," she says, laying her warm hand between his legs, "our parting gift."

"You've made it mine," he says. "You gave them names."

She removes her hand. "They have names."

"Take a couple weeks away from here. Let it cool down."

"There are two different groups of girls in there, John. Those like Maja—day workers whose own families condone the labor. Then there are the Bernas. Some of them chained. None well fed, nor looked after. Who knows what happens to them?"

"You can't bring her back."

She rolls away from him. "Get out of my bed!"

Knox sits up. Pulls on his jeans and gathers the rest of his clothes. He stands too quickly, banging his head on the ceiling.

She rolls back, pulling the sheet across her.

They meet eyes in the faint light of a spreading dawn. He looks away quickly, a reflex as he feels the power she now possesses.

20

Grace listens to the voice mail forwarded by Knox for the third time. Chief Inspector Brower's voice is calm and deliberate as he explains. The Special Investigative Services division of the KLPD has determined that two thousand euros used to purchase the radio-triggering device in the EU delegate car bombing is traceable to a single bank branch. It is information he is not supposed to possess, and therefore cannot act upon. The KLPD is itself unlikely to act, as the discovery surfaced as an unintended consequence of an ongoing investigation of its own, having nothing to do with the EU car bombing. The situation leaves the police and the KLPD in a bureaucratic tangle and has led to Brower's sharing the information with Knox and Dulwich. The euros were withdrawn as cash and paid out to the man who built the trigger for the car bomb, providing a possible trail to the person who ordered the bombing—the person behind the knot shop.

After her third listen, Grace stares pensively from the back window of a different Mercedes than the one she rode in the day before. Dulwich begins his day by renting a new vehicle, limiting the chance of a bombing. He has settled into his role as driver, looking comfortable behind the wheel, talking back to his Dutch-speaking GPS, and cursing the other drivers.

Grace is asked for her take on the message. Dulwich has listened only once.

"With the help of the Hong Kong office, we have a fair chance of breaching the bank's firewalls. It should not be difficult to determine cash withdrawals in amounts over two thousand euros in a given time frame. My guess is it will not be a terribly long list given that it is a particular branch."

"It will be a shell corporation."

"Perhaps. If they are in fact that sophisticated. It is possible, certainly. But you are overlooking the obvious. Whoever is running the knot shop will not use banks. Safe-deposit boxes possibly. But far more likely a private safe in a home or office."

"So this is useless information? To hell with that. We must be able to use it somehow."

"These people are not stupid. But their customers? More likely, this cash was paid *to* the shop. A withdrawal was made to cover the purchase of some rugs or drugs or whatever else it is they sell. That money was passed along to the knot shop and locked up in a safe. When it came time to pay off the bomb maker . . ." She doesn't finish the sentence.

"It's not the knot shop's money, but a customer's." Dulwich stops the car at a red light, throws his arm across the seatback as he turns to face her. "We identify the customer, have a little chat, and we're noses to the ground on our way to the shop."

"*I* identify the customer," she says, correcting him. "Knox performs the interrogation. More than likely the money leads to a middleman or agent. But we are closer, yes."

"Don't get all bitchy on me. It doesn't suit you. We're saying the same thing, and you know it."

"It is late in Hong Kong. I will need to speak to Dr. Yamaguchi or Mr. Kamat."

"Shouldn't be a problem."

"I will require high-speed Internet access. Not this café or hotel bandwidth. A legal firm, an investment firm. Something with some muscle."

"Understood."

"The light is green."

Dulwich drives more slowly than just a few minutes earlier. "I'll make some calls."

"As for tonight," Grace says, "they may be expecting me."

"I can arrange for a runner."

"Please."

The GPS speaks again. Dulwich consults the screen. "Two hundred meters. Keep the phone in your boot and the call open."

"Make certain you are seen. But not your leg."

"The trouble with Chinese is they speak too bluntly. You need to work on that."

"If you want an American, hire one."

The Mercedes slows and pulls to the curb. Identical four-story brick buildings populate every block in every direction. Only the street signs and bicycles and parked vehicles break the similarities. A blue and white real estate sign is taped to the inside of a vacant storefront window. To the right of the empty shop lies an antique toy train store; to the left, insurance.

The real estate agent awaiting Grace is in her late forties, wide of girth and heavy of bosom. She's dressed in solid-color wools. Her lipstick attempts to hide the purse-string wrinkles that have overtaken her mouth. They speak Dutch.

"I will wait!" Dulwich calls out, also in Dutch. He's a formidable specimen at any distance. The Mercedes looks suddenly smaller to both women.

Grace dismisses him with a wave of the hand. She has slipped the iPhone into her right boot where it's wedged between calf muscle and black leather. Dulwich will monitor the conversation as well as Grace's location in case there's an attempt to abduct her. The kind of space she has requested could raise some eyebrows. At least, she and Dulwich are hoping so.

Graces walks to the center of the shop. A counter sticks out from the wall two-thirds deep into the space. She goes through the motions of inspection, then asks if there's cellar storage. She's led down to an open common space into which storage cases have been installed. Like everything Dutch, the space is clean and tidy. It runs against Grace's Chinese heritage.

"I will be honest with you," Grace says. "I am looking for something . . . it need not be so upmarket as this. I must not have explained myself. You might call it . . . artist space. A loft will not do because I must have quiet. Cellar space would be ideal. Four to five hundred square meters. Street access, but it cannot be a busy street with difficult parking."

"Galleries and boutiques are moving into this neighborhood. It is why I thought of you."

"My needs are strictly work space. Not retail. I have a . . . a start-up in mind. You know the women in India who make useful art from plastic bags? Eco-art? It is along those lines."

"Light industrial."

"Emphasis on light. It must be fairly close to town, but in a more residential neighborhood. A place with schools and housing."

"An old paint shop or garage. Furniture store."

"That's the idea."

"But on a quiet street," the realtor says, reminding Grace of her own requirement.

"Yes. Perhaps you could pull up some comparison leases or rentals? Maybe that would give us a lead." Grace has reached the crux of the matter. "Rentals or leases made within the past twenty-four months."

The realtor nods contemplatively. "Yes. I am happy to do so."

"We could do this now?" Grace asks. "At your agency?"

"My pleasure." The agent fishes out a business card and hands it to Grace. "For your driver."

"Thank you." For now, no attempts to kidnap or assault. The return to a civilized meeting feels foreign to Grace. The iPhone is getting hot against her calf. "Perhaps we could let other agents know as well."

"Yes, of course. I made some calls initially, but I can expand upon that now that I have your needs more fully in mind."

"I'm in something of a hurry," Grace says. "Money is an issue, of course, but more than anything, I do not want someone beating me to the marketplace. First to the baker gets the freshest loaf."

"And the warmest," the agent counters, leaving Grace to wonder if she means anything threatening by it.

DULWICH FINDS a pooled office rental, one of six stand-alone offices, rented by the day, week or month, that share a conference room, printers, copiers and faxes, and a receptionist to run them. The Internet access is fiber-optic.

He, Grace and Knox meet there the following morning, with Knox in charge of runs to the kitchenette for coffee and tea orders. Dulwich has been awake since two, when the Rutherford Risk offices opened in Hong Kong. Knox has been up most of the night on the canal boat.

There's little conversation as Grace goes about her work. Knox dozes. Dulwich answers e-mails. The office is warm. Dulwich opens a window to the sounds of a city waking up. Grace has been supplied a VPN address, user name and password by the IT boys in Hong Kong. If she hadn't studied and trained under Kamat and Yamaguchi, she might have doubted the data would allow her access into the bank's network, but the two are like magicians and she the adoring apprentice. Yamaguchi's head currently occupies a video window in the corner of her screen. A Bluetooth headset adheres to her right earlobe like a piece of ugly jewelry. Overhearing the one-sided conversation, Knox has to stifle his chuckles that bubble up from ignorance; she's speaking the utterly indecipherable language of computers.

She puts Yamaguchi on hold to address Dulwich and Knox. "Only once I am in will we know if it will hold. If the system detects this as an attack, it will shut me out."

"I thought I gave you everything you need," Dulwich says.

"Yes. But Dr. Yamaguchi cautions me of the Ziegler Protocol—some institutional security maps a user's most commonly accessed pages as well as the hierarchy route adopted to access those pages. Think of accessing the *New York Times* online. One person might go directly to Sports from the home page; another might first scroll the entire page reading headlines and then go to Sports. Those slight differences define us as users. Dr. Yamaguchi suggests I take my time getting to recent cash withdrawals. The deeper I am in the system, the more complex it is to compare this visit to others."

"So? What's the problem?" Dulwich complains.

"The longer I am online inside the server, the more time we give the Ziegler Protocol to work."

"Catch-22," Knox says.

"Exactly so. We must make a choice—collectively. It cannot be mine alone. If we are locked out, Dr. Yamaguchi believes it could be three to five business days before he can regain access for us."

"Shit." Dulwich pulls the window shut. It's too noisy for him.

"Yamaguchi got us in," Knox says. "I think we ought to listen to him."

"If you go directly to cash withdrawals, how long to download that data?"

She shakes her head. "Not long, given that we are not looking back so very far. At these speeds, the download itself is a nonissue, which was the point of getting this kind of bandwidth in the first place."

"Give me a time, Grace."

"Under five minutes."

"And this protocol? How fast—"

"Instantaneous." Grace allows that to sink in. "Dr. Yamaguchi suggests looking at the company's current stock price first—the information of the most interest to executives. It will be on the home page, so he suggests I stay there for at least twenty seconds. This user account we are borrowing belongs to an investment banker. Dr. Yamaguchi has assembled a list of eight landing pages that are the most commonly accessed on the network. Once we are past those eight, he believes we can make a run at the cash withdrawals. Even then, we will have to be fast. If this particular user has never accessed such data, it will generate a red flag that could result in session termination.

On the other hand, the protocol may simply add the address to this user's library."

"Including the download?" Knox says.

"We will not know until we try. I have a screen capture program running. We will have a visual history of every page I saw."

Dulwich looks over to Knox for advice.

"One shot?" Knox inquires of Grace, who nods. "I'm with Yamaguchi, but it's your call, Sarge."

"Very well," Dulwich says, coming out of his chair. "We take our time."

Knox comes around as well, shoulder to shoulder with Dulwich behind Grace.

"Dr. Yamaguchi says hello," she informs them.

Knox feels stupid as he waves.

Grace's fingers are fluid on the keyboard. She doesn't stab or punch. It looks more like she's casting a spell than typing. The home page appears.

"I am in," Grace says.

Yamaguchi is watching a mirrored image of Grace's laptop. He speaks to her, but Knox can't hear. Grace opens a small window in the lower corner that shows a stopwatch timer. At :25 she waves over the keyboard and another page appears. She resets the stopwatch. At :15 she navigates to a fresh page. She checks the price of two traded stocks and moves on. Forty seconds are spent on that page.

Dulwich is sweating. He should have left the window open. Knox sips coffee. Office brew. He could never work in an office, a fact that won't make any headlines. Watching Grace operate is fascinating—her accountant-minded precision, her adherence to a plan. Seeing this, he better understands Dulwich's pairing of them. They are pine-cone weights on a cuckoo clock, juxtaposed but working in concert. She is surreally even-tempered and made for such work. Yamaguchi's mouth never stops moving as he speaks into her ear; Dulwich leans close enough that she can feel his breath on her neck. Grace robotically drills down into the site, page by page, resetting and restarting the timer to where Knox finds himself watching only the countdowns. He finishes the coffee, takes a three-point shot at the trash can by the door and sinks it. The noise stands Dulwich up like a gun was fired, but Grace—dear Grace—never so much as flinches.

"Okay, we're in," she announces. "Sorting by amount of deposit."

The column is longer than she told them it would be. At the top are amounts in excess of twenty thousand euros. She scrolls down through the high teens to the low teens on her way to four digit withdrawals. She is too good at what she does. The column blurs on her way to amounts hovering at two thousand euros.

"Too fast," Knox says. "I can't read them."

"Dr. Yamaguchi . . ." Grace says. "Security spiders . . ."

"We're busted?" Dulwich injects.

Grace navigates to the bottom of the page, where a blue-highlighted radio button reads: *Download Data*. She double-taps the track pad and a second window opens; she clicks *Save File*.

Behind the pop-up window the server page posts a red-letter warning that this is *Questionable Access*. It's followed by a yellow exclamation point and the triangular caution signs used for vehicles in the breakdown lane.

Grace yanks the PCMCIA card from the laptop, causing a second warning sign on the screen.

She turns to Dulwich. "I will need an external drive. Possibly a new laptop. Today. As quickly as possible. They will have back-doored my laptop. By now they know we're in this building, this office. We must consider there is an outside chance the police may be dispatched. Perhaps no action will be taken. I suggest we—"

Knox is already wiping down surfaces and door hardware. He fishes his paper coffee cup from the trash. Crushes and pockets it.

"Did we get it?" Dulwich asks anxiously.

"We got it. I think we got it."

"You think, or we did?"

"We don't need it," Knox says.

Both Grace and Dulwich are standing. Grace is packing up. Dulwich is at the window wiping down. But Knox wins the attention of both.

"Nine thousand five hundred euros," Knox says. "Somewhere on that page. You were scrolling fast. Maybe more, maybe less, but the amount doesn't matter."

"Because?" Dulwich says. "What the hell are you talking about 'the amount doesn't matter'?"

"Kreiger, G.," Knox says, believing he saw the name during the scrolling. "Gerhardt Kreiger."

21

The three separate as a matter of procedure. Dulwich drives off in the Mercedes. They have no idea what kind of heat, if any, the hacking will draw. They entered and departed the office building cognizant of security cameras watching, careful to avoid offering their faces. But they are in the security business and are made painfully aware of how much can be made of little. For twenty-four hours they will make no contact. Communication will be reestablished through coded text messages.

Knox returns to the houseboat via a circuitous and careful route. He doesn't know what to expect. He wants to find Sonia waiting for him, but is loath to admit it to himself. It's a romantic notion, one that doesn't come easily for him. He's greeted by the proprietor, a wiry man with an Abe Lincoln beard and the rheumy eyes of a morning drinker.

"She paid for a second night," the man tells Knox.

His sense of relief surprises Knox. He's inwardly giddy. "There's an envelope."

Knox hurries forward, nearly bumping his head. The envelope is sealed, no name written on it. He tears it open a little too eagerly.

You didn't pick up. I left you a message.

He silently compliments her on her lack of detail while chastising himself for not switching out his SIM cards and checking messages and texts. The events of the past two hours have put him off his routine.

John, I heard back from Maja's teacher with an address. Also, the name and address of another student who is also a possible. He notes her careful use of language; she divulges nothing in the message, yet conveys all that is necessary. *I will return later today, or call me.*

She picks up on the third ring.

Without introduction, he says, "I think a silhouette shot, the mother in front of a window or in a doorway. A kind of spooky anonymity might work very well."

"I can see that."

"Will you wait for me? Are you there yet? I'd rather you wait."

"If you get too protective, it's over."

"Noted. I'm an older brother. Cut me some slack."

"No, I will not."

"An address?"

She supplies the address and tells him if he's not there in twenty minutes, not to bother.

He's stuck with an audiotape loop running in his head: *I will return later today.* It goes around and around in her

Indian-accented English with him reading more into it on each replay. There are other places she could go than the houseboat. She not only wants to see him again, but has decided to see him again, a decision he can live with. Why any of this should matter to him, he doesn't know. Women are good company, sometimes a physical pleasure. With the constant travel that comes with his job, he has become a seaman or a door-to-door salesman. He has friends, not relationships. So, he can't help but wonder why he has already decided where he will be sleeping tonight, that he would not dare to let her down. He may be stood up; it may be nothing but an ill-conceived test on her part, but he's willing to play along. Is eager to play along.

He doesn't know how she got across town, but she didn't walk. He had the motorcycle, so it must have been a taxi or tram, and he bristles at the thought. He weaves his way through traffic taking chances he shouldn't, wondering if this is solely for the sake of the job or if there's something more to it, something that bears consideration. The camera bag slung across his shoulder now bounces in his lap. He's constantly checking the time.

He arrives with a few minutes to spare. Introduces himself to the plain-looking Slavic woman who answers the door and is shown inside to an apartment occupied by three generations of women. It's pillows and rugs, a television and two large futons strapped around the middle with bungee cords that tower in the corner like sentries. Two boys pass through the room on their way from the kitchen, one fourteen, one eight, both suspicious of Knox. They disappear into the apartment's only bedroom

and pull the door shut. A very old woman smokes a cigarette by a partially open window, harboring a comfortable distrust in her unblinking, quiet eyes.

Sonia sits cross-legged amid a pile of decorative pillows,
a notepad open at her ankles. Standing across from her is
Maja's mother, who greeted them at the door. In the
corner is Maja herself—sleepy-eyed but not missing anything. The girl's face is young—twelve or thirteen, Knox
is guessing—but her eyes contain an unshakable depth
that is twice that.

The Dutch is spoken rapid fire as Maja's mother objects
vehemently to the presence of a photographer, all before
Knox has unzipped his bag. Again, Knox admires Sonia's
calm under fire. She is unruffled, her voice steady and
deliberate as she explains nothing is going to happen
without the woman's consent.

Knox removes the camera, turns it on and shows her the
LCD screen on the back of the camera. "We will remove
any photographs you do not approve."

"I swear to it," Sonia says.

The mother settles. "I ask that you go now."

Sonia flashes a sideways look at Knox, who wishes the
camera did not make a shutter noise. He wants to capture
that agonized expression, finds himself thinking as a photographer. Wonders how long he can keep the truth from
Sonia.

Unfolding her legs, Sonia comes to her knees and
hands Maja's watercolor to the girl's mother. She sits back
down, indicating she isn't going anywhere. The mother
opens the drawing and squints her eyes shut painfully.

"How did they contact you, Yasmina?" Sonia inquires.

Yasmina shakes her head. The watercolor hangs at her side, pinched between two fingers. Her hands are rough skinned.

"Have you been to this place?"

"Please . . . go."

Knox trains the camera on the old biddy by the window, so ensconced she acts as if she doesn't notice. He adjusts the exposure for the gray glow on the window behind her, tries a shot. Then another. The third time is just right: a spiral of gray smoke, a faceless woman but one whose years are apparent. He is quick to delete the first two.

"Look at the artwork, Maja's artwork, once again. The girl in the leg iron. Please, look again."

Surprisingly, Yasmina obeys. Her eyes tick between Sonia and the watercolor.

"Maja," Sonia asks sweetly, "do you know this girl?"

Mother and daughter exchange glances. "No names," the girl says.

"What language? Do you all speak Dutch?"

"No talking," the child replies. "We talk with hands."

"You approved of this?" Sonia asks the mother.

"Do not judge me."

"I ask only what the agreement was going in. What you understood the working conditions to be. How it was they contacted you."

Knox captures an amazing shot of Maja, her knees to her chest. Yasmina wants to object, but is more concerned with Sonia.

"It is money. Steady money."

"Were you approached directly?" Sonia asks.

Yasmina looks afraid.

"The other mothers at the community center," Knox says, winning a fiery look from both women. "You heard from them." Sonia does not want him speaking; Yasmina is rattled by his accuracy. Sonia is quick to translate the woman's expression.

"We know about the community center." Sonia lies beautifully, something that is not lost on Knox.

"You hear things."

"At some point you must make contact, they must make contact." If Sonia is excited by their progress, she doesn't show it.

Yasmina corrects her. "The first day she is taken by a friend. After that, she knows the way and can go alone. Some of the mothers . . . if you follow your child . . . if you're caught . . ." The protective glance toward her daughter finishes the thought.

"Schooling?"

"She is enrolled, of course. The excuse is illness. We do as much work here in the evenings as possible. I do not expect you to understand. I do not want your sympathy. My Maja is an important part of this household. She helps us all."

The girl looks up from her tucked position proudly.

Sonia directs her attention to the girl. "You must know the names of some of the other girls."

"Turtle." Maja makes a fish with her thumb tucked into the fingers. "Bunny." Thumb and pinky finger raised.

She smiles awkwardly. "They call me"—she draws a finger across her lips—"Silence."

"The other times your father came to school, did he take you to work?"

Yasmina strains to contain her alarm. She is no actor. "Answer."

Maya's silence draws her mother's ire.

Yasmina turns to Sonia. "Which day was this?"

Smart enough to stay out of a fire she has herself started, Sonia bites her lip.

"Not my son," says the woman by the window, mournfully. "Who was this man, precious?"

"Not the girl's father," Sonia says.

Yasmina spins in the vortex created by her mother-in-law, Sonia and her daughter. She seeks sanctuary in Knox, but then sees him working the camera in his lap and holds up her hand to block her face.

"Get out!" she says.

Sonia collects the fallen watercolor and smooths it open with calm hands. "It is these girls we must save," she says, pointing to the leg iron. "These nameless girls."

"He wasn't her father," Knox says. "Then who? A man from the shop?"

"She disobeyed," Yasmina says, glowering at her child. "How could you do this to us? You know the rules!"

"By attending school," Knox says.

Sonia does not appreciate his participation.

But Knox is on a roll. "They tried to pull her out of school and put her back to work."

Yasmina sits down heavily, hands to her head. She's

talking to herself in a language Knox does not understand. She takes in each of them, including her mother-in-law, one by one.

"My husband is in jail. Two more years." It's all she says. It is meant as confession, justification and apology, all in one.

The old woman stares out the window as if this is an indictment of her. Her cigarette is burned down to the filter, still clasped between her fingers. Knox takes a lap shot of her.

"We ask that Maja take us close enough to the shop to point it out," Sonia says.

"Never! They have eyes everywhere. You understand nothing. The mothers who have tried . . . How close do you think they ever came? Absurd."

"We could show Maja a map," Knox says. "Photographs." He's thinking of Google's street view. The girl could lead them right to the door without ever leaving the room. "We can pay you three hundred euros."

Yasmina gives the offer consideration.

Sonia is ready to castrate John Steele for his interference.

"How many weeks must Maja work to earn three hundred? Ten? Twenty? She could be in school instead."

Maja sits forward expectantly, hanging on her mother's decision like an inmate at a parole hearing.

"And what after that, daughter?" the older woman says, aimed again at Yasmina, who cringes at the appellation. "We must resist the sin of temptation."

"I asked you to leave," Yasmina says, unable to look at either Sonia or Knox.

"And I ask you what is best for your daughter?"

"Take your poison and go!"

"The girls in the leg irons . . . ask Maja what happens to the pretty ones when they reach the age. What if Maja fails to come home one night? What then? Where do you look? To whom do you turn?"

Yasmina's face drains of color and her lips tremble as tears form. "Without her . . . we starve."

Her words seem to echo in the room. A dog barks down the block. The sound of the old woman working her lighter sounds like a cat scratching at the door. She disappears behind a cloud.

Knox fires off another lap shot, wondering how much the cigarettes cost.

"I wish to see the photos." Yasmina extends her hand to him.

But Sonia takes Knox's camera from him and together she and Knox show the woman the half dozen shots he's taken. It's good work, if he does say so. No faces. A good deal of mood and texture.

The mother selects two for deletion, simply exercising her power to do so. Knox resents losing them.

As they are huddled around the camera, Yasmina says softly, "You do not understand. These people know where we live. They . . . the things they have done . . ."

"Have you *seen* these things, yourself, or heard about them?" the journalist asks.

"Please leave." Yasmina once again avoids looking at Knox.

BACK ON THE STREET, John Steele and Sonia Pangarkar exhale at once.

"Damn!" Sonia says.

"We follow her," says Knox. "I can follow her. She will never know."

"And if you're seen? It won't be you who suffers, but she, a twelve-year-old girl. And her mother, and her grandmother. No, John."

But I won't be seen, he wants to say, but does not.

"You know what they would do to that poor girl?"

He does know, and by making the comment she pushes him to consider ramifications, which is not something that comes naturally to him. For whatever reason, he thinks of Tommy and how he owes him his daily call that often comes weekly. He thinks of Dulwich and Grace working behind his back to track the money embezzled from him. He thinks of bills he must pay and contracts he must honor. The reality of straddling two worlds comes crashing down on him out on a sidewalk in the Amsterdam suburbs where it's impossible to tell one street from another.

"Damn," he says, echoing her.

"We know more than we did," she says.

"'A little bit of knowledge is a dangerous thing.'"

"You need not remind me."

He'd parked the motorcycle around the block. He leads her there. She follows.

"Will you write something?" he asks.

"Not yet."

"Should I e-mail you these?"

"It is a good idea." She climbs onto the back of the motorcycle. "Are you going somewhere?"

"Now, or later?"

"You tell me."

"Now, to the houseboat."

"I am glad."

"It doesn't have to be Maja." He revs the motor and toes the bike into gear.

"Schools in the U.S.," he adds. "Visitors are required to check in at the school office. They must sign in. Pick up a name tag."

"The same is true here."

"Many public schools—our government schools—print a photo onto the name tag," says the photographer. "A vid cam shot at the reception desk."

Her hands go from around his waist to his shoulders. She shakes him. "The 'father'!" she shouts.

RUSH-HOUR TRAFFIC clogs Kinkerstraat as commuters use it to avoid the major surface streets out of downtown. Buses and trolleys use center lanes, choking the street to a single right of way, compounding the problem. Grace kills time at the postcard stand outside the Bruna bookstore, stealing glimpses between passing vehicles. The building across from her, just at the start of the tram stop, has a pink wall of mailboxes mounted between sets of doors. She watches long enough for someone to enter without use of a key or card.

"I am going in," she tells Dulwich over her phone.

"Copy."

There's no waiting for a break in traffic. She forces herself between bumpers, hesitates as a bus growls past, and reaches the opposite curb just before a cyclist would have paved her. Donning the mind-set of a resident, she enters through the outer door, then the inner door and finally an unmarked door to the building's stairway, identified by the discolored wear in the vinyl-tile flooring. She bounds up to the landing, turns and continues to the first floor.

"I am in," she says for the sake of her Bluetooth earpiece.

"Copy. Awaiting your confirmation."

She looks right and assures herself the hallway is clear. Turns left toward the pair of glass doors leading out to the balcony seen from the streets. It is common to a half dozen apartments, wraps around the Kinkerstraat and Ten Katestraat sides of the building and is dotted with television satellite dishes. The architectural glass outer wall is banister height. As she moves toward Ten Katestraat, a Kelly Clarkson song rises from the market street. She looks down onto the tent roofs of the street market stalls, intent upon identifying the one selling kitchen linens. She finds it thirty meters down, recognizes it not by its contents, nor its vendor, but by the beater Volkswagen hatchback parked behind.

"Go!" she says.

"Copy."

She steps closer to the corner, eyes down, awaiting the red baseball cap Dulwich has suggested she use to spot the runner he's hired. The red cap enters from the canal side of the street and pushes its way into the center of the scrum. It sits atop a head connected to broad but under-developed shoulders. Grace can picture the acne-riddled face of a boy sixteen or seventeen. He maneuvers through the horde of late-afternoon shoppers burdened with bags of fresh vegetables and fruits. He twists and turns and creates his own lanes, rising onto tiptoe in search of the vendor. He homes in on the stall in question. Dulwich has told him what to say.

Grace moves along the balcony as she monitors him, stopping as he stops. Waiting as he waits. She steps back from the low wall, exposing as little of herself as possible.

Marta, with whom Grace is all too familiar, takes time with each customer. Finally it's the boy's turn. He leans over the display of place mats. Grace can't see the vendor. He's stuck there for a long count.

"The lady asked you for a dozen names," the boy is saying by now. "You must give her at least three. I'm supposed to tell you things will happen if you don't."

Grace imagines: the boy is waiting for Marta to write down the names. The longer it stretches, the more hopeful she is that Marta has delivered.

Dulwich's large frame doesn't fit well in the market. He towers over the rest as he crosses through the thick crowd and vanishes beneath her. He's to deliver a raw potato to the Volkswagen's exhaust pipe should the boy come up empty. It will plug the car's exhaust, choking the engine and making it impossible to start; it's a warning shot. The repercussions will only get worse for Marta should she fail to deliver.

The signal is simple: if the boy should stay in the center of the lane, he has come up empty. If instead he heads behind the stall, accidentally bumping into Dulwich as he hurries—simultaneously passing him a list of names and addresses of young girls accepting Grace's offer of employment—the potato remains in Dulwich's pocket.

The red cap moves to the sidewalk. Grace looks on from above as the collision with Dulwich occurs. It's a neat little performance by both. Though knowing what to expect, Grace misses the pass. She stays even with the red cap as it moves back toward the traffic on Kinkerstraat.

"Got it," Dulwich confirms through the earbud.

"Copy," she replies.

"Any tail?"

"On it." The pent-up expectation surprises her. Scanning all four corners of the intersection as well as the entrance to Ten Katestraat and the throng of shoppers that belches into the street, she's aware that Dulwich's bad leg limits him to all bark and no bite. He can cover ground but cannot run, offering a form of backup but not true partnership. If she's in this, she's in this alone.

The two look far smaller from above than they did in the gloom of the tunnel outside the community center.

She has reimagined them as rough men when reliving the attack. But from where she stands they are just small bugs, ripe for the squashing.

"Two following," she says for the benefit of the open phone line. "Mark is across Kinkerstraat heading south on Ten Katestraat. I am on it."

"With you."

Grace is down the stairs and out onto the street within seconds. She crosses Kinkerstraat's traffic as if invisible. No horns sound. Turns down Ten Katestraat cursing the stupidity of the street kid Dulwich hired. Instead of staying on the busy sidewalks of the main avenue, he's isolated himself and is heading into a dangerously vacant neighborhood. He compounds his problems by crossing diagonally at the next intersection and heading into an empty kiddie park, Ten Kateplein. It's a quarter acre of pavement, slides and a spinning jungle gym. He appears to be using the park as a shortcut, but it serves to give his tails an open space to attack.

She catches up to the two black leather jackets as they reach the park entrance, a gap between a section of metal fence and stone block. From this perspective they are eerily familiar: not just shorter than full-grown adults, but walking with a cocky swagger that speaks of their immaturity.

"Geert!" she calls, not breaking stride. The name on the ID in the wallet Knox confiscated.

Geert glances furtively over his shoulder. She kicks him in the chest with the sole of her left foot and sends him ass over teakettle. The sound of his head striking the asphalt is sickening. He won't be trouble.

The other one is fast. Two strides and he's left her behind. A fraction of a second passes before a red baseball cap lies on the blacktop and their runner's throat is clamped in the elbow of a leather jacket while being dragged backward. Grace marches toward the assailant.

"Any closer," the assailant shouts, "I break his neck!"

The runner's face turns bright red. He's quickly deadweight in the choke hold. She checks once to make sure the first kid is still down. That felt good. Her limbs scream with adrenaline wanting an outlet.

"He is nothing to me," she says honestly. "Do as you wish. It is you I want." She waves him toward her, daring him. The man-child is twenty at best. His left eye is bandaged, his face scratched. His remaining eye possesses the cruelty of a person much older.

She remembers poking the eye of the one who'd groped her, savors that it has worked out this way. Suddenly possessed by an unrelenting sadism, Grace wants to torture him for what he did, sickened and embarrassed by the intimacy he presumed in touching her down there. A kick in the groin won't do. It goes well beyond the desire to inflict pain. There's a message that must be sent as well, a retribution. He must be taught a lesson.

His lack of one eye benefits her. She spends no time on negotiation. She leaps to his left, where he loses her to his blind spot before he overcorrects. She drives her right heel into his lower ribs, cracking them.

He drops his hostage and screams. Digs a blade out of

his pocket but fails to use it. Instead, he presents it as a threat, displaying it for her. He's pathetically ill-equipped. She flies to him, bends his wrist to his forearm and hears it snap. The blade falls. She delivers a fist into the center of his chest. His eyes bulge. He can't breathe.

She replays the hideous sensation of his cupping her pubis. Nothing she can do to him will atone for that violation. But she can try.

She slaps him, open handed, across the face. Right. Left. Right. Is careful not to break her hand as she drives a fist into his bad eye, and wonders if they could hear that scream in the market, wonders if Marta recognizes that cry. Dulwich stands off to her right, watching. The boy at the gate remains down.

The runner is up and gone. His red cap remains.

"Enough," Dulwich says.

"Bitch!" her victim grunts.

"Oh, shit," Dulwich says.

She strikes the bandaged eye a second time and watches the man's knees buckle. Half turns and heel-kicks him again in the cracked ribs. He's down on his knees.

She squats and clasps his throat while her free hand blindly finds the fallen knife.

"Enough!" Dulwich repeats, though weakly.

The tip of the knife finds the man's groin. He tenses and groans.

"One slip and you are peeing sitting down for the rest of your sordid life. You hear me?"

He nods.

She's rushing, so high she's nearly faint.

"Find a new line of work. You don't ever touch a woman like you touched me." She waits for his working eye to open. "A reminder, so you won't forget."

She slices him across the belly. A surface cut, but a bleeder.

"Jesus!" Dulwich says.

Her victim's too far gone to scream. He's in shock as he looks down at the wound as if it belongs to someone else. She uses his shirttail to wipe her prints off the knife, kicks it well across the play yard, its blade singing.

"I'm done here, if you are," she says to Dulwich as she walks past him, every nerve alive.

"WHAT THE HELL?" Dulwich says from behind the wheel, aiming in the rearview mirror in order to check her out.

"The number seven." She ignores him, studying the piece of paper the runner delivered. "No names, and a single phone number. A double blind."

"I thought you were going to kill him." Grace doesn't respond. "The vendor is pimping child labor?"

"No. She is the neighborhood's eyes. She's being cautious. When we deliver a place and a time to her, she will get the word out and the girls will show. They will have been told to give fake names and reveal nothing of their families."

"It doesn't get us any closer to the knot shop."

"It brings them to us. We will cut into their labor

supply. That, or we will create the demand for higher wages."

"You're a market maker."

"Why not?"

"They'll burn you out, or kill you. They're not going to make nice."

"I am telling you, sir, they are going to want to know my financing." She hesitates, wondering how confident she can allow herself to sound. "This is what I do."

"We have other, better, leads to follow."

"You backed me with John."

"I go against Knox as a rule."

"But you hire him."

"For all the same reasons I go against him."

"I do not understand."

"No," Dulwich says, slowing the car at a red light. "What's the progress on Kreiger?"

"Dr. Yamaguchi promises to have me inside the bank's servers again in the next few days. These things cannot be rushed."

"So what's bothering you?" Dulwich asks, focusing on her reflection in the mirror instead of the traffic.

Am I so transparent? she wants to ask, but says nothing. He would hold this against her, use it as further proof that she is not ready for the field.

"Something is bothering you."

"I overthink."

"I listen," he says. "Spitballing is good. Never be afraid to spitball."

She doesn't know the expression, but she doesn't let on—she gets the gist. "John meets with Kreiger. The next time, John is asking about rugs, and the next, he is sampling the merchandise. Kreiger moves with him in lockstep on this, never throws up a wall."

"So? They have history."

"Is Kreiger smart or dumb?"

"According to Knox, he's worked black market contacts for years. He can acquire most anything, move most anything. Girls. Drugs. Rugs. Profit is king. The good thing about the Kreigers of this world is they're predictable. You can rely on their greed."

He swings the car left and comes fully around the block, his eyes on both outside mirrors. He pulls over and double-parks, then backs out into traffic. He runs the engine hot as they speed down a side lane. He aims back toward the city, his eyes constantly in motion.

"You run a knot shop. You are selling rugs for one thousand euros that cost you less than one hundred to produce. It is a money factory. Along comes Sonia Pangarkar. You decide she will draw too much heat, but teaching her sources a lesson will prevent such a story from happening again. It is all about containment."

"I'm listening."

"You plan to kill the EU delegate in a way easily confused with a political message. A car bomb. Maybe you are committed to a large order. Maybe the cash from the knot shop keeps other parts of your business afloat. Much of that may come into focus once I am into the server for a second time."

"Tell me something I don't know." Dulwich sounds restless.

"If I represent a controlling interest in the knot shop, the way I throw suspicion off myself is to have funds I pay out to the knot shop traceable back to my account."

Dulwich waits through a red light without speaking. "Go on," he says, as the car rolls.

"I pay myself in cash. I make sure some of that cash is paid to the bomber. To authorities it must appear exactly as it appears to us: that I am a customer of the knot shop and that some of my cash has been used to pay for the bomb making."

"Removing all suspicion from me." He inhales sharply. "Genius!"

The adrenaline is being processed out of her system. She feels depressed and slightly hungover. Sad, not tired. She can't put her finger on what's bothering her, only that something is, and it's the inability to identify it, to see it clearly, that increases her sense of gloom. Dulwich likes her theory; she should be celebrating. But why, then, is her stomach wrenching, and why does she feel so antsy? She wonders if it's because she won't have another chance to feel as she felt in the playground for some time. All the talk of banks and money reminds her of the tediousness of her day job. John is the winner. John is the one who lives the playground every day.

She knows it isn't true. John spends most of his time negotiating over handwoven kitchen towels and chasing down container shipments. The realization makes her feel all the worse. The majority of life is mundane. Drudgery.

Time spent building up opportunity credit. Some spend such credit taking a cruise to Norway. Skiing the Alps. She wants the field.

"You okay?" Dulwich asks, attempting to reconnect with her in the mirror.

"Tired," she lies, her eyes to the car floor.

22

Maja does exactly as her mother has instructed. When she leaves the house—always in the thick of rush hour—she heads away from the shop, not toward it. Her mother may not think she understands, but she does. The visit the afternoon before has so rattled her mother that, judging by her sunken eyes and irritability, she didn't sleep all night. Kneeling, she held Maja by the shoulders and looked her directly in the eye, detailing the route she was to take, requiring her daughter to repeat it twice.

There was no choice but for Maja to report to work. Being discovered in school instead of home sick had brought down the hammer of discipline on all her workmates. A single child misbehaving meant hell for all, and this week it was Maja's hell brought upon them.

To lead reporters to the shop would be much worse.

Her mother might be killed. She might be put into the van that she has told no one about, including her mother. The girls driven away in the van never return.

Eight blocks north, she turns left at the intersection. Three blocks west, another left. She crosses the street to the opposite sidewalk and goes six blocks. On and on, exactly as her mother told her. Finally, she makes it to the canal. She takes a moment before crossing a dirt field and approaching the side door of a concrete building. Once inside, she crosses the oversized garage where someone had long ago built windows. One last door. She stops and knocks. A man's scruffy face peers out. She's admitted.

There are twelve stations. Three to six girls per rug squat on the floor alongside the work. A photo of the project is taped nearby where all can see it. Another, laminated in plastic, circulates hand-to-hand as needed. Some use a coat or sweater as a mat. Most are barefoot. The residents are identified by a ring of irritation or pus above the ankle, some rings worse than others. Maja has never spoken a word to any of them, but they know the hand signals—may have invented them for all she knows.

Overcome by the smell of wool and the unpleasant odor of men, she heads to her place and sits, feeling the weight of eyes upon her from the watchers and hoping she doesn't look as guilty as she feels. Light floods in through high glass panes. The electricity works—the men make tea—but the lights are never used. Over half the bulbs are missing.

She and the other girls have a secret: a crude language

spoken with their blurring hands. Barred from speaking, the girls use the sign language to communicate basic needs and alarms.

Maja is directed by a coworker to check out the same resident who was recently beaten severely after disappearing for a day. She had run away, presumably because of the infection from the ring. The sore began to smell disgusting, and when she returned, it looked worlds better, though her body was worse for wear. They are careful to never hit the girls in the face. They hammer the bottoms of their feet; pull their hair; pour salt or lemon juice into their eyes. They strip them naked and dunk them in cold water and tell them the horrible things they are going to do to them. It's all talk, and the girls know this, but it's impossible not to believe it.

The sick girl's ring wound is bandaged, but there's no hiding how bad it is. Maja can see it in her wan complexion, the lifelessness in her eyes, the slow speed with which she knots. The other girls are working to make up for her limitation; they've crowded next to her to hide her hands from the watchers.

Maja sees the shop differently today. She resents the reporter's visit. Why it should look any different is beyond her, but it does. The residents, especially. The reminder that those entering the van alone never return. Of the strict rules and harsh consequences when violated. Of her missing school for this. Of her mother's paranoia sending her off this morning.

She flashes a signal: *Bad?*

Her coworker returns it: *Yes. Trouble. You?*

Maja signals. It dawns on her: *Me. This place. The sick girl.*

The sound of the van's engine turning over resonates through all the girls. No one looks up, but they all tense. The timing is wrong. The van is used only at the start and end of the day to transport the residents from wherever they're kept. If it's being used at this time, it's to remove one or more of them.

Maja can't breathe. Her limbs are frozen.

A watcher crosses through the stations, heading directly for her.

23

The immediate reaction to Sonia's celebrity reminds Knox how difficult it will be to hide. The woman behind the counter of the school office can't contain her excitement; it explodes from her eyes and her suppressed grin. Bubbly and self-conscious, she knocks over a child-decorated tin can, sending pencils flying like pick-up sticks as she reaches for the phone. She can't stop staring.

Equally convincing is Sonia's calm and practiced reaction. She is gracious and polite. The two women shake hands. It settles the receptionist.

They are asked to stand before a webcam and have their pictures taken. Knox and Sonia exchange a telling glance. A sticker is produced for each that they affix to themselves.

"Not terribly flattering," Sonia says, patting her collarbone.

In Knox's photo, his camera hangs out of view, only its neck strap showing.

The phone call brings the head of school to the desk, a sad-looking woman in her fifties in need of a makeover. Her tired eyes speak of alcoholism or drug abuse. She strives to look interested but the effort is exhausting.

"Please," she says, motioning Sonia and Knox through and into the outer office. Heads turn toward Sonia. The woman's office reflects her personality, austere and unchanged for far too long.

To this point, Sonia has asked for nothing. She and Knox are the victims of ceremony. Knox believes the clerk out front would have given Sonia anything she asked for, whereas this woman may need a defibrillator if she's to speak a coherent sentence.

The head of school, Sienna Galbraith, according to the plastic stand on her desk, absorbs a lungful of air at great effort and says, "What may we do for you, Ms. Pangarkar?"

The royal *we*, Knox assumes.

"I am a repor—"

"I know who you are. We are . . . so honored to have you."

She looks over at Knox as if he's Sonia's Great Dane and therefore something to keep an eye on.

"I am working on a story—"

"Maja Sehovic."

The HVAC emits an occluded, throaty rasp. Knox catches himself looking over his shoulder, searching for the source of the growl.

The woman's connecting them to Maja disturbs both Sonia and Knox.

Why would you say that? appears to be on the tip of Sonia's tongue. Knox is grateful she doesn't ask the question.

The silence begs for someone to fill it. The head of school obliges. "We've had a call from the mother. I informed her that without police involvement there's really little to be done on our end. I encouraged her to involve the authorities, and as far as you're concerned, Ms. Pangarkar, that is the beginning and end of it." She's a woman accustomed to speaking down to students; she apparently can't help herself.

"It is a beginning, to be sure," Sonia says, conniving a smile for appearance's sake. "I believe I am in a position to get you ahead of something . . . problematic."

"Is this connected to the series on Berna Ranatunga?"

"I am flattered."

"Disturbing, what these people get themselves into. Using a child like that. Unforgivable, to exploit one's child in such a manner."

"Then you are sympathetic."

"I have a pulse, my dear. Of course I'm sympathetic!"

This is news to Knox. He's tempted to congratulate her.

"Whether a connection can be made between Berna and Maja . . . that remains to be seen. More pressing for you and the school is a certain visitor—a man who has made repeated visits, in fact—to this institution posing as Maja's father."

If it's possible, the woman loses a shade to where her skin is a lemony cream.

"Posing?" The woman's voice cracks.

"Maja Sehovic's biological father is serving time in prison. There is no male guardian."

The woman's blank expression confirms her greatest fears: this is potentially a career-ending oversight.

"In order for him to remove a particular student—" Sienna Galbraith stabs the computer keyboard like she's trying to crush a bug. Her face distorts as she drills deeper—apprehension, agitation, anticipation. "A visitor must be registered." She pauses. "In the system."

She spins her computer monitor dramatically for it to face Sonia.

"Father," Galbraith says.

The lens cap of his camera already removed—because he sneaked a photo of Sehovic off the screen—Knox springs into action. He coughs loudly to cover the shutter noise and fires a wild shot in the general direction of the monitor where a man's stony face looks back at them.

Do the math, Knox wants to say. If this man is Maja's father, he was a father at fourteen. He's darkly complected, with a nearly shaved head and a heavy shadow of beard. Greek? Turk? Slavic? Mixed blood. A Euro mutt with dead, angry eyes. It's the face of the enemy, and Knox identifies it as such immediately, reacts to it viscerally. Coughs again, taking another photo. He simultaneously memorizes the mobile number listed among the man's information, wondering if it's legitimate. Could they get that kind of break?

The head of school pulls the monitor back. "I cannot give out such information, of course."

"If it means possibly rescuing these girls?"

"To the police, of course."

"They are not involved yet," Sonia presses. "Whereas, I am . . . we are." She indicates Knox. "I am able to operate in ways the police cannot, as I'm sure you understand. This hastens certain investigative avenues that become restrictive for the police." While Galbraith considers this, Sonia continues. "How trustworthy is this individual's phone number?"

"As to that," the woman says, "it would have been verified at the time of registration."

"Verified?" Knox says, unaware of a mobile phone registry.

"We had . . . that is, the Amsterdam school system . . . There was a child pornography ring. They used one or two girls . . . horrible acts." She closes her eyes, recovers slowly. "For the photographs." She looks at Knox's camera. "They used dozens—hundreds—of local girls' faces. Digitally pasted onto the bodies to give variety to their customers. It was discovered that some of the head shots were taken on school grounds. Photographs taken primarily by mobile phone. It prompted a regulation to account for the mobile numbers of all registered visitors."

"So that number is valid?" Sonia asks anxiously.

"It was at the time of registration. Our receptionist personally calls the mobile at the time of registration. It was a horrible—despicable—case. Girls who've never been compromised in any way made to look like willing participants. The parents . . ."

"I remember the story," Sonia says. "I would very

much appreciate his phone number, Ms. Galbraith. I can do much more, far more, and much faster if I'm in possession of that number."

Knox has the number memorized. He wants to prompt her, but there's no opportunity. Sonia and Galbraith battle over the good of the whole weighed against an individual's privacy. It's too socialistic an argument for Galbraith. She works the keyboard, closing the file, no doubt.

"You will have to obtain this information another way."

"What other way?" Sonia objects. "It's a face. An unremarkable face at that. Every girl used by them is subjected to the disgrace and abuse you've just outlined for us. Certainly you see your own hypocrisy?"

"I will, of course, cooperate fully with the police. I promise to contact them immediately. It's the best I can do. You must have sources within the police?"

She's not only holding a gun to their heads, but has started a clock running as well.

"Might I suggest Chief Inspector Joshua Brower?" Knox's speaking seems to surprise Galbraith.

"By all means," Galbraith answers.

"Yes," says an incredulous Sonia, "by all means."

It was John Knox speaking, not Steele. He curses himself, but sees no reason to backtrack.

Sonia returns her attention to the head of school. "I cannot believe you would not have the child's best interest at heart," she says. "This will be reflected in my article. You understand?"

"I understand, Ms. Pangarkar, that my obligation is first and foremost to the child's family and the proper authorities, and so alerted I now intend to follow through with precisely those responsibilities. Providing the man's personal information to the press could hardly be called responsible or proper. However you choose to report that, I trust you will at least keep this in mind. And now if you both will excuse me, I have calls to make."

Sonia is unaccustomed to losing; it's a side of her Knox has not witnessed. He would not like to find himself on that side—he recognizes the fury of the scorned when he sees it. He takes her gently by the arm and she looks down at his grip spitefully. He lets her go.

He'd like to review what just happened. Not Sonia.

She's gone.

24

Knox occupies the seat of the motorcycle across the canal from Kreiger's latest hangout: a coffee shop/pot bar in the red-light district. A cold drizzle falls, causing him to wipe the visor of his helmet. It's not wet enough to want to get out of it, but he's hardly dry. It's nearing the lunch hour; Kreiger isn't in there to get high. It's business.

Three days of following the man and it's apparent to Knox that Kreiger has his hand in everything the city has to offer: a company offering walking tours; a private brothel where Kreiger keeps an office. This is the man's third visit to a "coffee shop" in as many days. The previous two he entered alone and left with a young woman. The city is working to eliminate the coffee shops and clean up the red-light district, a plan that can't sit well.

Knox switches out SIM cards and texts Sonia if she

wants to meet for lunch. She's been writing around the clock and could use the break. She texts back that she needs to keep working, showing her true colors. He envies her that kind of singular focus. He's more of a Ping-Pong ball in a cardboard box. The stakeout on Kreiger has tested him. It's getting time to bust some heads and take shortcuts. He understands why police detectives are such assholes.

"YOU'RE SCREWING HER, AREN'T YOU?" His only meeting with Dulwich in the past seventy-two hours. "That's a mistake." They're customers in a brown café near the Van Gogh Museum. Tourists go in every direction. Cabs are queued up. There are more people in the bar from the UK than the Netherlands.

"That's indelicate," Knox says.

"Find yourself another hole."

"And again." Knox fights the urge to jump across the table and shut him up.

"She's a source. *The* most important source we have. What happens when it goes south?" he asked rhetorically.

"Such confidence."

"We can't lose her, Knox. She's at the center of this storm."

"I won't lose her." He adds, "You've had that phone number for three days. What the hell?"

"We're using our Paris office. They're on it. The chip is a pay-as-you-go just like yours and mine."

"So map it."

"I said they're on it. When they have something, we'll have it."

"That's actionable intelligence," Knox says. "Three days."

"End it, nice and gentle, or you'll find yourself on a plane to Detroit."

"If I end it, we have problems. It wasn't planned, and we aren't . . . we aren't sleeping together. Not in the way you're thinking."

"Don't go all Bill Clinton on me."

Dulwich relates Grace's theory about Kreiger's using the money trail to hide behind.

"Where does she get this stuff?" Knox asks.

"Don't ask me."

"It's a blind?"

"It's a possibility he's using it as one. Yes."

"So we treat Kreiger as hostile. That's where he was anyway. No change."

"Agreed."

"I sit on him until something better comes along."

"And you stop her from sitting on you," Dulwich says.

"You're not going to enjoy where this goes if you keep that up."

A table of women laugh from the corner. One of them makes eyes at Knox, causing Dulwich to moan like he's sick.

"Have you ever had to work for anything in your life?" Dulwich asks.

He's ruined the moment. Knox can think only of Tommy, of all the work that has gone into saving for his brother's independence, of how far there is to go. He guzzles some beer. Dulwich notes the change from sipping.

"We'll find her," he says. Dulwich isn't referring to the knot shop.

"Soon, or it'll all be spent."

"She's an accountant—"

"A bookkeeper."

"She'll invest it. Purchase assets. It won't be spent frivolously. We'll regain ninety percent or better."

"Your lips . . ."

"Trust me."

Knox polishes off the beer and sets the stein down heavily. Says nothing. Doesn't offer to pay. Never looks back on his way out.

Grace's plan is fraught with risk. Knox wishes he and Sarge had spent less time on his sex life and more on how to best protect her. His concern for her takes a backseat to the embezzlement. He stews on establishing priorities as he endures the drizzle.

Across the street, Kreiger is on the move.

KREIGER LEAVES THE COFFEE SHOP with yet another young woman and they walk up the street to his electric silver Volvo C30. The car pulls out and Knox parallels him across the canal. Knox has left two messages for the man and has yet to hear back. If any of the man's appointments have to do with Knox's purchase, Knox has yet to make a connection.

With his earlier two attempts to follow the Volvo botched because of traffic and weather, Knox tightens the distance of the current tail. He backs off only at traffic lights. He detours to avoid a jam and ends up getting ahead of Kreiger, allowing himself to wait for the Volvo to retake him. The tactic works: he's got the Volvo in sight five minutes later as it slows for a parking space. Knox knows the final destination, having been here before. He drives past.

PRIVAAT CLUB
NATUURHONIG

The engraved plaque is mounted to the left of the stone stairs leading to the canal house's imposing front door. Knox has passed close enough to read it only once, and that was three days earlier. Natural Honey. It's the whorehouse where Kreiger keeps an office.

"Kreiger's earlier stops make sense now," Knox tells Sarge over the phone, watching the club from a distance. "The coffee shops sell drugs. Teens from all over Europe arrive in droves, get high and expect to find work. Instead, they run out of money, some more quickly than others. What better place than the coffee shops to recruit girls for a sex club? The manager keeps his eye out, calls Kreiger, and Kreiger pimps the girl to the club, taking a cut of her earnings."

"Unless he owns the club in the first place."

"There's that, too."

"Can you get in there?"

"The only thing private about the club is the cover

charge. Fifty euros to get through the door. Helps keep the window gawkers from Oudezijds Achterburgwal out."

"Your accent's improving."

"Kreiger knows me. If I'm spotted, I'm busted. But if I make a date with him that takes him away from the club . . ."

"If you're asking me to volunteer, the answer is unequivocally yes."

"Your job is Kreiger. I will set up a meet. You're my backer and you're sick and tired of all the delays with the rug deal. It's either yes or no, but you're not waiting around. It guarantees he's out of the building. Grace and I do this together: a couple shopping for a threesome. I get the office open, Grace does whatever she does and we find out if Kreiger is our guy."

"Fahiz identified his attackers as two Caucasians. Not Muslim, or Turks or Russians. Kreiger's Caucasian."

"That hasn't slipped my mind," Knox says.

"But it's too easy. We both know that," Dulwich states.

"We do."

"Shit like this doesn't drop into your lap."

"Grace teed it up for us. We have to swing at this one in order to get a mulligan." It was unfair but necessary to manipulate Dulwich through his love for golf. "We know it was his cash that reached the trigger man. It's not a matter of going after Kreiger, it's *how*—as a somewhat innocent bystander, or the big dick. Big difference."

"I'd rather be the one doing the legwork. Why don't you take Kreiger?"

"Who is going to buy you and Grace as a couple?"

"Up yours."

"He hasn't been answering my calls, so it may all be moot, but I'm sure he's getting them. If you imply it's now or never—"

"It *is* now or never," Dulwich says.

"But maybe not for him. I'll let you know."

25

"The last time we were together in a place like this, it did not work out so well." Grace's nervousness manifests itself as tightness in her body, even her voice.

"You're walking like a robot. Loosen up. Remember, this is exciting for us. We are flush with anticipation."

She snorts. "I may look the part, but I do not feel it. Do not set your expectations too high, John."

"So noted."

"Not exactly my area of expertise."

They've taken the usual precautions in order to be together. Grace has gone one step further—she has found herself a leather miniskirt, and a metallic gray silk shirt that's unbuttoned to her navel. She's wrapped in a silver trench coat and completes the look with black spike heels that give her the calves of a supermodel. He catches himself looking over at her yet again, not seeing her as a colleague, and looks away.

"You apparently like robots."

"Busted."

"I am flattered."

"You're nervous."

Of course I am. Another woman? "A threesome? I am not this woman, John."

"I'm open to suggestions. We can still call it off. I can do this alone, if you can coach me through the IT stuff."

"No one is requiring this. I will do what the job requires of me."

Over the course of the next city block, she transforms. It is the butterfly appearing from the chrysalis. There's a definite, defiant swing to her walk, and her spine straightens. Her posture is aggressive, but also alluring—even the sound of her high heels on the concrete is different, more certain, more determined. She has entered the zone.

GRACE IS WORRIED ABOUT HIM. She has witnessed his Messiah complex. Though honorable, it has no place here. They aren't here to save a prostitute. Together, they must buy each other time. She has set herself to that goal. She would like to avoid getting naked in front of Knox, though she's no prude. Her earlier sexual encounter at the hotel has prepared her well; nothing could be worse than an unfulfilling lay with a stranger.

Her focus must remain on the IT needs of the operation. Knox's job is to get her into the office; once there, the real challenge begins. Will there be a computer in the office? Wireless or Ethernet? Physical files to copy? A landline telephone?

She carries listening devices, line taps and cameras to install—all in a purse slung over her shoulder. The items are hidden in the bottom of her bag beneath a camisole, a cordless vibrator and a riding crop. She is a one-woman wrecking ball.

She mentally choreographs each phase of the operation. Her mathematical mind serves her well. Without any knowledge of what the room will look like, she nonetheless visualizes each stage of the job, rehearsing it. Knox has given her a limit of twenty minutes, promising to occupy their willing partner at least this long. It is barely enough, given so many unknowns. An hour would have been more comfortable—an hour with a team of two or three, better yet. She enters the job knowing they will not get everything they are after, that they will have to settle for less. She hates such compromise.

Knox pays the fifty euros to a fabulous beauty in a *Pulp Fiction* platinum wig and an elegant evening dress that shows off an abundance of smooth cleavage and nut-hard nipples that could be pasties. She has the body of a lingerie model, and the smile of a quiz-show hostess. Knox's gaze lingers a little too long on the cleavage; Grace is unsure if it's intentional or not.

The interior of the house is more contemporary than clubby. Dance music plays in the parlor to the right where a half dozen extremely young women show off their wares by dancing together. The smell of pot and tobacco commingle. Nonsmoking is the room to the left, where love seats, couches and coffee tables break the room up into more intimate spaces. The lighting is low and warm. A self-serve liquor bar and small buffet table divide the room. The management is smart: the couches are not crowded with girls. Instead, there are three or four in the room at a time, rotating constantly from a pool of girls at the back of the house. The exchange is done naturally. It doesn't come off as a parade, nor a runway, but feels more like a cocktail party that is moving between rooms.

The girls are young and very pretty, well groomed and fashionably dressed. Grace feels old by comparison. For everything it tries not to be, it is nonetheless a meat market: blondes, redheads, brunettes; skinny, plump, plus-sized; flat, busty, leggy, tough, cuddly. Grace has always admired the artistry of women's bodies. God was having a good day when he created woman. Regardless of taste, a man—or woman—could find the look of choice here. Everything is engineered to seduction. She is excited, aroused even. She can only imagine the conflict in Knox— rage versus desire. Repugnance mixed with hormones. Hell for him. Only now does she realize how difficult it must be for him to participate.

Grace clutches his arm. He guides her to a couch. She holds the short skirt as she sits, the hem rides up to where the slightest movement of her legs will flash her red lace panties.

Knox brings her a vodka on the rocks with a twist, three fingers deep. He has poured himself a single malt. She has to watch herself with the vodka; it can go down too easily.

They make small talk with a very-well-put-together brunette who goes by the name Usha. They begin in Dutch, but her Slavic accent makes her incomprehensible. Grace attempts Russian, but they soon settle on English so Knox can participate.

"You are together," the woman says, as if in surprise.

"We like adventure," Knox says.

"Don't we all?" the woman returns.

"Do you like adventure, Usha?" Knox asks. He takes hold of Grace's free hand to make the request more obvious.

"Yes, of course."

Grace doesn't approve of the look in Usha's eyes: the woman clearly favors Knox; Grace is an afterthought, which could complicate the job.

The woman never loses her bright-eyed expression. "You want Jin-Jin," she says, indicating an Asian hardbody who has a preference for dog collars.

Grace will not work with an Asian. "Perhaps not," she says.

"Veronique," Usha says.

The French African wears a rainbow of thin metal bands around her long neck. She has sharp collarbones and wide, square shoulders. Her overly large eyes are haunting; her body belongs to a marathoner. Her skin is so black it looks purple. She wears a side-split skirt open to her hip.

"*Magnifique!*" Knox pulls Grace to the front of the couch. "You will introduce us, please?"

"Pleasure."

Usha leads them. Two loud men enter and proclaim

themselves partiers. Grace feels Knox tense, and squeezes his hand to bring him back. Had he come alone, a fight would have already broken out.

Veronique grins at Knox across blinding teeth. But it's the heated look she gives Grace, her eyes first aimed at Grace's small skirt; she then makes eye contact and loses the smile to a pursing of her large lips. Not quite a kiss, but far from disapproving. She is curious. She is thinking.

She speaks with a British accent. Grace makes small talk. Knox works his way around to the reference of voyeurism. It's like asking a mechanic for an oil change.

"I can arrange a companion for you as you watch, if you like. For either of you, if desired." She checks out Grace.

"No, thank you," Knox says. "I prefer . . . to fly solo."

Grace says, "We'll see."

It's four hundred euros an hour and any portion thereof. Knox makes a cash down payment to a madam in her thirties. Knox and Grace are left to continue drinking while Veronique prepares the room.

"So far, so good," Knox says.

"I will need the full twenty minutes. Make sure you give me proper directions."

Knox says nothing.

"I know this is difficult for you," she says. "I remember Chongming."

Silence.

"We both are going to keep her busy, John."

A younger woman shows them upstairs. The decor is warmer. Knox nudges Grace and eye-checks the floor. Hand-tied rugs. A string of hallway runners. The Dutch oils on the walls look surprisingly authentic. The golden glow from the leaded-glass wall sconces. The sultry, deep-throated voice singing a jazz standard through unseen speakers.

As Grace takes in the rugs, she sees Knox surreptitiously look for the location of the webcams they assume are in constant operation. At these prices, with this clientele, it's doubtful the cameras cover the bedrooms. But if a girl runs, or a john tries a door other than the one he's paying for, someone needs to be watching.

"Anything?" she asks.

"No," he whispers.

She spots a staircase leading higher. An exit sign suggests the window at the end of the hall leads to a fire escape. It has Knox written all over it.

As Grace expected, the bedroom is small but well appointed. It's cozy, done in warm colors and soft lighting. A place one wants to spend time in. The girl's job is to push the companionship into a second hour, requiring another four hundred. The corner sink is a welcome sight. "Toilet?" Grace asks.

"Into the hall," says Veronique. "A second, up the stairs."

This will help Knox.

"Here's how it's going to work," Knox tells Veronique, laying out the rules. "Constance," he says, referring to Grace, "and you will get to know one another. You will show me . . ."

"It is the next door. This side." She points to the mirror on the near wall.

"Very good. I will join you later, at which time Constance will watch. You will arouse me but not allow me to climax. I am counting on your professionalism. Constance will rejoin us after that."

"This sounds like fun," Veronique says.

"We are in no hurry," Grace says.

Veronique locks eyes with Grace, who suddenly feels she might faint.

FROM THE MOMENT Veronique touches Grace's hair, Knox turns his back on the voyeur mirror. If he was in therapy or could drink away the memories, he might find them tempting, but there's a history buried within him that neither a shrink nor Scotch can ameliorate. And so: avoidance.

The observation room consists of a twin bed and a nylon mesh chair, the same cozy decor as the bedroom where the two women are currently undressing. He's about to leave as a second mirror in the room reflects Veronique stripping. Next is Grace. When there's nothing left but the red thong, his pulse races and his throat feels dry. Knox breaks out of his trance, aroused. He leaves the room and heads upstairs.

The room marked PRIVAAT is at the top of the stairs to the right. The toilet is to the left.

Knox carries a pick gun, an automated tumbler decipher that picks nearly any lock with the squeeze of a trigger, illegal worldwide and available on eBay. He removes it from the Scottevest pocket. There was a time a person needed actual lock-picking skills. He prepares the iPhone for camera mode and sets up its digital recorder to record from his Bluetooth headset. He's accustomed to ad-libbing, has to slow himself down to remember to ask for Kreiger if anyone's inside the office when he opens the door. He and Grace have worked through half a dozen contingencies.

VERONIQUE TOUCHES GRACE FIRST.

"No." She pauses. "Not yet."

"You are new to this," Veronique declares.

Grace feels her cover disintegrating. "I like to take my time. I will do the touching."

"Whatever you like."

Veronique lies back. Grace avoids intimacy but touches the woman's stomach and neck. She tries to appear interested. After a few minutes, Veronique turns to draw on Grace's abdomen, which contracts under the touch.

"Not yet. I'll let you know." Grace starts to pull up the sheet, but Veronique catches it and returns it to their knees.

"For him," she coos. "He's watching."

"Lie back, please."

Veronique lies on her side. Grace runs her hand over the woman's muscular buttocks and up from the small of her back and into her hair at the nape of her neck.

Veronique purrs, "A man lacks nuance," as Grace busies herself with both hands.

Knox opens the door without knocking.

Grace swallows a gasp.

He looks at her first, then quickly he settles his eyes on Veronique.

He smiles, immediately playing his role. "My turn."

WEARING A SILK ROBE with her purse slung over her shoulder, Grace listens to the voice recording Knox has sent to her phone. She flushes the toilet before leaving the washroom without having used the facilities. Although charged with adrenaline, she adopts a lazy stroll on her way down the hall to the office.

"The pick gun is behind the speaker to your left as you face the door," Knox's message said. "Laptop, front and center. Wireless router on the lower shelf to the left of the desk as you face it. Vaulted ceiling with natural light. Blinds on the lower windows were open. Now closed. Important you remember to reopen them before leaving. I swept it. No devices found. You'll want to do better. Twenty minutes. Less, by the time you hear this."

There's a text from Dulwich.

meeting wrapping up. unable to hold him.

It's time-stamped seven minutes earlier.

Now inside the office with the deadbolt locked, she texts:

how long?

Doesn't wait for a response. Her bag is open. Game on.

on his way there now

She slips into the office chair. The key tracking software will provide them with passwords that will allow her to attack Kreiger's laptop. She opens a port on the router to skirt virus security software. She video-bugs the top bookshelf where dust on the volumes tells her they're rarely touched. She wants the audio closer to home. She'll take over the laptop's microphone and video once she's inside.

She packs up her wires and shoulders the purse. Turning off the lights, she crosses to open the blinds. There are windows on opposing walls.

She twists the blinds open. A man on the sidewalk below jerks his head in her direction.

It's Kreiger. He's caught the movement in his own office windows. Whether instinctively or by chance, it hardly matters.

Without hesitation, Grace waves down to him.

He stops, head still aimed at her.

She waves again.

Kreiger waves back. He then marches furiously toward the front door.

"YOU ARE?"

Grace displays herself resplendently on his love seat.

Her best Mata Hari pose, borrowed from an Ingrid Bergman film she'd seen while getting her master's in criminology at USC.

"A friend of John Knox," she answers in English.

Kreiger waves off a bouncer and enters. He places down a briefcase that catches her eye.

"I lock my office," he says, not having moved. "It's marked 'private' in case you can't read. How, in the name of God, did you get in here?"

"I am a friend of John Knox," she says.

She wins a laugh from Kreiger. "Yes, well, that *would* explain it."

"I . . . I was interested in company . . . female company . . . and Knox recommended your establishment. He made me promise I would say hello." As she sits up she makes sure to let a good deal of leg show. He must be immune to such sights, but she tries anyway. The robe comes open far more than she would have wished, but she makes no attempt to close it. Let him ogle her. To her surprise, he does just that. Men.

"I would expect nothing less," he says. "Drink?"

"Vodka rocks, please."

She regrets having placed the video camera on the bookshelf. Of everything she's done, the video camera is the most likely to be detected if he gets suspicious. And how can he not? All the charm in the world cannot nullify breaking and entering.

He pours them both drinks, his back to her.

"He sent you to spy on me," Kreiger says, paralyzing Grace's diaphragm.

"I was to get the wholesale cost of the rugs, if I could," she says without hesitation. "I won't tell, if you won't?"

"Identify the wholesaler," he speculates. "Eliminate the middleman. Knox is not stupid. I might have done the same."

"He is annoyed at the time it is taking," she says.

"Yes. I've just spoken to his money man." A wave of realization spreads over Kreiger's face. "Oh, very good." He hands her the drink and pulls out a chair to face her. He shows no further interest in her body; she pulls the robe shut and ties it tightly. "He's a clever one, our Mr. Knox." He lifts his glass and they toast. "Now . . . what to do with you?"

She peers over the rim of the glass, attempting to look unaffected by his comment.

"I find it most instructive to send a message when such advantage is taken. You are bold to have stayed after I spotted you up here. Very bold indeed."

"I don't get paid unless I can deliver actionable intelligence. The laptop is password protected. The desk drawers locked."

"Hold your purse by the bottom two corners, turn it over and shake out its contents, please."

"Is that necessary?" she pleads. She has nothing with which to bargain. Sex is a nonstarter in a place like this. She can't buy him. This is the part of fieldwork she understands requires experience, and she has none. He sits between her and the door. To assault him would be easy enough, but would put Knox in a terrible bind. She's already done enough damage.

"Please."

She inverts her bag. Her knot of wires and cameras tumble out.

"How many of those were installed?" he inquires.

"One."

"Do you assume me so naïve?"

"If I'd had more time . . ."

"Remove it, please."

She uses a chair to access the top of the bookshelf and retrieve the video camera. The lens is smaller than a lentil. It attaches by a nearly nonexistent wire to a box half the size of a sugar cube. He has been staring at her legs as she climbed; he asks for it, and she hands it to him.

"Amazing," he says.

To her surprise, he returns it to her and tells her to pack the bag.

In doing so, she manages to check the time. She's been away from the room for thirty minutes. She has failed on all fronts.

"Tell Knox these things take time. His is a very large order. The manufacturer must carefully measure production before committing. There's no saying he'll go for the deal."

She's unable to tell if he's talking about himself in third person.

"You should keep in mind—*yourself*—as well as pass along to Knox, that this operation . . . these rug merchants . . . Let's just say they are acutely aware of, shall we say, the world opinion of their ethics. They are not the type to tolerate outside interference. You would have been raped and your throat slit by now if this had been their offices. I would not blindly follow everywhere Knox leads you, young lady. He would be quick to cut bait in a case like yours. You don't see him knocking down the door to rescue you, do you?"

"If I should scream," she says, "he will be through that door before you hear me." She smiles and stands.

Kreiger stands as well, blocking her.

"We can try it, if you like," she proposes.

A sheen forms on his face.

She marvels at the man's instant reaction to Knox. She hoists the purse to her shoulder. Tightens the robe's belt once again. Realizes she knows Knox in ways others do not.

"I'll have the office swept." He makes it a threat.

She looks down to the carpet. "It could use it."

She provokes laughter from him.

"I could use a woman like you," he says, smiling. "Here at Natuurhonig."

"Get in line," says Grace.

FROM THE OBSERVATION ROOM, Grace sees Veronique's wrists tied with bows to the bed frame, her lean, blue body stretched out elegantly on the bed. Knox has blindfolded her. She is smiling while he, in briefs, runs a feather across her.

Grace feels a spike of sentimentality. It's "us against the world" for her and Knox. She's beginning to care for him, despite herself. Not romantically, not exactly; she's unsure what it is she feels. She shakes off the feeling, but it's sticky and stubborn.

She recognizes the scar on him she helped to mend. One among several. Recalls the story of Knox dragging Dulwich from the burning wreck of a transport, wondering if any of the scars are traceable to that incident. Or the streets of Detroit? Wonders at those unseen, the kind she carries. She spends a few seconds longer here than necessary, causing her to question herself. She is not given to such nostalgia. What's happening to her? she wonders. She has loved before—loves, still—but this is not that. Is it? Not close. Then what?

An adrenaline hangover from Kreiger's office, she convinces herself. Blood chemistry, nothing more. A narrow escape. She pulls herself together, realizing she will likely have to dress in front of him.

She opens the door.

"Ah . . ." Veronique says, smiling. She hears Knox's belt buckle as he begins dressing. "What is this, please?" She unties herself, removes the blindfold.

"I am afraid I am not feeling well," Grace says, eyes to the floor.

"I did not please you?" the woman says to Knox.

"We have to go," Knox says. He reaches for his wallet.

"Not again," Grace says to him. "Please . . ." They both know she's harking back to Chongming.

He places a great many euros onto the bed. Many times what they owe. He keeps enough for cab fare.

"Find other work," he tells the woman.

Veronique stares at the pile of cash. Looks between Knox and Grace.

"It is not you," Grace says, nearly dressed. Struggling into the tight skirt. "He has this . . . it is an emotional problem. We thought tonight . . . that is, we had hoped . . ."

Knox has his hand on the doorknob, waiting impatiently. He holds the door for Grace, takes a fleeting look back at the naked woman stretched out on the bed and closes the door.

AVOIDING PUBLIC TRANSPORT, they pause to overlook the black, still waters of a canal. Pale light seeps from the cabin of a boat tied a hundred meters downstream. A tension holds between them.

"He caught me," she says, "inside his office."

Knox remains focused on the mirrored water.

She recounts the events down to the exchange of dialogue.

"And we come away empty-handed?"

"No, not at all. He will have the office swept and discover no more bugs. He will have his computer scanned but will find nothing."

"Is that possible?"

She sighs.

"I'm sorry."

"We will have video and audio as long as the laptop is online. We will monitor his keystrokes, allowing us to obtain his passwords as well as his correspondence. We are inside his head now, John. His cell phone number will be listed among his contact information."

"I have his number."

"There may be others. How many chips do you carry? It is possible he will list bank accounts, credit cards and other financial information in his contacts. Many do. We will have his browser history."

Knox whistles. The sound carries out across the water. "Less traffic out here," he says.

"Yes. It is quite peaceful."

"You must be wondering what I saw."

"You believe me so childish?"

"Then you don't care?"

"Do I look fourteen? I need to get started. We go separately from here."

They walk to the end of the bridge. Grace turns left, Knox right. As she reaches the curb, she stops and turns. He's standing across the intersection looking back at her.

"You do *not* look fourteen."

26

Knox has relocated them to another houseboat, this time on Keizersgracht, not far from the Amsterdam Hermitage. It's the same boat by the same manufacturer, the same layout as the first, but Sonia has been installed in the waterside cabin because Keizersgracht has a fair amount of foot traffic; Knox is taking no chances of an inadvertent sighting.

Perched on the berth, her laptop on her lap, Sonia clings to a glass of red wine, half full. It's a familiar sight; she hasn't moved from this pose in days. But it's not the same woman; one look tells him as much. Tells him more than he wants to know. The wine bottle stands close to empty.

"What is it?" He speaks at a low volume. Closes the thin wooden door gently behind him. Latches its brass latch.

Sonia plays music from her laptop to cover their voices.

Contemporary Top 20 pop. She's full of surprises. Knox sits by her ankles.

Her eyes wander to his, then roll into the back of her head and her pupils reappear. She stares him down with angry eyes. He looks back at the near-empty wine bottle. Its glass refracts and displaces the camera tucked behind it. His Nikon.

"Who are you?" she says accusingly.

"You've had too much to drink."

"Who—?"

"You know who I am!"

She spins the laptop to face him. "I needed to caption whatever photo I was to include with my article."

On the screen is a shot of a tall woman in a scarf entering an eatery.

"The camera keeps information on all the pictures," she says. "Date and time. So I ask again: who are you?"

"I followed you. It's true. But for your security. To look after you because clearly you were not looking after yourself."

"And this Chief Inspector Brower?"

Knox assumed he'd gotten away with that misspeak at the school. Her bringing it up now is a surprise. He's underestimated her.

"Brower?" He won't lie to her. Can't tell the truth.

"He's your boss, isn't he? You're police."

Knox grins. Wishes he hadn't. "No."

"Get out!"

"Listen to me. I was following you. Yes. To protect you. After your meeting, I tailed that woman," he says, pointing to the laptop, "into a park where *she* met with a man. As it turned out, a cop.

"Brower's men caught me spying on their inspector and brought me in," he continues. "I had to talk my way out. It wasn't easy." The truth. "Brower wants the knot shop shut down as much as we do. Brower will work with us. I thought if the head of school called into the police's main number, we might lose our hold on this, lose control of it. So I recommended Brower."

"We never had control in the first place."

"We have this guy who claimed to be Maja's father. We're ahead of everyone on this."

"Not we," she argues. "I . . . do . . . not . . . trust . . . you."

"Don't do this." Dulwich's warning echoes in his head. He adds, "Please."

She answers with hurt eyes. There's a boat motoring on a nearby canal, a barking dog several blocks away.

"Who is that woman?" he asks.

Her words slur. "I have very good instincts when it comes to people. My work depends on it. I was wrong about you. I know it in here," she says. "I don't know who you are, but I know when I've been lied to."

"Who . . . is . . . she?"

"An activist. All right with you? Google her, if you want. Christina Jorgensen. Swedish. Has been fighting child exploitation, worldwide, for nearly a decade. She read my article, okay? If she meets with the police, what do I care? The woman should be sainted!"

He takes this in. Christina Jorgensen could have been

watching the market stall where Grace got the tip that led to her assault. Jorgensen followed and saved Grace when the time came.

"We have a phone number for the man claiming to be Maja's father at the school," he says. "We—both of us!—have people who can help us with that. This impostor is one of *them*. Has to be. You understand how close we are? The first twenty-fours hours are critical."

"You even talk like a cop."

"I am *not* a cop."

"A photographer?"

He answers only with his eyes.

"An agent?" Horrified.

"We can finish this. We can close this."

"We? I don't think so. You followed her, didn't you?"

"Who?"

"Why bother asking? You'll just lie to me anyway." She revisits the wine bottle, sloshing more into her empty glass.

"Sonia . . . listen to me—"

"Shut up!" She fumbles with her phone and places it past the laptop faceup. She plays a voice mail for him.

It takes Knox a moment to recognize the hysterical voice as that of Maja's mother. *"What have you done? I told you not to follow her. I told you to leave us al—"*

"I called back. I recognized the caller ID and I called back." She absorbs a long draught from the glass. "She never came home. Because . . . you followed her. Who the hell do you think—?"

"No! I did not follow her!"

"Just like you did not follow me?" The image on the laptop glares back at him.

"A friend's house. School again."

"No. Yasmina has checked everywhere. Gone. She has no idea where to start looking. She can't contact the police, and she blames us."

"We'll get Maja back. But we have no time for this." He motions between them. His mind is cluttered with prepared dialogue as he rehearses what comes next. He can drop her into his world but fears the shock would push her even further away. He can abandon her, accepting that he used her as best he could. Rutherford Risk is already running the impostor-father's phone number. It's the best lead they've had. All things come to a useful conclusion, including the Sonia Pangarkars. He hates that Dulwich could have foreseen this.

"You followed her and don't have the balls to admit it."

In a moment of clarity, he sees through the alcohol, through her.

"You blame yourself, not me," he says.

"To hell with you."

He can't quite put his finger on it, but knows he's scored a hit. "For writing the original story. For getting these girls into all this trouble."

"You're an asshole."

"A photograph?" he says, thinking aloud now. "Captioning a photograph? That would be at the request of your editor."

"You little shit."

"You filed the story on Maja."

Her eyes burn into him.

"You filed, and then Maja went missing."

"No connection. Coincidence."

He waits her out, both impatience and intolerance gnawing at him. He enjoys getting drunk as much as the next guy, but has little time for drunks. He's never claimed to be fair. He eases the glass from her and sets it down.

"I filed the story around four this afternoon. It cannot possibly be the cause." She sounds resolved to the likelihood she's the cause of it all.

"You sent in one of my pictures without asking me?" It's important to remain in character, but he's losing John Steele to Knox's temper. How much of this conversation will she even remember?

She seems to have just noticed Knox. "The grandmother. The cigarette by the window."

"Which one? Which shot?"

"What do you mean, which one?" she asks.

"Are you insane?" It escapes before he can prevent it.

"There's nothing in that shot to give Maja away. It's a silhouette."

"There's *everything* to give Maja away," he counters. "It took three tries to get the f-stop right to account for the depth of field. In the first two shots, the background was *in focus*—a store sign across the street."

Her skin tone turns a sickly yellow. He reaches for the trash bin, but it's too late. She vomits onto the floor. Knocks the laptop and phone into the bedding and slips off the berth, heaving a second time, this time on target.

He catches her as she's heading for the floor. "You didn't know."

"Oh, God . . ."

He moves her out to the head. The proprietor's in the galley and tries to pretend he doesn't see them, hasn't heard them arguing.

Knox helps her out of the stained top. Pulls the bottoms down and places the clothes into the sink as he turns on the water and steps out of the room. The showerhead is in one corner, a drain in the wood floor.

Knox approaches the proprietor and asks for cleaning supplies, and after some discussion accepts the offer for the proprietor's wife to clean the forward berth. When Sonia comes out wrapped in a towel, Knox directs her into his room. He's collected her laptop and phone as well as his camera. Hasn't left anything for his hostess to come across.

A more sober Sonia sits on his berth, barely covered by the small towel. He offers her a T-shirt he's been sleeping in. She declines.

"She never came home. Can you imagine?" She whispers, but Knox does not like ears so close. He's already planning to move them again.

He puts a finger to his lips and they wait out the cleaning next door. It takes ten minutes. Feels longer.

The proprietor knocks. John answers the door and thanks him.

"Coffee," he says. "No milk. One sugar."

Sonia looks out from a curtain of wet, stringy hair over the rising mist from a mug of coffee. The mug is from

Starbucks in Oslo. As she tilts it, its bottom reads: MADE IN CHINA. "I'm sorry for what I said, John."

It hurts more than her accusations. "Listen—" The truth dances on the tip of his tongue.

She samples the coffee. "This tastes horrible."

"You're welcome."

"I have to see her. Yasmina."

"Never going to happen."

"We must get her back."

"Yes."

"You are distracted."

"Thinking," Knox says. "A lot to think about."

Her hand is occupied with the hot coffee, so when the towel falls open she has only the one hand to try to deal with it. Knox comes to her aid, reaching for the mug, but Sonia reconsiders and opens the towel fully. Finally, she passes Knox the mug as she lies back on the berth.

Knox locks the door.

LATER, AFTER SONIA HAS RETURNED to her cabin, Knox pulls out his phone—his version of smoking a cigarette.

"It's John," he tells the man who answers. *Daniel,* he thinks. But Daniel may have been the nurse before this. "John Knox."

"Sure. Hello. How can I help you?"

"Just wondering how Tommy's doing?"

"It's a rough patch, Mr. Knox. It'll pass."

"Physical, mental, or both?"

"Let's not limit him," Daniel says. When Knox fails to respond, he says, "The new medication is causing insomnia. That's triggering some of the old behavior. I have a call in to his doc."

"Which doc?"

"Foreman."

"Okay. Good. But he's okay?" Tommy's progress toward at least the guise of independence has been promising—even encouraging; any reversion to earlier behavior is a blow. The suggestion that Tommy hasn't progressed, his meds have simply improved, leaves Knox desperate.

"He's okay."

He's never loved Daniel—if that's even his name—but Tommy likes him. Daniel treats Tommy as an adult, which is more than can be said for the nurse that came before him.

"Can I call him?"

"A visit wouldn't hurt."

He remembers now why he doesn't like the man.

"Thanks for everything you're doing." Knox's version of a white flag.

"It's my job, Mr. Knox."

Knox ends the call, tempted to smash the phone.

Tommy's number rings right to the edge of when the live answering service will pick up. Tommy struggles with mechanics. The live service is a godsend. But at last he picks up and Knox says hello.

"Johnny?" Sometimes his brother can sound especially young.

"Hey."

"How ya doing? You sound kinda out of breath."
Tommy finds this amusing.

"Out for a walk," Knox lies. He doesn't like the sound
of this already. Blames himself for so few visits.

"Where?"

Tommy knows better than to ask.

"How about you? How goes?"

"Darkest hour is just before the dawn."

"Is it dark or dawn?" Knox asks, cringing. He knows
this pattern: random quotations, inability to find words
of his own.

Tommy takes the question literally, as always. "It's just
past three in the afternoon."

The time. That's progress, though Knox can't mention it.

"And how's business?"

"Dollars to donuts. Bob's your uncle."

"Tommy . . . Just hang on a second . . ."

"Just desserts. Rack your brains."

"Stay with me here, Tom."

"Stand and deliver. Silence is golden, duct tape is silver."

Knox plays along. "Keep the ball rolling."

A sudden silence.

"All's well that ends well." Knox checks the connection. As he does, a call comes in from Dulwich. Hanging
up will crush Tommy.

"Tom, I gotta run."

"Run amok. Run of the mill. Run out of steam."

"It's nice hearing your voice."

"You, too. YouTube," Tommy says.

"We'll talk soon."

"I miss you."

"And I, you."

"You said you were coming."

Knox silences Dulwich's incoming call.

"I'm working on it," Knox says.

"How much longer?"

"I wish I could say. Don't know. I'm being honest, Tommy. Treating you like an adult."

"I know."

"Your meds are off."

"You think I don't know that?"

"Daniel's working on it. Hang in there."

"It's noisy in here."

Knox isn't sure what to do with that. In his head? In his apartment?

"I'm here for a reason. For you, man. We both want the same thing for you—"

"But it costs money."

"I know you don't want to hear that."

"I want to see you."

Knox won't lie. His voice catches.

"I'll be there as soon as I can. That's the truth, Tommy."

"Truth hurts. Truth or Consequences. You can't handle the truth!"

It hits Knox in the chest. Jack Nicholson. A favorite film scene of the brothers.

"Gotta go."

Knox calls Sarge back.

THE EXTERIOR OF THE FIVE-STAR Sofitel Grand on Oudezijds Voorburgwal harks back to Europe's glory days a century or more before. Inside, its Gothic-arched ceiling is painted ceramic white and supported by massive columns. Two seven-foot-tall metallic vases hold purple alliums reaching five feet higher, a contemporary dazzle where form meets function and where blue jean–clad millionaires mix with the business elite. Sitting before the glass-enclosed gas fireplace, in two of the modern overstuffed seats, Grace and Dulwich sip a Pimm's and a lager as conversation blurs around them.

Grace is connected to the lobby's free Wi-Fi. Dulwich has one eye on the front door, the other on their escape route to the dining room.

"Your upper lip," she says.

Dulwich pats the perspiration away. This is the third time they have lounged like this around the city in as many days, sometimes for hours at a time. Grace acknowledges her boss's impatience. Dulwich comes out of fieldwork; he's not wired for stakeouts, physical or virtual. He's a leader of men, good at running supply convoys from the safety of Kuwait into the killing fields of Iraq. He's tough and durable, filled with titanium screws and pins and enough stitches to make a quilt. Apparently incapable of holding down a relationship, he is a single-minded workaholic. But sitting around in the lobby of a luxury hotel is anathema to him. The perfume, the piped-in classical music, the distant chiming of arriving elevators—everything here conspires against him.

"They are in," Grace says calmly. The moment they've been waiting for: Grace delivers it with all the aplomb of a telephone operator.

The announcement nullifies Dulwich's former sarcasm and disrespect for the process. Grace made the investigative procedure intentionally difficult. Too easy, and they would be suspected; too difficult, and the enemy would never connect the dots. It's a cat-and-mouse game, where the mouse can leave nothing but a scent and a whisker or two to follow.

Grace has been planting the crumbs to follow: the business card left with the real estate agent, listing an e-mail address; her persistence with Marta; the thumping she gave Marta's runners. All pieces of a whole—a woman looking to set up a sweatshop of her own. Dulwich, the doubter, failed to believe anyone would figure it out. But Grace knew. She would have. Knox, as well. Those who establish a beachhead can smell the enemy coming.

She's the enemy, and she awaits notice. An e-mail address she has used has led back to a service provider; the service provider to an ISP; the ISP accessed via a router; the router tracked to the hotel whose lobby Grace and Dulwich now occupy. Bread crumbs. Grace's firewall will require several attacks before submitting. This because it's expected.

The third time's the charm. The hacker opens a port on Grace's laptop. The hacker is so consumed with the attack he misses being outflanked. Grace has been expecting him.

While her hacker is downloading her files, she is a spawning salmon swimming up the data stream. Bytes are flowing in both directions.

"It is good," she says, trying to dissuade Dulwich from his penchant for worry. "The connection is established. We're in."

It's a double-blind: the data the hacker is collecting is disinformation, positioning Grace as a direct competitor. Piggybacked onto the raid, she is downloading pertinent data. A digital battle has begun. For all she knows, the data she's collecting is as bogus as the data she's dishing out. Time will tell. Data is only as good as the analyst interpreting it.

She can't appear to give the hacker endless access. It's a dance. She sends some bogus e-mails to dummy accounts. Suddenly the hacker is not downloading but uploading large packets of data to Grace's laptop. Too big for a virus. The deadliest trojans and worms are a tenth this size.

"Something is wrong. I am not sure exactly what. Data bomb? I cannot explain what I am seeing."

"Try." Until this moment, Dulwich has been like a boy coming downstairs Christmas morning. He doesn't understand the technical side of the raid, but has approved the strategy.

Grace closes her laptop, ending the connection.

"What the hell are you doing?" Dulwich is beside himself.

"I am telling you: it is some kind of sabotage I have

not seen." Her eyes land on a point beyond him. Dulwich looks there.

Two thirty-somethings in dark suits. Hotel security.

"We are blown," she whispers. "They may have tagged the laptop."

Money has been spread around the city to try to find Sonia. This has never been in question. It seems unlikely Sofitel's security team would bother a guest about hacking the hotel's wireless, as Grace has. Much of Dulwich's attention has been fixed on the front doors; a raid from within wasn't part of the game plan.

The security men stand before them. Dulwich is clearly considering a physical response, and though Grace will go along—especially given the man's bad leg—she hopes it doesn't come to that. The surprise raid could play in their favor. There's not time to explain it to Dulwich. Her disquiet comes not from the men facing them but from unexplained data bombs loaded onto her laptop. She can't explain that act; in Grace's world, numbers must add up.

"Good evening," the taller of the two says.

"Hello?" Dulwich returns. "How may we help you?" Ever on the offensive.

"May I see a room key, please?"

"We are not registered guests," Dulwich says. "We are awaiting some friends for drinks."

"I asked another guest for her log-on," Grace explains. "She gave it to me freely."

"I see. No problem. If you would come with us for a moment. Please." He tacks this on for appearances, but the man has made up his mind how this is to proceed.

"Concerning?"

Dulwich is already plotting their escape. She places a hand on his knee.

"It is all right. I am sure it is nothing."

"The hotel conforms to International Internet Usage Regulations, as explained in the wireless agreement. We merely wish to inspect the lady's laptop, as is our right. It won't take but a minute."

"Of course." Dulwich is still plotting.

"It is all right," Grace repeats. She stands, slipping the laptop into a stylish case.

"I will take that, if you don't mind," the security man says. "Just until this is all cleared up."

True hackers might have magnets in their case, or a way to erase the drive prior to detection. Her real laptop— not this substitute—possesses not only a general password but a second, unprompted security code. If the second code is not input within thirty seconds of other use of the track pad or keyboard, the drive erases. This man knows about such systems; he's concerned about timing.

She passes him the case and he wisely removes the laptop and returns the case to her. Dulwich stands. Other people in the lobby are now watching them. The security men—one in front, one behind—walk them to the elevator. They are taken to the mezzanine level and shown into an unimpressive office that has gone too long without a spring cleaning.

Dulwich and Grace take seats in uncomfortable chairs

while the one who has done all the talking walks around
and takes his place behind the desk. More troubling: the
second man stands behind Grace and Dulwich with his
back to the door. They aren't going anywhere.

The man behind the desk spins the laptop toward
Grace and says, "Password, please."

"No, thank you." Resistance now may offer her useful
information. She wants to see what's coming, knows how
important her anticipation is right now, but also doesn't
want to appear too willing.

"If you have not read the terms of our agreement," he
says, rifling a drawer, then another, "I can provide one."
He produces a printed copy of the three-page agreement.
The clause he points to is already highlighted in yellow:
Users grant the hotel access to their hardware and software. His eyebrows arched, he awaits her. "Any violation
of this agreement can result in criminal prosecution." He
leans forward and turns to the last page, stabs the penul-
timate paragraph.

Confiscating a business person's laptop could put the
hotel in a serious PR jam. But short of confiscating, how
does he hope to download the laptop's contents, a process
that could take an hour or more? Perhaps the plan is to
gain access to the machine and then spend at least an hour
in discussions. Maybe the man standing behind them is
a runner to be handed the machine the moment it's
unlocked.

"I have done nothing wrong," she says, playing her
role well.

"Perfect. Then enter your password, please—as required by the agreement—and let's have a look. You'll be gone within minutes," he says, an intimidating and insincere snarl overtaking his lips.

It's the "criminal prosecution" that's ringing in her ears. Dulwich's, too, judging by the look of him. If she fails to supply the password, they can, and presumably will, call the police. Whoever's behind the cyber attack on her machine knows this. The man speaking to her may only be doing his job, unaware he's part of someone else's plan; or he may be on the take, and part of it. All this is going through her head as she places her hands on the keyboard and enters the password.

"Thank you," the man says. He places a one-page agreement before her, writing the time of day as 20:16. The agreement grants the hotel the right to search the laptop and establishes what files were part of the machine when confiscated. She doesn't like the way this is going.

"I will now call up the most recent activity." He angles the laptop so that she can observe his actions.

Dulwich can't see and makes no attempt to join Grace, his attention instead on the man guarding the door. The vein in Dulwich's forehead is pronounced. His breathing is deep and controlled.

Oh, shit, she nearly blurts out, but holds herself back. The equal-sized data packets make sense now. She should have guessed their content by their size: Images. JPEGs.

Her computer screen fills with a photograph of a

girl—a naked girl no older than ten—touching herself. Grace's stomach lurches and she nearly vomits.

"It is *chilly* in here," she gags out, looking at Dulwich.

Her use of the safe word triggers an explosion of energy. Dulwich stands, bringing the chair he was sitting in up over his back, and plants it into the man at the door. Grace scoops a desk stapler up in her left hand and delivers it full force into the temple of the man behind the desk. She vaults the desk on her side, clearing the desktop, and careens into the lap of the stunned and bleeding security man. The bridge of his nose is crushed with the second blow from the stapler. She wedges her hand into his throat as together they ride the chair over backward. She drives his head down hard onto the thin carpet. It strikes with a thud and he's unconscious.

Dulwich has a bloody lip and a scratched cheek but his opponent is curled up in a fetal position and groaning. He kicks him twice to move him out of the way of the door. Grace grabs up the laptop before following Dulwich into the mezzanine.

"What the hell?" Dulwich says.

"Porn," Grace says. "Child porn dumped onto my machine so I could be arrested."

"Shit." Dulwich skids to a stop outside the door to the stairs. "Wait here." He can move well despite the leg when he wants to. He returns only seconds later with an employee ID card and lanyard in hand.

"Security cameras," he tells her. "We're all over them."

Grace now assumes hotel security was alerted to

porn-casters using their lobby's free Internet. The purpose
was to get Dulwich and Grace arrested by Amsterdam
police, to take Grace out of the sweatshop business while
learning as much about her and her financing as possible.

The hotel security footage represents their arrest.

A limping Dulwich leads the way down the hotel fire
stairs to the basement. She has spent a limited amount of
time with him in the field. She could easily take the lead—
his bad leg is a hindrance—but there's an alpha dog air
about him that cautions her.

From the back, Dulwich's thick neck and massive
shoulders intimidate. She has forgotten who this man is,
the past he comes from. His soft gray eyes and unrespon-
sive face belie the reality. She has been lulled into an
opinion of him that's shattered as she follows. He's a wolf
on a scent. The most she can hope for is to pick up a few
scraps.

He never checks to see if she follows; he doesn't care.
He whips the bad leg ahead of him, hurrying down the
bright, subterranean corridor, out to prove something.
To himself? To her? To others?

She can't figure out how he knows his way until she
realizes his upward head motion isn't part of dealing with
the leg. The ceiling holds metal brackets supporting dozens
of blue Ethernet wires, round black cables and phone lines.
They turn and terminate at the door he now stands before.
He slides the ID card into the door's mechanism; the
doorplate beeps, and a red light turns green. Dulwich pockets the card and leans against the door's lever handle.

He dispatches a middle-aged woman sitting before a

rack of flat-screen monitors by kicking her chair into the countertop and slamming her head down from behind. She's out. A second man, coming out of his chair, drops an iPad as Dulwich backhand-chops him in the throat, elbows him in the chest and throws him to the floor. No more than five seconds have passed.

"Thumb drives, hard drives, DVDs," he says. He must be talking to her, though he doesn't look in her direction. "Here!" He grabs the unconscious woman's purse, upends it, dumping its contents, and passes it to Grace. "Everything. Nothing left behind." He starts ripping Ethernet cables at random, concerned there may be a cloud backup in place. She's never considered him much of a techie, but Dulwich works methodically through the chilly room at a feverish pace, stripping it of any memory capability. They confiscate a dozen thumb drives, thirty DVDs and half that many freestanding external drives. Ninety seconds after they've entered, they're out in the hallway.

Five meters from the corridor's exit sign, the door beneath pops open. A black-suited security man with a shaved head and quick eyes emerges. He's outwardly suspicious of these two strangers, but forges a smile as he and Dulwich pass shoulder to shoulder. Dulwich stops at the elevator and slaps the wall button.

The security man continues toward the office. Ten meters . . . five . . .

Dulwich waits for the elevator. Grace can't believe this decision. It's costing them precious time. Worse, she has no doubt the elevator can be controlled from the security office.

The chirp of the door to the security office rings out. The man depresses the lever.

Dulwich darts across the corridor to the stairs as the elevator dings its arrival, Grace close on his heels. The leg is far more difficult to maneuver while climbing. Had he wanted to take the elevator, or was it only a ruse?

"How many on duty?" he says, rounding the first landing toward the lobby level.

"Six," she says.

"Correct."

In a bank of ten walkie-talkie chargers, five radios are missing. The woman dispatcher who won't leave the office accounts for the sixth employee.

"Four down," Grace says, "and the one we just passed, leaves one. Possibly more depending on the condition of the first two."

"Give me that!" He grabs the security woman's purse from her. Stuffs various pockets with samples of its contents. Returns it to her. "We separate from here. Rendezvous at Wing Kee on Zeedijk. One hour. You take the lobby."

"You've got the lobby," she says stubbornly. The leg will slow him down. The lobby is the quickest way to the street. She pulls the door open for him, and snags the ID card from his hand, balling up its lanyard in her fist.

He's about to object.

"One hour," she says, then nudges him and closes the door behind him. She climbs to the mezzanine level, where the ballrooms are letting out. She mixes into the crowd and leaves with others ten minutes later, walking within an arm's reach of the security man she'd passed in the basement who stands a sentry surveilling the crowd. His eyes go right past her. He'd locked in on the alpha dog.

For once, Grace doesn't mind being an afterthought.

27

The Taschenmuseum Hendrikje protects them from prying eyes. Unlike the tourist-jammed Van Gogh, here is a small museum dedicated to bags and purses. It is visited only by women on this day, tourists speaking everything from German to Urdu. Knox and Sonia occupy a padded bench in front of the case of jeweled clutches.

The map forwarded to Knox's iPhone by the Hong Kong office of Rutherford Risk shows dozens of small blue pins, each representing where Maja's "father," Mert Demir, remained in any one place for over five minutes. The pins are time-stamped and address-stamped and, if a business, listed by company name. What's readily apparent, and what is the focus of the e-mail message accompanying the map, is that huge chunks of time are unaccounted for, sometimes hours at a time. Time spent in the knot shop, Knox assumes. Time the man's phone has been turned off and/or its SIM card removed.

"Where did you get this?" Sonia asks.

"Yeah, right!" Knox has slipped up in his enthusiasm to share the data. "And you're going to reveal all your sources, I suppose?"

"I am a journalist."

"And I'm not, because I make pictures instead of sentences?" He waits, but she isn't going to let him off. "Okay." He vamps. "I have a friend very high up at the BBC. He/she has contacts in agencies that end with numbers. That's as much as you get."

Her eyes soften from outright distrust to vague suspicion.

As he studies the map, several things jump out.

First, the repetition. Patterns are schooled out of undercover cops and covert agents. Walk a different path every day in the woods and the hunter doesn't know where to lay his trap. Walk the same path, and you put your foot in it. Yet Demir—the name listed with the school and therefore most likely an alias—frequents a particular lunch spot, a smoke shop and a brown café close to downtown.

Second is the gaping hole left in the map by the *absence* of pins. The Hong Kong office has explained that the international carrier purges location data to storage in seventy-two-hour time spans. The data Knox is looking at represents the most recently stored seventy-two hours and includes a pin at the school, confirming its accuracy. Hong Kong is working on retrieving the archival information but is not hopeful.

"What's interesting," Knox tells Sonia, who's tucked in close to him to view his phone's screen, "is this area here. A whole section of the city he avoids."

"Or a zone where he pulls his phone's chip in order to keep himself off of the radar." She blushes. "But you already knew that."

"We have to consider it an area of interest."

"It is not small."

"No, it's not."

"We cannot go door-to-door hoping to find a knot shop."

"No. But we can watch for young girls walking alone."

"And get them killed? Like Maja?"

"They watch for people following the girls, not people in wait. It's like setting a tail from in front—impossible to detect."

"A photographer knows this, how?"

"I watch a lot of movies. Read a lot of books." He's too flip by a long shot.

She disapproves. "We are not putting the girls at risk."

"We know they walk to the shop on their own. We spend a day or two, early in the morning, watching from a coffee shop window for a young girl alone. No harm, no foul."

"The only way to see where they go is to follow them."

"You know leapfrog? We play leapfrog. You take her. I take her. We pass her off to each other. Difficult if not impossible to pick up on."

"No, John. No more girls go missing."

"Then it's Brower," he says, hoping to change her

mind. "It's us, or it's Brower. And he'll take some convincing, I would imagine."

"We get nothing out of Demir's arrest." She sounds frustrated and irritable, a different woman from that of the night before when the towel had come off. When the inhibitions had been dropped and the alcohol had inflamed another Sonia.

"We have two possible lines of pursuit: the girls, and Demir. If you're ruling out the girls, then it's down to Demir, and trust me, you and I are not going to handle a guy like that. If we do, it won't be anything you can write about. It's called persuasion by force. You wouldn't like it." He waits for her to school him. She does not. Instead, she seems to pull away. "Which leaves the police, because they're good with people like him. They know exactly what to do, which buttons to push. If we feed him to Brower, Brower owes us. We can bargain up front what we get in return. Maybe you get in on Demir's interrogation—"

"Never happen. Not the KLPD, not Brower."

"You know him?"

"Of course I know him. I'm a reporter here. I know everyone!"

"You never said anything."

"No." She lets that settle, wanting to drive home a point. "Joshua Brower is a climber. If he is working with you, it's because it helps him, nothing more. He is not to be trusted."

"He'll owe me for this." She huffs. "Maybe you observe the interview."

A pair of American grandmothers draws too close.

Knox stands and leads Sonia away to a display of shoulder bags.

He says, "We don't give him Demir without participation." He keeps his voice low. "Once we get past twenty-four hours, all bets are off for our friend. We act now. The girls, or Brower . . ."

Her eyes fill with distrust once again. Dulwich's warning hits home: it's doomed to fall apart. Grace's bugging Kreiger's laptop or the attack on her computer had better deliver. They need results. He needs to connect with Grace.

He's losing Sonia.

"I'll make the call," he says.

28

Having hacked Kreiger's laptop and its built-in camera, Grace watches as her computer screen plays live images of the man at his desk. She turns the laptop to Knox.

On the screen, Gerhardt Kreiger leans back in his desk chair. His necktie is loosened, and he's smoking either a hand-rolled cigarette or a joint. His left hand is held to his jaw, suggesting a mobile phone. He speaks in heavily accented English.

"It's me . . . Ya . . . Two? This is good. Send them, please." The "please" is an afterthought, a courtesy with zero conviction. "As to that other thing: yes, or no? It's a big order. I thought you would want that. My customer is . . . anxious. No more dicking around, okay? Just give me a yes or no . . . Do you honestly think—? I've done business with him many times. He is for real . . . Just yes or no. A price and a date . . . I have no idea what you're talking about. This is your problem, not mine . . . Okay, I'll tell him. As to the two, I will get back to you when I have an offer. Send me the pictures. *Ciao*."

Grace aims her laptop's screen at herself, steering it away from Knox, whose head is spinning from what he's heard. He chose the meeting place, a wine bar on Keizersgracht open well past midnight. The atmosphere inside is controlled drunkenness, a notch or two above that of a brown café.

"It may be possible for us—the office in Hong Kong— to get his phone records. If so, we will be able to identify the number he called. You get the point. We may have the dog by the tail. Short term it is a different story. I have been data-mining Kreiger's laptop. One of the problems with machines like his is the large capacity of hard drives. Eighty gigs. Three hundred gigs. Could take months to read everything. So I focus on three components." Grace sees Knox's eyes glaze over and wonders if she's causing his condition or if it's the beer. She can see he's not sleeping well, if at all. Wants to ask about the reporter, but she confines herself to her domain. She's warming behind the effects of red wine.

"First," she says, continuing, "e-mails, of course. Second, browser history. Finally, off-Web social media: Skype, iChat, SMS messaging. Each represents a specialized activity and offers unique information and insight." She can't stop herself from sounding like a technical

manual. Knox rocks his beer side to side, watching the
bubbles surface. "Eighteen minutes after this call, he
receives an e-mail." She angles the screen only slightly,
not sure he cares to look. Senses he'd rather be told than
participate. Wonders if his distraction is purely fatigue, or
is the reporter involved? "Two attachments. Photos, just
as he requested." She displays the photos side by side.

Now Knox is looking. "He said to—"

"Send them. Yes. 'Two,' he said. Then, at the end, he
said he would get back to him about *the two* after he has
an offer."

The screen shows the glum faces of two young girls.
She waits for Knox to find his breath, knows what he's
going through. The girl on the right is Berna. The like-
ness isn't perfect, whether the result of lighting or angle,
or her swollen right cheek, but it's Berna. Grace waits
him out.

"Less than five minutes later . . ." She types and moves
the cursor. "It's a social networking photo site called
Shutter Shot. He has it administered under password-only
access."

"He posted the girls' photos onto the Internet."

"Here's his scrapbook." She pages through several
screens of one, two or three girls' faces. Some are in their
late teens, early twenties, but the majority are just children. The names are fake, given that Berna is captioned
as Cindy.

"If there's more of a connection," Grace says, "I have
not yet found it."

"More? Berna's alive! They're posting her for sale. She's alive!" he repeats.

"Bidding," she says. "Your Mr. Kreiger is selling the girls, John."

He turns away from her use of "your."

"From what I can tell," she says, "there are only seven people able to access this scrapbook. The ISPs for all seven are distributed among Thailand, Indonesia and Russia."

Knox shakes his head. Over the past year she has seen Knox display any number of emotions—he's not shy when it comes to expressing his feelings. But never like this. The closest was a minute before they entered Natuurhonig. He doesn't speak what he's thinking.

"Not yet," she cautions. "Your Mr. Kreiger is useful to us."

"Stop calling him mine."

"Strangely enough, the phone call . . . his subsequent actions suggest he may not be directly involved in the knot shop. Just tangentially profiting by agenting their rugs and selling the castoffs. Berna is a liability. They mean to get her out of the city. We can be thankful they apparently have no plans to kill the girls."

"They might be better off," he says.

"No, John. You must not think so. As bad as this is, they can heal. They will heal."

"You can't know that. None of us know that."

"Our focus," she says strongly, "must remain on our objective. We will shut them down. I am not suggesting we overlook the more immediate concern for the well-being of the girls, but we must not allow ourselves to be distracted. One hand washes the other. We are close now." She hears herself sound so clinical.

She has lost Knox. He's retreated inside himself.

"Pressing Kreiger for information could backfire for a number of reasons."

"Who said anything about pressing?"

"First, he may not know the identity of the person who called. Second, even should he know this person's identity, he may be used as a firewall: by the time he gives us what we are after, the person is long gone. We do not know the structure of their defenses."

Knox broods, ready to take this out on her.

"My suggestion would be to monitor Kreiger closely. I am privy to all of his communications. If we learn of more dealings with the girls, of course we act. Presently, we continue to close in on the knot shop. Ultimately, getting Kreiger will not contribute to the endgame. It may, in fact, prevent it."

"Shut up. Spare me the 'Human Trafficking for Dummies' speech, would you? Jesus! Listen to you! Is there a human being anywhere inside there?" He glares. He seems ready to strike her.

It is as if he has pulled the batteries out of her. Grace the robot winds down. Her eyes flicker once and shut tightly. She fights back the need to cry; she will not give him that.

"I'm sorry. That was . . . I didn't mean that. I'm upset." She manages to nod.

"Seriously. I didn't mean—"

"The next step," she chokes out, clearing her throat, "is to trace the e-mail containing the photos—"

"An underling," Knox says. "You don't actually believe this guy would be sending the photos himself?"

"The routing may help us. They could have been taken with a mobile phone, for instance."

"So?"

"So that would do it. With Hong Kong's help, that might do it. Might lead us back to the nest."

"The older girls?" Knox asks.

"One would assume it has to do with what we saw at the coffee shop. Kreiger's stable at Natuurhonig. Perhaps we have it wrong about Kreiger."

"He's not putting them up for adoption," Knox says cynically.

"They are experienced labor. We don't know absolutely that they are destined for the sex trade. Perhaps we have that wrong."

"Yeah. When are you ever wrong?" He intends it as a compliment, but it stings her just the same. Runs his hand through his hair. Upends the beer and gulps.

She lays a hand on his forearm, having no idea why she's doing so. "It is progress, John. Think of it as progress."

He looks down at her hand and she removes it.

Knox isn't ten meters out of the wine bar when he hears, "I'll take my phone."

It's Sonia's voice.

Grace stops and turns to glance back but is smart enough to keep walking.

Knox doesn't move, his mind on damage control. He processes Sonia's request. There are a dozen things bad about this. No good can come of it.

He pats the various internal pockets of the Scottevest, realizing that she beat him fair and square—which makes it all the more humiliating. He finds her iPhone zippered into one of his many pockets.

"I underestimated you," he says. He underestimated the slyness of the wily reporter. Was sucked in by their intimacy and partnership, something that clearly escaped her.

At the purse museum she must have slipped her phone into Knox's jacket. She then used its lost-phone app to follow him to the wine bar. She has observed him with another woman, and she will know by the way they interacted it was not romantic, but professional. That has triggered a dozen alarms in her.

"Have you interviewed her already? Is that it?" he asks. The one way he can see clearly to get around this.

"My phone." Her hand extends. She's not taking the bait.

By doing so, she gives him his hold on her. He grabs the phone more tightly.

"That was clever of you." He wags the phone.

Her hand begins to tremble. Nerves, or fatigue? "Please."

"The woman—this woman—has replaced the murdered EU worker." He pauses. "That's why I thought you might have already interviewed her."

Her eyes twitch—at least he has her thinking.

"She has been nosing around herself. Has heard of

someone who's come in trying to make competition for these guys. Have you heard about that?"

"I'm not going to fight you for it. You're a pig."

"Interview her yourself!"

She gives him her backside.

He calls out. "Here!" He extends the bait, hoping to lure her back.

Her disgust calves off her. She can't look at him.

"What you're thinking; it's not right."

"Shut it." She reaches for the phone and he acquiesces. She slips it into her purse. "You could have told me the truth the first time."

"I am *not* a cop."

"You . . . and I . . ."

"Sonia—"

Her eyes glaze over. She purses her lips, shakes her head, discouraged. "Shit."

"You're at risk. I can protect you."

"You probably arranged all that, didn't you? Set me up so I needed you."

"Not true."

"I thought I'd seen it all."

"You're at risk!"

"You're a liar."

And she's gone. Words dance on the tip of his tongue, words he must swallow. She turns back. "If I see you . . . at any distance, I will have you arrested—if that is even possible."

He lets her go. As long as her phone is left on, Hong Kong can, and will, track her. He arranges it with a call to Dulwich, who, in a rare moment of compassion, doesn't rub it in. It's Dulwich's lack of condemnation that leaves the taste of crow. But there are other tastes that linger as well, ones he savored and is sorry to lose. He wants her back. Wants the knot shop closed down, Berna found and peace restored. A week with Sonia in Berlin or Bruges.

She'll go to the houseboat and clear out what few belongings she'd collected. Or maybe she'll avoid it altogether. If she returns to her apartment, he'll have to intervene, but he assumes she'll have the sense to find another houseboat, or a friend's place.

He is reminded that women bring a heavy heart, that he avoids investment because he can't tolerate the interest. That the weight of Tommy can't handle any more piling on. That he knows better. But Sonia's gotten to him. He pays for it in anger and frustration and shame. A self-loathing and self-pity that wells up in him like a toxin. He is poisoned. God help the next person to cross him.

He finds a bar and rediscovers single-malt amnesia. Anesthetized, he works through his phone chips, checking for messages.

"We should meet." Kreiger's heavily accented voice does not identify itself. Just the three words, but in an assertive tone that implies paragraphs. Knox knows too much because of Grace; he's reading too much into it. Impatience, determination, suspicion. He cycles out that chip, replacing it with the original. How long has it been? Five minutes? Thirty? But as the next SIM card logs on to the Dutch mobile carrier, there's already a message waiting.

The number is "UNKNOWN."

He slurps another Scotch down. Scarfs some bar nuts and chases it all with a beer. It's all so easy now—his throat doesn't fight it. An elixir. It pulls an opaque curtain across the past few hours, adds a dash of humor where none was possible. It allows him to acknowledge the babe at the end of the bar who makes eyes every few minutes. Doesn't know why he does it. Can't figure out who's doing this from inside him. He's possessed. He can blame it on the Scotch. He can blame it on Sonia. But he knows better.

The babe isn't interested, adding insult to injury. Or maybe she's on the meter and figures him light in the wallet. No matter.

Can't bring himself to retrieve the message. It's either Dulwich or Sonia. Painful, no matter what. But Tommy and Daniel have this number as well as others. It can't be ignored. He touches his shot glass, ordering number five. He's a big boy, he tells himself; he can handle it. He and everyone else leaning over the bar barely moving.

"For what it is worth," says the recorded male voice, *"I did not expose you. Out of professional courtesy. She is a celebrity here. You must know that. It was not so difficult to make sense of it, Mr. Steele, but you might have—"*

Knox hears nothing past the mention of his cover. It's Chief Inspector Brower's voice. Only now does it register. It's the confluence of two worlds, a *Twilight Zone* moment. Only Sonia calls him by that name. *She is a celebrity here . . .*

He drags the iPhone's blue time line back to listen again. *"—you might have warned me. I allowed her to monitor the interview of Demir. Unseen, of course. One-way glass. Her taking off like that. Most unprofessional. I expected some courtesy. I believe we had an agreement to work together, did we not? I would appreciate your sharing whatever it was he said that triggered that hasty departure. I believe you owe me that much. I am on the graveyard. Call me. Please."*

He bumps the Scotch, nearly spilling it, while going for his wallet. "How much?" In Dutch. The single malt is insanely expensive. He overtips the moment he sees the first of the five shots ring up on the register. Does the math in his head. Is out the door.

The bitch! The Scotch speaking. The Scotch working at his temples and his knees like an invisible kickboxer. Calls Brower back. Demir's interview was videoed. He's on his way.

Risks a series of trams. Feels a million eyes on him. Wonders how much is the liquor. Breaks his own rules. Hopes she has more sense than he.

Calls her from the third tram. It goes straight to voice mail. Calls Dulwich.

"I need a real-time fix on her, pronto. Code red, Sarge."

"Copy."

The call ends, Knox marveling at Dulwich's self-control, his not throwing a punch. Dulwich is the closest thing he has to a real friend, which is somewhat depressing. He fits Grace into that equation, but doesn't know how to assign value. She's more of a fixed variable. Dulwich is the common denominator.

Middle of the third tram ride, his phone vibrates.

"No joy," Dulwich says. "Device is disengaged or destroyed. No signal."

Disengaged, Knox thinks, ruminating on the word . . . *or destroyed*. Sonia is AWOL.

"On my way to Brower," Knox explains. "He may have something for us." He holds back from admitting the reporter has scooped him.

"Progress here," Dulwich says.

"Keep trying, will you?"

"You'll hear if I do."

Knox tucks the phone away. Takes a moment to look out a window. Catches his agonized reflection in the glass. Turns away from it.

BROWER COOPERATES, suggesting he's expecting a quid pro quo. It tells Knox that Demir's interview was inconclusive and that whatever drove Sonia from oversight of the interview is now the carrot they both seek.

Knox buries the ask, out of gamesmanship. No way Brower is giving him everything.

Finally, the opportunity comes around. "Maybe if I saw the interview tape . . . ?" Knox says.

"But I tell you, there is nothing. *Pfff.* I am preparing to begin the interrogation, and there is one of my men asking for her recorder back."

"Her recorder," Knox echoes.

"Exactly that," Brower concedes. "I never claimed to

know how to run the damn thing. Every one of them is different. Is it not so?"

"Every recorder," Knox tests.

"I had barely turned the thing on and she wants it back!"

"Could I see?"

"I tell you, there is nothing to see."

Knox is capable of being belligerent. Would rather not take it that far. Is warming up to it as Brower shrugs.

"Why not?"

The room smells of a cigarette veneer mixed with the acrid bitterness of electronics. Contrary to the state-of-the-art resources available to Rutherford Risk, this looks like a high school language lab. The video is low definition, though the sound quality is above average.

Demir occupies a fixed chair with his hands cuffed to a chain between his legs. Given that pose, he's doing everything possible to look bored and in control, but it's a losing effort. The chains rattle; he lets go two deep sighs as he works to calm himself.

"He's been coached, or he's been through this before," Knox says.

"Evidently."

"Does he have a record?"

"Not within the EU." Brower adds, "We are checking outside, including your FBI."

On the screen, the door opens. Demir is careful not to change his demeanor even slightly; he stares straight ahead like a man stuck in a long waiting line. Brower enters and sits down. He reads the suspect some legalese that pertains to his rights, pointing out that video and audio will be recorded and may be used as evidence. He slaps down a legal pad and proffers a Crayon.

Next, he withdraws a device from his pocket.

"Is that—?"

"I tape all my interviews. We . . . our department . . . has experienced some misfiling of certain interrogation recordings."

"Permanent misfilings?"

Brower doesn't answer.

On the video, Brower studies the device and works its buttons. The digital recorder plays instead of records. A male is heard speaking. The voice continues from the device as Brower works to stop it from playing.

"Damn thing," Brower says to Knox. "Buttons meant for a child!"

On screen, the recorded voice stops. Brower places the device onto the table.

"State your name and age, please," Brower says to Demir.

The interview door swings open. Sonia comes through the door, a female officer a step behind. Sonia leans in to Brower and whispers. He motions his officer away—clearly annoyed by the interruption—then whispers back to Sonia.

"She asked me who was on the device," he tells Knox.

"And you told her . . . ?"

Brower pauses the video.

On the screen is Sonia looking into the camera. Directly at Knox.

"What did you tell her?" Knox repeats.

"Kahil Fahiz," Brower says. "It was the interview with Fahiz following the assault. I didn't conduct the session, but following your and my initial conversation, I asked for a dub in order to study it."

"Could you play the video again, please?"

They watch it again.

The suspect Mert Demir's reaction is unmistakable. Upon hearing the voice his face fills with alarm. He is wide-eyed. He forces himself to recover from the shock, but it's too late.

A lie is the first thing to find Knox's tongue. But he swallows it. Brower is an asset, a friend of Dulwich's.

"Watch Demir," he advises. Brower plays the bit again.

"He knows that voice," Brower says, finally seeing what first Sonia and now Knox have. "He's afraid of Fahiz."

"Because Fahiz is actually—"

"*Kloten!*" Brower curses.

"The voice is completely unexpected by Demir. It paralyzes him." Knox pieces together the story. "Fahiz's guys find and punish the EU worker, killing him with the car bomb, hoping his death is taken as politics as usual. They can't find Sonia's other sources to teach them a lesson. But Fahiz has serious stones: he walks into your cop shop playing the victim to try to find out how much you know. If anything should connect back to him in the future, you'll doubt your findings—he's a victim, after all."

"He was assaulted! I've seen the photographs!"

"Was he?"

Brower is already typing on an adjacent keyboard. Fahiz's face appears, showing his injuries in three images.

Looking beyond the cuts and abrasions, Knox leans in and points out a curving bruise across the man's forehead.

"Wiekser!" roars Brower.

"That bruise is from a steering wheel," Knox says.

"First-year constables! They process this shit and don't pay a damn bit of attention to what it is they are looking at."

"He wrecked a car and saw it as an opportunity to introduce himself to you guys." Knox hesitates.

Brower says, "The sack on this guy!"

"He's a psych case." Knox blurts out without thinking, "Sonia's going after him." At the same time he's thinking there's a report sheet of traffic accidents on or before the date Fahiz filed the assault. That one of those accidents will tie directly to the man they're calling Fahiz. Brower has access to that information, but the excited look in Brower's eyes says not to ask. Knox doesn't want to give the man a head start.

"If we are to arrest him, I need more than Demir's look of surprise. We must locate him. Put him under surveillance. Build a case."

Knox has lost the ability to track her iPhone. She's responded to none of his messages. But maybe not Fahiz. Grace has a phone number the man answered, a SIM card from Singapore.

Brower clearly wants Fahiz for himself. He'll interrogate Demir for a second time as soon as Knox has gone.

There will be additional threats and plea bargaining incentives. If Demir plays along, Brower will jump ahead of Knox with little or no consideration of Sonia.

Knox feels himself being sucked down the drain.

He's afraid Sonia has already beaten him to it.

29

The call from the real estate agent is anything but reassuring. The woman has found a couple of properties that Grace "should see." Given that Grace has pressured the vendor, Marta, for a list of possible girls, has hacked Kreiger's laptop, and has downloaded the vitals from the computer that hacked hers, she's aware it could be a trap.

Knox sends the text message:

sit tight. on way

She has a decision to make. Knox's situation is radically different from her own; in the world of Rutherford Risk, initiative is capital. If she's to be rewarded with future fieldwork—with or without Knox—it will be because she has taken initiative while remaining part of a group. It's a fine line to walk. Dulwich's impressions and recommendation are critical. The very nature of Knox's text implies urgency; she can feel him about to influence the direction of the assignment.

The sleeping tiger never eats.

"We have an appointment," she tells Dulwich over her mobile. Like an obedient driver, he spends much of his time behind the seat of a rented Audi or Mercedes in the hotel's parking lot while on his BlackBerry. She explains the realtor's call.

"I'll pull around front."

She saw no indication the text had been sent to both of them. Dulwich's failure to mention it can mean several things, none of which matters to her once he agrees to drive her. Dulwich has his own master plan.

"What about the computers?" he asks from behind the wheel.

"I have enough to attempt to hack them. Kamat narrowed down the router location to a ten-block area."

"Still too big."

"Yes, but the smallest yet. We're closing in. If I ping the router, we will have it much narrower, but a ping would be detected. No way around that. We would have a matter of minutes. No more."

It has been the worry since the firewall breach from the hotel lobby. Any attempt on her part to reconnect could scare the rats from the den. It is a time for prudent decision-making.

"That could play into our favor."

"Agreed."

"The photos? The porn?"

"Carry a digital ID, yes, but unfortunately not a phone. Taken with a Canon PowerShot. Kamat is working a long shot."

"Which is?"

"Both photos were taken with the same camera—same digital tag in the code. If the camera happens to be under warranty . . ."

"Seriously? The camera is hot. Count on it."

"If Canon will cooperate, or if Hong Kong can hack their warranty database, we might come away with his full contact info."

"I wouldn't count on it meaning anything."

"I register all my gear."

"As do I."

"Something to think about from now on."

"If I go into the porn business," Dulwich says.

They're a good ten minutes from the hotel when she says, "John just texted for us to 'sit tight.'" She pauses to see if he calls her out. "He is en route to the hotel, I believe."

"Tell him to sit tight himself. We'll be, what? An hour? Two, at most." Dulwich reconsiders. "Better yet, text him the address of the meet. Tell him I need him as backup, ASAP."

"Yes." She doesn't dare go counter to Dulwich's instructions, though for a moment her fingers hover over the phone's screen without touching it.

The invitation to view the real estate could be an attempt on her life, an attempt to steal her laptop, an attempt to raid her hotel room while she's away. It might be used as a chance to photograph her, or the car, or Dulwich.

Her driver pops gum into his mouth and begins chewing furiously. She doesn't often see Dulwich nervous.

"Do you want to walk through this?" she asks.

"You keep your phone on and the line open so I can hear. What more is there to discuss? If we can wait for Knox we improve our odds—and then some." Dulwich has on several occasions referred to Knox by the name of a popular sitcom: *Two and a Half Men*. There's a seed of truth behind the jab, and all three know it.

"I doubt that will be possible." She would rather do this herself. Knox has a way of sucking the air out of a room.

"You can stall her. Ask long-winded questions that demand long-winded answers. Realtors love to sell. Let her do her job."

"I refuse to believe this woman could in any way be tied to our principals."

"She doesn't have to be. It could be a coworker. Another realtor who's heard what you're looking for. You did everything but tell this woman you were setting up a sweatshop. It won't take a genius."

"I suppose."

"Your street market pal could have gotten the ball rolling. Your beating the shit out of that guy may come back to haunt us. If you're looking for child labor, you need a place to use it. It's all a piece of the same pie." He adds, "Remember, by your own admission, these mothers, people in these neighborhoods, *rely* on the knot shop. If you go into this meeting expecting trouble, you might just come out of it."

She didn't need that. She wants to tell him so. Maybe her silence does.

THE PLUS-SIZED REALTOR WEARS a matronly wool outfit again despite the fact that the day doesn't demand it. A warm front has moved in; it's bearable outside and in. One look at the woman's clammy complexion and darting eyes puts Grace on alert and wishing she could send Dulwich a warning without invoking the safe word.

There are too many possibilities: from the benign to the overt. Grace is out on the ice and hears it cracking.

"Impressive," Grace says, after the usual pleasantries.

The cellar space is large, supported by steel posts. The glow is from tube lighting; there's no natural light. Grace walks the perimeter of the room while the realtor babbles, exactly as Dulwich anticipated. Grace is looking for the best defensive positions. No natural light means no windows; no escape routes beyond the two doors, one on either end. She's trapped, and judging from the realtor's anxiety, it's to be more than a photo or eavesdropping session.

"Only the two doors," she says, for Dulwich's ears.

"I understood you were looking for privacy."

"Absolutely. And where does this second door lead?"

"You expressed interest in access away from busy

streets. This door leads to a common parking area behind the building."

"Excellent!"

"Yes, I thought it fit your needs quite nicely."

"Proximity to a tram line is a potential problem," Grace says. "But more to the point is the apparent absence of toilets, running water and heating. I am not running a sweatshop, you know? It's to be an artists' work space. It must be habitable."

On the off chance she's being listened to by people other than Dulwich, she has thrown out this treat.

"The landlord is amenable to negotiate improvements, providing—"

"He is aware it is to be month-to-month?"

"Well . . . I thought, perhaps . . . That is . . . allow me to show you around before we discuss too much detail."

If she had any sense, she would mop her brow. It's not the wool suit or hormones causing her to overheat.

"Very well."

"The parking. Please." She motions to the second door.

Grace holds her ground, studying the exposed ceiling with its pipes and conduits. "You have to admit it's *chilly* in here."

"I find it quite pleasant," the realtor answers.

"If I may say so," Grace says, "you look warm. Are you not feeling well?"

She has given Dulwich as much as possible. She allows the realtor to open the door, revealing concrete steps leading up into darkness. The realtor nervously tries a light switch.

"Oh, I am terribly sorry!" the woman says. "The light appears to be out. *I will lead the way.* Please follow me."

The woman could not be a worse actor. It doesn't merit a high school performance.

"That is all right. I would like to see the exterior of the building anyway. I will meet you around back."

Grace moves with deceptive speed toward the original entrance. It's impossible to predict Dulwich's reaction to her having spoken the safe word. He might be about to come through that same door, or he may have pulled the car into the back lot. As she's five strides from the door, she hears them coming for her. *Two or three of them,* she thinks, not looking back. Stealthy, and well trained, already fanning out to surround her. *Two,* she decides. She recognizes this as her "be careful what you wish for" moment: her chance to earn herself a field promotion, to be considered more Knox's equal, but it's fraught with risk. She didn't wish this upon herself, but doesn't shy from the knock of opportunity.

The two have closed in on her quickly, both approaching from her blind spots behind. If she turns to see one, she invites assault from the other. They are anticipating her going for the door. The idea is to use their strength and advantage as weakness and vulnerability. Never moving her head, she bounds three strides straight back, splitting them and forcing *them* to turn.

Her target is the nerve running from the knee, up the thigh and into the lower back. She uses her hips, not her leg muscles, to thrust her upraised knee into the sweet spot on one attacker's thigh. Cupping her left hand, she smacks his right ear, disorienting him, then drives the outside of her left elbow into his jaw. His right leg won't move; he's semiconscious and immobilized, though still standing.

Her right hand goes out like a two-fingered claw. She misses his collarbone, connecting instead with the powerful chest of the assailant to the right.

He's fast. Bats her arm away while simultaneously digging his fingers into the flesh of her forearm. She screams involuntarily and drops to her knees, succumbing to the pain.

Grace head-butts his kneecap, cups her right hand and swats his groin.

He curses, knees her in the face, and the lights go out.

The Indonesian in the parking lot jumps back as Knox, aware he's late to the party, hollers in Dutch for him to get out of the way. Up until that moment, the man had been changing a tire on his Nissan. But Knox scares him back, hip-checks the Nissan and knocks it off its jack. Knox grabs the jack like it's a drumstick and marches for the unmarked, black metal door.

He's through the door. Shoves some librarian in a wool suit so hard she flies to the concrete floor a good distance from where she started. She won't be getting up soon.

Grace is over a goon's shoulder like a sack of potatoes. The other one is on his knees doing an imitation of Jerry Lewis seeing stars.

"Stop! Or I kill her."

Knox stops.

"Seriously?" Knox returns in Dutch. "I'm supposed to care? Who the hell is she?" He looks between the two men. "I didn't come for her, asshole. I came for you."

The man dumps Grace off his shoulder while reaching for his back and a concealed weapon. Grace hits hard, headfirst, which results in Knox going all primal. He uses his core to launch the car jack javelin-style, a two-foot spear of Japan's best steel. It flies on a frozen rope and strikes with so much force that Knox hears a crack and a pop. *That would be the ribs and the lung.* The handgun discharges.

Grace's body elevates off the floor two inches like someone lit her up with 220 volts.

The jack clatters to the floor. It has torn a hole in the guy's chest.

His partner tries to stand, but tilts to his right on a numb leg and falls over. Starts crawling toward the back door while going for his own handgun. Knox has the punctured guy's gun. He shoots the crawler twice—two taps, chest and head.

Knox pistol-whips the coughing mess, dropping him. Then kneels next to Grace, his chest tighter than the fallen man's. Feels for a pulse. *Strong.* Her face is a bloody mess, but wiping it off, it's nothing more than a broken nose. He feels down her chest and abdomen for an entrance wound.

"Pervert," she gags.

He hears himself exhale.

"Left leg," she says, her attempt at a smile wiped away before it materializes.

"Another couple inches, you woulda been a nun," Knox says.

The wound is a through-and-through on the inner thigh of her left leg, four inches below her crotch. The bullet is flat on the concrete in an island of flesh and tissue. Not much blood: it missed the femoral artery, which is something of a miracle given how little there is of Grace. He tears open her pants. She tries for modesty, but he slaps her hand away.

"Easy," he says.

The exit wound isn't pretty. The size of a quarter, it's taken a plug out of her.

Dulwich comes through the street-side door, prepared to finish what Knox started. He has the entire picture with one look.

"Can she be moved?"

"Yes," Knox answers.

Dulwich drags the unconscious realtor to inside the darkened stairwell leading to the parking lot.

"There's a guy out back changing a tire," Knox hollers. "Or he was."

"Got it."

Dulwich leaves the realtor in a pile. She'll awaken soon and take off—won't dare head back inside.

Dulwich crosses back and hoists Grace into his arms. He stands.

"Brower?" Knox says. "The shots could have been heard."

"Doubtful. I didn't hear them," Dulwich says. "A big no to Brower. Grace and I are wanted for questioning.

Don't worry about Grace. We have friends who can help her." He turns Grace toward the door he came through. "Put the prints on this guy when you're done with him. Wipe down the jack." By not speaking what is on both their minds, Dulwich has given Knox carte blanche to interrogate the one who shot Grace.

"Thanks," Knox says.

"WHERE AM I?" She speaks Chinese. Corrects herself to English, repeating the question.

Knox answers in Shanghainese. "You will heal."

"Smells like a dentist's office," Grace says.

"She knows what she's doing. Sarge arranged it. She's a legitimate surgeon. And yes, it is a dentist's office. Two to three weeks, you're on your feet again."

"So long?"

"You were very lucky. Could have been far worse."

"We do not have three weeks."

"Not your problem. You need to rest."

"You waited for me to awake," she says. It just comes out of her; she attributes it to the medication.

Knox says nothing at first. He looks at her and smiles. "Wanted to see if you'd cry."

"Sure," she says.

"You didn't," Knox says in the warmest voice he's ever used with her.

"You should go. With all that happened . . . They could pack up and move."

"It's Fahiz." He explains it to her. "They don't know what happened. Not yet. At best they have a pair of men missing."

"What about Ms. Pangarkar?"

Knox winces. She sees deadness in his eyes, a mixture of grief and regret. She wants to ask him to explain, but lacks the strength. "That's a disconnect," he says.

"You must get me my computer. I can help you."

"You need to rest."

She repeats herself. "I am close. More information will be coming from Hong Kong. Between Kreiger and the attack on my laptop . . . You were told of the camera registration?"

"Sarge caught me up."

"I can help. From the bed. As I am."

"We'll move you to a houseboat."

"By now Marta—the street vendor—will have completed her list for me. One of the mothers on that list will take cash for information."

"Good to know."

Knox is not about to go door-to-door. She can hear it, see it. He shot a man. She doesn't dare ask what happened to the man who shot her.

"He was muscle," Knox says. She feels a chill at the coincidence of thought. "The one I shot was a driver. The other guy mentioned a van. A white van. He rode in the back with the girls. They move the girls to a safe house each night. It's on a canal. He didn't know which canal. He was useless."

"Not entirely."

"No, not entirely. He was inside the shop daily. Gave me a decent description. That could help."

She doesn't ask about the outcome of the man he interrogated. She doesn't want to know. As much as she wants the fieldwork, there are places people like Dulwich and Knox will go that she will not. If that disqualifies her, then so be it.

"Is it Pangarkar? What is troubling you?"

He smirks. "What could possibly be troubling me?"

"What is her status, John?"

"AWOL," he says.

"You have every right to be worried."

She has upset him. Whether the drugs, the shock or exhaustion, she feels something she can't decipher.

"My computer," she says.

"Yeah, I got that."

"They will not kill a journalist," she says, the devil's ventriloquist. "We know them to be smart, John." She adds, "She is also smart, eh? This is not to be overlooked."

Dulwich enters. He has been on the phone with Hong Kong continuously.

"We're done here," Dulwich announces.

Knox stands there, paralyzed.

"How can they do that?" Grace asks like a defense attorney.

"The client is satisfied with Brian's decision to turn it over to the Dutch. Given all the data we've collected and our collateral losses," he says, looking down at Grace, "it's the right call."

"Bullshit," Knox says, spittle flying off his lips.

"Of course it's bullshit," Dulwich says, aiming at disarming Knox. "It's the bullshit I'm paid to say, and the bullshit you're paid to do. Happy clients mean more business. This is over. Brian wants us out of here before he has to explain your death to Tommy."

"And you?" Knox says. "What do you want?"

"Don't push it."

"Sonia's in the wind."

"And no one saw that coming."

"Stop." Grace can see the fight about to erupt. She manages to sit up, but the pain is excruciating. The two men face each other like wild boars, paws scraping the dirt. "Time line?"

"Less than twenty-four," Dulwich says, never taking his eyes off Knox. "They're sending the jet. Coming up from Istanbul. Late afternoon. Early evening at the latest."

"We make use of this time," Grace says, concentrating on Knox. "We do not waste it having such arguments."

Knox reminds Dulwich of the promise of backup teams if the case progressed.

Dulwich responds, "What case? The client is satisfied."

"Will he be satisfied when the journalist who started all this is found floating in a canal?"

"She's smarter than that. She'll attack with words."

"Which will require an interview."

"Which he won't give," Dulwich says. "Collaring a guy like this is going to take the Dutch . . . Interpol . . . who the hell knows?"

"She will press this. She has a number he checks."

"We have most of a day," Grace interjects. "We should be planning, not arguing! You two are idiots."

"You don't know her," Knox tells Dulwich, who can barely contain himself.

"Not like you do."

"Will someone please get me my laptop?" Grace hesitates. "Now!"

It breaks the mesmerism. The two men stop the staring contest.

"Late afternoon, early evening," Dulwich repeats.

"We'll see."

30

W ell, that complicates things."

The two men have moved Grace from the surgery to a hostel west of downtown in the Audi. It's a bare-bones backpack establishment with a kid in dreads behind the counter, ten minutes from the KLM Jet Center FBO used by corporate jets.

They've taken a room with a set of bunk beds and an open-shelf dresser that holds a sink basin. The mirror is bolted to the wall. The room is registered under a Dulwich alias.

Grace was carried up a back stairwell by Knox, the limping Dulwich trailing. That Dulwich curses his failure to heal completely goes unspoken. He's boiling over on a daily basis, no more so than at times like this when Knox can do what he cannot.

The door is closed and locked. At Grace's request Knox

has taken ten minutes to splice into a co-ax cable found in the hung ceiling. He seems impressed Grace would know such a cable would be found there, impressed that she understands it will provide them access to the hostel's closed-circuit security cameras.

Dulwich never takes his eyes off the parking area. Knox's iPhone plays Jimi Hendrix from Museeka.com as loud as it will go. It isn't much, but it covers their hushed voices.

Grace has an e-mail from Kamat in Hong Kong. The Canon PowerShot used to photograph Berna and friend for their Internet posting was indeed under warranty, but to a man in Paris—stolen on a trip to Amsterdam six months earlier.

"There is more," she tells them.

Dulwich continues to surreptitiously watch the parking lot. Knox scrapes off a fleck of bloodstain from his water-resistant jacket.

"The model of camera carries geo-tagging."

Both men look over at her sharply. She's propped up in the lower bunk, her laptop open. "The feature was functional at the time the photos were shot, with the coordinates embedded in the code."

Dulwich gasps. "Coordinates?"

"The operator was likely unaware of the feature. Kamat is making every effort to log the chip's usage for the past two months."

"We can follow *a camera*?" Knox asks. Technology is not his long suit.

"We know the approximate location of the girls on the day they were photographed, six days ago."

"Approximate?" Knox asks.

"Geo-tagging is not always perfect. We would be mistaken to kick a door based on these coordinates. That said, we should be within a radius of one hundred meters of where both photos were taken." She spins the laptop toward them. "I have marked the geo-tag with the red star. Please notice it is well outside Demir's mobile usage hole."

Knox marvels how she can sound like a robo-telephone operator.

"One supports the other. The dormitory is nowhere near the knot shop. I believe we can trust the geo-tag," she says.

"It's either the knot shop or the dormitory," Dulwich says.

"Still in a hurry to fasten your seat belt?" Knox asks.

"Shut it," Dulwich responds.

"Boys . . ."

DULWICH DRIVES. The men don't speak two words. Knox rechecks the handgun lifted from the corpse along with a box of self-loads found in the man's front pocket. Dulwich glances at the weapon uncomfortably. Says nothing.

Masts of a great ship appear dead ahead as Valkenburgerstraat nears the tunnel entrance to Noord. The merging of old and new. The car's interior goes dark as they enter the tunnel; the overhead lights strobe against the dash. Still, not a word.

As they emerge, the evening sky is the same endless

pewter it has been for days. Knox catches himself grinding his teeth. Dulwich has previously complained about the sound. Not now. Not today. Knox tries Sonia's mobile for the thousandth time. And for the thousandth time it's out of service. Will she turn to the pen or the sword? Given the mood he last saw her in, he's thinking the latter. He'd assumed she would cool off and reach out to him. He's wrong.

After a mile, they pass woods on the left. The suburbs are giving back to the farmland they were stolen from. Up ahead, low-rise apartment blocks loom like something from the Cold War, juxtaposed by all the vegetation. The Audi slows to a satisfied purr.

"There won't be a neon sign, you know."

Knox doesn't speak.

"Until we know exactly where it is, you could do more harm than good."

Knox connects a wire between his iPhone and the car's stereo. "All the windows down. Play it loud."

"You're dreaming."

"Someone has to." Knox jacks a round into the handgun, clicks out of the seat belt and stuffs the weapon into his lower back.

Dulwich conducts a drive-by. Dozens of four-story apartment complexes crowd Cleyndertweg, all nearly identical, all separated by landscaping screens.

"It's too upscale."

"Not for this city. It's perfect," Knox says. The look of the buildings and the parklike environment support Dulwich, but the apartment density and the older cars parked outside suggest a blue-collar bedroom community with residents who have too little time to pay much attention to the neighbors.

"We're talking ten to fifteen girls. Someone's going to notice!"

Knox says, "We have no idea how many they board. It could be a handful. They're here. Somewhere."

"It lacks a double egress."

"The bike path to the west," Knox says, "and through the trees, more surface streets. They covered themselves well."

Dulwich snorts.

"Drop me at the first parking lot. Don't hit the iPhone until you're alongside the pin." Knox has marked the geo-tagged location on the car's navigation system.

"Yeah, yeah."

"This will work," Knox says.

"You act on this, and it blows up in our face. If word gets back to the knot shop, it's blown."

"Sixes."

"Keep it in your trousers."

"Keep the engine running."

"You can't undo what's done," Dulwich says, throwing salt into the wound of the Sonia breakup.

"Right here," Knox says.

Dulwich pulls over.

KNOX CHOOSES A LINE OF TREES with an unobstructed view down Cleyndertweg. He could stand here for a week and no one would notice him. Dulwich and the Audi roll one block. Two. The car windows open smoothly in unison.

The downloaded singsongy catchy tune plays loudly, sounding like bells and trumpets. Ten or twelve notes that repeat in an obnoxious loop: a call from the most popular ice cream truck company in the city. Dulwich lets it repeat for the length of the block, then shuts it off and turns right at the next intersection.

The geo-tag is tied to an apartment building in a west-running cul-de-sac on the north side of the street. Knox has a view of it and three other four-story monstrosities, all with a string of brightly painted garage doors at ground level. The call-to-arms draws two curtain views and causes another woman to step out onto a small balcony to look for the truck. From an adjacent structure, two more balcony visits. All of these are disqualified by a ripped man in his early thirties who emerges at ground level. He's close to Knox's size, and carries a don't-mess-with-me air that's as much a part of him as the neck tattoo that opens to engulf his left ear. It's not his body-building or the tattoo that interests Knox, but the fact he's come out of one of the many doors that are tied to a particular garage, and that a white van is backed up to the garage door. Dulwich has schooled him to challenge coincidence, that trusting a single piece of evidence can get a man in serious trouble. But this is the trifecta: the geo-tag, the Gold's Gym guy, the white van.

The guy has come outside to buy ice cream for his captives, testimony to the monotony of routine, boredom and a human heart buried below all the muscle. His charity has exposed him.

The man checks the street in both directions. Knox stands stock-still at a good distance. When the guy retreats into the garage, Knox reaches for the pick gun sequestered in an inside pocket and begins walking calmly, but inexorably, toward the door, Dulwich's warnings ringing in his ears.

THE SENSATION IS THAT of a diving bird as Grace advances the satellite image toward a tiny circle within a triangle. She is invited lower by her innate curiosity. *Click. Click.*

It's the only sound, this click of her laptop's touchpad. Something's not right: the hostel is an active, noisy place.

She swipes three fingers to reach the next screen: the matrix of eight black-and-white security cameras in use. Camera 7, lower right of her screen: a police car. She envisions herself in a similar black-and-white CCTV frame beating the snot out of the man in the playground.

Yanking the wires from her laptop, she snaps its lid shut as she slides out of bed and onto the vinyl floor. The room is a bunker of painted concrete block with no place to hide. She drags her bad leg, the laptop balanced on her stomach. Crab-walks to the door. Snags the key. Stretches to get it open. Is outside in the hallway.

One cop will ride the elevator; one will climb the stairs. They will converge on the room.

She backpedals too fast. The laptop slips off, forcing

her to stop and balance it for a second time. Her eyes tear up, involuntarily responding to the pain. Despite dragging her injured leg, the groin muscles contract in partnership with her active leg and it's like someone is pinching and squeezing her stitched wound. There's no finding a rhythm, no doing this well. She's a three-legged stool trying to carry a laptop while moving blindly backward.

The elevator dings: she's not going to reach the toilet. She slides behind a cleaning cart, draws her wounded leg into a tuck, biting down on her lower lip to keep from screaming. The resulting noises tell her the elevator has arrived, the door to the stairs has come open. The swishing of the pressed uniforms implies running. A key turns. A door bangs open.

She wonders what they'll make of the length of co-ax cable reaching up into the ceiling, or the bloodstained bedding, and the bloodied gauze in the trash can. Does it give her time to try for the toilet? Given the presence of the cleaning cart, is there a custodial closet unlocked and open? It must be closer than the toilet at the end of the corridor. She stays along the wall, screened by the parked cart, and tries for it.

The next sounds are of a struggle. Angry voices, barking out commands, first in Dutch, then in German.

No custodial closet, only doors marked with room numbers.

The struggle stops. Grace won't make it to the toilet to hide.

She slams her back to the concrete wall, stretches out

both legs and opens the laptop, immediately typing, a disgruntled roommate using the hall for privacy.

The two cops—a female and male—assist a pair of German boys whose wrists are tied off with plastic ties. They start for the stairs, then turn and head to the elevator. Both cops look directly at Grace. The male smirks apology. The boys are cussing in German. The skinny one uses an epithet on the female cop that results in the male driving his riot stick into the boy's lower gut.

He looks in Grace's direction a second time. A flicker of recognition. Is she making this up? Or has he realized he's seen her face before?

The elevator doors close. A moment later, several residents poke their heads out of room doors and, seeing only a woman on the floor with a laptop, retreat back inside.

Grace moves the laptop to see the surgical pants she's wearing are bloodstained at the crotch. Her automatic thought is: menstrual. It takes her several seconds to understand she has reopened the wound.

ACUTELY AWARE OF HIS SURROUNDINGS, having absolute confidence the dormitory will possess perimeter security cameras, head held down, Knox uses the pick gun to gain entrance to the adjacent garage. Penlight in his teeth, the semiautomatic in hand, he scans the interior: piled cardboard boxes, a baby stroller, a bike with training wheels. A tarp conceals a Suzuki GSX650. Knox searches it for a spare key, but comes up empty. Works through the junk to the shared wall and puts his ear to it. Takes him a moment to realize he's hearing a movie or television sound track. Another few seconds to identify the canned laughter and kids' voices—Disney or Nick. Tommy watches both stations incessantly.

Carefully moving a stack of boxes, one at a time, he clears access to the wall and pushes on it gently. It flexes easily—quarter-inch drywall, as cheap as it comes. He's assuming the use of vertical metal studs—two-by-fours, a panel of drywall on each side. Like punching through tissue paper.

He wants badly to think this through, as Dulwich would ask him to. Moving too quickly can put the girls of the knot shop in danger, and Fahiz on the run. The responsible option is to put the garage under surveillance, to follow the white van in order to locate the sweatshop, if not Fahiz as well.

Knox squints his eyes closed, takes two powerful strides and lunges his shoulder through both walls. He ends the life of the guard in the chair across the room, trains his weapon on a second man to his left and moves through the hanging chunks of drywall looking wraith-like, covered in white chalk dust.

Ten doe-eyed girls on sleeping bags and bamboo mats look away from a small TV. Not one screams.

The guard goes for a weapon. Wanting to avoid another gunshot, Knox puts the sole of his size 15 double-Es in the man's gut and manages to send him into the drywall that fronts one of the metal studs. A *whoosh* of air is expelled. The man can't breathe, can't move. He sinks on weakened sticks.

One of the girls grabs the man's fallen gun and, before Knox can stop her, turns it on her captor and squeezes the trigger. The weapon is safetied; her thumb fails to find the small lever. Knox offers his open hand and the girl surrenders it.

There's an open box of twelve-inch plastic ties used on the girls at night. Knox binds the fallen man's wrists behind his back and gags him with a small T-shirt.

Ten expressionless faces stare at him with blank eyes. Sonia is not among them—he'd been secretly hoping to find her. She could be eating dinner at this hour, or arguing with an editor, or floating in a canal, but he'd expected her here. Berna is absent as well. He'd hoped for her, at least.

"You make rugs?" Knox speaks Dutch to the girl who wielded the gun.

She nods.

"Not anymore," he says.

31

A bloodied woman drags herself down the hostel's corridor, a laptop pushed on the carpet ahead of her. As she passes the stairwell door, it rattles. An insignificant vibration to anyone but Grace. The door's movement indicates another door in the stairway has opened and closed, the airtight vacuum of the space responding to a slight change in pressure.

It might be anyone. Could be a guest leaving at ground level. But Grace's internal alarm has sounded: it's the cop. He's come back for her, the flicker of recognition having blossomed into full suspicion. He takes the stairs knowing the elevator signals his arrival.

She's no match for him; her only hope, flight. She pulls at the rough, industrial carpet, moving for the elevator. Only as she looks back toward the stairway door does she see the blood smear trailing her, pointing like an arrow.

A plan takes shape, the pieces all there. He last saw her down the hall in front of a different room. The blood arrow points to the elevator. She has to stand, no matter the pain. She claws her way up the concrete-block wall, her wounded leg throbbing and feeling like deadweight. She hops to her door, pain screaming through her. Feeling faint, she manages to get it open and drag her way through just as the stairway door opens, casting light across the hall. She eases the door shut. Locks it, and turns the deadbolt. Looks to the top bunk and the hung ceiling where Knox spliced into the co-ax.

Footfalls speed past her door. She hears a person slapping the elevator call button.

She slips the laptop between the mattress and the bunk bed's plywood. Snatches her phone from the bed, texts 7-6-7 as she simultaneously climbs the back of the bunk, the pain so intense she can't stop tears from running.

She looks up at the panels in the ceiling.

She hits SEND.

32

T he solution of one problem brings us face-to-face with another,'" Dulwich quotes as he surveys a garage cluttered with ten teenage girls, a dead man and another man gagged and bound.

"I want to say: Jefferson," Knox says.

"Martin Luther King."

Dulwich's phone purrs and he reads the text. "Grace. An SOS."

The two take another long look at the mess they face. No time.

"We give it to Brower," Knox says, proposing the next step for the dormitory girls.

"He'll come after you for the kill."

"No choice."

Dulwich's face is a knot of concentration. "We move

the girls in the van," he suggests, "dump it, and call in
its location. We leave this guy in the passenger seat. It
works out to a tidy little bundle for Brower. The guy's
prints have to be all over the van."

"The other one?" Knox asks, wondering about the man
he's killed.

"Our friend at the dentist may need an organ donor.
That keeps him off Brower's radar."

"We'll have to raid the knot shop by morning. When
the girls don't show in the morning—"

"We can do that," Dulwich says.

"What keeps Brower quiet?"

"My relationship with him is different than yours. He
will work with us as long as there's some carrot left out
in front."

Knox recalls Sonia's mention of Brower's ambition.

Dulwich doesn't await Knox's further agreement; his
mind made up, he taps his screen and brings his phone
to his ear, stepping outside. The call is to Brower.

Knox says to the girls, "Does anyone speak English?"

All ten hands raise at once, trembling to be chosen.

"I need a hundred thousand euros," Knox says
from the backseat.

"Who doesn't?"

Knox marvels at Dulwich's driving. They are flying down
streets without the slightest sensation they're even moving.

"Cash. Before noon tomorrow."

"Dream on."

"They can fly it in, for all I care, but I need it."

"We're in an abort, Knox. We won't get a dime. Free airfare. Peanuts and drinks. Get a clue."

"You've got to get me the money. I pay Kreiger for the rugs, he's going to deliver the money. That leads directly to Fahiz. No question."

"Follow the money? Never going to happen. There is no money. We're supposed to be buttoning up." Dulwich pulls over a block from the hostel. It's like they've ridden a time machine.

"Tomorrow morning, at the latest, they find out about the dorm. After that, they're in the wind."

"And whose decision was that?"

Knox's face burns. "Is that all you've got?"

"You don't want all I've got." Dulwich uses the remote to lock up. The car's lights flash and it's like a starting gun for both men.

"I take the stairs. I'll enter from the back. Open phones," Knox says, slipping his mobile into its interior pocket and connecting a wire.

They hook earbuds into their left ears. Knox's wire is concealed in the windbreaker's collar. Dulwich feeds his from his suit coat pocket. They test the connection while Dulwich works the weapon gained in the raid and tucks it into the small of his back.

"Ready," Dulwich says.

Knox mutes his phone in order to hear Dulwich without interruption. He nods.

"No heroics," Dulwich says. "If she's compromised—"

"We shoot anyone, including the messenger."

"Copy that."

KNOX STEALS UP THE STAIRS like a jungle cat. The Slovak semiautomatic is nearly concealed in his right hand, only an inch of muzzle showing. If he swings a fist while holding the gun, it will take his opponent's jaw off his skull at both mandible joints. A ventriloquist's doll.

He reaches the first floor in seconds, with no interference. Tests the hallway. Empty. Twenty minutes have passed since the 7-6-7, an eternity. He senses they've let her down; his stomach's in a knot. First Maja. Then Sonia. Now Grace. Attrition is an anticipated part of any of Dulwich's operations. People like Brian Primer speak of "reasonable loss," "erosion" and "attrition through enforcement." Knox is visibly angry as he approaches the room where they last left Grace. He's frustrated to have to wait for Dulwich, who has the room's other key card.

Dulwich disembarks the elevator. He seems to take forever reaching the door. He keys it open.

Empty.

Knox's stomach drops.

"Shit," Dulwich says.

"Someone close the door," says a female voice through the ceiling's acoustic tile.

GRACE HAS STRUNG CO-AX CABLE between sprinkler pipes as a makeshift hammock. The two men help her down. Dulwich can't stop mentioning all the blood. Knox wipes her hair back off her face as Grace materializes from her cocoon. It's a touching, loving gesture. She squeezes his upper arm, amazed at the iron feel of it.

"Jesus!" Dulwich can't get over the blood.

"I broke some stitches. Some tape, I am fine."

"The hallway," Knox says.

Dulwich has no idea what he's talking about, whereas Grace looks impressed.

"Fahiz's people or—"

"Police." She explains the coming and going. The returning. "I knew they'd search every room, and they did." Looking down at Dulwich from the top bunk, she says, "Under the mattress?"

"It's here," Dulwich says, her laptop in hand.

They help her to the floor and lay her out on the bed.

"Pants off," Knox says.

"I'd rather do this myself."

"Tough. Warm water," Knox tells Dulwich, "and hand me the gauze and tape."

The cop has dumped the bag of supplies out on the floor in disgust, having found the bloodied bedsheets. Dulwich collects them for Knox as the water runs.

"Quid pro quo," Knox tells her, helping her out of the surgical pants. They are both thinking back to Shanghai when Grace tended to him.

She opens the laptop and places it to cover her lap. Knox nudges the computer up slightly and pushes her underwear leg seam higher.

"Easy," she cautions.

She's right about the busted stitches. He leaves them in. Cleans and dresses the wound. Tests his work and wins a wince and a small yelp. No blood.

"You can't wear those," Knox says.

"To hell I cannot!"

"We'll buy you something," Dulwich says.

Knox helps him to lift her, and together they wrap a towel around her waist.

"Here," she says, spinning her laptop for the two men to see. "This is where I was . . . what I was working on before the police. You see the dead zone in Demir's usage? It is basically all of the Oud-West district; a good part, if not all, of De Baarsjes; and the south half of De Krommerdt, from Jan Evertsenstraat to the canal." She pauses, drawing the area with her bloodied finger. Knox rinses the towel and she cleans herself up, but the reminder of her injuries burdens them all.

"I conducted a fly-over using satellite mapping. My first thought was this blue area, here." She leans to look at the screen and indicates an area on the satellite image she closes in on. "Turns out it is a tennis court at a school."

"You're looking for . . . ?" Dulwich asks.

"A water source."

"Berna's pant legs," Knox reminds Dulwich. "The photo taken in the ER. Wet to the knees."

"But that's—"

"Significant," Grace says, cutting off Dulwich's dismissive tone. "The girl escapes. She finds her way to a clinic, arriving in bad condition. At some point she got her legs wet. Wet enough, recently enough, that they show up that way in her admittance photo."

"During her escape," Knox says.

"So, a water source," Grace explains.

"For the record, I'm not buying this," Dulwich says. "You want water? For the record, Amsterdam has a few hundred miles of canals." He's pushing Grace to show off her knowledge of the centuries-old Dutch battle against the flooding of low-level lands, the Wonders of the World system of dikes that holds seawater at bay, the adoption of Archimedes' screw in flood control and irrigation. Offhanded remarks like Dulwich's provoke her, but she keeps her cool and stays on point.

"I combined the two," she reviews for Dulwich. "Demir's phone records, revealing a . . . donut," she says, finding Knox's word, "in his usage. Along with a water source." She grabs the map and drags it lower, exposing more of the north. She double-clicks repeatedly. With each action, the camera draws closer to the earth's surface, like a zoom lens.

"A circle in the triangle," she continues.

Dulwich is noticeably anxious and agitated. An advertising flyer lies on the floor. He picks it up, rolls it and taps it against his open palm like a cop with a nightstick. "We need to move. We can do this anywhere."

"Please . . ." Grace says, annoyed with him. It's a rare display of emotion, and it is not missed by either man. "A blue circle in a triangle of green."

"A fountain," Knox says, "in a small park." He's captured by her constrained excitement.

"With a bonus." She runs the cursor in a blurring circle around five dull brown rectangles that look like pieces of pastel chalk in a box. They lie adjacent to a massive horseshoe-shaped structure that abuts a canal to the northeast.

Dulwich beats the newsprint against his hand annoyingly, his impatience grating.

"Warehouses," Knox says to Grace.

"Or garages. Storage. Manufacturing?"

"The knot shop."

"Escaping, she passed through this fountain." Grace points to the blue circle. The cursor moves street to street, arriving eight blocks away, and stops. "The medical clinic."

"I'm not saying it isn't interesting," Dulwich says carefully. "But it's a theory, nothing more."

"Worth looking into," Knox counters. "There have to be more girls. The van isn't going to show up tomorrow morning. If they are there, this will be the last time they are."

"Then we have lost them for good," Grace adds.

"You can't lose what you don't have." Dulwich's frustration surfaces as anger. Toeing the company line is killing him. He addresses Knox. "Pangarkar is not in that building." He convinces no one, perhaps not even himself. "More to the point: Fahiz is not in that building."

"It's possible," Knox says, "that at night, no one's in the building."

"To Brian's point: we can give the address to Brower. Closing the shop does nothing to stop Fahiz. And do *not* tell me," he says, raising a finger to Knox, "that Pangarkar can lead us to Fahiz, because *you* lost her. Not Grace. Not me. *You!*" The pressure and fatigue claim him. His face florid, his eyes bloodshot, his frontal vein bulging to bursting, he puts his face into Knox's and beats the rolled newsprint against Knox's shoulder. He's dangerously close to starting a war. "You were right; fine. She *was* our one asset, our one ticket? Well, *you punched that ticket!*"

Knox swipes the newsprint from Dulwich's hand with deceptive speed. He's about to throw it to the floor when he sees it's a pennysaver, the back page crammed with personals and classifieds. Time stops. Dulwich is poised defensively, expecting Knox to hit back; Grace holds her breath. Knox is locked in time travel, rooted back in the claustrophobic confines of the houseboat's forward cabin.

Sonia sits with her laptop open . . .

Knox checks his watch. "What's the time difference between here and Mumbai?" he asks.

"Four hours, thirty, ahead," Grace says without consulting her computer. "Tehran and India both adopted the added thirty-minute difference in their time zones." She silences Knox before he doubts her. "Do not ask me why."

He does the math. Stares down Dulwich. "I'm going to need Winston's help."

"What the hell?"

"He needs to make a phone call for me." He adds, "For us."

"Because?"

"Because if he makes it, the publisher will listen."

"I got that much."

"Because I need to place a classified in Mumbai's morning paper, which is about to go to press, if it hasn't already." He stumps Dulwich. "And I need you," he says to Grace, "to post an ad on Craigslist right this minute."

"What the hell?" Dulwich says.

"No matter what, she reads the classifieds *every* morning," Knox says. "She reads them looking for her niece's initials."

"I don't want to ask who, do I?" Dulwich says.

Knox answers, "I promise you, we can take this to the bank."

33

It's past midnight by the time Grace has been resettled and Dulwich drops off Knox at the Kwakersstraat bridge, on the eastern bank of the Bilderdijkkade canal. He heads away from the canal and his intended destination across the bridge and sits outside on a plaza in a rattan chair at the Grandcafé for an espresso while others around him drink beer. There's cigarette smoke and conversation in the air. Any other night Knox would be happy to spend a few hours here, but tonight it's about appearances.

If the area surrounding the knot shop is being watched or monitored by camera, Knox has taken a moment to blend in. But not too long: by now Brower and the police could be interested in him. Amsterdam is an easy place to remain anonymous, but Knox can't be careless; some police could be on Fahiz's payroll.

After five minutes, he crosses to the south side of Kwak-ersstraat and holds close to the buildings, pausing in shadow at the corner facing the bridge. The espresso fires up his hunger—he can't remember when he last ate—and overcharges his battery to where he needs to expend some energy. He kills nearly ten minutes waiting for foot traffic across the bridge. It's a group of eight from the Grandcafé, arms slung over shoulders, voices carrying off the water. Knox follows a few meters behind.

The line of structures, garage doors facing the street, is staggered like stair steps. Holding to shadow, Knox moves into a hard-packed dirt parking area. The moon-less, cloud-covered sky blackens the area, preventing Knox from seeing clearly through the grimy windowpanes. What little he can make out, without using his Maglite, tells him the space is empty. As does the next. And the next. The fourth facade is wider than the first three. It sports an oversized garage door, the windows to which are papered over from the inside. The butcher paper is white, not yellowed. The door entrance is to the right. By the dust and debris pushed up to the weather stripping, it hasn't been opened in weeks, possibly months.

A vehicle approaches, heading for the bridge. Its hal-ogen headlights throw off a sterile bluish light, creating a sharp shadow that conceals Knox. His eyes stray to the sand and dirt, and his heart catches. Dozens of shoe impressions, all of them child-sized. They point to, and disappear around, a corner ahead, past the last of the warehouses. He's nauseated and viscerally moved by the sight. The footprints of small ghosts. Some are gone and will never be found. Others, like Maja and Berna, are in limbo, their status unknown. They are like dinosaur tracks fossilized in stone.

It is the Pied Piper following the children as Knox's large shoes obliterate some of the tracks. It only makes sense the girls would not be allowed in through the front where they would be easily seen from the street.

An extremely narrow alley runs to a back parking area behind the buildings. This was once a complex of no fewer than ten interconnected buildings. Most are in decay, their windows broken and boarded over. Some carry realtor and leasing information on placards. A high brick wall with rusting wrought-iron fencing and gates surrounds nearly the entire compound—the equivalent of two city blocks. The impressions of small shoes and bare feet flow like water to a single door.

Knox flattens himself to the wall and works to steady his breathing. These are Tommy moments, where he considers what will happen to his brother if . . . He never goes there, never fully admits the possibility of his own demise; part of one's success requires a superman attitude. But the raven sits on his left shoulder.

The pick gun unlocks the door, but Knox does not open it. He turns the device left, relocks the door and steps away. The door could be rigged to blow the building.

He steps back into darkness. All of the structures in the satellite image showed long sections of skylight. The abundance of glass roofing suggests the buildings were originally used for manufacturing. Fahiz would not want an electric bill tied to an abandoned structure.

In the alley, toward the front, Knox locates a shed roof over hardened bags of cement. He shimmies a supporting post and pulls himself up onto the slick metal, writhing like a snake to get across it without slipping off. Reaches the rain gutter and hauls himself onto the roof. A tile breaks free beneath his weight. He pounces to stop it before it cascades off. As he stands, his face flashes with blue.

Two police cars are parked, engines running, outside the Grandcafé. The white van containing the girls has been found. One of the girls has mentioned a large American. Brower has read the all-points and knows whom to question.

Cops are methodical and predictable. While workers in cubicles somewhere study CCTV footage, the two patrols will expand their search area. An entire block of abandoned buildings will not go unnoticed.

Knox stays low and counts the rooftops as he moves from one to the next. But he needn't count: on the third, a string of six solar panels have been crudely installed. He doesn't risk the flashlight; he's found the knot shop. Frustration mounts as, searching the twenty meters of skylight, he discovers every pane is fixed or sealed shut. Short of breaking the glass, it offers no access.

The strobing blue light intensifies: one of the two cop cars has pulled to the curb on Bellamystraat. The thump of two car doors tells Knox he's outnumbered. He can't imagine them searching the roof; a perimeter inspection at best. But if the CCTV cameras picked him up climbing, these two may be holding the scene until backup arrives.

Knox has no choice but to get down. Now, ahead of reinforcements. And not the way he came: he would drop into their laps.

He moves judiciously, step by step. The tile is no match for him. The first to crack splinters into several pieces. He squats and stops most of them. But one sizable piece slides, falls and shatters into the gutter. A starting pistol.

One cop calls to the other. A flashlight beam illumines like a searchlight. Knox moves away from it, tiptoeing at first, then running as the tiles dislodge. The faster he runs, the harder he lands on the fragile tiles. He slips and falls, saving himself by catching his fingertips on some flashing. A waterfall of broken tile cascades, setting off a cacophonous explosion.

A cop appears behind him shouting in Dutch. Knox hunches, reaches the end of the skylight and rolls over the peak, sliding down to the joined gutters of the abutted structures. He runs atop the flat of the gutters, hidden in the valley. Can hear his pursuer stumbling and sliding.

Knox arrives at the steep brick wall of a higher building that's perpendicular to those along Bellamystraat. Climbs a downspout, throws a leg up over the gutter.

A nightstick catches his trailing leg. The second cop has materialized out of nowhere. The cop grabs Knox's numb leg and pulls sharply. Knox falls, rotating to face the man as he drops. Takes him by the shoulders and thumps the man's head off the tile. Releases him. There's no way off the roof but up. Again he takes hold of the downspout. Again he climbs, throwing his knee up and over the gutter.

The cop in pursuit has Knox in his beam. He's shouting at Knox while working his radio. Seeing his fallen partner, he's scared. Cops and fear do not mix.

Knox scrambles up the steeper roof, like trying to climb a sand dune.

A gunshot slaps. The bullet misses Knox only because he slips. Shards of roof tile rain down onto the constable, who shields his eyes and moves into the wall to avoid the fallout. Knox reaches the apex and vaults to the other side. He slides on his ass, falls off the edge and sticks a dismount in a valley between two lower roofs. He follows this west, leaps down to a flat roof and can't stop his momentum as he falls off, dropping fifteen feet to asphalt. Tries to loosen a turned ankle by running, but is hindered.

He's in an L-shaped back courtyard that once held landscaping in what are now large planters topped with weed-infested dirt. He can't find a way out. Is forced to reverse himself and run east. Hears another gunshot after it has already missed.

The courtyard is fully enclosed; he finds no door to the street.

"Canal side, A-SAP!" he tells Dulwich via his earbud wire.

He hears the constable land hard, just as he did. But close by. Knox kicks a door, forced to use his less powerful left leg because of his right ankle. The door holds. He kicks again, while glancing over his shoulder. The cop is getting to his feet, reaching for his holster. Again, he crushes the door. The door is holding fast, but the jamb has pulled free of the grout. He has no choice but to put his shoulder into it—a move likely to break a collarbone or dislocate a shoulder. He leads with his left. The entire door frame falls like a hatch; the door remains locked. Knox falls facefirst, rolls and, unable to see, is forced to reach for the flashlight. Makes himself an easy target as he dodges machinery, wooden pallets, buckets and patches of slick slime where the roof has leaked.

The cop does his best. Closes the gap by half as Knox launches himself through an interior door at the end of the building. He demolishes it. Somersaults into the next yawning space. Less equipment. Good for running. Bad for cover.

A gunshot sets his neck on fire, grazing it below his chin. The wound bleeds warmth down his neck.

He faces a final exterior door. Skids on the sandy floor as he fishes the semiautomatic out of his back. Stuffs the muzzle into the jamb at the door handle and fires three times.

The cop gets off a poor shot that lodges in the wood trim to Knox's right.

The door swings open.

Knox runs on the bad ankle across an open courtyard filled with sand. Mountains of it rise from the northeast corner. He's slow and an easy target. He dives, tucks, rolls and comes back to his feet like the beach volleyball player he sometimes is. The opening to the street is past a crane to his right. He uses the crane as a shield.

The Audi is already moving, passenger door open, as Knox reaches it. He stuffs himself inside as a gunshot rings out.

Dulwich is ducked low, peering through the steering wheel. He fishtails the vehicle left and crosses the Kinkerstraat bridge.

"Well?" Dulwich asks, steering nearly blindly.

"That's the place," Knox says. "Empty for now. But tomorrow morning the rest of the girls will be back."

"And so will we."

"They'd better have a quick sale. Tomorrow's closing day."

THE TWO MEN ARE COMFORTABLE together in a vehicle. Many hours have been shared like this, one behind the wheel, one as an IED spotter, on the sand-blown roads between Kuwait and Iraq. Dulwich drives twice the legal speed limit, passing cars and sliding through turns, without so much as a scratch to the rental. It's a full-blown high-speed chase, but inside the Audi it's two men driving to a ball game.

The Audi speeds down an extremely narrow street, a canal to the right. Dulwich lost the cop car two turns ago. He slows, though not by much.

"It's an ideal setup," Knox says conversationally, dabbing his neck wound. It's going to need a butterfly bandage or several Band-Aids to hold it closed, but it's manageable for now. "There's a market street to the west, giving an excuse for the girls to be in the area. They disappear inside the abandoned complex. Reappear when the market is shutting down. No one's going to see them or question them being around."

Dulwich taps the brakes, slides through a changing traffic light and nearly collides with a tram. He times it perfectly, sticking the Audi on the far side of the tram where anyone following would no longer see them.

"There's a coffee shop on the corner. And the market itself. I need to be there early."

"You're out of your mind. They made you."

"We don't know that. And it's guaranteed they won't be looking for me anywhere around there. I'd be crazy to go back there."

"My point exactly." Dulwich slows the Audi to the proper speed limit. "We'll be all over the traffic cams. I need to return the car, pronto. I'll use the key drop. Rent another in the morning."

Checking his phone, Knox says, "Drop me with Grace, or someplace near."

Seeing the phone in Knox's hand, Dulwich says, "You didn't really think that would work, did you?"

"It's three in the morning," Knox says. "Ain't over 'til it's over."

"Kreiger's the better play."

"Grace is all over that."

Glancing back at Knox's phone, Dulwich takes his eyes off the road. "Give it up."

"Not a chance," Knox says.

"You poisoned it, same as every woman you've ever been with."

"Says the man who can't carry a relationship beyond a drink order."

Dulwich chuckles, takes a right and an immediate left, narrowly missing an oncoming car. "Got that right."

"It will have taken her a day or two to reach Fahiz. Maybe more. Based on the way he dealt with Grace, his curiosity won't allow him to deny her."

"That's bullshit."

"She'll bait him. Sonia's a pro. She's not inviting him to tea."

"You're dreaming."

"You get close to somebody, you get to know them. You ought to try it sometime."

"He'll stuff her into the back of a van and dump the body."

"Not if we're there to stop him."

"You're talking shit. When was the last time you slept?"

"What day is this?"

Dulwich can't summon it. He starts laughing from the gut, a contagious laugh that Knox tries hard to escape, but can't.

"I'm stopping at the next light. You're out of here," Dulwich says. "Wheels up at sixteen hundred. You want your paycheck, you're on that plane."

"I thought you're coming back with a different car."

"In case I don't."

"Screw that." Knox knows it's impossible, but he hears the dashboard's digital clock ticking. He needs sleep. And food.

"You get Grace onto that plane."

"Shut up."

The car stops at the light. Knox climbs out with difficulty. His ankle's frozen, every muscle tight or bruised. The Audi peels out. Dulwich never talks smack in an op. Embattled by the Turkish mob on one side and the Amsterdam police on the other, he's dropped out of the Optimists' Club. He comes from an operational mind-set, a pragmatism Knox can't afford. He's placed his bet: the three of them won't make the plane. Someone, or more than someone, is going to be left in the jet's backwash. He's suggesting it will be him, but only out of politeness. He knows it'll be Knox, or Knox and Sonia. His mention of Grace was a not-too-subtle statement that said she would be on the plane no matter what sacrifice it requires. Of the three of them, she's the most valuable to Brian Primer and Rutherford Risk. She's the mathematical savant who can change into the cape in the phone booth and double in the field. She's Primer's rising star, and it's Dulwich's job to protect her.

Primer has barracks full of John Knoxes. The Grace Chus come around rarely.

Knox keeps his head down for the sake of the CCTV cameras. It's a long walk back to Grace. He starts humming Paul Simon's "Graceland." It helps his ankle, improves his mood.

Dawn is suggested as a pink dust against the gray clouds behind him, but Knox doesn't see it. He's focused on the traffic, the next street corner, and every shadow within fifty meters.

34

The service apartment on Goudsbloemstraat, northwest of the city center, is warmly furnished in a contemporary style. With a full working kitchen and washer/dryer, living room and bedroom, the suite's opulence bothers Grace. For all her Westernization, she still feels uncomfortable when alone in such places. With the deposit, it cost Dulwich over fifteen hundred euros—a month's rental for a suite of rooms they intend to occupy for less than a full day. But it's in a quiet part of town on a narrow street where people apparently keep to themselves. She doubts there's been more than two people at a time out on the sidewalks; she rarely hears a car drive past.

Stretched out in bed, having taken a long hot bath to clean her wound, and an oxycodone to wash away her pain, she navigates her laptop through the company's

VPN, a Web proxy server called Hide My Ass, and a
second Australian proxy service she learned about from
Kamat. Trying to find her now would be like searching
for Nessie. She finds the meds calming. The lack of stress
is so foreign to her that she briefly experiences a kind of
mental vertigo, only to find herself giddy. Instead of
foggy, she's intensely focused and mentally nimble. Gig-
gles at the sound of her fingers tapping arrhythmically on
the keyboard.

A few minutes past four, Gerhardt Kreiger's face appears
in an open window on the laptop's screen. Natuurhonig,
his brothel, has closed for the night. When the ladies head
home, Kreiger is seen counting a good deal of cash. Her
screen-capture software reveals that he examines the electronic credit card charges as well. He matches amounts
with girls, leaves nothing to chance. She envisions a business where shorting the house is commonplace. He
removes the cash from the desk; there are noises—he's still
in the office. He returns to the desk empty-handed.

Another open window monitors Kreiger's data console
in a scroll of green numbers on a black screen. A long
search string resides in a tiny box, and the automated software routinely checks for a match. When a set of numbers
goes, a bell tone sounds, drawing Grace's attention.

She hears the door come open. Her right hand finds
the weapon below the sheets. Her finger lays across the
trigger.

"It's me," Knox calls out. He's carrying a grocery bag;
his neck is patched up with four flesh-colored Band-Aids.

She lets go of the gun.

"Good timing," she says. "We may be onto some-thing." Her eyes dart among the half dozen open win-dows on her screen. For her this is like a game of Sudoku, establishing patterns by supplying missing pieces while trusting all along that those pieces fit. Computer traffic and data flow is no more random than vehicles in a city at rush hour. It *appears* chaotic, but every vehicle's driver has a destination; there is a logic to the routes they take. So it is with each piece or packet of data: someone directed it, someone else received it. For her to break every encryp-tion used by Kreiger would take months, perhaps years. So she allows his machine to do this for her; she merely captures the incoming stream, and mirrors the resulting images on his screen, reading or viewing, or listening to it, just as Kreiger does.

Knox starts into the first of two liverwurst sandwiches he's brought with him and chugs down a beer while sit-ting on the side of her bed.

Grace does not look up from her screen. "The hacker who dropped that kiddie porn on us? That happened after I was already drilling him . . . data mining him."

"I love it when you talk sexy," he says through a full mouth.

"I trapped the MAC address and have had it tagged since. It just surfaced again, five minutes ago."

Knox stops chewing, cheeks like a squirrel.

"On Kreiger's laptop," she says.

"Simplify," he says. "Spying for Dummies."

"I had established a defense against a particular hacker. That hacker engaged Kreiger's laptop, not mine."

"Hacking Kreiger?" Knox places the sandwich down.

"No. It is not adversarial. A text message was sent via Skype. Today's date. Eleven P.M. This was followed by the number three. Meaning unknown."

"A meeting? Fahiz?"

"We can assume the computer in question is in some way related to the man we call Fahiz. As to the purpose of the message: a meeting, a conveyance? It could be something as benign as a television program on Channel Three."

"We haven't got until eleven o'clock."

"Yes. Of course. I only meant to point out that whoever hacked into my laptop has contacted Kreiger."

"A rug shipment would have little reason to go out at that late hour," Knox theorized. "What about the number? The three?"

"If it involves Kreiger's laptop, I will most certainly pick up on it. Otherwise . . ."

"Sarge should have fought for more manpower. He rolled over. I didn't expect that."

"The client dictates the endpoint."

He flashes her a disapproving look. He doesn't want to be read from the manual. Knox's size, his barely constrained power, can terrify her at times. She tries to never show him that he has such an effect on her, but wonders. It's important that Dulwich see her at least as Knox's equal.

"Where is David?" She had expected him to follow in behind Knox.

"Switching out rentals."

"At this hour?"

He explains the events at the manufacturing compound.

"We found it? You withhold such a thing from me?"

"We . . . I need to watch the place this morning. For the girls arriving."

"The white van will not arrive."

"Exactly."

"Fahiz will be notified."

"Possibly."

"Their mobiles . . ."

"Would help."

"You cannot attempt this alone. It is foolhardy, John."

His smirk tells her she's misused a word, or amused him with her choice. "They'll call the two in control of the van first. One's dead, the other's in police custody by now."

"We have their mobiles," she says.

"Yes," Knox agrees.

"They will do this before contacting Fahiz."

"Of course," he says.

"What am I missing?" She can see it in his eyes.

"The same thing they are: the van."

KNOX REACHES DULWICH at the off-airport Avis counter and lays out the plan. The painfully long silence that results suggests Dulwich's resistance.

"Brower can handle this."

Knox ends the call. Not because of the string of expletives that jump to his tongue, but because he's receiving an incoming call from a number his phone doesn't recognize.

He's sitting in the parlor of the apartment, the doors shut to the bedroom where Grace has fallen asleep with her laptop atop her.

"Yeah?" he says. Waits. Is about to repeat himself when his dulled brain kicks in.

"Don't hang up," he says.

"You bastard!" Sonia says.

"I had to reach you."

"You . . . It's so *unfair*."

"A horrible thing to do," he admits.

"You gave me hope. You used her initials."

"I had to reach you. We raided the dormitory. Ten girls. All safe now." He hopes to appeal to the journalist.

"You tricked me in the most horrible way imaginable."

"We've located the knot shop. Have you heard from Fahiz?"

"You are a monster."

"I'm an operative for a private security firm." He gives that time to sink in. "My employers are backing out of the op, shutting us down today. If we're going to find Berna and Maja, if we're going to stop Fahiz from packing up and doing this same thing to other girls someplace else, then we need each other. You and me. Now." Against his better judgment he adds, "You want to talk about a story . . ."

"You think me so crass?"

"Fahiz has the balls to leave his number with the police so he'll be notified if they close in on his own operation.

You've contacted him," Knox states with certainty. He waits. Nothing. "If you go to him alone, it's the last any of us will see of you." He adds, "That's unacceptable."

"You think me so stupid?"

"Fahiz agreed to a phone interview," Knox speculates. "He'll trap your number. Your location."

"You played upon my emotions with that classified ad. My niece has been missing four years now. How could you do that?"

He reminds himself that she wants Berna alive. She wants Fahiz punished. Why, after discovering he tricked her, has she stayed on the line?

He's overly tired. He's allowed himself to believe she cares about him. It takes him added time to process her voice sounding apologetic instead of accusatory, time to realize that she still hasn't hung up. She's kept him on the call. A trapdoor opens beneath him and he falls.

You think me so stupid? echoes in his head. Sonia isn't interested in a story. She wants Berna back. Fahiz has agreed to a trade. Sonia knew exactly who had placed the ad. She's offered up Knox in exchange for the missing girl.

One glance out the window confirms it. A sedan double-parked at an angle. The heads of two men running toward the sidewalk.

He moves as if he's rehearsed this a thousand times: a chair is used to wedge the apartment door; he's into the kitchen, stripping the refrigerator of its shelves and drawers.

"John?"

He's awakened Grace.

The crisper drawers go under the sink. The shelving goes under the bed as he scoops up Grace and runs her into the kitchen. He deposits her into the refrigerator in the fetal position, places his gun onto her lap. "Count to three after you hear it. Then open and shoot."

Grace stares back with koala eyes. Fresh from sleep, she cannot process any of this.

"Breathe shallowly. Not much air in here." He shuts the refrigerator's French doors, entombing her.

Grabs a knife on his way to the kitchen's only window as the first jarring blow is absorbed by the apartment door. He opens the window and slides out on his belly so his chest is against the brick. Jabs the knife into the grout and, hanging by one hand, pulls the window shut with the other.

A second and third crash as the door is kicked in.

Knox hangs by his fingertips from the window ledge, the knife stuck between the bricks above him. He doesn't look down; it's two broken legs or shattered ankles if he lets go. In his mind's eye, he sees two men searching methodically, surprised to find the apartment empty. Has every confidence they will not open the refrigerator. The living room glass is fixed.

He violates his own rule, glancing down to see if the men have reappeared at street level. That's when the window slides open and a man sticks his head out. Seeing Knox so close, the intruder jerks away instinctively, catching his neck on the open window frame. He's dazed.

One-handed, Knox liberates the knife and cuts open

his opponent's neck. Stabs the knife back into the grout, grabs hold of the man's collar and pulls. The body stops halfway out, caught at the waist. Blood runs down the brick like bunting.

A second face appears in the window. A gun is raised. Knox swings one-handed as a gunshot rings out. Knox bounces off the brick and returns like a pendulum to where he was. The second man's face smacks against the glass and he slides down, dead before he reaches the floor.

Knox drops the knife and claws his way up with two arms.

Across the room, Grace is coiled in the open refrigerator, the semiautomatic in hand. She's dazed and in shock. Climbing back through the window, Knox draws his victim fully out, and the body falls to the sidewalk below.

He eases Grace from the refrigerator. "We're out of here," he says, taking her into his arms.

She nods.

"Your first kill?" he asks.

She looks up at him, then rolls nearly out of his arms and gags. "My laptop," she chokes out.

Knox places her on the bed, returns to the kitchen and searches the second man, lucky to find the car keys on him. He takes the man's weapon. At ground level, he places Grace in the backseat. Retrieves the knife and wipes it down. Leaves the gun Grace used under the fallen man. The scene won't add up for forensics, but this way it will take them longer to make sense of things.

Knox drives the car he's borrowed from his attackers four blocks before pulling over and taking a breath.

"John," Grace says. He turns to see she's pointing at the dash.

His eyes light on a GPS device suction-cupped to the windshield. A GPS used to find a waypoint established by Knox's monitored phone; a GPS that would most likely have come *from* wherever Fahiz is hiding.

Knox works through the menu, instructing the device to direct them to the origin of the last trip.

"Is it the knot shop?" Grace asks expectantly.

"No."

"Then it's him. Fahiz."

"Could be." Knox stares at the guidance system, wondering if Sonia's hatred has led him to Fahiz.

"How could they possibly have found us?" she asks.

"Don't know," he lies. All he can think is that Sonia sold him out for Berna's return. *A woman scorned* . . . Or Berna along with Fahiz's full story.

Knox can picture her with her knees up, laughing at him in the warm light of the houseboat's cabin. He underestimated the damage done by running the classifieds using her niece's initials.

Twenty minutes later, the stolen car rendezvouses with Dulwich in a church parking lot less than a mile from the knot shop. Knox beams as he bumps the car into the lot.

To his surprise, Dulwich has done as he requested: he's behind the wheel of a rented white van.

GRACE IS POSITIONED across the sedan's backseat with a view of the park containing the fountain, the street market and the building with the knot shop beyond. Her mobile phone is connected by a Bluetooth earpiece; she hears Knox's breathing and the low rumble of the van's engine. They left her here in the car, with the keys in the ignition, but Dulwich took her laptop "for safe keeping." A reminder that, with her leg wound, she is the most vulnerable.

"Three small girls in the market," she reports.

"Copy," Knox says.

The choice of location seems so obvious—so perfect—now that she sees it in person. A natural barrier of a canal to the east; a market where the girls can mingle and blend in before disappearing into the abandoned buildings beyond.

She wonders if this market is where the vendor, Marta, first spotted the girls. First wormed her way into a role of scout and recruiter. Eventually moved her stall to a different market to increase Fahiz's reach across the community. Is reminded that to many who live in the area, she and Knox and Dulwich are the enemy, not Fahiz.

The white van arrives, turns into the dirt lot and disappears.

"Nothing unusual," she reports, keeping watch for police or a Fahiz guard.

"Stand by," Knox says.

DULWICH HAS THE DRIVER'S SEAT pushed back to where he can't be seen in profile. Knox is crouched facing the van's rear doors, but the space is not meant for a man his size. His legs are cramping.

Dulwich throws it into park and waits. Knox has the dormitory girls to thank for knowing how the drop-off works. The white van he and Dulwich occupy stops outside, just as a different white van always does. A moment later, the van's rear doors will be opened. The girls would normally climb out and be escorted inside—sometimes two at a time, sometimes all at once. In this rental there is a curtained divider in place that separates the driver from the girls, just as in the regular white van. Its back windows are covered by newsprint. A man from the knot shop escorts them; a guard in the back of the van will help to escort them inside. At least two other men remain inside the shop.

Knox doesn't appreciate the wait. The van they're in is a newer model than the one confiscated by the police. How will the men inside react? The girls claimed the van changed occasionally, but the lack of response to their arrival is troubling.

"What's going on?" Knox asks.

Dulwich has the building's rear door in his outside rearview mirror. *"Nada."*

Knox's thighs are killing him.

"Back it up," he says. "Make like we're bailing."

Dulwich pulls the visor down to help screen his face as he eases the van into reverse and lets it roll backward.

The door to the shop opens immediately. A man waves for the van to stop. He has a short black beard and hair to match. He wears blue jeans and a New York Giants sweatshirt. He's short, but strong.

Dulwich is more visible from having backed up, putting

him and Knox at a disadvantage. He forces himself back into the seat, and leans his head back, hoping not to be seen.

After a moment's hesitation, the man in the doorway reaches around to his back.

"Gun!" Dulwich shouts, popping open the driver's door. He rolls out of the driver's seat as the first shot penetrates the windshield. He has failed to put the van into park. It rolls back, still in reverse. Knox throws open the rear doors and jumps out. His cramped legs won't hold him. As he attempts to stand, he collapses. The van backs up and Knox flattens, crawling out of the way of the rear axle's differential, forcing himself into the space between it and the wheel. The front tires are turned slightly. Knox has to belly-crawl to the center of the undercarriage to avoid being paved by the right front tire. The van passes over him. Knox gets a clear shot at the shins of the man who's put three more rounds into the door panel. His second shot shatters bone and the man drops like a broken bar stool.

Knox pistol-whips the fallen man and slides his handgun to Dulwich.

"*Gracias,*" Dulwich says. Hampered by his bad leg, he has every reason to fear a firefight.

The van continues backing up, colliding with the wall and scraping and grinding its way along the brick. It comes to rest, the driver's door mirror bent and angled, its engine straining, back tires spitting dirt as they spin out. The engine stalls.

Top 40 music plays from a radio inside, the only sounds.

If there are girls, they are eerily quiet. Knox scoots back along the wall below rows of fixed glass panes the size of bathroom tile. Has no intention of firing into a room full of young girls. Wonders if the two men inside know this. Are counting on it.

Bruno Mars is singing about grenades.

"Anything?" Dulwich says.

Knox shakes his head, only to realize Dulwich is speaking to Grace.

Knox has long since lost his earbud. The white wire dangles from his jacket.

Dulwich hand-signals Knox: *No sign of the two men.*

Knox works his way back to a narrow column of brick separating the sets of windows; he stands, his shoulder blades pressed to the wall.

A flicker of movement to his right. It takes him a half second to realize it's coming from the van's bent mirror. It shows the bridge of a nose and the peak of a man's forehead. He's as flat to the interior wall as Knox is.

Knox ducks down and works his way back to the van. Slips out of his jacket and wraps it tightly around his right hand, switching the weapon to his left. Eases his way up the brick, sweat breaking out everywhere. Dulwich knows better than to look in his direction, but has followed Knox's every move.

Knox swings out, smashes through the glass with his wrapped hand and catches the man by the throat, pinning him to the wall. Hears a gun drop as the man reaches to fight the choke hold, but works against himself. In a deceptively fast move, Knox shifts the man's throat to the inside of his elbow; Knox drops his weapon and, pulling the man to the window, effects a choke hold with both arms. He has the advantage of six or seven inches and fifty pounds. He hauls the man off his feet, breaking glass with the man's head and shoulders. He extracts him, finishes the choke hold and drops the unconscious man to his feet.

"We've got one in the wind," Dulwich reports, receiving notice from Grace. "Heading west on Bellamystraat."

"Can she drive?" Knox calls across to Dulwich, who relays the request.

Knox risks a quick look through the broken glass. The place looks empty. He steals a second look inside. Moves to and past the door, gaining another angle. For the first time, he sees a girl prone on the floor by a stack of wool, her hands over her head. Then, another.

"Are there any more men?" Knox shouts in Dutch. One of the girls, with about the saddest eyes Knox has ever seen, looks up at him and shakes her head. Not afraid—sad. Knox kicks open the door fully, waits and then rolls inside, coming to prone with his weapon extended.

Two dozen brown eyes stare back at him from where the girls lie on the floor.

IT WASN'T EASY DRAGGING HERSELF behind the wheel. There are two kinds of pain at work—a dull, bone-penetrating throbbing, and an electric-sharp pang from the wound itself as her thigh muscles contract. The two combine to blur her vision with unwanted tears and steal her breath as her chest goes tight. She turns the key.

Thankfully, it's her left leg and therefore not involved in the act of driving. But even small inconsistencies in the roadbed send her shuddering with chills.

She picks up her mark easily—the fool is locked in an awkward stiff-legged walk on the south side of Bella-mystraat, glancing back with terrified eyes every twenty meters. He must be expecting someone on foot, for he misses Grace's slow patrol.

For how long, she can't be sure. He goes left at the next street. Rather than follow, Grace drives past, though slowly enough to determine he's just running scared. This is a bedroom neighborhood he's trying to find his way out of.

Grace, too. The next turn is a dead end. The one after that, a short lane that connects with a street perpendic-ular, forcing her to turn east toward where she last saw him. She passes a Caribbean restaurant, only to realize he's nowhere in front of her. Swings a U-turn and an immediate left, and there he is crossing Kinkerstraat against a traffic light.

He's come full circle. The knot shop is a block ahead on the left, and she briefly wonders if it's on purpose, if he intends to return. These questions are put to rest when he boards a tram and rides toward the city center.

"The one who escaped is heading east on the number seven."

Dulwich answers that he copies.

"Police," she says, as a string of the flashing lights race toward and then past her.

She hears Dulwich repeat the warning to Knox. There's a discussion between them but she only gets Dulwich's side. He's adamant that the white van they're driving is a liability, that it's time to notify Brower of where they're heading—a saved location on the GPS device Knox liberated from the car she's now driving. Knox must be arguing for more time to find Fahiz on their own.

"We're close," Dulwich tells her. "A few blocks south of here."

"That does not match with my mark," she says, but then corrects herself. "Stand by."

The man she has followed has ridden the tram all of one stop. He disembarks on the far side of the canal and walks back a half block. She's forced to give him more credit than she believed due. He rode the tram in order to get a look back for any tails. She continues past Bilderdijkkade to not fall into his trap. Maintains her speed while keeping watch in her two rearview mirrors.

"The mark is heading south on Bilderdijkkade."

"That's interesting." Dulwich relays the information to Knox.

"I am turning south now," she says, having reached another canal and not wanting to cross the bridge.

"Negative!" Dulwich commands. "Hang back."

He's concerned about her wound, her condition. He sees her as vulnerable, perhaps even a liability. The thought of that frustrates and angers her. She must not be seen as the soft forensic accountant who's in over her head, the *woman* who can't handle fieldwork.

She realizes too late it's none of that. Dulwich has the

GPS: the street she is on runs out ahead, forcing her back
to the west—aiming her directly at her mark. Seeing him
walking toward her in the distance, she does exactly what
she shouldn't do: she stops the car.

He stops. Perhaps he even recognizes the car as one of
theirs. He breaks into an all-out sprint, turning right and
crossing over a canal bridge.

"I am made," she confesses, feeling an obligation to
the team. Crushed by her own stupidity.

"Run him down!" Dulwich orders. "Stop him. Now!"

He doesn't want the mark tipping off Fahiz.

She accelerates, tires peeling, and fishtails onto Bilderdijkstraat and across the canal. He begins climbing a
chain-link fence into a construction site. Grace accelerates
across the bridge and crashes the fence, knocking him off.
He bounces onto the hood of her car.

But her collision has torn the chain link, and he's
through it like a mouse into a hole. Grace kicks the car
into reverse and swings right past the site, catching her
left headlight on a retaining wall that defines a tunnel
entrance to underground parking. The car lurches right,
and she's gunning it down a narrow passage between the
wall and the chain link toward a concrete bunker of a
municipal building. The mark vaults the next fence effort-
lessly and sprints across a sand lot where the construction
trailer is parked.

She slides through the next turn and accelerates across
the lot, closing on him.

"Shit," she says for Dulwich to hear. "A footbridge!"

At the end of the lot are red-and-white-striped stanchions that prevent vehicles from accessing a divided bike and pedestrian path that cross the canal she's paralleling. If the mark reaches the footbridge, she's lost him.

She throttles the engine, takes out a section of chain link and a lamppost as she avoids the red-and-white barriers, connecting with the mark's legs. He's thrown up onto the hood of her car and across the windshield. She can't see.

The next thing she knows, the car no longer feels solid. It is dancing and weaving. Her feet are cold. The front dips forward.

Water.

THE GPS DIRECTS THEM the long way around, taking them down the west side of Bilderdijkstraat canal instead of Tollensstraat. Dulwich realizes the mistake too late. But it's from Bilderdijkstraat that they see a black car at a distance as it crashes through a chain-link fence and plunges into a canal.

At this same instant, a silver Mercedes races from the bright red door of a garage. It's headed away from them, to the west. Its speed alone tells them it's Fahiz. Dulwich hesitates only a fraction of a second—then floors it. Straight ahead, toward the near side of the footbridge.

Knox is out before Dulwich skids the van to a stop. The canal bubbles eerily. No sight of the car. A man swims frantically for a nearby houseboat. Dulwich makes surprisingly good time in that direction, despite his bum leg.

Knox climbs between struts and drops into the murky

water. The windbreaker, laden with its pockets of tools, weighs him down and he sinks quickly.

The car's daytime headlights draw him. It's landed on its side, the driver's window facing the surface.

Knox tries his Maglite. To his amazement, it comes on.

A leaking air bubble stretches from the back window to the windshield. The trunk has opened on impact. The depleted airbag waves against Grace's head. She's out of the seat belt, sucking the remaining air while fighting the water pressure that holds the door shut.

Her eyes go wide with fright as Knox puts his face to the glass. He's running out of air. He motions her back and tries breaking the glass with the butt end of the Maglite, but it just taps against the glass.

Grace returns to the pocket of air, her hair floating eerily. Knox holds up a single finger. Then he swims for the surface where his bursting lungs find relief. He sees Dulwich boarding the canal boat to capture the escapee.

He's alongside the car again. More than half the air has leaked out. He pulls on the door. Nothing.

Bubbles of air burst loose and he's blinded. He tries again to break the glass, but he lacks the proper force.

He leaves her. Grace pounds against the glass desperately. But Knox is headed for the car's trunk. He pulls it farther open. Still no access to the backseat, to Grace. A floor mat floats into his face, startling him. He exhales most of his reserve air, digs for the tool kit, unscrews a large wing nut and takes hold of the tire iron.

As he comes around to the driver's window, Grace is gone, lost behind a curtain of silver bubbles. He swims to the hood. Her face is pressed, eyes shut, into a tiny pocket of remaining air.

He takes out the driver's window with three consecutive blows. The safety glass finally shatters, though in slow motion: small, brilliant cubes cascading down like ice crystals.

He takes her by the shirt and pulls. She breaks his grip, caught unaware by the contact. A second later, her hand gropes for his and they join. Knox draws her from the car.

Together, they kick for the surface.

35

Three or four minutes, max," Dulwich says, referring to the distinctive police sirens closing in. Grace and Knox lean against a brick wall, both panting. "With my leg, I won't even make it to the van in time. And she's not going anywhere."

Knox absorbs what he's being told. He suspected all along that the three of them would not make the jet. But he didn't see it working out this way.

"Bullshit," Knox says.

"Pangarkar gave you up, Knox. Get while the getting's good. I can try to keep Brower from going to the press on the knot shop, at least overnight. After that, bets are off. It doesn't mean they won't be after you," Dulwich adds. "But shut this sucker down, and maybe you buy us some favors."

"Two minutes, tops. Go. I've got this." Knox bends

and pulls Grace gently toward him. She's conscious, but the consistency of a rag doll. "Try to hold the jet. Work Primer for leverage here. Maybe it works out."

Knox is on his feet. He takes in the hostage by the van, the van itself, Grace's condition. Dulwich is of military stock. Because of this, his thinking doesn't always fit the situation; it's Knox's job—his duty to Grace—to make certain this is the right call. With so little time, it comes down to instinct. He bends and kisses Grace on the cheek.

"You okay?"

She touches his hand and pulls it to her lips. "Go," she says. "Keep my laptop. They mustn't find it." She provides him her password.

He rubs her hair, meets eyes with a surprised Dulwich. He jogs to the van, where he retrieves the laptop and the stolen GPS and power cord. Sirens bearing down on him, he recrosses the footbridge and hurries past Dulwich and Grace without acknowledgment.

LOSING FAHIZ HITS HIM MUCH LATER. He walks in the direction of the airport having little idea of where else to go. His iPhone is wet and dead. If he can find a store, he can buy a pay-as-you-go. Grace's laptop must offer something, but he's too dull to know exactly what.

As each obstacle is addressed by a possible solution, the trauma subsides, freeing up more of his mind to work out additional complications. The web is woven from the center, out.

He's following along a tram route that will lead back

to Centraal Station. Despite the likely presence of police there, a train is the fastest, most anonymous route out to the airport. He spots an electronics repair shop—the perfect place to inquire—and enters, setting off a dull buzzer as the door opens.

The woman behind the counter is Armenian or Eastern European. She's in her mid-twenties. The store is filled with everything from used toasters and blenders to tube televisions and plasma screens. Several of the televisions are running, each tuned to a different channel.

"I am looking for a pay-as-you-go mobile," he says in Dutch, resting the laptop on the counter.

His clothes are damp, his hair matted. His shoes squish and have left a trail across the floor. "Oops," he says. He proffers his iPhone. If she has an iPhone, all he will need to do is switch out his SIM card. If not, he has plenty of other SIMs to fit whatever she may offer.

She nods and moves to a counter display of dozens of older model mobiles.

And there's Sonia.

It's a small color television, some kind of portable model with an extending antenna. It's a local news piece. A weary-looking Sonia Pangarkar—the pride of Dutch journalism—stands with her arm around a shy, bashful girl, as her colleagues stand to ask questions. The sound is turned down. The girl is Berna. Behind the two is an image of a newspaper's front page—a preview of tomorrow's morning edition, if Knox has his Dutch right. She has an exclusive interview with the leader of a child labor ring. *Fahiz*.

The merchant must speak to him repeatedly to win Knox's attention. She can't understand his fascination with the television.

"You like?" she asks in halting English. "Good price, just for you."

One John Knox equals Berna's freedom and an interview. It means something more to him: Sonia negotiated with Fahiz. She made contact. She knows things he wants to know.

The merchant offers an iPhone 3GS, but it takes a different SIM than the 4. He settles on a RAZR that will accept two of the other cards he carries. Pays twenty euros for it.

The shot of Sonia was a short piece for a news program. It's replaced by a traffic pileup, which segues into weather coverage.

"Do you have Internet?" he asks.

She directs him to a coffee shop two blocks away.

He notices two shelves of car electronics, including a dozen GPS devices. Digs into his jacket's many pockets, producing the cigarette lighter wired to the stolen GPS.

"Can you power this?" They've settled on English.

"Of course."

He has to battle the device because it can't lock onto a satellite, but the woman comes to his assistance. He borrows a pen and paper and takes down the last nine recent destinations that Fahiz's men had driven to. Six are street addresses. The remaining are numbered one through four and represent latitude/longitude coordinates. He repacks his jacket and tips her five euros.

Smiling, the woman calls after him on his way out, "God be with you."

He can't stop that blessing from ringing in his head as he closes in on the coffee shop.

A police patrol diverts him. He enters a dress shop, where even he knows he doesn't belong. A giant of a wet man holding a laptop, his windbreaker bulging improperly. He doesn't try to explain himself. Looks for a back door. Finds a narrow staircase, ducks his head and ascends, arriving into a kitchen where an elderly woman is smoking an unfiltered cigarette while drinking from a demitasse.

"Toilet?" he says in English.

He might as well be from the moon, and she, chiseled in stone. He retreats down the staircase, where he's met by a silent but incensed shopkeeper. He leaves. The police car has moved on, allowing him to cross the street.

Something catches his eye, nearly stopping him mid-street. He doesn't know what it was. Arriving at the curb, he surveys the buildings' facades—the store names, windows, doors. What stopped him? What was it he saw?

He can't spend time so exposed. He enters the crowded coffee shop, wishes he could order a beer, but settles for a straight coffee, no adjectives. Turning on Grace's laptop is like stepping into a cockpit. He clicks on the browser. He uses her password for a second time and is presented with a stable browser frame offering a search window.

He calls up an interactive map of Amsterdam and begins plotting the locations from the GPS. Nearly simultaneously he uses Grace's interoffice mail system to send Brian Primer a message about the likely arrest of Dulwich and Grace, the schedule of the jet transportation and an appeal for assistance.

He has decided on a course of action: he's going to ring every ounce of information from Gerhardt Kreiger concerning Fahiz and leave it to Brower to mop up what's left.

For a moment, he's not sure if the coffee is too strong or if he's actually thinking clearly. He knows firsthand the aftereffects of shock and trauma. In a hallucinatory vision he's able to see not only the light at the end of the tunnel but what's beyond the light. He stands, leaving Grace's laptop on the table, and moves automatically to the shop's door. He moves outside, through the parked cars and nearly into the oncoming traffic as he surveys the shop facades. Something here stopped him and he has a sense of the answer, though he does not know what he's looking for.

And there it is: an address plate. A small tin rectangle above the shop to the left of the coffeehouse: *3*. There's a bird on the gutter looking down, mocking him. It tells him he's stupid for having missed this.

Back inside, he cuts a direct line to his table and Grace's laptop. He does not go unnoticed, his size and determination nothing to mess with. His work is clumsy, his fingers too big to type easily. He pecks out a website address, lays down the list he copied from the stolen GPS.

It must be the coffee: his heart rate is palpably quickened and sharp, painful. *Is this how Grace lives each day?* he wonders. He feels high. The possibility he might be right drives him like a whip. These few minutes are wildly exciting for him, parked in a chair in a coffeehouse. Of all things. It's impossible. Yet it's not going away.

He enters the latitude/longitude for the GPS location labeled 3. His middle finger hovers over the RETURN key. He knows this is right; he's no longer searching, he's merely confirming. It's a foregone conclusion.

The blue pin drops onto the Google map. Knox gasps aloud, drawing attention to himself. He saves the map to the computer's desktop.

Swift movement approaching.

He has the grace of a gymnast as he takes hold of the chair, raises it and lowers it onto the head of the policeman coming up behind him. The chair doesn't splinter; it thuds like a club. The cop falls to his knees. People scream as they jump away. Coffee flies.

Knox blocks the cop's attempt to reach for his hardware belt; blocks him from taking hold of Knox's leg. Doesn't want to hurt the guy, but Knox is mechanical, robotic. He drives his knee forward, stomps down hard and a gush of surprise erupts from the onlookers. Two blows: the cop is down.

The laptop folded shut, his note stuffed into a pocket, Knox heads out the back, away from the cop car parked out front.

From behind the counter, a barista dares shout out for him to stop. Knox keeps walking. He feels surprisingly good, the brief confrontation helping to release some of his pent-up excitement.

The train is out. He's closed that door on himself. Taxis are no good because of Fahiz's network.

He's chosen a ubiquitous VW Passat. Dark blue.

Knox heads for the airport, adjusting mirrors as he goes. The car's ceiling is too low, but he's used to it. As in all European countries, the Netherlands traffic cams report registration plates in real time and are searchable. From the moment the stolen car is called in, Knox is driving a time bomb. The highway to the airport will be lousy with traffic cams, less so on the surface streets. So he takes the slower route, paralleling the highway where possible, keeping it available if he's pursued. He does all this without a second thought, again marveling at what he's become. Would he have known to do this two years earlier? If he'd known, would it have been so automatic? Dulwich has shaped him, has gotten what he wants. He's turned him into an adrenaline junkie who'd rather outrun cops in Amsterdam than go on a shopping spree in the Cambodian jungle. He resents it, but doesn't resist it. Drives on, his eyes ticking from one mirror to the next, ready for anything thrown at him.

KNOX MAKES THE CALL under an overhang outside the KLM Jet Center. He parked the stolen car in a long-term lot a half mile away, walked here in a light drizzle, but still keeps a weather eye for police cars or anything unusual. Having the Dutch police after him is less than reassuring. He knows European security to be swift and efficient. He must stay a step ahead and never linger in one place for too long.

"Brower," the man answers.

"John Knox."

A brief pause. Knox can picture the man signaling his subordinates to trace the origin of the call. Knox keeps track of the time on his wristwatch. He's giving himself thirty seconds. Twelve are behind him.

"Get yourself to the nearest constabulary and turn yourself in. It will go far easier for you."

"I have a deal to propose."

Knox ends the call, switches out the second of the three SIM cards that fit this phone. Calls back.

"Brower."

"I give you a human trafficking ring, complete with kidnap victims and a person responsible. In all likelihood that person gives up the ringleader of the knot shop. You put my friends on a plane, no charges, no hidden agendas." He adds, "You've got fourteen seconds."

He waits.

"Seven seconds," he says. "No more calls."

"Done."

Knox ends the call, throws his head back and steps out so the rain strikes his teeth.

He has spent time before in the waiting areas for private jets. The jet centers spoil their corporate customers or anyone waiting for them. Knox gets a catered meal, more coffee and a shower. Pays cash.

He calls his brother, but wakes him and promises to call back later. The clock grinds slowly toward three P.M. Much of the time—all of the time—is spent with pieces of a plan spinning in his head, coming together only to separate and refuse to bind like same-pole magnets. There's much to accomplish.

Grace's laptop comes to his aid repeatedly. He watches live video of Gerhardt Kreiger's empty office as he navigates into the man's contacts list. It takes him nearly thirty minutes to locate what he's after, primarily because his written Dutch is so poor, and the online translators so confusing. But even this piece comes together for him, and he's beginning to sense the tide has turned; losing Fahiz, the arrest of Dulwich and Grace, all marked the crest of the wave breaking. Now he rides calmly to the beach without need of paddle or sail.

Satellite maps and the jet center's complimentary printer allow him to compile not only a plan of attack but an atlas of pages with highlighted routes, notes about timing and Sharpie notations pointing to possible obstacles.

Brower will attempt to burn him—never trust an ambitious cop—making Knox's job all the more problematic, demanding impeccable planning. He establishes relief valves and a time line that will invoke aborts. He projects three different competing perspectives, making a plan for himself, one for Brower and one for Gerhardt Kreiger. He looks for intersections and competition.

At last, he tries several times to channel Fahiz, wondering if he needs to be included. And again. But Fahiz hides behind a two-way mirror, impossible to see. Knox knows the unaccounted-for is what scuttles any op. Yet no matter how hard he tries, he can't fully account for Fahiz, his knowledge of the man so limited as to be useless.

The plane has landed. Knox greets the captain at the door, a wiry man with flinty eyes and a soul patch who gives the impression of once having been a long-rifle sniper.

"The others are delayed," Knox says.

"Wheels up, sixteen hundred."

"One needs medical attention. It's imperative she make the flight."

"Which'll work fine as long as she's here by sixteen hundred."

"I need twelve hours."

"You need another plane."

"You're our plane."

"I'm on a schedule."

"Just put in the request for me. Can you do that?"

"There are rules. Hours aloft, hours of rest. Can't be messed with. This crew is at the end of a run. We miss the wheels up, we don't fly again before oh-four-hundred."

"Twelve hours from now is oh-three-hundred," Knox presses.

"What are you, my dispatcher?"

"Oh-three-hundred," Knox repeats.

"You have any idea of the expense of parking the bird and the rest of us overnight? No way my dispatcher's going for that."

"Have her contact Brian Primer's executive assistant. Give me two minutes to send an e-mail. Then you can make the call."

"Is that right? And can I have your permission to take a dump while you're sending your precious e-mail?"

"Works for me," Knox says, straight-faced. "And take your time."

He begs God: Give the man a hemorrhoid the size of a walnut.

"THE VEHICLE YOU WERE OPERATING struck and injured a man." Chief Inspector Brower is fashionably dressed in a white Oxford button-down and a gray zip-neck sweater under a black corduroy sport coat. He looks remarkably well rested for a man who must not be. He drinks tea from a plastic travel mug.

"I lost control of the vehicle," Grace says.

"It was captured on CCTV, you know? Coincidentally, you took down a man with a lengthy criminal record."

Grace is unfazed by the attempt at a staring contest.

"You have a bullet wound in your thigh. We have blood stains at a perplexing homicide crime scene that I would be interested in testing against your own. Do you wish to explain your wound?" When Grace fails to answer, Brower continues. "One of two such homicide scenes."

"I do not envy you your job. I am sure you are very good at it."

"I am."

"We all have our jobs to do."

"And yours is?"

"I am employed by the European Union. But surely, you must know that by now."

"It is a good cover. Very strong. I must compliment David."

"I have no idea what you are talking about. Cover? It is my job." She adds, "My wound was a foolish mistake on my part during training. My colleague, as I am sure you are aware, was the victim of a bombing. I was given training in the use of a handgun, should the need arise. I was careless."

"Then the blood at the scene will not match yours. I am sure you would be willing to allow us to take a swab."

"My government will be wondering why I was treated like a common criminal. I cannot help but wonder how that will affect and influence your superiors. Their opinion of how you handled the case." Despite her EU cover, she is a Chinese national, a fact she believes will help her situation if the worst comes. No one likes to upset Mother China.

"I have two staged homicides, a vehicle at the bottom of a canal, and a woman with a fresh bullet wound. All of this needs explaining."

She knows that Dulwich gave Brower both the dormitory and the knot shop, that his star has risen substantially since Knox came along, that he can't possibly want to muddy the waters. She expected the interview to be by the numbers, a video and report that could be filed away to cover his ass if the need arose. His persistence is a surprise to her. Dulwich would not sacrifice her. So it's John he wants. Dulwich is willing to let Knox go if it means saving her. While that thrills her, it sickens her as well, and she wonders how far she's willing to go, how much she's willing to play along.

"I am sure you will make sense of it all."

"You have the night to think about it," he says. "I suggest you consider cooperating with the investigation."

A continuance. The night ahead means something to Brower. And then she has it: the message intercepted that was sent to Kreiger—the date and time. Tonight.

She has to fight back a grin. Knox has sent them a message through Brower to give this time to play out.

He's up to something.

36

The lat/long saved as "3" on the stolen GPS is due north, across the river. There is no easy or quick way to reach the remote waterfront location.

He knows the knot shop girls who have served out their usefulness are resold through Kreiger to Asian markets. Connecting the information they have, he assumes there are three rendezvous locations for the girls' transfer. On this night, according to the message Kreiger received, it's to be number 3.

Knox rides the motorcycle he left near the Keizersgracht houseboat several nights before. It feels much longer than that. He doesn't dare go within half a kilometer of the desolate spit of industrialized waterfront for fear of forcing an abort. The roads become unpredictable once he's off the major thoroughfare. Interrupted by water and bridges, dead-ending at piers and docks, Knox hangs a U-turn and seeks an observation point.

He finds it thirty minutes later: the Noorderlicht Café, a bizarre greenhouse affair on a dock in the middle of nowhere. It specializes in organic, farm-raised meats and vegetables that cater to the platinum-card set despite its docklands location. It couldn't be better situated for Knox's needs: it sits on the western bank of a man-made inlet across from the spit of sand and cranes indicated by the GPS's coordinates. A five-minute swim, but at least a ten-minute motorcycle ride. The rendezvous location is so well chosen as to madden him. No way in or out without being spotted, and a long way from anywhere.

To make matters worse: the restaurant closes in an hour, leaving him with time to kill. One hundred meters inland, the canal is lined with trees on both sides.

His mind made up, he orders the skate with creamy polenta and a stein of lager.

The last supper.

THE NOORDERLICHT CLOSES AT TEN, an hour before the rendezvous. A kind waitress serves him a beer beneath an outside umbrella as the restaurant lights go out and the last of the kitchen staff heads home. The sky is broken cloud and light from a half moon. The flashing lights of jet aircraft play hide-and-seek up there.

Knox wasn't made for stakeouts. Once he might have had the capacity for such boredom, but roadside IEDs and Tommy's condition have advanced his path down the time line. He can handle watching the occasional football game with friends. But most television leaves him antsy and with the feeling he's wasting his life. There are probably meds he should be taking. For now, the beer will have to do.

Worried about the outcome of the next hour, Knox checks the time difference and calls Tommy.

"I always know it's you because how long the number is," Tommy says, answering.

Knox doesn't need to ask "How's it going?" because the tone and focus tell him the new meds are working better.

"Just called to say hi."

"Hi."

"Miss you."

"And how," Tommy says. "Hey, we're up six percent for the month over last year."

Maybe it's the fatigue, maybe that they're carrying on a real conversation, but Knox chokes up. Wipes his eyes as a sky full of lights blurs.

"Remember that trip to the Wisconsin lakes?"

"Boy, do I. With Mom and Dad."

"Yeah," Knox says. "I'm looking out on water like that, only there are lights and stuff, but it reminds me of you and me sitting out there on the dock."

"The mosquitos."

"No shit."

Tommy laughs. "Website traffic is up nearly twenty percent. The Google ads."

"Good deal."

"I was thinking . . . You think I could maybe get a Segway? You don't need a driver's license, and it's not like I'm going to use one of those sit-down things the fat people drive."

"Worth looking into." Knox can't believe the progress. It's like he was never diagnosed. A bigger part of him knows it won't last and he hates himself for not just thinking it but knowing it.

"You remember the girls across the lake?"

"If we'd been caught, we'd have been locked up as pervs." Knox has to hold the phone away, and he gags himself with his free hand and thinks of all the bum luck. That his kid brother had to go off the rails. That the world is an unfair place. That he can't bring himself to be Tommy's caretaker and how he knows that's wrong and how it's never going to change. His selfishness creates this debt between them that cannot be bridged.

"Are you *crying*?"

"Windy here, is all. I should probably go. Just wanted to hear your voice."

"This is my voice."

"I like hearing it."

"You must be tired."

"Very."

"So come home."

There's the word. "Working on it."

"Work harder."

"Later."

"Later."

The red and white lines of taillights and headlights streak across a bridge in the far distance. Container ships and canal boats jump into frame and disappear. Directly across from him, nothing. The lumberyard—or is it concrete beams or steel?—sits as the spindle on a phonograph; the world spins around it. Knox enters a meditative state, part coffee, part beer, part full belly, part winsome recollection of what he's left behind in the red-light district café.

He swallows deeply, fearful he's left the import/export business behind as well; that, like a drug dealer, Dulwich has dared him to sample the product and now he can't quit. As a man who eschewed "causes," he's frightfully close to caring. This final chapter isn't about justice or Fahiz or Kreiger. It's about Maja.

At 10:35, he removes the Scottevest along with his shoes, his wallet and the change from his pocket. He wraps it all in a ball and stashes it near the motorcycle. He leaves his watch on, empties the plastic takeaway bag holding his leftovers, and wraps the mobile and the handgun. All of it automatic, like a painter laying out his tubes and preparing his palette.

The water is colder than he expected. He's allowed himself enough time to swim slowly, holding the wrapped phone and gun at head height, soundless and serpentine. He's chosen a crossing deep into the inlet, away from the yard's extended docks. He arrives at a stand of trees clinging to a muddy bank, beyond which rise stacks of logs and concrete light poles. He shivers in the copse, awaiting warmth, then steals among the stacks, crouching and moving stealthily, looking for the best spot to light. His feet are tender against the splintered wood and chunks of bark, an unexpected liability.

The yard holds three massive rows of timbers running north/south, with two wide dirt aisles between them; these lead to two more shorter piles running east/west and a wider dirt area that feeds a one-lane bridge wide enough for a tug. The bridge connects to a barren man-made island twenty meters square, off of which are tied several empty barges. Knox assumes the boarding will take place off the island; it's a location well chosen for its exposure. Having returned to the cover of the trees, Knox looks for opportunity. Any vehicles or boats headed toward the yard will be spotted well in advance of their arrival, giving the human smugglers time to kill the girls and sink their bodies. Anyone trying to cross the bridge in an attack is defenseless and vulnerable—a sitting duck.

And what if they don't use the island? Another two empty barges are secured in the inlet between the island and the yard. Loading from these barges would be more difficult to see from the café side of the canal.

His watch's hands glow green in the dark: 10:45. He conducts additional reconnaissance, realizing his mistake. He can hear Dulwich schooling him, can feel the choking heat of the desert: "Watch for the choke point, or it'll be the last thing you see."

It is only with leverage he's able to budge a stray timber from the swollen grass that cradles it. Once it's out onto the asphalt, it rolls easily as he applies an iron pipe to its side. The log waddles left, then right, refusing to go straight and consuming unnecessary time to keep it on track.

He phones Brower, waking him. Recites the lat/long, having no idea of the street names or how to explain the area.

"Wait for us," Brower says.

"If you don't make this public, I can deliver the ringleader." He ends the call; he knows better than to trust the police's handling of hostage situations. It's why a company like Rutherford Risk is kept so busy. Has no idea if he can deliver what he's promised, but it was all he could think to say.

Knox gets the log rolling with his arms, still battling its wandering.

A blink of white light to his right through the trees. One last push of the log; it partially blocks the entrance, angling in, pointing toward the open yard. Knox moves to the hidden side of a warehouse office building. Is finally able to look at his work.

It's pathetic. He might as well have written a sign declaring his intentions. With no time to correct it, he hurries around the far side of the warehouse and into the lee of a storage trailer. He'd like to make the stand of trees by the gate, but there's no time.

The approaching vehicle slows. It's a dark minivan, the kind that looks like it's come out of a metal crusher, forcing it high and narrow. On the water, Knox sees a boat slowing toward the yard's canal. They have this timed to the minute, suggesting radio or cell phone communication.

The van rounds the turn into the yard and the driver brakes immediately upon seeing the log.

Knox hears the driver going for reverse. It's too far away—ten meters or more—forcing Knox out into the open, into the headlights. No choice. If the driver gets the van turned around, Knox will be shooting into the back of the vehicle—and into the hostages.

He braces his hands against the corner of the building, sights the pistol and pops off two rounds through the driver's side of the windshield. The angle is wrong for the passenger side, exposing too much of the van's interior should Knox miss.

The van continues backing up, but at idle speed, indicating that the driver is impaired or dead.

Knox rounds the corner in a squat. He moves to his left to get a better angle as an arm protrudes from the passenger side. The telltale white muzzle flash commands Knox to go limp. His right shoulder flashes hot and his fingers release the handgun.

He starts rolling before he ever hits the ground. Hears three more reports, all evenly timed, the product of a cool and collected shooter. Rolls toward the van, requiring the shooter to come up out of his seat to acquire a shot. If the man isn't wearing a seat belt, Knox is dead. But he hears the restraint engage, a man curse in Dutch, and before the gun discharges at close range, Knox stands behind the open window, his hand on the man's throat, crushing his windpipe.

The weapon appears, forcing Knox to release the man's

throat and go for his wrist. As it discharges into the sky, the door behind Knox slides open and Knox spins—one hand battling against the weapon, his left grabbing for the sliding door's handle and pulling the door shut. The sliding door thumps, not closing fully, and a man screams from inside, his forearm crushed.

A semiautomatic holds eight to ten rounds. This weapon has fired five. Six, as another flies high. Knox creeps his hand up the man's wrist. The shooter mistakes this for an effort to angle the gun away; he pushes against Knox, who allows it to move, shortening his reach to the trigger guard. Knox pulls the man's index finger twice— two shots out through the windshield. Then swings his fist, crushing the man's nose.

His left arm is not as strong as his right. The man in the back is winning the tug-of-war with the sliding door. Knox applies the same strategy: he runs to his left, pulling the door open, assisting his opponent. He reaches in, grabs for clothing and pulls.

He throws a small girl onto the asphalt. The mistake stuns him. Freezes him, half turned in her direction.

A gunshot from behind. Knox spins and drops as a body falls on top of him. The driver was not killed. He's fired a round into his own man who was moving to jump Knox. The jumper has a golf-ball-sized hole in his upper chest. The exit wound of a hollow point. Holding the jumper as a shield, knowing the hollow points won't pass through him with killing velocity, Knox carries him into the van, pushing him toward the wounded driver, who fires two more rounds into his colleague.

The passenger turns in his seat, sticks the barrel of his weapon to Knox's temple and pulls the trigger. It clicks. Knox pounds a fist into the man's face, flattening his nose for a second time, delivering the man unconscious. He heaves the dying man forward into the driver like a stuffed doll, and the two wrestle with the wounded man between them. The van's horn sounds as Knox dislodges the weapon, the driver weak from taking one of Knox's two rounds.

The girls flee the van behind Knox.

"Wait!" Knox calls out in Dutch.

The driver is stubborn. The now-dead man between them sinks out of the way and the two pummel each other, Knox pounding the sticky wet area in the man's chest until at last he goes limp.

Knox collects the weapons and tosses them out of the van.

The boat has turned and is heading away. Knox slumps down onto the asphalt, knowing he must make the swim before the police arrive. He calls out, but the girls have fled. Screams Maja's name, implores her to come back. But the girls have scattered into the dark, putting as much distance behind them as possible. They are left to find their way back into the city and be reabsorbed into another sweatshop or brothel. The lucky ones like Maja will find their way home; though what, if any, promise that holds remains uncertain. Marta, and recruiters just like her, litter every street corner.

Exhausted, limping, he makes his way to the water as police cars close in, slips into the blackness like a crocodile and swims quietly for the far bank.

37

Knox is on foot on the streets of the city center, his stomach full, his mind alert. He's on the hunt—he feels exceptionally good. Time is against him, but he understands the value of patience. This can't be rushed.

Without the girls who fled the van, he has nothing to trade Brower for the release of Grace and Dulwich. By now the constables have taken the injured delivery team into custody; without hostages, the police may lack enough evidence to hold them for long. Knox has this one night at most.

He is presented with a choice: turn everything over to Brower and hope to win favor, or deliver the prize no cop could resist: Fahiz. The knot shop ringleader.

Grace's work has been unable to specify a source location for the incoming messages to Kreiger, and has explained that an outgoing data stream would improve their chances. He needs Kreiger to contact Fahiz directly. It would allow him to track the e-mail through an ISP server to a particular router, to identify a city district, possibly narrow it down to a few blocks.

Knox walks the length of Kreupelsteeg, the alley that contains the entrance to Kreiger's Natuurhonig. Circles fully around a long block, canal to canal, and back to the alley's southern entrance, a fifteen-minute walk. It's growing dark. The sex tourists are out in droves. The red-light district is hopping.

The pale, scantily clad girls stand in the windows like mannequins, smoking cigarettes, talking on cell phones, credit card processors on a table, ready to go. It's the Gap of prostitution. It all reflects in the black water of a canal, doubling his distaste.

He crosses the canal in order to look back and get a wider view of the block that houses Natuurhonig. He's taking into account every drain pipe, every intersection of architecture. It doesn't look promising. Old Amsterdam is a warren of abutting, narrow brownstones without logic or reason. Many of the blocks contain courtyards common to all the buildings. He assumes there must be fire egress from upper floors of commercial buildings like Natuurhonig, but there's little evidence from the outside, and he saw nothing while inside. He would have liked to leave by the front door. He's not so sure about that anymore.

He buys a souvenir, an expandable duffel bag with a gold marijuana leaf emblazoned on it. He takes up

position on a bench and makes a call. He gets an automated answering voice that repeats the number called but
gives no indication of the owner's identity.

"If this reaches you," he says, "I forgive you. Berna is
safe. But I need you if we're to save the rest." He names
a restaurant/bar a half block away and a time: an hour
from now. "Alone, or I can't help the remaining girls."

The time passes agonizingly slowly. He switches SIM
cards, checking for messages: nothing. The dinner crowd
flows into the red-light district; a few windows are lit,
scantily clad girls reflecting green neon. Many more stand
dark, awaiting a later hour. Knox has not moved. He
measures the body language and the look of every new
face. He looks to see if she has compromised him. He has
four routes of egress available and a handgun tucked into
the small of his back. Warmed by the adrenaline pumping
through him, he rides it like a drug. He feels exceptionally
right and good. This is where he thrives. Dulwich now
owns him.

Sonia arrives alone. Knox first feels nothing beyond a
negotiator's appreciation that the deal appears to be going
through. That acceptance causes a rush of grief and disappointment. He waits a long time, on alert for surveillance. He accepts the futility of it. She could be
electronically marked. It could easily be a trap.

The bar isn't busy. She sits on a stool. Knox passes her
and takes a table for two, his back to the wall, where he
can see the front entrance and a back hallway marked as
an exit. She joins him after her drink arrives.

The cold in her eyes isn't an act. She's eager to be gone.

"They tried to kill us," he says.

"He said a warning. I swear."

"You negotiated."

"I did. But, I swear——"

"I saw you on television," he says, interrupting. "I suppose congratulations are in order."

"What other girls?" She must know about the discovery of the dormitory and the knot shop by now. She has nothing to say about his successes.

"I can't be in two places at once," he says, tapping Grace's laptop. "I need you to monitor the laptop while I do something."

"Such as?"

"I'm going to shut him down." He doesn't need to tell her whom he means. "It's what we all want and what I happen to need. You just do the monitoring. Keep the laptop safe."

"You cannot possibly trust me for such a task. How can you possibly do this—whatever your name is?"

"Knox. It's John. And yes, I do trust you to do this. I'm afraid there's no other way."

"You are desperate."

He shrugs. A gnarly-looking waitress arrives—half sex kitten, half dominatrix. Amsterdam. Knox orders a coffee; Sonia waves the girl off.

"It's over," she says.

He takes that to mean many things, none of which he wants to face. Nor is he sure how to respond. She is beyond beautiful, without trying; she amplifies the light emitted by the pathetic candle that's trying to stay lit. The sound of her voice is music and he's suddenly so bone-tired he wishes he could just put his head back and listen to her speak. She could read the menu for all he cares.

His coffee arrives. It's freshly brewed and surprisingly good.

"I want to hate you," she whispers, hanging her head.

"That's a start," he says.

"No. It is an end."

"It's better than nothing."

"It is less than nothing."

"For now," he says.

She looks up through glassy eyes. "We both got what we wanted," she says.

"Not even close," he tells her.

"What do I do?" She's looking at Grace's laptop.

"Mainly, keep watch. I can't very well set it on a table and hope it will be there when I return. It must remain on, connected to the Internet. Running. There's a screen capture key that I need you to operate. It will shorten the analysis time." They spend nearly twenty minutes at the keyboard together. Knox works her through what little he knows.

"Natuurhonig," she says.

"Why would you say that?" He has trouble keeping suspicion from his voice. He fears a second betrayal.

"It is less than two blocks from here."

"She's a coworker, nothing else. This is her laptop."

"She's under arrest."

Sonia knows more than he suspected. She must be in

direct contact with Brower to know their status. "There have been shootings. Deaths. It is serious for her."

"For all of us," he says.

"Natuurhonig," she repeats.

"The less you know, the safer for you." He wants to avoid the melodramatic because she'll call him out for it. Sees no other way. "If I'm not back, if you don't hear from me within the hour—"

"Oh, please."

"You need to get this to her. Don't even think about hacking it—it'll zero itself with any attempt at that. You turn it over to Brower, or anyone else, and it's useless. In her hands, only."

"There is no way I can accomplish this."

"You'll think of something."

Some of the ice is gone from her eyes, but there's a veil of self-preservation in place that feels impenetrable.

"It's operating now," she points out. "Unlocked. If I take it, I do not need the password."

"Which is why I need someone I can trust."

She stares.

"I can end this."

"It's over."

"You don't believe that. Not for a second. You want it over or you wouldn't have come."

He finishes the coffee. Removes Grace's power cord from the Scottevest. "In case it runs low on battery." He adds, "I'll give you exclusive rights to the story."

"You do not know me so very well."

"I'd like to," he says.

He leaves by the back door, pausing at the narrow hallway to look back at her. She's looking at him, her face unreadable.

Knox is not built for second-story work. He's more of a ground-floor man. The Kreiger tactic is a risk. Calculated or not, he cannot allow it to backfire; there's more to accomplish.

Using the pick gun, he enters a darkened souvenir shop, and turns to relock the door as the security alarm begins beeping its warning to enter the alarm code. He's upstairs in a matter of seconds. The alarm begins *whooping* moments before he's out the third-floor window, which he carefully returns to closed. He's methodical, having rehearsed this in his mind a dozen times.

With the front door relocked, it will look like a false alarm, which accounts for over ninety percent of such calls. The interlocking roofs remind him of being above the knot shop. He walks carefully, avoiding breakable tiles, staying to the structurally sound and supported valleys and seams. It seems much farther than it should be, but at last he faces a peaked roof sandwiched between two flat, tarred roofs that are hidden behind ornamental Dutch facades. The skylight to his left offers a clouded aerial view down into Kreiger's office.

He makes the call while watching the man at his desk.

"Ya?" Kreiger answers.

"I have the contents of your safe," Knox says. "You know who this is. Either get me the goddamn rugs, or some people are going to be very angry with you." He ends the call.

Below him, Kreiger heads directly to a large Asian floor

urn. The urn separates at the rim. The silk plant rotates out of the way. Kreiger leans over. Knox sees only the man's back as he's leaning over the urn. He never for a moment doubted that the hyphenated number at the bottom of the man's own contact information was a safe combination, but he gambled it was an office safe and not in the man's home. Grace's work has borne fruit. She reported watching over the computer's webcam as he counted a great deal of cash, of hearing noises, and his return to the desk without the cash.

Kreiger returns everything as it was and leaves the office, presumably to have a talk with Usha.

Knox has just minutes. He retraces his steps, jimmies one of the windows in the peaked roof and lowers himself through. All the third-floor bedroom doors hang open. The brothel won't be at capacity for another several hours. Business is confined to the second floor for the time being.

He can only hope the damage to the upper window won't be noticed in the next few minutes. He's into the man's office and has the safe open on the first try. Empties it into the marijuana duffel, relocks it and slides the plant back into place.

He leaves a handwritten note on Kreiger's keyboard. He winks at the screen, assuming Sonia is watching. Taps his wristwatch to let her know her part in this has come.

Returns to the hallway, the duffel slung over his back. There was a good deal of money in the safe, along with a pair of external hard drives and, more intriguing, no fewer than a dozen plastic bags containing what appear to be pubic hairs.

He'd planned to stash the duffel, surprise Kreiger by

being in the man's office upon his return, and to later leave by the front door. But he has misgivings about such brashness. He can hear Grace cautioning him.

The hallway's overhead window is too high, even given his enormous reach. He jumps, trying to catch his fingers on the window frame, but it's no good with the duffel awkwardly weighing him down.

The sound of someone climbing the stairs drives him into one of the open bedrooms. There's an antique hand mirror on a dressing table; Knox uses it at an angle to scout the hallway.

Kreiger arrives at the top of the stairs and returns to his desk, where he sees the note ahead of when Knox would have wanted. It reads:

Nice banana plant. Get me the rugs.

Kreiger checks his safe. Roars to where the building shakes. Lumbers quickly downstairs shouting in Dutch.

Knox slides a chair into the hallway to make up the height he needs. Climbs up and out the jimmied window, the duffel over his shoulder. Knows the chair's placement will give him away.

"YOU MISSED THE SHOW." Sonia has succumbed to a glass of red wine and a calamari appetizer. Maybe two or three glasses, because she looks entrenched and comfortable, her earlier trepidation calmed. She emotes an air of respect for him.

"Did I?" Knox signals the waitress and orders a coffee. Maybe it's all an act, adrenaline giving way to shock. Or a fatalistic surrender. But she's eerily stable as she crosses her legs and treats him like they're out on a date.

"No beer?"

"No beer."

She angles the laptop in his direction. Knox is watching the restaurant's back exit, the foot traffic in front on the sidewalk and, across the canal, the mouth of the alley that leads to Natuurhonig. One eye finds the laptop.

Kreiger's office chair is empty. Suddenly a man screams.

"That would be Kreiger checking his safe," Knox says.

Four minutes later, the florid-faced, winded man deposits himself into the desk chair and begins typing. Knox borrows Sonia's wineglass and upends it. She covers her smile. When the waitress delivers the coffee, he orders her another.

Knox now divides his attention to include two smaller windows open on the laptop screen. The first scrolls code he doesn't understand. The second shows a map where a red line stretches from Amsterdam to Berlin and back to Amsterdam.

"I captured these screen shots," Sonia says. The resulting screen shots play out like a slide show. The last shows a district in Amsterdam as an island of pink. Knox studies it long enough to get its street boundaries.

He tests the temperature of the coffee and then drinks down half the cup. He can feel her watching him.

"You are not going to tell me," she says.

He passes her the duffel. "To help Berna and the other girls. I'm assuming the hard drives will give you a story worth publishing, including human trafficking. Enough evidence to bring down Kreiger. Hopefully, Fahiz. That's a work in progress."

She unzips it, peers inside at the cash and gasps. Zips it back up. "I cannot," she says, aiming the strap back at Knox. Her eyes stray to the bag repeatedly. She consumes a good deal of the wine as it arrives. "Jesus! It's so much, John."

He studies the laptop one more time to make sure he has it right. The Dutch street names drive him nuts. Alphabet soup. He enters several numbers from Grace's contacts into the new phone: Primer's direct office number; the tech center; Dulwich's mobile; the Rutherford Risk emergency number. Some of these he has memorized, but the mind does strange things when juiced on adrenaline. Knox knows what's coming.

"I want to help you," she says. He won't look at her. Knows the power of those eyes.

"Then get as far away from me as possible. Go to ground. Write your story. The pen is mightier, and all that."

"And you are the sword?"

"I'm dull, but I'll have to do."

"Not dull," she says, "just not honest."

He nods. Finishes the coffee. It's not as good as the earlier cup.

KNOX DROPS THE LAPTOP into the canal as he crosses the bridge. Feels its loss in his chest for it signals the end-game, a point of no return. There might be a dozen routes to the same end but he can only think of the one. Having started it in motion there's no going back, even if he wanted to. This is what he tells himself, though a voice of conscience suggests otherwise; there's always time to change plans. But he's robotic, preprogrammed. His pace increases, his demeanor intensifies. He passes the curious and the creeps, the Indiana innocents and the perverts. The full-length windows are alight with wan skin and scant under-clothing, navel rings and wigs. The air reeks of marijuana, tobacco and perfume. Of Indian food and motorboat exhaust. A dozen songs compete, Euro-rock to The Fray. Oddly enough, it's the perfect place to hide—all attention is on the window girls and the promise of depravity.

He reaches the front door to Natuurhonig. Thinks back to his and Grace's entrance. The receptionist, the gorgeous Tarantinoesque blonde. Doesn't recall a male bouncer, but assumes that he—or they—blended in with the customers. But Kreiger is a cheap son of a bitch: there will only be the one bouncer.

"Good evening," he tells the attractive receptionist, as he hands her fifty euros. Perhaps she remembers him. But his sour smell and sweat-stained face and hair must set off an alarm, along with the fact he doesn't wait for her to admit him.

Knox is facing the stairs when a wide body in designer jeans and a mock turtleneck crosses toward him.

"Nice shirt."

An amateur, the guy reaches out to grab Knox by the forearm. Knox pins the man's thumb to his wrist and drops him to his knees. Crushes his nose with his own kneecap, then toes him in the solar plexus. The bleeding man collapses to the floor unable to breathe. Knox has barely broken stride. He climbs the stairs, two at a time, turning right at the top.

He shuts and locks Kreiger's door and is behind the man's desk before Kreiger has the desk drawer open that contains what turns out to be a .45. Unloaded, after Knox handles it.

He strips the man's sport coat partially off his shoulders, pinning Kreiger to the office chair. Ties the man's hands with phone cord. Pulls up a chair and sits cross-legged facing Kreiger.

Hears heavy footfalls coming upstairs.

"Tell him everything's fine," Knox advises.

Kreiger has only now begun to process what's happening. The smell of pot smoke alerts Knox to the man's dulled condition. Following the discovery of his empty safe, he blew a blunt.

The one in the hall sounds intent on bringing the door down. Kreiger calls out and assures him everything is okay. It takes two tries. The man calls back that he's not leaving. He's waiting outside the door.

Knox shakes his head at Kreiger, who then instructs the man to wait downstairs.

"I will get you the rugs," Kreiger says pleadingly.

Knox offers a winsome smile.

It takes an inordinate amount of time for Kreiger's stoned brain to process what's happening. "Oh, shit."

"Now you've got it," Knox says. "You know that e-mail

you just sent to Fahiz—or whatever name he goes by?" Knox smiles a shit-eating grin. "He called himself 'Fahiz' to the police. He's a clever one. But you just gave him up, Gerhardt. He's done. Which means you have one, and only one, play. You work with the police and maybe they protect you. Maybe, just maybe, they save your life."

Kreiger is green. It's a bad high. He's wishing he hadn't taken those last two tokes.

"Work with me," Knox says.

Kreiger's eyes wander to the open safe.

"I have the hard drives."

Kreiger shakes his head.

"We know each other, Gerhardt. We've done business together for what, four, five years?"

Kreiger can't speak, or knows he shouldn't.

"And I am the guy you think I am. A simple business-man like yourself. Right?"

Kreiger rattles off a string of profanities in Dutch. Knox doesn't know them all, but recognizes one as a piece of female anatomy.

"Stop me when I'm wrong," Knox says.

Kreiger simply stares back at Knox.

"Gerhardt?"

Kreiger pretends he doesn't hear.

Knox takes a stapler off the desk, bends Kreiger's head back while cuffing the man's mouth. He punches a staple into the man's forehead.

Kreiger's cry sounds like a cough.

"Nod," Knox says, placing the stapler to the man's nose.

Kreiger nods vehemently.

"Better?"

Kreiger nods again.

Knox settles, straddling the ladder-back chair. Kreiger is crying.

"Oh, please," Knox says. "Let's skip the good parts, shall we?"

Kreiger nods obediently.

"You recruit some of your girls from the pot shops. The good-looking ones who are out of money."

Kreiger hesitates. Knox reaches for the stapler.

"Yes," Kreiger says.

"Provide them work."

"Yes."

"Get them off the streets."

"Exactly!"

Knox is no stranger to such interrogations. A graduate of the Navy's SERE course—Survival, Evasion, Resistance and Escape—one of just a handful of civilians to take the course, he knows both sides of the chair. He works to loosen up Kreiger by establishing a rapport. Surprisingly, even though this man knows what Knox is up to, the offer of camaraderie will overpower other instincts.

"What benefits one, benefits all," Knox says.

"I couldn't have said it better."

"The man who runs the knot shop . . . the rugs . . ." Knox waits for Kreiger to supply the name. Allows his eyes to wander to the stapler.

"Berker Polat," Kreiger says.

"Spelled?"

Kreiger spells it out for Knox.

"You . . . what? . . . Agent his goods." It's a statement.

Kreiger nods.

"You ship his rugs. You agent them, and ship them."

"Correct."

Knox weaves his fingers together to keep himself from using his fists. Feels his throat dry. "Polat uses child labor."

"I don't ask. Never have. Don't want to know."

"Of course you know," Knox says. He seizes the stapler and sinks two staples into the man's thigh. The sound of Kreiger screaming brings Rudolf-the-red-nosed bouncer banging on the office door. A perspiring and terrified Kreiger tells his man to go away and stay away.

Knox is feeling insanely good. He cautions himself, wondering if it's the pot smoke hanging in the air. Knowing better.

"The girls, yes," Kreiger says. "I have never been inside his shop. I have no knowledge of the conditions or the—"

"You sell the girls for him."

Knox hadn't noticed the ceiling fan, but the resulting silence emphasizes its lazy rotation, suspended from the overhead ridgepole.

"Careful," Knox says, withdrawing the gun from the small of his back. "No more stapler."

Kreiger tries to swallow. Between the marijuana and terror he doesn't have a drop of saliva. He sounds like a toilet refusing to flush.

He nods.

"As sex slaves," Knox says, his finger absentmindedly finding the trigger.

Kreiger's shock is authentic. Knox knows this by how quickly it transforms into wide-eyed alarm.

"Is that what you think?" Kreiger would have spit if his mouth wasn't so dry. "Sex? No! No!"

"You're a charitable organization, I suppose. Putting those girls onto the ship so they can pursue higher education."

The first takeaway is that Kreiger is surprised at the depth of Knox's information. The second is that he's determined to resist any admission of guilt given the gun in Knox's hand.

"I'm a little short on time," Knox says.

"I abhor child pornography, the kiddie sex trade. Berker does as well. In this we are together, he and I. It is true: some of the girls he takes against their will. I do not deny this. Others, many others, are recruited with their parents' agreement. He runs a business. I do not deny this. I do not ask. But as to the girls—"

"The auctioning to Asian buyers."

Kreiger's astonishment is manifest by his sudden hyperventilating.

Knox is a glutton. Loves shocking him like this. Wishes Grace were here to share it with him. Thoughts of her and Dulwich remind him of the clock. He must keep a step ahead of Fahiz or the man will flee the city.

Knox makes a buzzing sound. "Time's up."

Kreiger rushes his words. "The girls who come of age, the girls who menstruate—Polat can't abide them. He weeds them out—I don't know how! I swear!—and removes them from his shop. Says the hormones and the mess are bad for business. Ten- to twelve-year-olds—that's his stable. The castoffs . . . Yes, it's true. I auction them. Asian buyers. Yes. How you can possibly know this . . . but yes. But not for what you think! These buyers have been carefully vetted! It's a very, very small list. The girls go into work as laborers, with the caveat they will never be sold into the sex trade."

"That's horseshit."

"I swear it."

"You can't possibly know what becomes of them. You, of all people! You're in the business."

"Not children, not ever."

"You sack of shit. This is how you justify it? Do you seriously have yourself fooled into believing this?"

"I vet these—"

"How? You follow up, I suppose. Visit Indonesia often, do you?" Knox realizes it doesn't matter: inmates take a dim view of crimes against children.

"You have much of it right, Knox. I swear you do. But not this part!"

"Uh-huh."

"Not the girls."

"Right."

"They leave here as skilled laborers. They are moved to the sewing shops. Athletics. Knockoffs. Good positions. Decent treatment!" He sucks in a lungful of air.

"The saddest part," Knox says, "is if you actually believe that."

38

In attempting to match addresses from the stolen GPS to the area to which Kreiger's message was sent, Knox has two possibilities. He conducts drive-bys of both. Amsterdam's homogeneity doesn't help any: both are nearly identical four-story brick apartment buildings that make up the thousand city blocks west of Singelgracht canal.

Knox must pick one. He selects the second property, for no other reason than this address is the farthest out of the addresses on the GPS, and is well located near a bus and train station.

Concerned there may be hidden cameras, he stays away from the building. He parks the bike around the corner, from which he takes a long hard look at the four yellow doors. He counts eight mail slots alongside each of the four yellow doors. The red doors separating the yellow appear to be ground-level storage or a shared laundry room. Residents of thirty-one of the thirty-two apartments are innocent bystanders. Fahiz is, in effect, using human shields.

He could call in Brower and his men. Would information alone be enough to win his colleagues' release? But the reason firms like Rutherford Risk exist is in part due to law enforcement's ineptitude in hostage situations. He can picture a SWAT team charging through corridors. Fahiz will have countermeasures in place—an escape route at the very least.

He anticipates no fewer than two men with Fahiz, possibly several times that. He's tired and hurt, his shoulder wounded. He likes the odds.

He considers smoking them out, but abhors the risk of innocent casualties. The most effective means would be to ask a resident, but that's a crapshoot at best; if Fahiz has ingratiated himself with his neighbors, it's suicidal.

He circles back around to consulting Brower. Denies himself again the easy out.

He collects himself; thinks it through. How would he and Dulwich do it? Where's the point of egress? Given a raid, where's the out? Leans around the corner and studies the building again.

Four yellow doors, each servicing eight apartments, four to either side of a common stairway, judging by the curtainless windows rising in a column over each door. The only other windows without curtains are small ones at head height on the ground floor. Storage. No visible fire escape. It makes the top two end apartments ideal safe houses. Your enemy can only reach you by coming up the common stairs. With eyes on the door and stairs, there are no surprises.

But where's the out?

He walks completely around a neighboring structure, identical to the others. Each apartment has a balcony.

And there's the out: in the event of a raid, Fahiz can quickly escape by lowering himself from one balcony to the next until he reaches ground level. There's even a downspout outside the balcony for an express route should the back prove to be guarded.

Dulwich would have a camera on the yellow door and two more inside: one looking down from the first landing; a second, from the highest landing, making the castle impenetrable to a surprise attack. Dulwich would not bother to put eyes on the egress; an escape route exists only in case of an assault—a frontal attack.

He would put a man on the ground.

KNOX MAKES A SECOND PASS around the apartment building, this time from a wider radius, alert for a guard he might have missed. Seeing none, he convinces himself a guard in such a quiet cul-de-sac would only attract attention and arouse suspicion, no matter how carefully placed. It is the solitude, the remoteness, of the setting that makes it so perfect to its purpose.

He double-checks the handgun, hoping to find more than the four rounds left in its magazine. Reminds himself it isn't just Fahiz he's after. Despite circumstantial evidence connecting Kreiger to Fahiz, and Knox's hope that Kreiger's external hard drives may further implicate Fahiz, he needs hard evidence to trade to Brower. A captive girl is unlikely—the girls were meant for the shipment Knox interrupted. There could be rug or fiber evidence linking the man to the knot shop, accounting, phones or a computer. Any and all of it is equally as important as the man himself. He can't trade half a package.

Satellite dishes hang off the half balconies in the back, including the first-floor corner balcony that is Knox's destination. A blue glow behind the gauze curtains warns him that a television is on in the bedroom, just on the other side of a double-glazed glass door, also curtained from the street.

The drainpipe is a cheap aluminum; he rethinks the idea of anyone using this as a fire pole; it won't support him. But it provides enough of a grip to allow him to extend himself as he jumps, and catch hold of the balcony's concrete platform. He pulls himself higher, takes hold of the banister rungs and gets a knee secure beneath him. He can hear a sound track and dialogue traveling less than a meter, can ill afford a neighbor crying out an alarm or calling the police. He holds to the very edge of the tiny concrete balcony, climbing up onto its south wall in order to reach the balcony directly overhead.

An irritated voice from inside freezes him. The music and dialogue have stopped as well. It takes him several seconds to process that his legs are now blocking the dish, have interrupted the satellite transmission. He pulls and swings his legs high just as the door opens. Knox is parallel to the balcony below, stretched along the outside of the next balcony's rail. An African man passes just feet below him. He bends to inspect the dish just as the music and dialogue start up again and a woman calls out in Dutch that everything's fine.

The door shuts and locks.

Knox climbs from the second to the third balcony; from the third to the fourth. He's suddenly more mechanical, more in control. He places his ear to the door as he slips the pick gun into the lock and pulls its trigger. Tumblers are caught. With a slight wiggle, the pick gun turns. He rids himself of all expectations. This is his gift: the ability to exist entirely in real time. It allows him to be prepared for anything, for nothing, for everything. He takes what he's given and has the evolved nervous system to react with split-second timing.

The room is dark on the other side of the glass. He closes his eyelids and waits for his pupils to adjust. Slips the gun from his lower back.

The door opens slowly and he peers in to see a loveless room with a floor mattress, alarm clock and cheap lamp. He is exceptionally careful closing the door behind him, aware that even a small gust of wind could reveal him.

A knife blade of light cuts beneath the bedroom door, beyond which the murmur of male voices carries. Knox stretches out on the tile floor, closes his right eye and peers beneath the gap with his left. The smell of cigar smoke taints the air.

Three pairs of shoes, a few feet away, around a table set with four chairs. The heels aimed toward him are

polished, the seams tightly stitched. To the right, black
Reeboks size 12 or 14. Barely seen: the toes of a pair of
black military boots, exceptionally wide. Like the Reeboks, they look big.

His index finger slips through the trigger guard, finding the trigger. He practices swiveling the barrel from
right to left—the Reeboks to the military boots. He must
keep his face away from the recoil, knows he'll be momen-
tarily deafened by the reports.

His vision refocuses: two sleeping teenagers on mats
beyond the military boots. Enfolded in a tangle of blanket.
Knox catches two of the spoken words: French. North
African French at that. The men are playing a game of cards.

"I need a piss," a voice says in French. The polished
shoes turn toward Knox.

Is it Fahiz? Does he have the wrong apartment?

Knox rolls out of the way of the door coming open,
stands and tucks behind. The man who appears in the
soft light invading from the adjacent room is African, not
Turkish. He spots Knox out of the corner of his eye and
his voice catches. Knox eases the door back toward the
jamb with his heel as he seizes the man by the throat and
lifts him off his feet, one-handed. The door clicks shut.

Knox walks the flailing man into the bathroom. Closes
this door as well. Runs the water. Indicates for the man
to remain quiet—the gun aimed into the man's forehead.
He smells shit in the air; the man has crapped himself.

"Turks?" Knox says, speaking French. "This building.
Men. Possibly small girls."

The man nods. He would have agreed if Knox had mentioned green-tailed aliens, but Knox takes it as progress.

"Where? Which apartment?" He cautions, "You call out, and it's your last, my friend."

The terrified man points over his shoulder.

Knox eases his grip on the man's throat. "Across! Across the hall."

"How many?"

This adds to the man's horror: he doesn't have the answer.

"One man? Three?"

The man shakes his head violently. "More than one, certainly."

"They live here long?"

Another denial. "Come and go. Not so often."

"Turks?"

The man nods. "Not nice, these men. Never speak."

Knox studies the bathroom: concrete walls. It's a bunker.

He says, "We will go into the other room. You will tell your friends it's okay. The children and your friends . . ."

"Brothers. They are my brothers."

"You, all of you, must come in here. Stay in here. It's safe in here, these walls." Knox reminds the man of the gun in his hand, and the man nods. "Silently. No sound. These are bad men."

Another quick nod from the man.

Knox keeps the man in front of him. Together they pass into the room, and his hostage speaks rapidly, telling the two younger men, "It is all right!" The men are on their feet, the tension thick. The kids come awake.

"No heroics," Knox speaks in French.

His hostage serves as his ally. The panic is diffused. Knox takes their cell phones, not wanting any emergency calls made. The men cooperate, surrendering their phones. The five lock themselves in the bathroom. Knox hides the phones in a drawer.

He's not going to climb any more balconies. His nerves are electric with the events of the past few minutes, and he can't afford a post-adrenaline slump.

He peers through the security peep. The webcam is a round piece of plastic mounted in the corner by the opposing door, aimed toward the stairwell.

The door will be locked, likely barred from the inside as well. He's not going through it; they will have to open it for him. Too late for a pizza delivery. The idea of climbing the balconies resurfaces, but his patience is worn thin. His batteries overcharged, he wants to do this now.

He sees the ball cap hanging on a peg.

Opens the door, plasters himself to the wall and hurries across, hooking the cap over the camera. Rolls to his left, back to the wall, the shut door alongside.

If they're asleep, if no one is watching the screen, he'll need to start climbing. But if they're awaiting confirmation the girls are gone, they don't have it and nerves will be high.

He hears a man approach the other side of the apartment door. Likely eye to the peephole from where he won't have a view of the dysfunctional camera. Knox waits for the sound of the lock turning, the door coming open.

Nothing. *Too smart for that,* Knox thinks.

He suffers a panic attack. He can hear Dulwich say, "Always beware of unintended consequences."

He has scared the rabbit from the hole—and there's no one watching the hole.

He crosses the landing back toward the mistaken apartment. A shot rings out and takes a chunk from the door in front of him. Mistake number 2: the man at the door had not left.

Knox dives and rolls into the apartment. One of his hostages has fled the bathroom in search of the phones and is hunched over, hands over his head. The man drops to the floor and crawls. Knox leaps over him and reaches the balcony door. They will escape by the front or back balconies, forcing Knox to choose, and he's chosen the back because this is what he would do.

And there they are: two men, already lowering onto the second-floor balcony, two below Knox's level, toward the middle of the structure. As one careens into a patio chair, he turns and takes a wild shot at Knox.

This is the starter's pistol for Knox, the game changer. He doesn't like being shot at. He turns and goes for the fireman's act on the downspout to make up time. The downspout obliges by tearing loose from the wall, and Knox goes down like a pole vaulter. It bends and then snaps, dropping him the final fifteen feet.

Two more shots ring out, but they're chaff, meant as countermeasure, trying to force Knox to keep his head down. He braces his forearm in a prone posture and puts one of his four bullets into the man firing the weapon.

He takes out a piece of the man's buttocks, spinning him and causing a horrific scream. It's a lucky shot at this distance; he's not about to waste any of his remaining three.

The downed man is in a ball of pain and out of play.

Knox rises to his feet. The remaining man bursts through a hedgerow and vanishes. Knox leaps through the line of shrubs, ducking and rolling in case his opponent has used it to set him up. The move costs Knox by taking him off his feet. The man had no intention of pausing to shoot; he's making for the line of parked cars.

He's too far away for Knox to get off any kind of accurate shot. At which point Knox realizes his gun feels light. One touch confirms he's lost its magazine. The handle stock is crammed with dirt. He has one round in the chamber, if that.

The car starts, its headlights switching on automatically. It rams the vehicle behind it as the driver cuts the wheel to escape the parking space. Knox is going to lose him.

The car's engine whines as it overraces. The tires shriek. Knox runs for the lane. Vaults a row of large rocks that create a boundary between the parked cars and lawn.

The car speeds toward him. *Twenty meters . . . Fifteen . . .* He aims the handgun, but it fails to fire. He drops it and reaches down. Takes hold of the nearest rock—the thing is massive—and hits it, dislodging it. He kneels, wraps his arms around and maneuvers it out of the stubborn earth. His muscles tearing, his chest and head exploding, he pins it to his chest, turns and gets one knee up.

Ten . . .

Then his second knee. He squats like an Olympic weight lifter. Shuffles his feet forward a matter of inches.

Five meters . . .

Grunts as he struggles to stand. Feels something pop in his gut. Heaves the rock. It travels about two feet, no more. Takes out the front bumper and right headlight, but has the desired effect: the airbags deploy. The driver is slammed back in his seat, like a fist to the face. The car plows into the rear end of a puke orange hatchback, and rebounds back into the lane.

Knox throws open the passenger door, grabs Fahiz—it is Fahiz!—by the arm and pulls him across the front seat like a toy. Elbows him in the jaw. Hears a crack. Places the stunned man's right arm against the dash, rotates the shoulder out of its socket and delivers a blow to the reversed elbow, dislocating it.

Hears a shot. Takes cover behind the car. Comes around behind the wheel and the collapsed airbag and floors it. Both car doors shut from the forward velocity. A bullet cleanly pierces the rear side window.

Fahiz—Polat—looks like a mannequin dropped from a third-floor window. But the guy is not going down easily. He tucks his knees, swivels and kicks Knox into a different time zone, pressing him into the driver's door.

The car drifts through a corner. Fahiz kicks the steering wheel. The car crosses the lane and bounces off a retaining rail. Two more vicious kicks beat Knox's head into the driver's-door window. The gun is lost. Fahiz straightens his arm, grabs the wheel and throws himself backward, pulling his dislocated arm out far enough to reset it into the socket. He screams. Regains enough use of the arm to throw a punch, connecting with Knox's temple. Fahiz screams again, but a curl of a smile takes to his wounded face.

"About time," Fahiz says.

His left arm raises. But the elbow is dislocated so that the forearm flaps, with Knox's gun roughly aimed at Knox.

Knox shoulders the gun out of the way, gropes between the seats. Fahiz slaps away his efforts. The car scrapes along a row of parked cars and Knox manages to keep it on the road. The gun discharges. Knox is instantly deaf.

His fingers search blindly between the seats, with Fahiz pounding and slapping away his efforts.

But Knox wins: he yanks the parking brake. Fahiz and the weapon are thrown forward against the dash. The car slides through an intersection and is T-boned on Knox's side by a slow-moving tram. The vehicle is pushed down the street, spins and is dumped into oncoming traffic.

Knox punches Fahiz in the previously dislocated shoulder. He then takes hold of the man's left forearm and reverses it like it belongs to a gummy bear. Fahiz opens his mouth to cry out, but there's no sound. The man is past pain. His eyes roll in his head. He waves the gun at the end of his rubbery arm up to head height—Knox sees the barrel's dark hole out of the side of his eye.

Fahiz pulls the trigger. *Click*. Empty.

Fahiz is all whites where his eyes should be. He slumps.

39

The exchange is made outside the Jet Center. Brower arrives with only his two prisoners, Grace and Dulwich. He can't be seen making such a trade, but possesses the authority to release them.

The phone call leading up to the dawn exchange was not easy sledding. Pushed by Brower, Knox admitted a lack of hard evidence but informed the man that Sonia possessed Kreiger's hard drives. Something has changed between that call and now, two hours later. Perhaps Kreiger has been arrested and is already talking. Whatever it is, Brower wears his fatigue well.

"Christ!" Brower says, seeing Fahiz's condition.

"We took a tram for half a block," Knox says, indicating the car that looks as if it shouldn't run. "The airbags had previously engaged."

Fahiz says, with difficulty, "You arrest me, you will anger much of Oud-West."

"Thank you for that input," Brower says. He replaces the shoelaces that bind the wrists of Fahiz's bizarrely twisted arms with a set of handcuffs. "That has got to hurt."

"I feel nothing," Fahiz says.

Knox pats him firmly on the dislocated shoulder, causing him inordinate pain. "A real soldier, this one."

"There is money. Much money." Fahiz addresses both men. "Besides, you have nothing."

"We have Gerhardt Kreiger," Knox corrects, feeling no shame in giving up the man. "It's going to come down to who gets in front of this, eh, Brower?"

"Just so. Always the same."

"To hell with all of you!"

Brower makes sure to use the man's arms while putting him into the backseat of the unmarked car.

"There will be warrants for your arrest," Brower says. "I wouldn't return to the Netherlands for some time."

"I'll miss it," Knox says. "I like it here."

"If you expect me to thank you, that's not going to happen. You've left me a mess to clean up."

"I have limited expectations," Knox says. "I'm pretty low maintenance."

Brower's had enough. He circles the car and drives off.

Dulwich collects a wheelchair from inside the Jet Center, and together the men wheel Grace through the automatic doors. Nothing is said among the three; barely a word is spoken. A first-aid kit is provided and Grace tends to Knox's shoulder wound. The hernia will have to wait.

Dulwich disappears into the business center, spending time on the computer and phone. His eyes find Grace and Knox from time to time, like a school principal.

The flight team arrives. The pilot gives Knox a disapproving look. Grace doesn't ask. But she can read Knox's mind, as it turns out.

"She tried to get us killed," Grace reminds him.

"There is that." He doesn't think of himself as a particularly forgiving man, but he has let that go easily enough. He keeps seeing the parts he wants to see, remembering the moments he wants to remember.

She might have told him something encouraging, but she doesn't try. This is what they do. Who they are.

Knox falls asleep waiting to board the plane, the pilot taking an inordinate amount of time preparing and filing the flight plan.

Now strapped in one of the eight seats, he nods off again.

He's forgotten to ask where they're headed.

40

The island of Patmos is covered by cascading white buildings set against the azure blue of the sea, mirrored by cumulous clouds in a matching sky. It's an active monastery, Saint John the Theologian, housing one hundred seventy-five monks who farm their own food, raise goats and grow their own wine on outlying acreage.

Grace and Knox have been debriefed on multiple occasions by interrogators too pale to have been on the island long. Dulwich is nowhere to be seen. The warm sun soothes wounds inside and out. Grace has turned nearly black in a yellow bikini that seems to shrink by the week. Knox has stopped himself from staring repeatedly, reminded of their evening in Natuurhonig.

He nearly can't remember the abdominal surgery, but has a bandage to show for it. Grace has conquered Sudoku. Knox has caught up with company paperwork that has plagued him for months. But it has lost its luster—not the paperwork but the thought of import/export. Dulwich has won, and Knox resents it deeply.

"Here is what we know," Grace says from the chaise longue beside his. A fountain of two cupids peeing into a birdbath gives a pair of butterflies a place to dance.

Knox is expecting more on Berker Polat, who at last mention had been refused bail by the Dutch and was said to have been badly beaten by inmates when it was leaked he mistreated young girls.

But Grace, being Grace, surprises him.

"We found and tagged the forty-seven thousand," she says, as if picking up a conversation they'd started over lunch. "I can have that back to you, but do not recommend it. She is very good, this Evelyn. If this is her first time, I would be surprised—and that may aid us in our search. Her past, whatever it may turn out to be. If, or should I say when—because you will instigate this—she moves the forty-seven, it will assist me in tracking the remaining funds. This is the heart of forensic accounting: a person's tendency to repeat himself. The transfer of the forty-seven will bear a fingerprint, maybe three stops? five stops? the degree to which it is laundered. Believe it or not, this will allow me to go back in time and match similar patterns to your remaining funds."

"Are you saying it can be recovered?"

"I have told you as much all along."

"Cheerleading," he says. "I thought—"

"You doubted me."

"I doubted you."

"I told you I will find your money. I will find your money. It may go well beyond that, John. In my experience: this isn't her first time. We will find more than just your money, and when we do . . . finders keepers."

It strikes him as such a Western expression. Wonders at the changes in her, worries she will be fast-tracked within the company and that this may be the last they work together. He feels like they're just getting started.

He drinks from a sweating beer bottle. Burps softly and excuses himself.

She chuckles.

"Oh, come on."

"Not the burp, John. The apology. This is new."

"Is it?"

"David will find her. When he does, your actions will trigger the withdrawal of the forty-seven. It must be carefully planned, carefully thought out."

"My action will be to cave her head in."

"No, John."

She has taken him literally. Again. He's about to try to straighten it out when she lays the chaise longue back flat. Knox can't help himself from looking. Again.

"Not going to happen," she says.

He looks away at the peeing cupids. "In your dreams," he mutters.

"Mine or yours?"

Several minutes pass. Side by side.

"You miss her," Grace says to the sky. "This is understandable."

"What makes you the expert?"

It takes Grace another minute to answer.

"My broken heart," she says.

41

Three weeks and four days later, Knox stands outside a duplex in Hamtramck, Michigan, ready to keep his promise. The air smells clean thanks to an overnight rain. He toes the cracked sidewalk where a tree root is exposed, trying to write a script in advance, to have himself prepared for whatever arises. He remembers when the tree was only as tall as he is now. All his size and powerful body, and yet he feels so small.

He wonders why he stalls, what necessitates such preparation. *Catch as catch can,* he reminds himself. But he answers: because it's smoking in a fireworks factory. It's a life that centers around him like he's the sun. It's this unrelenting burden and responsibility that he resents and that he loves, that he welcomes and resists. Where does the temptation to turn around and return to the rental car come from? How can a gun fired not terrify him the way standing here does?

He climbs the steps and rings the doorbell.

1

Two men await a delivery van. Nameless men. Professionals. Proficient at blending in. The man with the camera—call him Alpha. The man who stands in the camera's frame is Beta.

A white FedEx minivan appears in the camera's field of view. It serves as the starting gun. Alpha eases the Nikon onto his chest. Turning away from the Merkez Mosque, he is jostled by Istanbul tourists posing for the perfect picture. It's nearing the end of the day. Slanting sunshine slices through the smog playing across the mosque's stone dome and adjacent minaret. Hell of a photo.

Beta, looking so much like Alpha they might be mistaken for twins—each in a navy blue knit cap, black leather jacket, blue jeans—sees the camera lower and moves toward the curb. He cradles a canvas messenger bag beneath his right arm.

The van double parks in front of a pharmacy, its emergency flashers pulsing.

Alpha walks incrementally faster, entering the pharmacy only seconds behind the FedEx deliveryman. His job is to provide cover. Beta opens the van's panel door and slips inside. After five days of surveillance, they know the delivery kid, always in a hurry, never locks the van in this part of town.

THE PHARMACY SMELLS CHEMICAL. Alpha reaches the FedEx kid and, as if trying to slip past, allows himself to be tripped. He brings down most of the contents of a shelf as he falls. Turns and pulls the deliveryman along with him.

There is shouting as employees hurry to help. Boxes of medicine are spread across the floor, causing the employees to tiptoe as they approach. The delivery package has slid out of reach of both men.

The lens hangs broken from the camera's body.

"Idiot! You clumsy bastard!" Alpha speaks English in an Eastern European accent. More training. The deliveryman is young, red faced and unsure. He spouts apologies in Turkish.

BETA SEARCHES THE CONTENTS of the first of six plastic bins arranged on the van's open shelves, his fingers flipping through the packages like a collector in a vinyl-record store. He knows exactly what he's looking for: he has its clone in his messenger bag.

Bin two. Bin three. An internal timer runs. The op calls for an abort at thirty. He's at twenty-seven when his fingers stop at the air bill listing:

Florence Nightingale Hospital
Abide-i Hürriyet Caddesi
Istanbul, Turkey

Seven packages. More slowly now. The third shows the sender as a Swiss address. He makes the swap, his for theirs.

Forty-three seconds and counting . . .

No reaction. No adrenaline or concern or anxiety. The lapsed time is merely a statistic to be noted. It's filed and processed. He stuffs the switch package into the messenger bag and comes out of the van with his back to the sidewalk. He walks the curb like a balance beam. No one has shouted at him. No one has approached. He slips out his phone and sends the text. The signal.

ALPHA'S PHONE DINGS at his hip.

"My fault, my fault!" Alpha says. He helps the cautious deliveryman to his feet, making sure to keep the man facing away from the windows. In tourist Turkish, he manages something close to *Uzgünüm.* Sorry.

He inspects his broken camera, trying to force the lens back into place. He and the deliveryman exchange agonized looks. Alpha extends his hand, a peace offering. The deliveryman is delighted by his change of heart. They shake.

Alpha says in English, "All for some toothpaste." A shared moment of tense humor.

Leaving the pharmacy, Alpha reads the text. It's a smiley emoticon. Success.

He makes a phone call. Hears a click. No voice. He keys in a five-string number followed by three pound signs. Hears a second tone.

"It's done," he says in Hebrew.

2

A veil of fog obscures the steep steel-and-glass-clad marvels that rise out of Hong Kong harbor. From the twenty-second-floor offices of Rutherford Risk in the Chamberlain Tower, John Knox thinks the trolleys and cars look like toys. On the glass, pinpricks of mist collect and join, growing into drops and skidding down the glass in a race, obscuring the view. It's not raining, but it will be within the hour.

Knox steals a look at his own reflection while behind his image, another appears: an imposing figure of a man, older by a few years, unable to disguise a brutal intensity that impressed Knox when the two first met in Kuwait, another Knox ago. David Dulwich still walks with a limp,

although his gait has vastly improved since the car accident in Shanghai two-plus years ago. The men embrace.

"This way," Dulwich says.

Knox notes the lack of small talk, wonders if the brief
phone call that detoured him to Hong Kong was as much
of the personal stuff as he and Sarge were going to bother
with.

The starkly contemporary offices of Rutherford Risk
reflect the tastes of company president Brian Primer, whose
warm side only surfaces when a client is present. Knox
knows Primer as a calculating son-of-a-bitch who concerns
himself exclusively with margins and profitability—often
at the expense of his assets, like Knox.

Down the corridor, the maple office doors, marked only
by a number, rise to ten feet and are a full meter across,
ensuring that any visitor, no matter how large, feels physically insignificant.

Primer, a proponent of Frank Wisner's "Mighty Wur-
litzer," required his architect and interior decorator to
work with a team of psychologists. Wisner, the first director of the CIA, created front organizations and planted
media stooges in order to "play any propaganda tune
needed." Primer can work a meeting.

To Knox's surprise, he's led not to Primer's office but
to the secure elevator. It drops thirty stories so fast he
feels like he's floating. He's ridden it only once before.

Hong Kong high-rises are anchored deeply into the
mountains. Lessons learned from mudslides a century
earlier have prompted the creation of structures able to
withstand both the ground giving way and the pummel-

ing of typhoon winds and rain. Twenty meters below grade, storm shelters and storage rooms are carved into the hillside. It's here, outside a door marked PRIVATE, that Dulwich removes anything containing metal—coins, wristwatch, Bluetooth device, smartphone, belt. He places the items in a cubby, turns the lock, and asks Knox to do the same. Knox does so and pockets the plastic key.

Dulwich swipes his ID card and admits Knox to a small vestibule, where they must wait for the door to close before a second can be opened. A body scanner hums. A green light indicates that they are clear.

"The red room," Knox says. "So cloak-and-dagger."

Still, Dulwich is silent. The barrier is seven inches of steel and insulating concrete, weighing three hundred pounds, yet it moves fluidly, clicks shut and locks electronically. The red room is a twenty-square-foot bunker with pale green walls and a strip of exposed overhead lights. The furniture is clear, ensuring that nothing can be hidden inside it. Knox saw it once during an early tour of Rutherford Risk.

"I've never had the pleasure," he says.

Dulwich checks his watch. "We don't have long." He produces an A4 manila envelope. Knox can't believe he didn't see it, marvels at how quickly one can lose one's edge. He's been back to import/export for a matter of months; the operation in Amsterdam is still fresh in his memory but apparently not in his skill set.

Dulwich slides the envelope across the table like it's radioactive.

"Your schedule, not mine." Knox says. He finds the

red room claustrophobic. He can handle small spaces; a top secret facility, impenetrable to all eavesdropping technologies, causes undue pressure.

Dulwich taps the envelope.

David Dulwich is usually not the melodramatic type. It's one reason Knox doesn't mind doing the occasional piece of work for him. The rest of his time, John Knox is a trader, traveling the world for rare goods, in business with his younger brother, Tommy. Dropping into a James Bond movie is a little much.

"Sarge?"

"They're of you. The pictures. You love looking at yourself, Knox. So go ahead."

"Moi?" Knox fails to entertain his host. "Why?"

"Why what?"

"I have plenty of pictures of myself, all of them stunning."

An uncomfortable smirk crawls across Dulwich's lips. "Not like these, you don't."

Knox suppresses the urge to take the bait. He wants more from Dulwich, who knows that Knox is a reluctant freelancer. His brother, Tommy, isn't in the best shape—the experts call him cerebrally and physically impaired, autistic, mentally challenged. He is, in fact, highly functional with the medication and care. Knox can't risk leaving him alone on this earth, but he's attracted to the work Dulwich offers for more than just the money. He has a savior complex that probably bleeds over from caring for his damaged sibling.

Still, he's in no hurry to screw things up by rising to

the wrong fly. Dulwich will eventually play the money card. Knox has been robbed, embezzled from by his company's bookkeeper. Things are tight. Have been for some time.

But Dulwich doesn't start there.

"I don't go in for drama," Dulwich says.

"An understatement."

"This is an in-and-out—a week tops—that can do a lot of good."

"Good, like Amsterdam?" Dulwich understands which buttons to push.

"No, not like Amsterdam. Not even close. Frog and the scorpion. Open the envelope."

Knox doesn't understand the reference but doesn't want to appear ignorant. He wants to open the envelope—oh, how he wants to—but there's commitment that accompanies the act, and he can't bring himself to do it without knowing more.

"Political?" Knox wishes he had hidden the astonishment in his voice. Like all private contractors, Rutherford Risk's bread and butter comes from U.S. government jobs: guarding convoys of supplies, providing security details, moving funds, interrupting the Internet, burning drug crops. It's the occasional insurgency Knox wants no part of.

"Open the envelope."

"Wrong guy."

"Turns out you're the only guy, or we wouldn't be locked in the red room."

"Maybe you should unlock the door."

"Maybe you should open the envelope. There are good

guys and bad guys on every team, Knox. Even good teams have their share of bad apples. But I wouldn't put you on the bad team. Not ever. Now, goddamn it, look—"

Dulwich takes the envelope back, opens it, and slams down a handful of 8 × 10s. Shot with a high-powered telephoto at a good distance.

Knox can't pretend it's not his profile. It takes him several long seconds to digest the look of the café and the apparent location: Bethany, Jordan. That gives him the other man in the photo, a man with Jordanian and Circassian blood: Akram Okle.

"I was never told flat-out," Knox says, defending himself, "that the piece was black market. Every antiquity has passed through too many hands to count. Sometimes that includes mine. I'm offered a piece; I know a buyer. More like a matchmaker. I can see how that might be politically embarrassing, but I don't work for you, Sarge. I'm not your employee. I'm a contractor. I—"

"You are so off-base you're running around the outfield." Dulwich flips through the stack of photographs. Three show Knox and Okle engaged in what Knox thinks must be their most recent deal; more troubling are the final two photos, which go back eighteen months earlier. There's no way Knox has been followed for eighteen months; he keeps track of such things. So it's Okle who's being surveilled.

"Okay, I give up. The frog and the scorpion?"

Dulwich arches his eyebrows as if Knox should know this one. "Frog and a scorpion meet on the river bank. Scorpion asks for a lift to the other side. Frog says why would I do that, you'll sting me. Scorpion says he won't and they sign a treaty. The frog carries him on his back. Halfway across, the scorpion stings the frog. As they're both going under, the frog says, 'Why would you do this? We're both going to die!' Scorpion says, 'It's my nature . . .'"

"Akram's a good client," Knox says. "I see certain pieces, I think of him first. He only buys the rarest of the rare. There aren't many people who can afford such things. You go where the market is."

"He's a middleman."

"None of my business."

"It is now."

3

Rutherford Risk pays out six figures to employees at various Internet security companies on top of the seven figures budgeted for their own hackers, who roam cyberspace probing for firewall vulnerabilities. When a back door is discovered in an existing operating system, Rutherford receives an alert before Microsoft or Adobe or Sun or Apple can identify the issue, a day or two before they can offer a patch.

During that window—hours, or minutes sometimes—people like Grace Chu, a private contractor based in Hong Kong and specializing in forensic accounting, are able to slip through the back door undetected.

Thanks to other sources on the inside of those companies, Grace Chu is also told when to get out.

Most of her days are spent poring over spreadsheets or money wire transactions, establishing trails and hard evidence for the client, most typically Rutherford Risk. Today she works like a day trader, jumping in and out of the market, seizing opportunity, playing margins. She's attempting to establish and trace an individual's net worth. It's a nerve-racking exercise not meant for the faint of heart. A moment's hesitation and the SEC or FBI will have her location. Get out too quickly and she loses her only chance at access.

Today she's inside the server of a Jordanian bank; tonight or tomorrow, if the current back door holds, an Iranian investment firm. She's curious about the op. Yesterday, Dulwich instructed her to data-mine this man's financials. Dulwich wants her travel plans left open. He sounded uncertain. It's new territory—Dulwich at sea, running her personally. Success will mean promotion; she can taste it. To prove herself as a field operative capable of on-the-fly intelligence gathering and analysis will put her in a class by herself. She knows of no one at Rutherford Risk with this particular hybrid skill set.

She works wirelessly using a "hopper"—a cellular Wi-Fi device that jumps between three carriers randomly, the same technology that makes her jailbroken iPhone impossible to eavesdrop on. It costs her some speed, but she has grown accustomed to the pauses.

She's working from the downtown campus cafeteria of the University of Hong Kong, meaning her IP address is shared by a few hundred at a time, making a quick trace difficult, if not impossible. She's stolen a user ID and password off a nearby, far-too-casual user.

The bank's firewall is impenetrable. The last effective

cyber-raid was in 2004. This back door they've been given is far more benign—it's for the bank's local area network, which includes all web searches, most e-mail traffic, video conferencing data as well as the security server.

Grace monitors the cafeteria's visitors, studying the face and body language of each new arrival. It's lunchtime and therefore busy, which is both a blessing and a curse, but she chose the time slot to help support her cover. Her fine features—she's been described as "haunting"—win the attention of males over twenty, many of whom underestimate her age, which is well north of that. She keeps her laptop screen angled slightly down; it wears a layer of plastic film that limits side views, but there's a sweet spot she found from just above head height that concerns her.

She types a long string of commands. A year ago, she was fairly new to this cyberplay, made anxious by it. Now she eats it up. Over the months she's grown addicted to these short bursts of information theft, much the way she imagines runners treasure their endorphins.

Working with remarkable speed, she moves through the root directory hierarchy, navigating to the security servers. In her mind's eye, it's like going down ladders and through tunnels, into anterooms and on to other tunnels and more ladders. Throughout the process, she raises her eyes, tracking newcomers, accounting for those already in place. Her memory is superior. Her mind has been trained to be nearly photographic. She has identified the two men back by the soda fountain, the woman by the trash can, another woman eating alone. Any of these could be a threat. There's a male student who looks like he's hoping to see up her skirt. She'd like to flip him her middle finger but keeps it on the keys.

One thing she's learned about security servers: the systems are organized to accommodate and account for the intelligence level of those meant to operate them. Not every security guard is a Bill Gates in waiting. The video stream is labeled KAYMARA. Camera.

In seconds she's opening a dozen video feeds, like surfing a traffic-cam site. She closes them as quickly as they open. She's not interested in the teller windows or the safe or the safe-deposit boxes. Not interested in the elevator interiors, the back hallway, or the six exterior cameras.

All the while a stopwatch app runs in the upper corner of her screen. She's been online 2:07 minutes and counting. Even using a back door, she may be sniffed and identified for having an IP address outside the known database of approved users. She should be safe staying within five-minute usage intervals.

At 4:22, she clocks off.

The second hack, she heads directly to the camera list.

Her third breach hits gold: the camera is mounted behind four desks, with a view of the teller windows' left side. One of the desks is occupied. Her fingers fly across the keys as she builds a macro that logs in, clicks through to the proper security camera, takes a video screen shot, and logs out at the four-minute mark. The macro will loop until she shuts it down.

She hits ENTER, angles the screen lower, and is caught off guard by the young skirt-chaser's approach.

Terminate or continue? These are the decisions that

define her: when to run, when to admit temporary defeat, when to trust her instincts. Right now couldn't be better— the hack is clean, the macro running flawlessly. She has the op teed up perfectly. She just needs the other two desks filled following lunchtime breaks.

This guy's a problem. He asks in Cantonese if the seat is taken. It's a dialect she has nailed but an accent she finds tricky even after two years living in the city. Her rebuff of him is polite but firm; her right pinky finger hovers over the F12 key while her left index finger covers the FN. These two keystrokes combined will log off the laptop and send it into a double-encrypted sleep mode that would require seventy-two hours on a Cray computer to have a hope of gaining access.

Appearances mean nothing. The boy's approach is taken as a high-level threat. If he lifts a finger, she'll break it like a twig, and his arm along with it. Apologies to cock-motivated boys like him are cheaper than excuses to Dulwich.

He offers a smile he's practiced too many times in his dormitory mirror.

"Listen to me, cousin," she says, losing her accent slightly to her temper. "I don't appreciate boys . . ." she lingers on the word, savoring it, "looking up my skirt, or trying to. If you haven't seen one before, I'm not interested in you, and if you have, then you know it's a woman's secret treasure and she doesn't wear it like a Shanghai billboard. If I wanted to share pictures of it, I'd post them on the corkboard over there by the register, neh? Back up and leave me alone or I'll put my heel so deep in your crotch you'll have shoe leather for a tongue."

His sallow skin tone drains to the color of talcum powder.

The fact that he remains there, standing his ground, is cause for worry: he's a cocky bastard.

She detests the thought of logging off when everything is going so well. She can't bring herself to do it without further provocation. But her instinctive reaction is impatience and she's trained to guard against it. Good things come to those who wait. She'll have another shot at this data, she reminds herself.

So why can't she bring herself to log off? It's him and his obstinacy; she's taken it as a gender challenge and she's not about to cave.

She's angled the screen too low to see what's happening at the bank. The boy's flirting will provide good cover, but the distraction has cost her: she's lost track of who's entering or exiting the cafeteria. Her best chance now is to keep this boy engaged for the sake of anyone who might be watching. The longer she has him with her, the longer her computer continues recording the bank's video camera.

"A woman's secret treasure, or her secret pleasure?" he says now, and draws the opposing chair back with his shoe, making space to sit.

"Pleasure cannot be kept secret," she returns, suddenly enjoying the wordplay, "whereas treasure can."

Keeping her prior threat in mind, he estimates the

length of her extended leg and moves the chair far enough back to accommodate. He sits.

"Origin EON-seventeen-S," he says.

She wishes she could stop the blush that floods her face. John Knox has told her it's a tell that could get her killed.

The boy has been lusting after her boutique laptop, not her crotch. She's made a fool of herself, and he's so smitten with her electronics that he's played along.

He rattles off specs and she counters with the upgrades she's opted for. Lunge. Parry. His eyes go wide—and then wider. His upper lip is sweating.

Has she misjudged his age? Is he too old to be a student? Teacher's aide? Grad student? Or is he a risk-taking thief, who dresses well and chats up girls on college campuses, snatches their laptops and disappears before they can rise from their chairs? The Origin is worth over four thousand U.S. Mainland gamers would pay that or more.

If he manages to steal the unlocked laptop, she and Rutherford Risk would suffer. She plays the odds, pressing the two keys and protecting the data. She's angry over being forced to do so, is tempted to knock the guy across the room.

Quoting a proverb, "'Man's schemes are inferior to those made by heaven,'" Grace casually closes the Origin. It's heavy, but she one-hands it into the Trager Tru-Ballistic case.

"I was admiring it. And you. That's all, cousin."

"Next time you might consider antiperspirant on your upper lip, cousin."

He holds up both palms in an act of surrender. Behind his eyes, he hungers to test her threats. That look convinces her he intended to steal the laptop. She has to wonder if he was hired.

She slings the case over her head so the strap, which will hold up to any box cutter or razor, crosses her chest, separating her breasts.

"I think I'm in love," he whispers as she passes.

From #1 *New York Times* Bestselling Author
Ridley Pearson

KILLER SUMMER

Sun Valley, Idaho: playground of the wealthy and home to an annual wine auction with enough rare bottles to lure high-rolling connoisseurs from across the country—as well as an inspired and ingenious team of thieves after a particular collection. Sheriff Walt Fleming's attempt to prevent the heist uncovers a far more sinister plan. Outsmarted, and forced to play catch-up, Walt finds his mettle tested when the crime suddenly turns personal and the stakes ratchet higher. With his private life unraveling, undermined by unforeseen obstacles, Walt walks a dangerous line, struggling to remain above the law he's sworn to uphold.

"Pearson serves up steady suspense
and a compelling setting."
—*Booklist*

"Ridley Pearson writes thrillers,
the kind that try to yank you to the edge
of your seat and keep you there."
—*Boston Sunday Globe*

penguin.com

M844T0311

NOW IN PAPERBACK FROM
#1 *NEW YORK TIMES* BESTSELLING AUTHOR

Ridley Pearson
KILLER VIEW

"Put *Killer View* on your summer reading list."
—*St. Louis Post-Dispatch*

When a skier goes missing from a Sun Valley mountaintop, Sheriff Walt Fleming's crack search-and-rescue team becomes a target. Waist-deep in snow and knee-deep in lies, Walt suspects that people of great wealth and power—including a former state senator—want to keep him where he started: out in the cold.

M646T0210